Lionel Barrymore

LIONEL BARRYMORE

Character and Endurance in Hollywood's Golden Age

Kathleen Spaltro

UNIVERSITY PRESS OF KENTUCKY

A note to the reader: This volume contains images of an actor wearing theatrical makeup and costuming to portray a character of a different race. Discretion is advised.

Copyright © 2024 by The University Press of Kentucky

Scholarly publisher for the Commonwealth,
serving Bellarmine University, Berea College, Centre
College of Kentucky, Eastern Kentucky University,
The Filson Historical Society, Georgetown College,
Kentucky Historical Society, Kentucky State University,
Morehead State University, Murray State University,
Northern Kentucky University, Spalding University,
Transylvania University, University of Kentucky,
University of Louisville, University of Pikeville,
and Western Kentucky University.
All rights reserved.

Editorial and Sales Offices: The University Press of Kentucky
663 South Limestone Street, Lexington, Kentucky 40508-4008
www.kentuckypress.com

Library of Congress Cataloging-in-Publication Data

Names: Spaltro, Kathleen, author.
Title: Lionel Barrymore : character and endurance in Hollywood's golden age
   / Kathleen Spaltro.
Description: Lexington, Kentucky : The University Press of Kentucky, [2024]
   | Series: Screen classics | Includes bibliographical references and index.
Identifiers: LCCN 2024010120 | ISBN 9781985900509 (hardcover) | ISBN
   9781985900523 (pdf) | ISBN 9781985900530 (epub)
Subjects: LCSH: Barrymore, Lionel, 1878-1954. | Motion picture actors and
   actresses—United States—Biography.
Classification: LCC PN2287.B37 S63 2024 | DDC 791.4302/8092 [B]—dc23/eng/
   20240318
LC record available at https://lccn.loc.gov/2024010120

This book is printed on acid-free paper meeting
the requirements of the American National Standard
for Permanence in Paper for Printed Library Materials.

Manufactured in the United States of America.

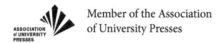

Member of the Association
of University Presses

For John, my beloved husband for these many years
Cor ad cor loquitur
"Heart speaks unto heart"

Contents

Introduction 1

Act One: Artful Dodger
1. Disorder and Early Sorrow, 1878–1893 11
2. Twenty Years, Two Apprenticeships, 1893–1912 17
3. Escape into Films, 1911–1917 26
4. The Valley of Indecision, 1917–1925 34

Act Two: Chameleon
5. Silenced, Again, 1925–1928 57
6. Talkies Stardom and Detour into Direction, 1928–1931 64
7. Scene Stealer, 1933–1935 80

Act Three: After Life
8. Year of Disaster, 1936 99
9. Mike and Jake: Exit Jack, 1942 106
10. Radio Days and the Taxman Cometh, 1934–1954 111
11. Brilliant Grouch: Dr. Gillespie and Other Roles, 1937–1951 125
12. The Best Wine for Last, 1945–1953 139
13. Compensations, 1937–1954 152
14. Down the Valley of the Shadow, 1954 164

Contents

Acknowledgments   173
Notable Films and Radio Performances of Lionel Barrymore   177
Further Reading   181
Notes   183
Bibliography   205
Index   221

Illustrations follow page 124

Introduction

In a radio tribute broadcast soon after the death of Lionel Barrymore in 1954, MGM head of production Dore Schary declared, "There were stars before Lionel Barrymore. There will be stars after him. There will be none more talented and vital." Schary's high esteem, echoed by many others, makes the absence of a biography dedicated solely to Lionel Barrymore seem like a sin of omission. Just as Lionel Barrymore was overshadowed and overlooked in his family because of family elders' favoritism for his siblings, Ethel and Jack, he has not been served well by the previous biographical analyses that conjoin him with his siblings. There, too, Lionel tends to be overshadowed and overlooked because of the greater glamour of Ethel and the substantial notoriety of Jack. Yet the perennially overlooked Barrymore is nevertheless the Barrymore most familiar to contemporary audiences. While twenty-first-century viewers may not know much about his stage work, his silent films, or his Oscar-winning (Best Actor, 1931) performance in *A Free Soul*, fans of classic radio remember his yearly turn as Ebenezer Scrooge, and everyone has seen his Mr. Potter in *It's a Wonderful Life*. The American Film Institute poll on favorite heroes and villains listed Henry F. Potter as number six among viewers' most cherished villains. Humphrey Bogart, Edward G. Robinson, and John Huston fans also savor Barrymore's acting in *Key Largo*.[1]

He is always praised as a superb character actor. That equivocal praise in itself explains the lesser attention given to his achievements. In the family pecking order, Lionel was the introverted, quiet son left alone to amuse himself by drawing or left behind on his father's Staten Island farm when their maternal grandmother summoned Jack back to her care, which John thought was "cruel." In the acting pecking order, Lionel was the praised character actor, whereas Ethel dazzled as a leading lady, and John fascinated audiences as a romantic lead. The lesser value given to character acting resulted from the long-lasting distortion of values created by the studios' star system that

LIONEL BARRYMORE

exalted "star types" or movie star personae. Other performers noted with awe how Lionel the actor *became* the character he played, but greater prestige went to actors whose supposed "real" personalities became the basis of their star types: in effect, the fictionalized personality of a real actor *became* the character the star played. A 1958 article "What Is a Star?" quoted Louis B. Mayer's frank account of the star-making process: "A star is created, carefully and cold-bloodedly, built up from nothing from nobody. . . . We could make silk purses out of sow's ears every day of the week." Gleefully mocking the extreme artificiality of the star-making process, Evelyn Waugh's *The Loved One* depicts Sir Francis Hinsley of the studio press office first transforming starlet Baby Aaronson into "Juanita del Pablo" and then, when the Catholic League of Decency objects to Juanita's amatory excesses, remaking Baby into an Irish colleen with dyed auburn hair, dentures, and a carefully manufactured brogue. Lionel himself lamented the emphasis on star "personalities" in creating and marketing films: "it would have been better for the industry if there had been no stars or very few of them. But the public wanted them and demanded to know who they were. . . . If an actor suddenly makes a hit as a cowboy we are expected to believe that he was born in Texas and that he had once been a cowboy, and so on. Actors in the theatre never resorted to this type of advertising; indeed, they would have been laughed at had they done so."[2]

Although the elevation of the movie star and the star type came to define the American film industry in the studio decades, this was not inevitable. Essentially, it was an accidental consequence of marketing. Stars who really were talented actors felt frustrated, for talented character actors were undervalued. *Duel in the Sun* (1946) can serve as an example of how the star-making process was unfair to Hollywood's character actors. The star whom producer David O. Selznick was trying to exalt, Jennifer Jones, gives a bad performance. The film's ridiculous plot notwithstanding, most of the character actors (Herbert Marshall, Lionel Barrymore, Lillian Gish, Charles Bickford, Walter Huston) are fine. Gregory Peck has a grand time as a baddie. But the focus on its star, the film's overriding purpose to create a star, detracts and distracts from the excellence of its character actors and sinks the movie.[3]

In such a system, acting ability was almost beside the point. Therefore, while Lionel Barrymore's exceptional skills attracted praise, he was still an also-ran, not really a top "movie star" for most of his time in Hollywood. Nonetheless, his career encompassed, in a rare and, indeed, unique fashion, the three basic categories of "star," "character actor," and "supporting player."

Introduction

He was a lesser star because of his sheer excellence and his surname, a character actor in his assumption of the persona of curmudgeon as Scrooge and Mr. Potter, and a supporting player in less constrained character roles. In so doing, he foreshadowed the fate of contemporary actors who have largely escaped the confines of star types and range between leading, character, and supporting roles depending on their film assignment. His accomplishments as an Oscar-nominated film director also foreshadowed the aspirations of modern actor-directors.[4]

While the American stage also distinguished between lead actors and supporting performers, the intense marketing of films by Hollywood studios in the Golden Age exaggerated this distinction by publicizing fictional personalities for its star players that defined their performances to meet prefabricated audience expectations. Nonetheless, for playwright and theater critic Stark Young, the difference between leading players and character actors explains differences in acting technique. According to Young, the force of a leading part depends on the actor's *displaying* the actor's self, "acting straight from the actor's self," working from *within*: "it is his visible self, objectively seen, that he puts into the person's place." Asserting that "the medium ... is the actor himself as he appears in life," Young included John Barrymore and Ethel Barrymore as exemplars of this stage technique of creating a star persona identified with the actor's public personality. In contrast, Young argued, character acting does *not* exhibit the actor's self, but fashions something distinct from the actor's own personality. Whereas the leading actor depends on an emotional and *internal* process, the character actor employs *external* means, such as mimicry and makeup, as the actor "creates a personage who is distinctly diverse, who is arranged, objectively seen, shaped up." Young continued, "Character work cultivates the sense of imitation, the duplication of external details, a certain distinct articulation and mimicry. This mimicry is the healthful and sound basis of the actor's art as the gift for seeing accurately the visible world about him is of the painter's." Writing just after Lionel had suffered through three stage flops, Young contrasted Lionel with his siblings by classifying him as a character actor not well-suited to leading parts: "Mr. Lionel Barrymore's three efforts of last season show how he can sink when he tries to give us himself, and at the same time what technical and laborious contributions he could bring to the study of a character part whose definite outline and external aspect were imposed upon him." Writing just a few years after Young's book appeared in 1926, Rudolf Arnheim in 1931 distinguished between the character actor who plays "man as he is" and the

3

heroic lead who portrays "man as he would like to be." Perceiving star parts as more prestigious and idealized, Arnheim thought that they consequently are more constrained by heroic convention and therefore less individualized than character parts inspired more by "real life." Observation of "man as he is" underpins character acting.[5]

In the twenty-first century, leading parts have often become character parts, blurring this hard line drawn between heroic, idealized, often romantic star roles and ordinary, realistic character roles. Consequently, it has become less obvious why the leading actor would draw inspiration solely from within, whereas the character actor would rely exclusively on externals. This gradual breaking down of the distinction had begun late in Hollywood's Golden Age, as revealed in a comment by character actress Gladys George about acting technique: "I believe in basing a part [on] life—on little things that you've seen people do. The dramatic schools are all right when they talk about digging down into a character and finding it. But even at that, if you don't copy life, your performance hasn't the punch that makes people say, 'I know somebody just like that.'" Acknowledging that even a character performance could draw from an actor's internal exploration of feelings and personal experiences, George nevertheless insisted on the value and the superiority of the external approach to portraying a character part. When Lionel was in his prime as a stage and screen actor, however, the distinction still held fast, and he adhered to it.[6]

Lionel actually did employ, both in the theater and in films, the external technique described by Stark Young as characteristic of the stage character actor and implied by Rudolf Arnheim's comments. A maternal uncle, theater star John Drew, praised his achievement in a 1902 stage production: as the "organ grinder in *The Mummy and the Humming Bird* his work was a revelation." Part of Lionel's technique involved trying to grasp a role authentically through careful observation and questions; besides talking with other actors, he researched his parts. This long-standing practice began with *The Mummy and the Humming Bird*, for which he patiently discerned regional differences in dialect and behavior among Neapolitan, Umbrian, and Sicilian waiters in New York City restaurants before opting for a Sicilian characterization for his organ grinder. Later cast in *The Copperhead* on stage and on film, he studied Civil War history and memoirs. Preparing to play Dr. Leonard Gillespie in a long-running movie serial many years later, Lionel constantly read about medical practice. Theatrical producer Arthur Hopkins in 1949 expressed his view that Lionel surpassed all other character actors in artistry by

Introduction

transcending his own personality to evoke the characters he created on stage or screen. In 1905, Jack had told Ashton Stevens that Lionel was "a wonder today, and one of these early tomorrows he will be great. . . . Lionel is a paradox in that he is both delineator and analyst. He's receptive, and he can impart. He's bigger than his mere personality. He doesn't depend on his personality. When he plays a part, he makes a character of it." Praising Lionel as a consummate character actor, Ludwig Lewisohn observed that Lionel played very different roles that "had nothing in common but his intelligence, his powers of observation, his ability to project what he had grasped and seen. . . . To imitate [him] is to have a just and fruitful notion of the actor's art." His movie colleague Marie Dressler envied "his consummate art" as an actor. Their great contemporary Lillian Gish asserted that "Lionel could play any character." As early as 1918, discussing the Barrymores when reviewing *The Copperhead*, P. G. Wodehouse confessed, "Lionel is the one that fascinates me most. . . . Just when you think you are never going to see him again, up he bobs once more and makes everybody else look like enthusiastic amateurs reciting pieces at church sociables."[7]

Despite the high esteem expressed by many for his acting, Lionel became a superlative character actor only very reluctantly. Turning as a last resort to acting because it provided the easiest way to avoid starvation, Lionel had wanted to support himself instead as a visual artist. His was the fate of many other people, famous or obscure, who spend their lives earning their sustenance by doing uncongenial work. Despite his extraordinary talent as an actor, he did not find that it expressed his individuality or met his need to create. To a perceptive interviewer in 1922, Lionel admitted that his natural bent was for acting, whereas his more congenial and enthusiastic artistic endeavors did not achieve as much. Yet he wanted to be himself, not a Barrymore: "My forebears, for generations back, were actors. So I suppose we were born with a natural instinct for acting, just as collie pups are born with an instinct for herding. But human beings like to think they are free agents; that they are *themselves* [italics in the original], not merely sort of hand-me-downs from the shelves of the past. . . . That's the only way I can explain my wanting to be a painter." Thwarted in his preferred vocation as a painter and illustrator, he used his artistry instead to portray many characters on stage and in films with great and increasing skill. Nonetheless, Lionel periodically and vehemently restated his view of acting as "a miserable and obscene way to make a living." "I dislike it—but no more intensely, perhaps, than I dislike any other form of work," Lionel asserted to Gladys Hall. "If I had a million dollars I would stop tomorrow. I would never again do anything on stage or screen or radio. As I have not a million dollars I will die with my prop shoes on, no doubt, or die shouting into the ether, perhaps. Die working, anyway." After Lionel shared these laments, Hall sought to question their negativity: "But the smell of greasepaint . . . isn't it true that it enters the blood?" Lionel insisted steadfastly, "The smell of greasepaint is a stench in my nostrils. I would run from it if I could." The interviewer in 1922 had observed his profound indifference to his acting accomplishments and his lack of any sense of them or of himself as anything special: "his whole attitude toward himself is one of insisting that he neither is nor does anything extraordinary. . . . Here was a man who is admittedly a great actor. . . . Yet, because his whole heart was not in it then, the things he did meant so little to him he scarcely remembers them."[8]

An earlier interview from 1905, when Lionel was twenty-seven, established his views of great acting, leading roles, and character acting. "To be great, an actor must be a sublime egotist," Lionel informed Ashton Stevens. "I have no hope of attaining to greatness." Moreover, he stressed his dislike of stage acting; first nights distressed him with acute anxiety. He greatly preferred being a character actor to being a leading man, which he characterized as posing very difficult challenges and as being undermined by character actors: "The leading man is the most abused creature in the world. He has to carry the whole play. He not only is, but he must tell, the whole story." When Stevens complimented him as "a man who had worked, had invented, for every success of his life," Lionel countered with, "My work has been largely subconscious. I've never had that good and proper feeling that comes from a good day's work—that is to say, I can't nail anything."[9]

Having opted for the easier choice of character acting and then denied that his success as a character actor was really to his credit, Lionel also expressed his never-changing dislike of the theater. His final years on the New York stage only exacerbated these attitudes. As a leading man, he failed to satisfy the critics, not only in *Macbeth* but also in such a play as *The Piker*, which had attracted him as a theatrical piece expressing grave truths about life. Its detractors filled him with indignant contempt. "Nothing profound or moving or tragic or terrible or pathetic or grotesque can happen to a citizen of New York," he sarcastically protested. "[If the situation in *The Piker*] isn't the spirit and substance of great tragedy, then the Greeks never wrote one. The ineluctible [*sic*] vengeance of the gods is here. . . . To me it seemed a masterpiece. It still does." Added to his doubts about his acting ability, his

Introduction

denigration of character acting and of his own efforts, his visceral hatred of the stage, was his disappointed belief in drama as a means to convey human truths.[10]

Repelled by the egotism of the leading man, Lionel sought refuge in character acting as a way *not* to reveal himself. Uninterested by acting, he sought instead to express his individuality through visual art and music. Perhaps his lack of personal investment in his acting actually improved its effectiveness because he concentrated not on self-expression but on accuracy of representation. He disappeared into his part, always. No one on the track of his actual personality ever found any revealing spoor to trail. In a world overrun by showy actors and overbearing personalities, Lionel impressed with his invisibility. He was so much The Man Who Wasn't There. Paradoxically, his achievement as a character actor, however unrewarding he found acting, established his individual genius in performances that have endured.

Besides defending against anxiety and fear of failure, this reluctantly drafted but conscientious character actor who scoffed at his own record of achievement was protecting the privacy and integrity of his innermost self. Stefan Zweig noted in *The World of Yesterday* that fame disturbs the equilibrium of many people: "It becomes a force which tends to influence, to dominate, to transform the person who bears it." Whereas confident and self-assured people may react with "a greater measure of self-assurance, a heightened self-confidence and ... the conviction that special importance is their due in society, ... [and] they inflate themselves in order to attain in their person the volume of their external achievement," "whoever is naturally distrustful of himself regards every kind of outward success as just so much more of an obligation to preserve himself as unchanged as possible." In other words, the reluctantly famous person resists identifying with the public persona in order to preserve an inner equilibrium. Zweig compared a human being's name to the band of a cigar: "a means of identification, a superficial, almost unimportant thing that is only loosely related to the real subject, the true ego." Lionel Barrymore's stage and screen fame, as well as his membership in the Royal Family of Broadway and Hollywood, may indeed have been profoundly unrelated to his inner self and consequently fundamentally unimportant to him, a matter of chronic indifference. His fame as an actor, as well as his place in the Barrymore constellation of stars, forever remained ill-fitting garments that vexed him and that he longed to discard.

Act One
Artful Dodger

1

Disorder and Early Sorrow, 1878-1893

Georgiana Drew Barrymore, descended from English and Irish performers, was beautiful, witty, charming—a talented American stage comedian. Maurice Barrymore, himself English and educated in England, was handsome, witty, charming—a talented American stage actor and playwright. To their children, they were idols rather than parents. Maurice was a friend, a pal to his sons, not a father. Georgiana had more awareness of her duties as a mother, but she was often absent while performing. As Ethel expressed it, "I was brought up in the interim of busy lives, lives of the theater, where children had to be set aside and cared for by others, so my most vivid memories of the beginning are naturally those connected with the rare times when the family were together." For Lionel, Ethel, and Jack, their real parent was their beloved maternal grandmother, Louisa Lane Drew, herself an actress since girlhood and a formidable upholder of the family's theatrical legacy. With their actor parents usually elsewhere, the Barrymore siblings found their only settled home at 140 North Twelfth Street in Philadelphia with Louisa—or "Mum Mum," as they called her. Their bond with her, their parents, their other older relatives, and one another was one of loyalty and respect. Yet because they were separated from Mum Mum and one another very early in life, the Barrymore siblings behaved with formality and distance. "[Mum Mum's] was the only home we ever knew together. We were to be separated very early in our lives by various circumstances," Ethel explained. "Consequently, when we met later in life we were rather formal with each other and very, very polite. It appears that rather terrified observers. I remember Lionel telling me that a friend of his who was present when I dined with him once said to him, 'My God! Don't you know each other?' . . . we didn't know each other well enough to quarrel." To Mum Mum the siblings owed whatever feelings of childhood security they experienced as well as the crushing expectation that each would carry on the family tradition of stage acting. None of the siblings wanted to be an actor. Lionel and Jack pursued dreams of being visual artists, while Ethel aspired to becoming a concert pianist. She shared with interviewer Ashton Stevens in 1907 her intention to retire from the stage to pursue opera singing. Jack commented to Stevens in 1905, "I still draw and paint—for myself—and it isn't with a feeling of mere dilettanteism [sic]. . . . Acting comes easy and pays well—that's the narcotic. . . . If I had my choice, I'd give up the stage." Perhaps, the glamour of being members of the Royal Family of Broadway was and is felt more by people who take for granted the protective care provided by dull parents than it was felt by the Barrymore siblings themselves. Parental absence, the pressure to become actors regardless of their own preferences, emotional distance, and the family dictum to avoid talking about anything important—all would have distinct consequences for each sibling. Elaine Barrie Barrymore, Jack's fourth wife, appointed herself witness for the prosecution by asserting that the Barrymore children were "brought up in a house of horror" by parents who had "the ugliest of marriages." Elaine's bitterness toward Lionel and Ethel subtracts some credibility from her condemnation; however, who knows what Jack told her in private? His and his siblings' public accounts of their early lives vary in detail, with Ethel's being the most perceptive and comprehensive.[1]

As Ethel narrated and various Barrymore biographers have elaborated, Georgiana's brother John Drew had joined Augustin Daly's theater company in New York City, the Fifth Avenue Theatre. There, John Drew met another actor of minor parts in the company, Maurice Barrymore, who subsequently married Georgie Drew in 1876. The first of their three children, Lionel, was born on April 28, 1878, at 119 North Ninth Street in Philadelphia and named after a Londoner admired by Maurice. (In his memoirs, Lionel misreported his birthday as April 12.) Louisa Lane Drew, an actor-manager who led a stock company and managed the Arch Street Theatre in Philadelphia for over thirty years, brought in the most steady income, so naturally Georgie and Maurice's three children lived with her on Twelfth Street in a house they called the "Tomb of the Capulets." After two years in England financed by others (Maurice had already dispersed his legacy with characteristic thoroughness), the children returned to Philadelphia. Lionel, who had attended London's Gilmore School in Warrington Crescent, then enrolled for five months of 1887 in Episcopal Academy, where Uncle John Drew had been a

Disorder and Early Sorrow, 1878-1893

student. A short stint in a nearby public school followed. At the Tomb of the Capulets, Lionel built ship models, sketched, dueled with Jack by using fly swatters, and pursued imaginary Iroquois in the nearby grounds of the Academy of Art. Then the elder two children went to boarding school. Sent to New York State's St. Aloysius Academy for Boys of Mount Saint Vincent (Eugene O'Neill also attended this school), the miserable Lionel ran away twice—most memorably in February 1888 by walking past oncoming trains in the darkness of Grand Central Terminal to exit through Grand Central Station and find his parents' hotel, Sturtevant House, at 1586 Broadway—a walk of thirteen miles. Eventually, in 1889, Lionel was sent to Seton Hall Academy in South Orange, New Jersey. Supposedly, Seton Hall expelled Lionel after he fought with another boy who had insulted Georgie, but no extant Seton Hall records substantiate this anecdote. In the summers, the children often saw each other and Mum Mum, with occasional glimpses of their parents. Georgie's serious respiratory illness necessitated a trip to Santa Barbara in California with the barely adolescent Ethel as her caretaker. Saying goodbye to Maurice, Georgie begged her husband not to forget her; during the trip, Ethel also overheard her mother crying, "What's going to happen to my three kids?" After Georgie's early death in 1893 in Santa Barbara from tuberculosis, Ethel brought her mother's body back east by train. Mum Mum later recalled, "The keenest sorrow of my life came to me in '93, when my dearest daughter, Georgie, died in California, whither she had gone in search of health, and only found death." Within months, Ethel learned of Maurice's remarriage, and Mum Mum announced to her that Ethel would now go on the stage: "suddenly, there was no money, no Arch Street Theatre, no house, and I must earn my living. No one talked about it; no one talked about it at all, ever." Mum Mum was famous for playing Mrs. Malaprop in Richard B. Sheridan's *The Rivals*, in which Ethel was now given a minor part. Mum Mum responded to Ethel's request for acting guidance with the rebuke, "You should know that without being told." By this time, Mum Mum had forsaken Philadelphia to live with John Drew in New York City. Fifteen-year-old Ethel lived with her uncle and grandmother at the Sherman Square Hotel and trudged around town looking for acting jobs with scant success. "I went on the stage," Ethel confessed, "because I did not know how to do anything but act—and I did not know how to do that. I had not become an ambitious actress. In fact I never have." For Lionel, too, Georgie's death meant an enforced draft into stage acting. Their grandmother apparently had envisioned their theatrical careers as early as 1882 when a newspaper interviewer recorded that Mrs.

Drew "lives for her two grandchildren ... who are being educated by her for the stage." This was probably evidence more of her aspirations for them than of any actual training. Four years later, in 1897, Mum Mum died in Larchmont. Maurice would die in 1905 after being committed by Jack in 1901 to institutional care for the complications of tertiary syphilis.[2]

Ethel published her memoir, *Memories*, in 1955, after both Jack and Lionel had died. Jack had recorded his recollections twice: in his 1926 memoir *Confessions of an Actor* and in a four-part series published by *American* magazine in 1933, "Those Incredible Barrymores." Jack in the twenties described his beloved Mum Mum at great length, told some funny stories about Maurice, and noted that he barely remembered Georgie. He did repeat, both in *Confessions of an Actor* and in the *American* series, the story of his dying mother's lament, "Oh, my poor kids, whatever will become of them?" Louisa Lane Drew dominated his account in *American* as well: "we were always moving—from this school to that, from one house to another.... Our grandmother took care of us, mostly.... Some months, when my father remembered to send money, we had fine clothes and lived in luxury. Mostly, however, we were poor." Once, when returning from a tour, Maurice arrived home with no money for necessities but with a bear cub that he had splurged to purchase. Maurice was the unending source of apparent amusement, Georgie a shadowy figure, and Mum Mum "part Drew, part Solomon, and part owl."[3]

Like Ethel's *Memories*, Lionel's autobiography, *We Barrymores*, was published late in life, in the fifties. His was perhaps the most reticent account published by the three siblings. The self-deprecatory humor that governed his very readable and enjoyable narrative also constantly served as an instrument of deflection. Lionel slipped here into his role as master raconteur, which did not allow for dwelling on the tragedies of the past. (An exception was his self-condemnation for destroying his marriage to Doris Rankin, which is more impressive considering that Doris was by then dead and no one could have challenged any excuses. Lionel apparently felt that he owed to Doris's ghost the recompense of his mea culpa, mea maxima culpa.) Lionel portrayed himself in boyhood as being uninterested in either acting or being formally educated. Lionel told funny stories about Maurice, referred to Georgie very briefly, and portrayed himself as a child whom his elders could leave to his own devices if they provided some drawing materials. Not only did he rapidly skate away from the tragedies of Georgie's and Maurice's deaths, but he also omitted crucial details from his own boyhood: most importantly, that

Disorder and Early Sorrow, 1878-1893

he ran away twice from St. Aloysius Academy and specifically that he walked for thirteen miles on a February day through railway tunnels and city streets to find his father. Admitting that, as a youth, he was constantly in fights, he did not say that he hit a Seton Hall classmate for insulting his mother, nor did he mention his 1895 arrest in Long Branch, New Jersey, for assault, which made the front page of the *New York Times*. While he emphasized the security provided by Mum Mum and recognized that his parents were not really parents, he excused their failings and stressed the sad effects on Jack while minimizing any mention of himself.[4]

Instead of expressing any disappointment or disapproval, Lionel chose instead to focus on his liking for Maurice and on their good times together. These included, according to Lionel and to Maurice's biographer, visiting the circus or lying in bed with his father and brother as Maurice narrated tales from his early years in India, where he had been born. As Maurice had become a prominent stage star and playwright, his acquaintances included many famous people of the day. Lionel unknowingly encountered Pyotr Ilich Tchaikovsky, watched Maurice spar in a gym with John L. Sullivan, and memorably met Mark Twain. Passive and uninterested when Maurice introduced him to a Mr. Clemens, Lionel suddenly revived when he realized that he was talking to the author of his beloved *Huckleberry Finn*; then Lionel relayed to Twain the entire plot of his own novel. The boy's naive enthusiasm brought tears to Twain's eyes. Their parents absent, Jack and Lionel enjoyed a chaotic summer existence at Maurice's weed-infested Staten Island farm, where they ran riot with thirty-five dogs descended from the four huskies given to Maurice by Commander Robert E. Peary after his 1891 polar expedition. Edward Briggs, an African American they called "Edward the Black Prince," supervised them. As Jack told an interviewer in 1933, "He never made us wash our faces, we never made the beds or washed dishes, and had a magnificent existence—the three of us and the 35 dogs.... There was practically an acre of dogs. They swarmed all over the house, sharing the beds, chasing cats and yelping at the moon and passersby. Often the larder was pretty low, but Edward, by the terrific force of his personality, wangled enough food from the town grocery to keep us alive."[5]

This preference for the misleading positive memory may well reflect the elderly Lionel's acceptance that his parents, especially his father, had lacked the capacity, as well as the time, to fulfill their responsibilities. Maybe he knew that Maurice was always a man with a fragile hold on reality, as when Lionel noticed at Georgie's funeral that Maurice had sunk into denial of her

LIONEL BARRYMORE

death. And yet Lionel's own record of being an outsider amid intimate strangers, of being neglected or ignored at home and abandoned to boarding schools, of fighting and getting arrested, of possibly being expelled, of walking thirteen miles on a February day through dark railway tunnels and on city streets to get away from school and to find his parents when he was not quite ten years old—all these attest to unexpressed yet potent anger, sadness, loneliness, and grief. Ethel described his plight more fittingly than Lionel did: "He ran away twice from that school, walking through the tunnel into the old Grand Central Station, no flashlights then—in fact, no *nothing*—except monstrous trains bearing down on a small boy in the blackness."[6]

2

Twenty Years, Two Apprenticeships, 1893–1912

Like many other intellectually curious and creative people, Lionel left formal education as soon as he could. Perhaps his exodus from residential schooling also partly resulted from his desire to reconnect with his family members. But a need to live among Drews and Barrymores did not, for Lionel, indicate the slightest ambition to take up the family profession. Yet, having to support himself, he found the theater to be his most ready employer. So Lionel reluctantly trod the boards, but he always cherished as his genuine creative interests both music and visual art. Twice, he expended considerable effort and time to obtain training as a painter—first at the Art Students League in New York City; then, a decade later, at the Académie Julian in Paris. Yet, despite his determined evasion of the theater, monetary pressures eventually turned him back to the stage. His two competing pursuits—theater acting and painting—consumed the twenty years between the end of his schooldays and the start of his serious involvement in film acting and direction. In retrospect, from 1893 to 1912, Lionel served parallel apprenticeships as a character actor and as a visual artist. In prospect, however, he was always trying to reject acting for painting. Sailing for Paris, Lionel remembered almost a half century later, meant "I had broken loose from the stage.... I considered it a complete, logical, and irrevocable break."[1]

From 1893 to 1895, while he lived with his father and his father's new wife, Marie Floyd, in New York City, Lionel attended classes at the Art Students League. In the 1893–1894 school year, he attended "Preparatory Antique" with either J. H. Twachtman or Carroll Beckwith as well as "Morning Painting" with William Merritt Chase. In the following school year, he resumed taking "Morning Painting" with Chase and "Preparatory Antique" with Twachtman. "Morning Painting" was simply a painting class scheduled in the morning, while "Preparatory Antique" instructed beginners in drawing shapes and understanding the components of visual art. It preceded classes in "Antique" (copying plaster casts of classical sculpture) and life drawing. A few years later, Lionel also pursued musical studies with Agnes Morgan, and composer-conductor Henry Hadley, a crony from the actors' Lambs Club, tutored him.[2]

When composing his memoirs, Lionel amusedly recounted how he was ejected from Twachtman's "Preparatory Antique" class for brawling, a chronic habit of Lionel's in his pugnacious youth. An argument with fellow student Ferdinand Pinney Earle precipitated a fistfight that wrecked Twachtman's classroom. Retiring to a bar and consoling themselves with alcohol, the reconciled combatants learned of their enforced, immediate, and permanent exile from "Preparatory Antique." Lionel gloomily concluded that this death sentence condemned him to life in the theater. The kind intervention of a fellow student, however, paradoxically got Lionel admitted to Kenyon Cox's class instead, which struck the dazzled Lionel as a thoroughly undeserved promotion and reward for bad behavior.[3]

The years from 1893 to 1900 also featured Lionel's initial appearances as an adult on the stage—first as a member of the Drew theater troupe and then as an employee of Georgia Cayvan and Company, Augustus Pitou, Sol Smith, Augustus Thomas, the Bond Stock Company, and, most consequentially, McKee Rankin. *Sag Harbor* in 1900 concluded this novitiate. Before his real debut in 1893, Lionel had engaged in a few juvenile appearances. Drafted at the age of five to replace an ailing child actor in a St. Louis production of *As You Like It,* Lionel had let loose a frightened yell that disgraced his premature debut. When he was a few years older, Ethel had persuaded him and Jack to appear in her juvenile production of *Camille* that netted thirty-seven cents unequally distributed among the three siblings. In a Staten Island barn, Ethel played Camille; Lionel (to his outspoken distress), her lover Armand; and Jack, the Count de Varville after Ethel had announced to her brothers that "it's about time we were doing something in the theater." (Lionel would play Armand again in a 1917 film about a *Camille* production on tour, *The End of the Tour.*) Other amateur productions that summer produced compensation in the form of ice cream. Jack remembered, "Until we were a good many years older, Lionel and I were in the theater mostly because of the ice cream."[4]

Lionel both engaged in and recorded his first adult acting experiences with scant enthusiasm. Hired in 1893 by his grandmother and her son, his uncle Sidney Drew, for a minor role in Richard Sheridan's classic comedy *The*

Twenty Years, Two Apprenticeships, 1893–1912

Rivals, Lionel evaluated his own performance as wretchedly poor and openly rejoiced when his grandmother, in a note written with purple ink, tactfully eased him out of the production. Emancipated from the theater for the time being, Lionel, as he told Hedda Hopper much later, "made myself useful to Uncle Sidney with martinis. See, he wasn't supposed to have them." He continued, "If it wasn't for Uncle Sidney, I wouldn't have had any acting career . . . [he gave me] a perpetual job—the only one I had." Still, Lionel told another late-life interviewer, Uncle Sidney "was a tough son of a bitch." Besides refining his skills as a mixologist and sampler of mixed drinks, Lionel continued to appear at intervals with the Drew troupe in *The Road to Ruin* and *The Bachelor's Baby*. Georgia Cayvan featured him in *Mary Pennington, Spinster* and *Squire Kate*. For Augustus Pitou, he acted in *Cumberland '61*. Uninspiring in and uninspired by these experiences, Lionel then hooked up with McKee Rankin, an actor-manager previously with Mrs. Drew's stock company who had created an acting team with his wife, Kitty Blanchard. The elderly Lionel claimed, "Nobody but Mr. Rankin would have given me a job in the theater." In Minneapolis in 1898, Lionel performed as part of Rankin's troupe in several productions: *A Wife's Peril, Magda, Oliver Twist, East Lynne*, and *Camille*. Mentorship by Rankin acclimated Lionel to stage acting, in which he gingerly began to take an interest. Always averse to acting in romantic leading-man parts, Lionel later recalled that he vigorously protested to Rankin that he would never play Romeo in a curtain-raiser balcony scene: "I'll be shot if I play Romeo." Rankin replied, "I deserve to be shot if I allowed you." Rankin fired Lionel's roommate, Frank Butler, who then secured a temporary job as drama critic for a Minneapolis newspaper and proceeded to savage Rankin's current production as well as to single out Lionel in his small part. Recalling the gist of Butler's notice of Lionel's performance as "the audience lived all through the entire evening in terror lest he return," Lionel chortled that this was "the funniest goddamned thing that ever happened."[5]

After working in Sol Smith productions of *Uncle Dick* and *The Honorable John Rigsby*, Lionel toured for Augustus Thomas in *Arizona*, in which he was cast as an old man. The Bond Stock Company also featured him in *Rain Clouds, The Rivals*, and *An Arabian Night*. Although Lionel remained unimpressed by his own performance in *Arizona*, actor-producer James A. Herne thought well enough of it to hire Lionel for *Sag Harbor*. Noting this 1900 staging as his debut on Broadway, Lionel deplored his own performance as a young (rather than an old) man, a sentiment shared by the kindly Herne, who flattered Lionel out of his cast: "I should be ruining your career, which is going to be brilliant, if I did not urge you at once to drop this very poor role and take a vacation." When Lionel was later appearing in *The Letter of the Law*, he recalled Herne's sage advice that Lionel should always play character roles as "the turning point of my life." When, as Milt Shanks in *The Copperhead*, Lionel delivered a very long speech, he took as his model Herne's performance in *Sag Harbor*: "My memory of his acting is one of my most valuable possessions."[6]

Enforced but welcome respite from acting ended when Lionel's meeting with Sam Shubert in 1901 arranged for him to join the cast of *The Brixton Burglary*, the Shubert brothers' first Broadway production. Once, when Lionel skipped a rehearsal to remain in bed, an enraged Sam Shubert hunted him down. Ethel subsequently persuaded theatrical producer-director Charles Frohman more than once to cast Lionel. Her elder brother performed in several Frohman productions in succession between 1901 and 1906 before leaving the stage, as he then thought, forever: *The Second in Command*, *The Mummy and the Humming Bird*, *The Best of Friends*, *The Other Girl*, and *Pantaloon*. These were the parts in which others first discerned Lionel's great gifts as a character actor. Regarding *The Mummy and the Humming Bird*, the *Indianapolis Journal* noted that Lionel, as Giuseppe, "mutters in his native tongue while gesticulating in his own rude fashion, and yet makes himself understood and wins the sympathy of his audience.... His was a performance of great artistic merit." The *Inter-Ocean* enthusiastically headlined "Triumph of Lionel Barrymore" and later reported that early rehearsals had been lackluster, with everything going wrong and the cast (including Lionel) expecting failure. Sitting next to an Italian count during a performance, Ethel was amused at the count's indignant correction of Ethel's description of Giuseppe, "He is *not* an Italian. He is a Sicilian." She commented wryly, "Probably the best notice anyone ever got!" *The Best of Friends* impressed Jack: "He seems to check his personality like an overcoat whenever he goes into a part." Augustus Thomas wrote *The Other Girl* for Lionel: "In the theatre his happiness is in delineating character and he goes at each new subject with the technical interest of an artist interested in surfaces and in the face behind them." The *San Francisco Call* headline for a notice about a production of *The Other Girl* declared "Young Actor Is Heralded as a Genius."[7]

Despite theater critic Ashton Stevens's admiration for Lionel as "the foremost American character actor of his years," Lionel minimized his achievement in a 1905 interview with Stevens. He confessed that the expectations

Twenty Years, Two Apprenticeships, 1893–1912

created by his newfound stardom frightened him. He did not know if he could satisfy them. By nature, the very opposite of the "sublime egotist" that he described "the Great Actor" as being—humorless, impervious to criticism, entirely absorbed in his own artistry—Lionel confessed his fear of the first night: "It's a nightmare. It takes me two nights to know what happened on the first." Stardom would only worsen his fears: "being the whole table d'hôte instead of the entrée puts you hard against it for nervousness." He joked about the inconsequentiality of some of his parts: "Why, I was at the theatre, but I didn't see you in the play," a friend said. Lionel replied, "You must have winked."[8]

Acting being the family business, like plumbing or lawyering, Lionel had halfheartedly sought stage roles only because it was the easiest way to get a job and make money. After a decade of experience, *The Mummy and the Hummingbird* (1902) and subsequent stage productions brought him some acclaim in his unchosen profession and the respect of those who recognized his great ability. However, acting in the theater also created such terrifying anxiety that he would forget his lines while onstage.[9]

In 1904, the year before he confessed these qualms to Stevens, Lionel married Doris Rankin, the daughter of McKee Rankin and actress Mabel Bert, not of Rankin's wife, Kitty Blanchard. In 1887, Bert retreated to her native England to give birth to Doris but eventually left their daughter with Rankin. In 1893, Lionel's grandmother Louisa Lane Drew had reconciled Rankin and Blanchard, and Blanchard had taken Doris into her keeping. The cast of a touring production of *The Rivals* had included Rankin, Blanchard, and their daughters Gladys (who was married to Sidney Drew) and Phyllis (who married Henry Gibbs and later Harry Davenport) as well as Louisa Drew, Sidney Drew, and eventually Maurice Barrymore. A summer 1894 Rankin troupe on tour included Gladys and Sidney Drew, Phyllis and Henry Gibbs, Doris Rankin, and Ethel Barrymore. In 1898, Lionel had joined the Rankin company for several productions in Minneapolis. Six years later, while visiting Phyllis and Harry Davenport's farm in upstate New York, Lionel fell in love with sixteen-year-old Doris, whom he married in June 1904 in New York City at Saint Francis Xavier Church.

Lionel had reportedly already engaged himself in 1898 to actress Angela McCaull, daughter of the founder of the McCaull Comic Opera Company, Colonel John A. McCaull, and he was still engaged to Angela in 1903. Maybe someone was pressuring a reluctant sweetie to announce. Perhaps geographical separation or lack of money or transient enthusiasm had indefinitely postponed these permanently deferred nuptials. Some newspaper accounts of the Rankin marriage reported that people felt surprised by it because they thought that the McCaull engagement was still on. Called "the quintessence of all that is dainty and fascinating," Angela apparently was not fascinating enough for Lionel actually to marry her, but she later wed film and stage director James Gordon Edwards.

Doris enthusiastically supported her new husband's desire to be a painter, Lionel persuaded Ethel to finance his endeavor, and the couple sailed for France in the spring of 1906. While they lived in Paris and Lionel studied painting at the Académie Julian, Doris allegedly gave birth to a short-lived daughter, Mary, in 1906. She certainly gave birth to their daughter Ethel in 1908. Most probably, there were only two daughters who did not survive to adulthood: Ethel (who was born in Paris and died in New York State) and an American-born Mary (who was born later in New York State and who also died there). The evidence for a baby born in 1906 is only anecdotal; searches in Parisian records (birth, death, burial, and baptismal) for a French-born Mary turned up nothing at all. Her purported existence likely resulted from confusion or misunderstanding. Unless and until someone finds a birth, baptismal, death, or burial document, her existence is merely hypothetical and probably bogus.[10]

A French birth certificate *does* establish Ethel's birth in Paris on August 9, 1908, and Pennsylvania as well as New York State official documents note Ethel's death in Manhattan on March 24, 1910, after Lionel and Doris had returned to live in New York. Filling out a biographical questionnaire late in his life, Lionel himself recorded the lives and early deaths of only two daughters, Ethel and the later Mary, who died on March 19, 1917, in New York State. (A New York State record documents that a "Mary Barrimore" was born in Manhattan on June 5, 1915.) He wrote that Ethel died as an infant (she was nineteen months old) and that Mary died at the age of two. Cameron Shipp's 1957 account of working with Lionel on his memoirs mentioned that Lionel and Doris lost *two* young daughters. In addition, reminiscences by Ethel published in December 1923 mentioned that Doris gave birth to her and Lionel's *first* baby in the summer after Ethel appeared in *The Silver Box* (1907) and then went on summer tour in *Captain Jinks and the Horse Marines* and before Ethel appeared in *Lady Frederick* (late 1908). Baby Ethel was born during her aunt's visit to Paris. Regardless of whether Lionel fathered two or three girls, he loved children, and the complete absence from his memoirs of his own children suggests how painful he found his memories of their brief existence.[11]

Twenty Years, Two Apprenticeships, 1893–1912

Just as his two daughters are unseen ghosts in his memoirs, there is scant mention of either of his two wives; neither Doris Rankin nor her successor, Irene Fenwick, appears in great detail. These ellipses of memory indicate the degree of Lionel's sorrow. Under pressure from his collaborator, Cameron Shipp, Lionel provided somewhat more detail about Doris Rankin, but he still mentioned Doris relatively little, given that they were married from 1904 to 1922—for almost twenty years. For the record, despite their eventual divorce, others had regarded the Rankin-Barrymore marriage as loving, even exemplary. Blanche Oelrichs, whose 1920 marriage to John Barrymore made Blanche Doris's sister-in-law, remembered, "Jack told me, and I could see, that Lionel adored his wife. . . . I saw him surreptitiously kiss her cloak as he laid it across her shoulders." Ernest Blumenschein, who painted a portrait group of Lionel, Doris, baby Ethel, and a nursemaid in Paris in 1909, admired his friend Lionel's "very beautiful, young and exquisite" wife.[12]

A friend with whom Lionel would keep in touch for many decades, Blumenschein, too, was associated with both the Art Students League in New York and Paris's Académie Julian. Both men had enrolled for classes at the Art Students League in 1893. Both had found teacher J. H. Twachtman somewhat uncongenial. Both had pursued musical as well as artistic passions. Blumenschein, however, had embarked for France long before Lionel, in 1894, where he had enrolled in the famous Académie Julian for two years before he returned to New York to work as an illustrator. Back in Paris again when Lionel and Doris lived there, Blumenschein expressed his liking for Lionel in a 1909 letter: Lionel was "jolly good company, very entertaining. ([W]e spend a great deal of time when together in giving imitations of orchestras)." Blumenschein and his wife, the artist Mary Greene, returned to New York in May 1909; not long afterward, Doris and Lionel left Paris for home with baby Ethel, disembarking on August 6, 1909.[13]

Although Lionel mocked his own alleged lack of talent as a visual artist, his failure to earn a living as an artist after sustained efforts undoubtedly frustrated him deeply and not only because succeeding would have allowed him to escape the theater. As he told an interviewer many years later, "I returned to New York and set up in business as an illustrator. Well, pretty soon I found that beginning illustrators didn't eat as often as they felt hungry." Obviously, if Lionel did not eat, baby Ethel and Doris did not eat either. His only sustainable option was to revert to being a theater actor, a profession in which he had some prospect of being employed but that he loathed. Almost a half century later, Hedda Hopper asked Lionel, "Do you enjoy acting?" to which he responded, "No. Not at all. I just don't like it." Hopper persisted: "If you could have made a living painting would you ever have become an actor?" "No," he stressed. "If I could have made a good living digging wells, I never would have become an actor." He grumped that he played his famous role of Scrooge only because of "that constant urge for dinner."[14]

Lionel had received some acclaim for returning to the stage in Charles Frohman's 1909 production of *The Fires of Fate*: his performance was hailed as "unusual acting . . . really wonderful," but then he suffered an alleged but dubious episode of appendicitis. News reports recorded that he left the Chicago company for an operation and convalescence in New York. To Ethel's horror, Lionel then joined his father-in-law, McKee Rankin, as well as Doris, Sidney Drew, and Gladys Drew, for some forays into vaudeville. From 1910 to 1912, Lionel acted in *The Jail Bird*, *The White Slaver*, *Bob Acres*, *Stalled*, and *The Still Voice*. McKee Rankin wrote the one-act farce *Confusion* "especially for Lionel Barrymore, McKee Rankin, and Doris Rankin"; they played it during the 1910 tour. A few years later, after her daughter's birth in 1912, Ethel herself began touring in vaudeville and changed her opinion of it. Dismissing as "snobbish" the disregard for vaudeville expressed by "legitimate" stage people, Ethel found vaudeville very demanding of quality work: "It is a real taskmaster because there are so many acts in it, like slack-wire artists, for instance, that require absolute perfection. . . . The vaudeville public is an exacting one and nothing must ever be slurred for them, perfect in the afternoon and perfect at night, over and over again for weeks and weeks." Indeed, *Variety* cited the demanding vaudeville audience's lack of enthusiasm for *Bob Acres* (excerpted from *The Rivals*) as proving that Sidney Drew and Lionel had chosen a poor vehicle for vaudeville. Despite their excellent performances, "A vaudeville audience waits for nothing so as a result the curtain silently fell on the first scene notwithstanding the dialog of old time wit indulged in by Drew and Barrymore." Presenting *Bob Acres*, *Variety* felt, wasted their time.[15]

Like his much-praised earlier role in *The Mummy and the Humming Bird*, *The White Slaver*, written by Lionel, featured him as an Italian immigrant. Doris played Lionel's niece or daughter, while Doris's actual father, Rankin, had the role of "white slaver," or sex trafficker. After a successful opening in Atlantic City, *The White Slaver* went on tour: "All three actors won praise from the very demanding vaudeville audiences." Sniffy about the unpalatable subject matter, *Variety* nonetheless praised Lionel's "splendid bit of acting. Dialect, gesticulation and bearing are perfect and he makes the illusion complete." Again praising "Barrymore's great work as the Italian [that] really makes this act," *Variety* did express some reservations about his character's physical violence: "While Mr. Barrymore may be carried away in his fury to stab the owner of his daughter several times, and perhaps more, once is enough on the stage. Just give him one good stab, and let it go at that." The *San Francisco Dramatic Review* called Doris "a clever little actress." *The White Slaver* being "a medium for some splendid acting," Rankin was "inimitable," Doris was "effective," and Lionel's "interpretation of the part is one of the best of the kind it has been our good fortune to witness."[16]

When *The White Slaver* closed in vaudeville in New Orleans in March 1911, Rankin celebrated fifty-one years of stage work, but he was now "a worn-out and forgotten matinee idol" toasted by "his illegitimate daughter and his penniless son-in-law." Even so, Rankin would prove to be a godsend to Lionel. By sending Lionel to the Biograph Company, on Fourteenth Street in New York City, to meet D. W. Griffith, Rankin had offered Lionel a means of escape from stage and vaudeville work. Lionel's defecting to the movies—although it horrified Ethel even more than the misuse of the talents of "the genius of the family" in vaudeville—rescued him from his terror of stage work.[17]

3

Escape into Films, 1911–1917

The Hollywood studio system in which Lionel eventually worked for thirty years was born out of the resistance by independent entrepreneurs to Thomas Edison's Motion Picture Patents Company (MPPC). In defiance of the MPPC, in 1910 the independents formed the Motion Picture Distribution and Sales Company. Struggling mightily against these independents, Edison's patents-based trust or monopoly finally failed in its efforts to control film production, distribution, and exhibition by exacting licensing fees. In 1915, a federal court found the MPPC guilty of violating the Sherman Antitrust Act. But the film company that Lionel joined in 1912, Biograph, had belonged to the MPPC since the MPPC's formation in 1908. Founded by Edison's defecting inventor William K. Dickson in 1895, the American Mutoscope Company changed into the American Mutoscope and Biograph Company in 1899 and further evolved into Biograph in 1908. The genesis of the Edison attempt at monopoly was Edison's ownership of many patents related to components of film production. He demanded payment for licenses by competing film producers, as well as required their exclusive use of patented Edison film and technology. Building on that foundation, the MPPC trust attempted to control film production, distribution, and exhibition. One means of control was the acquisition of other patents on film equipment and the imposition of licensing fees on independent competitors. The MPPC required distributors and exhibitors to feature only trust-produced films and to use only trust-patented equipment. Producers had to pay for trust film stock. The General Film Company created by the trust in 1910 promoted the distribution of trust-produced movies and threatened the distribution of nontrust films.[1]

The trust was based on the East Coast, so most early movie production occurred in New York and New Jersey, with some filming in Philadelphia, Chicago, and Jacksonville, Florida. Later, the independents' Southern California

Escape into Films, 1911–1917

location provided geographic distance from trust enforcers. California offered, in addition to plentiful sunshine, inexpensive and nonunionized labor as well as the varied landscapes vital to the efficiency of factory-style film production. The independents finally defeated the trust for additional reasons. In early trust-produced films, the stars were anonymous, but audience attachment to the players drove the shift to star-focused production and to an industry built around star promotion and control. The trust had also resisted producing feature-length films, but the independents had seen their potential. The focus on star players by feature-length movies transformed the industry, with the public's obsession with star actors remaining the controlling element for decades: "it shaped the industry.... Every advance in technique, every important development, could be attributed to it, from the close-up to the introduction of the feature film." When Lionel joined Biograph in 1912, however, these fundamental changes were still in the future. Biograph actors, however famous some of them became later in feature films, were still anonymous players in very short movies.[2]

Lionel was just starting in pictures, and his esteemed Biograph director, D. W. Griffith, and costars Lillian Gish and Mary Pickford were also relatively new to films. Pickford had acted in her first movie in 1909, whereas Gish began her film career in 1912 after her old friend Pickford introduced Gish to Griffith. A failed stage actor and playwright, Griffith had begun film work as actor Lawrence Griffith at Edison in 1907, and he worked as an extra in his first film for Biograph. Griffith directed for Biograph, as well as supervised production, from 1908 to 1913. With cameraman Billy Bitzer, Griffith created numerous short films and experimented with techniques that formed the armamentarium of the new medium. In over 450 short films, his stock company of actors included, in addition to Gish, Pickford, and Lionel, Dorothy Gish, Blanche Sweet, Mae Marsh, Harry Carey, Henry B. Walthall, Mack Sennett, Florence Turner, Constance Talmadge, and Donald Crisp. Harry Carey told the story of how he and Lionel, haunted by process servers hunting them after an investment in a show had withered, decamped to California to work for Griffith. Promised eventual payment, the manager of the New York City hotel in which they were staying helped them escape through a basement exit. Trying first to go east to New Jersey and "relax[ing] on a quart of bourbon," they mistakenly boarded a westbound train that kept them vulnerable in New York State: "We spent the rest of the trip till we passed Buffalo, N.Y., locked in the men's room every time the train stopped."[3]

Along with Universal Studios, the Fox Film Corporation, Goldwyn Pictures, Metro, and the Solax Company, Biograph established production facilities in Fort Lee, New Jersey. Maurice Barrymore had once lived in Coytesville, north of Fort Lee, and raised money there for a local firehouse, Company No. 2. In Coytesville, Lionel may have made his movie acting debut as a film extra in 1911 by performing in Griffith's *The Battle*. He signed on with Griffith's company in 1912. Acting with Pickford, Lionel had a major role in *The New York Hat*, shot by Griffith in 1912 in Coytesville and Fort Lee. George Cukor many years later asserted, after watching Pickford in *The New York Hat*, "[Her] acting is so modern. . . . She invented motion picture acting" because "[the other actors] were doing what they did on the stage . . . ranting and raving. . . . And then she began founding the tradition of motion picture acting."[4]

Until Griffith left Biograph two years later, Lionel acted in many of Griffith's short films in addition to writing scenarios for some and directing a few short films for the company. Noting that "Lionel could play any character," Lillian Gish remembered that Griffith felt pleased when Lionel joined their troupe. "Lionel found films interesting," Gish also explained. "Perhaps because of his ambition to paint, composition and lighting fascinated him." Perhaps using his strong visual sense by directing films satisfied a little his thwarted ambition to become a painter.[5]

Griffith's 1911 Civil War short *The Battle* is often listed as Lionel's first film acting gig, although some dispute whether he appears in it at all. Other sources cite Griffith's *Friends* (1912, with Pickford) as Lionel's first film acting job. Viewing himself in *Friends*, Lionel felt distressed enough by his own rotundity that he vowed to give up beer. Among the many other Griffith films in which Lionel acts, *The New York Hat* (with the Gish sisters and Pickford) was based on a scenario mailed to Biograph from California by Anita Loos, who became a prolific contributor. "I was the one writer he felt comfortable with," Loos recalled many years later about Griffith. "He'd loved me from the beginning. He was a terribly shy man, and terribly sensitive. . . . I would have done anything for him, because I adored him, although I never saw him but I always felt he'd given me my start." *Motion Pictures Today* in 1927 questioned whether "Harry O. Hoyt and not Anita Loos sent the scenario [of *The New York Hat*] to Mr. Griffith," when this "superb old thing" was revived at the Fifth Avenue Playhouse. Four years earlier, Biograph had conveyed all rights to the film to Pickford, and she gave permission to the Museum of Modern Art in 1935 to show the film. When, in 1938, Pickford donated a print of *The New York Hat* to the National Archives, she also sent National Archives certificates to Lionel, Loos, and Griffith. In 1959, Loos remarked,

Escape into Films, 1911–1917

"It's still run at the Museum of Modern Art. I often go to see it with the Gish girls and other people." Lionel is also among the cast of *The Burglar's Dilemma*, *The House of Darkness*, and *Death's Marathon*. When Griffith was still a stage actor in 1906, McKee Rankin had hired him to play in Ibsen and Shakespeare. Rankin's stage production of *Judith of Bethulia* was a precursor of Griffith's last Biograph film of the same name (1913), a four-reeler in which Rankin's son-in-law Lionel appears as an extra. The exterior scenes for *Judith* were shot in Chatsworth, California, where Lionel would later live for many years on a ranch. Lionel also worked with other Biograph directors, such as Anthony O'Sullivan, director of *In Diplomatic Circles*. Reporting in 1913 about Lionel's "fine portrayal of the Japanese Ambassador" for Biograph, *Variety* noted that "when Mr. Barrymore works for Biograph's 'Irish Players' he drops the latter end of his name to be in the 'atmosphere.'"[6]

Given his perennial, oft-repeated assertion that he disliked acting, perhaps Lionel enjoyed more his other contributions as a scenario writer and a director. "I never really wanted to be an actor," he repeated in 1941. "I tried to get away from it during the Paris stay. I tried to get away from it in New York [during the Biograph and Metro years]. I tried to get away from it in Hollywood by directing." In 1912 and 1913, as a Biograph employee, Lionel wrote (for Griffith) the films *The Burglar's Dilemma* as well as *The Tender Hearted Boy*, and (for Anthony O'Sullivan) *The Vengeance of Galora*. Recalling two decades later that Griffith paid him $25 for the scenario for *The Tender Hearted Boy*, Lionel teased Anita Loos that she should have gotten more money for her screen writing. Lionel himself estimated at different times that he wrote between fifty and one hundred scenarios for Griffith. Gish remembered that Griffith encouraged his actors who needed more income to write film treatments. As for Lionel's directing Biograph films, his credits include five movies from 1913 to 1914: *Chocolate Dynamite*, *His Secret* (with Donald Crisp), *Just Boys*, *No Place for Father*, and *Where's the Baby?*[7]

As early as 1920, Lionel expressed his respect for film artistry and his disappointment in the low quality of movie product tailored to the taste of mass audiences. He thought of these issues by remembering his early excitement over working with Griffith. "The Biograph dramas of the old days marked the high-water mark of the screen," Lionel asserted in 1920. "The production of pictures was then in the hands of the few and Griffith could force his public to take the kind of drama he wished to make. Griffith is a genius. Today he is curbed and hemmed in by the innumerable limitations which have grown up around the film." For his part, Griffith remembered that "Lionel Barrymore was vivid in those old Biograph days" and, in 1948, named Lionel, as well as Spencer Tracy, as the best actors around. Lionel recounted memories of these pioneering days as a film actor with his characteristic self-deprecating humor. Asked about his early appearances in westerns, he laughed: "I was the sheriff. And, goddamn, I'd never been on board a horse in my life before.... I always hated the guts of horses just like I hated acting, but I always had to do it, had to get on a blue roan, goddamn ... [and] some crazy girl used to race the train with him. This was my horse. Sheriff's horse. Boo!"[8]

During this first phase of his long but intermittent involvement with motion pictures, Lionel also worked for some independent producers and distributors. For the production company Colonial/distribution company World Film Corporation, Lionel performed in *The Seats of the Mighty* (1914); for World Film Corporation as both producer and distributor, in *Wildfire* (1915); for producer/distributor Kinetophote, in *The Span of Life* (1914); for the producer Life Photo Film Corporation and distributor State Rights, in *The Curious Conduct of Judge Legarde* and *A Modern Magdalen* (1915); and for the production company Wharton and distribution company Pathé, in *The Romance of Elaine* (1915). (*Variety* reported that Lionel also directed *The Curious Conduct of Judge Legarde*, but he is not credited as its director in filmographies.) Much later, Lionel reminisced to Ed Sullivan about *The Seats of the Mighty*. Director T. Hays Hunter—"A great friend of mine—never had an address except his office, and slept in Turkish baths"—needed five hundred extras to stage the Battle of Quebec, but Hunter's agent had mistakenly hired one thousand extras, "500 bums picked up in lower New York." Hunter enlisted "Barry" to redirect the five hundred unneeded and unpaid extras to Peter Burns's tavern in Fort Lee. Fearing a riot when the men eventually realized that they would not get paid after all, Lionel "sat on a balcony, ate a sandwich, and watched" while the tiny Fort Lee police department and fire department scattered the mob. "That night they robbed every hen roost within 10 miles, and stole everything in sight. But Hunter got his shots."[9]

Most of his non-Biograph work in this period, however, was for Metro. In 1915, Richard Rowland and Louis B. Mayer founded Metro as a distributor of movies produced by Solax. One of several other production companies whose output was distributed by Metro was Rolfe Photoplays. Metro-Rolfe had signed Ethel to a five-film contract for the two years between 1915 and 1917. As Ethel had previously intervened to secure stage work under Charles Frohman for Lionel, in 1915 she now secured for him a Metro-Rolfe

Escape into Films, 1911–1917

two-year "star at large" contract as well. When Ethel signed on again with Metro-Rolfe in 1917, her contract specified that Lionel would write and direct one of her five new films, *Life's Whirlpool*. In all, Lionel made ten films for Metro-Rolfe in these two years.[10]

Rolfe was the production company for most of these films, whereas Metro was usually the distributor: in 1915, *The Flaming Sword* and *A Yellow Streak* (produced by Columbia Film Company and distributed by Metro); in 1916, *The Quitter, Dorian's Divorce, The Brand of Cowardice,* and *The Upheaval*; in 1917, *His Father's Son, The End of the Tour* (produced by Rolfe and Columbia Film), and *The Millionaire's Double,* which Harry Davenport directed.

However, for the five-reel *Life's Whirlpool* in 1917, Metro was both producer and distributor, while Lionel did not act in the movie but wrote and directed it. Now a lost film, *Life's Whirlpool* is significant as Lionel's first major attempt at direction. The *Los Angeles Herald* reported that he had spent two years writing it. Exterior scenes filmed at Ethel's actual home at Taylor's Lane in Mamaroneck, New York were a selling point for the movie's publicists, who noted the desire of thousands of Ethel's fans to see her house. Alan Hale was Ethel's costar. *Variety* unenthusiastically noted that *Life's Whirlpool* "showed little or nothing to warrant comment," recycled well-worn material, but did feature Ethel and Hale to advantage. Contrariwise, the *Chicago Daily Tribune*'s reviewer enjoyed several of the performances and stressed, "You're SURE to like Miss Barrymore!" The *Sacramento Union* went so far as to consider Ethel's acting "one of the greatest depictions that has marked her career as a stage or screen star." *Photoplay* praised the "profundity about her understanding of the realities of life that sets her apart." The memoirs of neither Barrymore sibling mentioned *Life's Whirlpool* at all.[11]

Lionel's memoirs did mention D. W. Griffith at length. Lionel knew Griffith both near the beginning of Griffith's directorial career and at the end of Griffith's life. His in memoriam tribute declared in 1948, "Griffith was a genius. . . . I feel honored to have been associated with him in the smallest way although, bless him, he always tried to make one feel his contribution was great even though it might have been piffle. He was my dear friend, and I salute him with all my heart." Decrying Hollywood's neglect of this pioneer, Lionel minimized his own contributions to Griffith's films. Yet these first appearances as a screen actor, as well as his own first efforts to write film scenarios and to direct movies, were consequential for Lionel, if not for these early films themselves.[12]

LIONEL BARRYMORE

Acting in films rescued Lionel from the considerable stress he experienced from stage acting: "I find it an infinitely easier life, in the sense of physical strain, than the theatre." But more than simply feeling more comfortable, he also felt challenged. Acting in films stigmatized performers. When Pickford disclosed plans to return to the stage, Griffith warned her of the stigma: "You have disgraced yourself by being in motion pictures." Being open to the new medium in a way that many other theater actors were not, Lionel did not perceive movie acting as an inferior substitute for stage acting. Rather, he viewed it as a form of acting that requires novel approaches. He rejected any comparison between them as fundamentally misconceived: "The two mediums are different; the techniques ... are in essence unalike." Although the stage actor's experience is still valuable simply as training in acting, a role in films constitutes a "fascinating" exploration that widens an actor's scope. Although Lionel understood that an actor might miss the connection to a live audience, he denied that the absence of a live audience keeps the actor from correcting the performance. The actor can benefit from consulting with the film's director and evaluating the rushes during shooting. Challenged as an actor, Lionel also found in the movies greater scope for his creativity as a writer and director. Both in these early films and later, Lionel learned to collaborate with his actors to create the result he envisioned: "the good director comes to the making of his picture with clear ideas of what he wants, but ... he wants intelligent and constructive contributions from all his players. He is eager to hear their ideas, and discuss his with them." Decades later, after a half century as an actor, Lionel would recall that, "It was in the early days that the movies were great to work in.... Every Monday morning we started a movie. Every Saturday night we finished it. And there were many first-class bars in town for relaxation after work." Even with the greater satisfaction provided by movie acting, Lionel had sought to forsake acting for directing, beginning with these early silent pictures. But, eventually, he relinquished his directorial ambitions: "It was too much for me, working all day and worrying all night, and making decisions at meal time. I returned to acting, and I have been sorry for movie directors ever since."[13]

Despite the wider scope for his varied abilities that he encountered in the film industry, Lionel eventually developed and maintained a deep skepticism about industry product. Interviewed in 1928, early in the sound era, he dourly expressed his opinion of the new talking pictures: "I doubt if they can be any worse than the silent kind." The problem, in Lionel's view, was the low standard of entertainment tailored to mass audiences. If art probed beneath

Escape into Films, 1911-1917

the surface or depicted life realistically, it lost money. Instead, the studios pandered to the lowest passions of the audience and then restored a shallow moral order by tacking on unconvincing, contrived endings. Turning to the movies to survive financially, Lionel accepted his powerlessness to alter the public's appetite for dreck and the industry's eagerness to profit from that appetite. In it for the money needed to finance his private artistic and musical endeavors, Lionel nonetheless, in the words of his interviewer, "never fails to deliver the knock-out performance of every picture he plays in. He does it in his sleep." Disliking acting, whether on stage or on film, Lionel nevertheless impressed viewers with his performances. Undervaluing his own achievement, he nevertheless could not help expressing his nature as a superb artist in this least favored of his artistic outlets. What Lloyd Morris observed about Griffith applied to Lionel as well: "He had no respect for the medium in which he was working, but his temperament compelled him to treat it as if it were an art. The result was that he made it one." As early as 1916, reviewers noted Lionel's versatility: although known on stage for his "serious and heavy dramatic parts," Lionel transcended his stage reputation in his early films, for "it remained for motion pictures to bring out the true worth of this great artist.... A serious role was punctuated with comedy bits, and it was found that Mr. Barrymore was a supreme artist in this line."[14]

All of that disenchantment lay in the future. For now, from 1917 until his last New York City stage appearance in 1925, Lionel would return to the boards for his most momentous and protracted struggle with his theatrical heritage. There he would unexpectedly experience the manic-depressive thrills and agonies of his greatest stage triumphs and his most frustrating stage failures.

4

The Valley of Indecision, 1917–1925

Despite Lionel's disillusionment with much screen output, working in the movies had provided a respite from the stage life that he liked even less. Preferring acting in films to theater roles, writing and directing films to any form of acting, and painting as well as composing music to any of these vocational necessities, Lionel perhaps agreed with a character in Mary Astor's novel about actors, *The O'Conners*, that "as an artist, I was creative. As an actor, I was not satisfying the need to create. . . . Acting is not truly creative. An actor is the middleman between the playwright and the audience. If he is a good actor, he may supplement, enlarge what the playwright has on paper, or the action a director suggests—but he cannot work alone, create something completely his." Lionel nevertheless wandered back into the theater in 1917.

Lionel had much more than professional frustrations to trouble him. His elder daughter, Ethel, had died in Manhattan on March 24, 1910, after Lionel and Doris had returned from Paris to live in New York. Now, in 1917, on March 19, the death of Lionel and Doris's second daughter, Mary, in Long Island grieved her parents again. Performing in vaudeville in *The White Slaver* at Hammerstein's in New York on March 18, Lionel and Doris appeared again on April 19 at the Alhambra in New York and in Hartford on April 27. Mary's death occurred about a month before Lionel appeared with Jack at the Republic Theatre in New York in *Peter Ibbetson* on April 17. Her burial record for Mount Vernon Cemetery in Philadelphia noted a touching request from the unnamed owner of the cemetery plot to place Mary as close as possible to her sister. The telegram making this request came from California. Was Lionel on the way to the West Coast to film for Metro when Mary died? Of his 1917 films, *The End of the Tour* (produced by Rolfe and Columbia Film) was released on February 5, 1917, *His Father's Son* on March 19 (the day Mary died), and *The Millionaire's Double* on April 30. Directed

The Valley of Indecision, 1917-1925

by Harry Davenport, *The Millionaire's Double* was filmed at least in part in New York in late March, presumably after Mary's death. Lionel's memoirs mention neither daughter's death nor, indeed, either child's very existence. His silence indicates his profound devastation. He did not want to revive these memories.[1]

Nor did Lionel want to act again on the stage, but he was persuaded against his will by his and Jack's friend the playwright Ned Sheldon. (Late in his life, Lionel would describe Sheldon as "one of the finest friends I ever had.") In 1907, Sheldon had graduated from Harvard magna cum laude after taking George Pierce Baker's very influential playwriting course, The Technique of Drama, turned, in 1912, into the then-famous Workshop 47. Sheldon earned a master's degree as well from Harvard in 1908, the year of the production of his play *Salvation Nell*. The *New York Evening Sun* exclaimed, "To say that *Salvation Nell* created a sensation is putting the situation mildly. Playgoers may take our word for it, that . . . they will witness a production which is not alone extraordinary but unique. . . . It was, in a word, a very remarkable production of a very unusual play." Much later, Michiko Kakutani asserted, "Sheldon's craftsmanship raised the melodrama of the day to a new level, and in doing so provided later generations of playwrights with intimations of the theatre's possibilities." Sheldon continued in the vein of *Salvation Nell* by creating other innovative plays that depicted social issues. F. K. W. Drury, compiler of *Some of the Best Dramas*, gloomily summarized in 1917, "There was no American drama before 1890, and there has been very little since then," but he included Sheldon among the dramatists listed as honorable exceptions. By 1913, Sheldon had veered into a different direction and scored his greatest theatrical success with *Romance*. John Barrymore had played in a 1911-1912 production of Sheldon's *The Princess Zim-Zim*. Reencountering Jack in Venice in 1914, Sheldon encouraged Jack to seek dramatic roles, as in John Galsworthy's *Justice* and John Raphael's *Peter Ibbetson* (directed by Sheldon). *Peter Ibbetson* had been one of their father's favorite novels; Maurice was asked to star in a stage production of it, but he never did. For the 1919 production of *The Jest* with the Barrymore brothers, Sheldon rewrote an Italian original, and he adapted *Richard III* for John Barrymore's 1920 appearance as the Wicked Uncle, the "bottl'd spider." John Barrymore recalled in his memoir: "The first thought of my playing Richard III came about in an odd way. I was at the Bronx Zoo one day with Ned Sheldon looking at a red tarantula which had a gray bald spot on its back. This had been caused by trying to get out of its cage. It was peculiarly sinister and evil looking; the personification of a crawling power. I said to Sheldon: 'It looks just like Richard III.' 'Why don't you play it?' was his only comment." Lionel fully credited Sheldon's perception of his brother's potential. In Lionel's view, Sheldon exceeded everyone else in perceiving Jack's unrealized potential, his latent genius, despite Jack's drinking as well as his lack of both serious experience and sophisticated vocal training.[2]

While Lionel enthusiastically recounted Sheldon's positive influence on his brother's aspirations, he had resisted any attempts by Sheldon to persuade him to resume his own stage career. Yet, determined to cast Lionel, first in *Peter Ibbetson* (1917) and later (1919) in *The Jest*, Sheldon extracted a promise from Lionel after the ingestion of much beer and the enunciation of much persuasion: "Ned Sheldon was in love with the theatre, as an ardent man may be in love with a lovely woman. When you were with him you almost believed that you too liked the theatre." This equivocal comment revealed Lionel's bedrock ambivalence. Yet he yielded. Sheldon rewrote *Peter Ibbetson* for Constance Collier, Jack, and Lionel. Jack won some financial backing from Al Woods by telling Woods, "Lionel calls me a bastard and I hit him over the head with a club and knock him cold." "You're on, Kid. I'll take it," Woods agreed. Lionel fretted miserably about his part until he gained inspiration by watching Herbert Beerbohm Tree portray Thackeray's Colonel Newcome. He added to his characterization by drenching himself with a vile scent to accentuate the loathsomeness of Colonel Ibbetson. Reviewing *Peter Ibbetson*, Alexander Woollcott greeted Lionel as "a most welcome prodigal of the stage." Constance Collier remembered Lionel's extraordinary presence: "The part of Colonel Ibbetson was played magnificently in London by Henry Ainley. It needed a really great actor! It was perhaps the most difficult and exacting role in the play to cast, as it had not the sympathy of the audience and depended entirely on brilliant acting. . . . Lionel Barrymore was persuaded to return to the stage to act it. He gave a truly amazing performance—subtle, cruel, gay, with a certain horrible charm. He drenched himself in scent—musk or patchouli—to give himself atmosphere. It made me shudder." After the great success of *Ibbetson*, Sheldon's adaptation of *The Jest* also proved to be very popular. After Jack's death, W. C. Fields recalled Jack's telling him that, before both *Ibbetson* and *The Jest*, Lionel and Jack had planned to go hunting together and had assumed that they would appear in each show for only a few weeks. The trip was perennially postponed. "To my mind," Fields commented, "the incident stood as something of a symbol to them both—a symbol of all the things they meant to do but in a crowded life never got

The Valley of Indecision, 1917-1925

around to." (In between *Ibbetson* and *The Jest*, Lionel had appeared incognito in the last three performances of *Redemption*, an adaptation of Tolstoy, as a heavily disguised substitute for the ailing actor who had played Jack's confidant.)

Audiences and critics expressed great appreciation of both Lionel's and Jack's performances in *Peter Ibbetson* and *The Jest*, but Lionel's favorite stage role proved to be *The Copperhead* (1918). Eventually, he left the tour of *Peter Ibbetson* to star in the stage production of *The Copperhead*, and he left *The Jest* to star in the film of *The Copperhead*. As he explained to reporters, "Making the pictures, involving as it does mostly scenes in the open air, is a distinct relief from the monotony of going through the same role every evening in *The Jest*." (*Variety* reported as "silly" the rumor that Lionel and Jack had quarreled during the stage run of *The Jest*.) Ironically, Lionel had become the lead actor in *The Copperhead* only after Richard Bennett allegedly had rejected the role without even reading the play carefully. (However, Bennett reportedly complained in 1918 to Cincinnati newspapers that he had been "doublecrossed" out of the role.) David Warfield also had declined the part, and further staging difficulties caused the author, Gus Thomas, to consult producer John D. Williams, who secured Lionel's release by the Shuberts from *Peter Ibbetson*. A very creative, curious person with wide-ranging interests, Lionel was attracted to the role of the despised Confederate sympathizer/actual Union secret agent Milt Shanks partly because of his deep interest in American history and particularly in the Civil War. Reading a biography of Colonel John Singleton Mosby, the Confederate "Gray Ghost," helped Lionel to play Milt Shanks. He also believed that *The Copperhead* was "a genuine work of art." Doris was Lionel's costar in two roles, as Milt Shanks's wife and, after he aged, as Shanks's granddaughter. Jack so wanted to witness Lionel's triumphant turn as Milt Shanks that he offered to buy out the entire house for his own scheduled performance that night in *Peter Ibbetson*, but Lee Shubert generously turned down Jack's proposed payment. Producer Arthur Hopkins perceived that Jack highly respected Lionel: "There was no touch of envy, only complete admiration." Reviewers of *The Copperhead* shared that admiration, if not for the play itself, certainly for Lionel's acting. "The audience rose as an individual and cheered and cheered again," recorded Burns Mantle. "The actor who had made the scene the finest, most moving bit of character portraiture any American actor has offered these many years." "Mr. Barrymore brings us the complete illusion which is the reality of art," the *Chicago Daily Tribune* declared, "[Lionel's acting] is the real, the very rare thing." *The Jest* inspired similar accolades. Alexander Woollcott, amid "a large and spellbound audience," witnessed Lionel and Jack "give us their extraordinary performances in this absorbing play of revenge."

The Famous Players–Lasky Corporation announced in 1919 that the studio would engage all three Barrymore siblings for a movie version of *Peter Ibbetson*, "which was a sensational stage success in New York last season," but nothing came of this plan. Jack later explained the demise of this project as due to a failure of funding but stressed Ethel's surprising enthusiasm for the idea. Barrymore expert Spencer Berger expounded further: "[After *Variety* announced the all-Barrymore film of *Peter Ibbetson* on February 21, 1919], such rumors recurred in *Variety* on 3/7, 3/21, and 4/18/19. But . . ., Famous Players sought a less expensive cast. Released 10/21, the silent *Ibbetson* had Wallace Reid (soon dead of dope addiction) as Peter, Elsie Ferguson as the Duchess of Towers, and Montague Love (later John's antagonist in *Don Juan*) as the Colonel. Critics were respectful but not overjoyed." In 1924, J. Gordon Edwards announced plans to film *The Jest* in Rome with foreign actors and with Lionel in his stage role, but Lionel did not eventually appear in such a film.[3]

Asked late in life about his favorite stage roles, Lionel listed only *The Jest* and *The Copperhead*. If he had been less profoundly ambivalent about his theatrical career, these triumphs might have led him to new heights of accomplishment. Although he enjoyed critical acclaim for some later plays, *The Jest* and *The Copperhead* turned out to be the mountain peaks that he did not scale again. Such reluctant success as he experienced did not resolve his deep dislike of the theater; instead, any failures compounded that dislike and festered within him. His ambivalence could not be lessened by success, and it could not weather the failures that awaited him in the near future. Failure heightened his fear of failure, but so did success. He seems to have experienced both fear of forgetting his lines and a sense of being an imposter whom everyone was about to find out. (Ethel remembered the emergence of his "nervous terror" during the 1905 production of *Pantaloon*. Her memoirs recounted her own dismal experiences of stage fright.) Stage acting seems to have both terrified and bored Lionel. After his permanent emigration from the stage to the cinema, he commented, "Standing here on the stage, one is horribly isolated. Much more so than before the cameras." As a perceptive interviewer would note in 1922, "Here was a man who was admittedly a great actor. . . . [But] the things he did meant so little to him that he scarcely remembers them." Lionel explained to the interviewer: "[The actor] knows

The Valley of Indecision, 1917–1925

that if he doesn't make good he's a dead one.... Being an actor is pretty much like being chased by a bull." Meanwhile, he had another, lesser, success in *The Letter of the Law* (1920), a play that allowed him to act with Doris again, and they worked together in several movies as well. Perhaps this constant proximity to his beloved wife frayed their relationship while his ambivalence toward the theater degenerated into open misery even before Lionel's catastrophic failure on the stage in *Macbeth*. Lionel later accused himself of destroying his marriage to Doris because of his artistic unhappiness and emphasized that the fault was his alone. Marital strain had existed even before the catastrophe of *Macbeth* and the advent of Irene Fenwick, who would become Lionel's second wife. In addition, even if Doris and Lionel had partly recovered from the death of Ethel in 1910, their grief over the loss of Mary in 1917 very probably revived and intensified their profound sadness.[4]

Besides these personal troubles, Lionel was exposed to professional strife when several members of the Barrymore-Drew family, including Lionel, were prominent among the actors promoting the 1919 Actors' Equity strike on Broadway. The Lambs Club, incorporated in 1877 in New York City, was much more established than the six-year-old Actors' Equity Association, and Lambs Club members constituted almost all of those elected to the first Actors' Equity Council. Their grievances mounting, stage actors wanted to rectify their poor negotiating position and to obtain a standard contract—a demand that the Producing Managers' Association had stalled. Underestimating the union's appeal, "The producers looked upon actors as silly children," according to Tallulah Bankhead, "vain, illogical, capricious, even slightly demented. How could artists hope to function in something so plebeian as a union?" The standard contract proposed by Actors' Equity included provisions regarding paid transportation to and from New York when on tour; limited unpaid rehearsals; after one week of rehearsal, prohibition of unpaid dismissal; two weeks of notice; payment for additional performances; full pay for weeks of performance; reimbursement for some costume expenses. After the producers had rejected this proposal, Actors' Equity on August 7 called for a strike. Cast members walked out of thirteen shows; an additional thirty-seven shows eventually shut down, and sixteen others did not open. Producers' offers of incentive pay to scabs did not weaken the striking actors' resolve. Ethel had deftly parried a threat from her producer to replace her in an upcoming production with Mrs. Patrick Campbell: "I'm sure she will be very good." Indeed, such clumsy and heavy-handed intimidation by the producers backfired and actually greatly increased the number of actors joinings the union. Broadway was shuttered for a month, and the strike also went nationwide, with organized stagehands dealing a lethal blow to producers in September. The American Federation of Labor offered its support. Finally, the Hotel St. Regis summit meeting between Actors' Equity and the producers resulted in an actors' victory that included a standard contract and future representation by the union. Playwright Augustus Thomas, who had played peacemaker, announced that the strike had ended, and producer Arthur Hopkins confirmed the settlement.

John Drew, a Lambs Club member for almost forty years, had joined the strike on its first day and had announced the solidarity with the strikers of his nephews Jack and Lionel and of his niece Ethel. Funds had been needed to support Actors' Equity as well as the performers who now lacked an income. The first benefit show, on August 18, featured Marie Dressler and Eddie Cantor, with W. C. Fields as master of ceremonies. Lionel and Ethel played together in the second act of *Camille*. Stage manager for the Equity benefit performances, Edward Arnold, later remembered that the Equity *Camille* also featured Doris Rankin. Prevented by the Shuberts via court injunction to participate on the Equity stage, Ed Wynn, encouraged by applause, did his act in the aisles instead. As he would later do in George Cukor's film of *Camille*, Lionel played Duval, and he returned to the benefit stage during the strike to perform a scene of *The Copperhead*. Ethel remembered that Lionel was "superb." *Shadowland* enthused: "A scene from *Camille*, done by Ethel and Lionel Barrymore and Conway Tearle [as Armand], will stick in our memories for a long time to come. Lionel's portrayal of the father is a remarkable bit of work and a masterly example of make-up, while Ethel, seemingly ten years younger in her new slenderness, now and then struck a moving and poignant moment as the ill-fated heroine." Heywood Broun found Lionel hypnotic in his benefit performance of *The Copperhead*. Unpaid, like the other benefit performers, they also pledged personal contributions to the fund. After commenting that "the Barrymores can never fail to be the big event on any bill on which they appear," reviewer Dorothy Parker reported a prounion exclamation by Lionel: "We're proud to be here. We'll be here forever, if necessary." Most probably, this declaration of solidarity with union members proved to be a somewhat embarrassing memory for Lionel in his future metamorphosis into a conservative harrumpher. The Actors' Equity strike episode is absent from his memoirs. Devoting several pages of her own autobiography to the 1919 strike, Ethel, on the other hand, seemed to revel in

The Valley of Indecision, 1917-1925

the memory of her being, in the words of Anita Loos, "the glorious queen of the rebellion."[5]

After the strike's end, Alexander Woollcott called Lionel's acting in 1920's *The Letter of the Law* "distinguished and adroit" and pronounced him "clearly a master of his craft." Thinking Doris an actress with too-limited range for this play, Woollcott thought Doris was miscast. In contrast, he declared that "Lionel Barrymore is the kind of actor whose stage portraits are not easily forgotten." Doris received more positive notices for her "notable performance" in the film version of *The Copperhead*, while Lionel was "unforgetable [sic]." Unforgettable as well for Lionel during the filming of *The Copperhead* was his ploughing his way directly into a hornet's nest. A *New York Times* reviewer hoped that Lionel would make more movies, for he "possesses the rare talent for making himself intelligible by silent acting, yet without crude extremes and exaggerations of gesture or expression. He has subtlety and restraint, without the sacrifice of force and precision." Agreeing about Lionel's "achievement in repression," the *Chicago Daily Tribune* declared his appearance "a masterpiece." More restrained praise from the *Chicago Daily Tribune* greeted Lionel's solo turn in *The Master Mind*, but Doris received some accolades for *The Devil's Garden*: "she is always real and makes every flicker of an eyelash count." The newspaper's reviewer also enjoyed both of them in *The Great Adventure* and in *Jim the Penman*. *Boomerang Bill* and *The Face in the Fog*, produced by Cosmopolitan and distributed by Famous Players-Lasky/Paramount, would feature Lionel without Doris. Cosmopolitan's publicity material featured a supposed incident in New York's Chinatown during the filming of *Boomerang Bill* in which Chinatown residents, aghast over being photographed and consequently losing their souls, rained down on the players and crew bricks and bottles cast from rooftops. Filming resumed nearby but with the same consequence. Thereupon, Cosmopolitan replicated a street in Chinatown in its studio lot. Amusingly, other publicity mentioned Lionel's difficulty smiling during the film's production "because Mr. Barrymore's stage work for the last few years has been of such a gloomy sort that he has almost forgotten how to smile in character except to grin sardonically." Famous Players-Lasky/Paramount had both produced and distributed *The Copperhead*, filming it in Elmhurst, Long Island. *The Master Mind*, *The Devil's Garden*, *The Great Adventure*, and *Jim the Penman* had fulfilled Lionel's contract for four pictures produced by Whitman Bennett and distributed by First National. His father had acted in the first stage productions of *Jim the Penman* in both London and New York. During the filming of *The Devil's Garden*, Lionel rescued an extra playing a fireman when the man's coat was unexpectedly ablaze. Another accident, during the production of *Jim the Penman*, threw Lionel and ten other actors into the icy Hudson River when their boat sank. Interesting in light of the black eyes and bruises reported in Ethel's testimony during her 1923 divorce suit from Russell Colt are Lionel's ferocious denunciations of the spousal abuse committed by his character in *The Devil's Garden*: "Uncontrollable temper is the greatest curse of man, and the fellow who beats his own wife is lower than the lowest form of dumb animal. Wife beaters ought to be sent up for ten years. The workhouse is too good for them. Our present laws are altogether too lax, and statistics from many cities show that wife-beating is just as popular a practice as it was in the prehistoric days before prohibition."[6]

The 1921 stage production that starred Lionel as Macbeth had to wait until Lionel had fulfilled his contract to act in Whitman Bennett pictures filmed in Yonkers. Lionel also had to dispute an eventually unsuccessful lawsuit filed by the producer of *The Copperhead* and *The Letter of the Law*, John D. Williams, to keep Lionel from appearing in *Macbeth*. Williams had also in 1918 secured the rights to stage Ibsen's *An Enemy of the People* with Lionel, but this staging was never produced. The New York State Supreme Court in 1921 denied to Williams his injunction to prevent Lionel's working under other management. About *Macbeth*, this disastrous modernistically designed "futuristic spree," Jack teasingly consoled Lionel, "You've done everything but paint your scrotum green." Edmund Wilson judged Lionel to be "a most unfortunate Macbeth." Instead of impersonating a sympathetic chieftain tempted to evil, Lionel portrayed Macbeth as an "uncouth lout" with whom the audience could feel no sympathy. Undecided whether Lionel's Macbeth was a scoundrel or a half-wit, Wilson yet felt certain that Lionel's Macbeth was not Shakespeare's. Extrapolating his criticism from this to all of Lionel's performances, Wilson judged crushingly, "It would seem to be a bad plan to entrust Mr. Barrymore with characters of much subtlety or complexity." "Deeply and reasonably disappointed," Alexander Woollcott declared that Lionel's acting in *Macbeth* was "workmanlike but by no means distinguished." James Whittaker sorrowed with "the ghost of Shakespeare, uneasy and forlorn." Considering Jack's triumphs in *Richard III* and *Hamlet*, Lionel might well echo J. Alfred Prufrock, "I am not Prince Hamlet, nor was meant to be." Yet Lionel had enthusiastically anticipated Jack's *Richard III*: "I am very much interested in seeing Jack as Richard. He should be fine. Jack has a mediæval nature and always has had. As a boy, the margins of his school books were

The Valley of Indecision, 1917-1925

covered with his pencil sketches of the mediæval characters of his imagination." However, the producer of *Macbeth*, Arthur Hopkins (who also presented Lionel in *The Jest* and *The Claw* and had wanted to cast Lionel in Eugene O'Neill's *The Fountain*), dissented vigorously from the critical dismissal of Lionel's performance. Almost thirty years later, Hopkins still defended Lionel's interpretation of Macbeth as worthy and powerful. And *Variety* had given the production an appreciative review. Having reported on February 4 that the upcoming event "portends as one of the biggest of the season," *Variety* on February 25 portrayed the Hopkins-Barrymore *Macbeth* as being over the heads of both critics and audiences. "It shatters all the stage traditions of Shakespeare," *Variety* argued, "and the result is absolutely breath-taking." The *Variety* reviewer praised Lionel as Macbeth: "His command of the classic role was apparent from the first big scene, . . . and he never lost his command of the character or his audience." Acknowledging the defeat of this minority view, *Variety* noted on March 4 that it was "the season's most disappointing failure," with some brokers ripping up its tickets. Agreeing with his detractors that he was miscast, Lionel later joked that Ethel should have played Macbeth. He enjoyed repeating drama critic Kelcey Allen's witticism voiced on opening night to ticket broker John McBride: when Lionel delivered the line "Lay on, MacDuff," Allen whispered to McBride, "Lay off, McBride."[7]

Demoralized by this debacle, Lionel was then cast with Doris and with actress Irene Fenwick in the more successful 1921 stage production of *The Claw*, with Irene (but not Doris) receiving star billing with him. The *American* declared that, in "one of the most extraordinary delineations this generation of theatre-goers has seen," Lionel had "achieved a genuine triumph" as an older man duped and ravaged by his passion for "a selfish and unscrupulous girl." The reviewer emphasized how Lionel conveyed the physical and emotional collapse of his character: "the devastation of the man is complete. Notice the details which indicate his mental and physical collapse: the vague look in the eyes, the sagging cheeks, the open mouth, the drooping shoulders. The hands are inert, the knees fall outward, the ankles give way. The man is gone. What remains is like a thing that has burned out; the ashes still keep something of the original form and there remains a faint trace of fire in them. It flickers a little—then goes out; and the ashes crumble in a dead and formless heap." Lionel shared with the interviewer the habits of observation that undergirded his impersonations: "I've always studied people—all kinds of people. Then I seem to put them away in a pigeonhole of my mind; and when I want them, there they are.... An actor ... must suggest things to his audience; and then they do part of the work by supplying what he wants them to see." He explained, for instance, that a young man would unthinkingly reach for the saltshaker, whereas an old man would begin a process of slow deliberation. The same would be true for the old man's getting up from a chair. To illustrate the serenity of some older people, Lionel even cited characters portrayed in D. H. Lawrence's novel *The Rainbow*. Colgate Baker's long review of *The Claw* declared that Lionel "acts like a virtuoso playing a Beethoven sonata on the piano, for everything he does is worked into a harmonious whole ... in which the entire story of the play is embodied, great truths are revealed and the telling of destiny is heard through it all. ... [He produces] the uncanny illusion of reality, the art that conceals art." Woollcott declared that "Mr. Barrymore's virtuosity ... is extraordinary and lends to *The Claw* its only interest." Praising Lionel for "playing with uncommon skill," Woollcott also noted that "Irene Fenwick acquits herself handsomely as the wife." *Variety* crushingly described *The Claw* as "a bitter and tragic story that has no appeal to either sex" yet acknowledged it with backhanded praise as "an extremely unpleasant play supremely acted by Lionel Barrymore." Judging Lionel's performance as even greater than his Milt Shanks, *Variety* asserted that Lionel's triumph in *The Claw* erased his failure in *Macbeth*.[8]

Having supplanted Doris as Lionel's leading lady in *The Claw*, Irene also soon displaced Doris as Lionel's true love. Whatever Irene's and Lionel's emotions had been, their physical affair apparently did not begin until *The Claw* went on tour. Doris's sole recorded comment was, "I would gladly give several years of my life if ... he [had in seventeen years] looked at me just once in the same manner as I saw him look at that woman." Given that Lionel had been a devoted husband to Doris and that he would be, in turn, a devoted husband to Irene, this comment suggests one reason for his betrayal: while he probably still loved Doris, his romantic feelings toward Doris had given way to his overwhelming passion for Irene. In addition, by his own account in his memoirs, his professional frustrations had weakened their marital bond by making him an unpleasant and discontented husband. He did not mention their shared grief over the loss of two daughters, but some bereaved parents, finding their continuing sadness unbearable, flee the marital relationship in order to escape the deep pain.[9]

Jack's second wife, Blanche, whose own marriage was foundering, took Doris off to Europe in June 1922 and noted Doris's sorrow and bewildered hope. But Blanche also recorded that Doris "felt that here was the

The Valley of Indecision, 1917–1925

opportunity of our lives to achieve a foundation of confidence." Resenting the intrusion of Irene, the Barrymore family supported Doris who was, after all, related to them by more than one marriage as well as by long professional as well as personal association. Neither Jack nor Ethel ever liked Irene Fenwick Barrymore or expressed the barest respect for her. One recurring accusation was that Irene was a gold digger. Irene's first two husbands had been millionaires, but the money-indifferent and inept Lionel seems like a strange target for a gold digger. Wouldn't a gold digger desert Lionel for a millionaire, not the other way around? Irene's increasingly skeletal appearance was mocked; however, anorexia and bulimia are serious illnesses, not character defects. Her alleged sexual looseness was obsessively attacked, especially by Jack, with whom she had been previously involved. Failing to dissuade Lionel from marrying Irene, Jack told Lionel, "I've fucked her.... She's nothing but a whore." Biographers of the Barrymore family have generally echoed these characterizations in a chorus of hearsay and gossip. Noteworthy, however, are two facts: (1) Lionel adored Irene until he himself died, almost twenty years after anorexia killed her; and (2) many articles attest to their status as an unusually happy couple for Hollywood. One could dismiss the press coverage as nonsense peddled to sentimental and gullible moviegoers; nevertheless, Irene is pictured extremely differently there than she is in the biographies, which portray her as la belle dame sans merci with Lionel completely in her thrall.[10]

More than this, the "facts" recounted about Irene are often disproved by inconvenient dates and also undermined by biographers' inconsistencies. Irene married Felix Isman in 1906, and she divorced Isman in 1909. Saying that Irene had a "youthful" fling with Jack "when he was the mustached Lothario of Rector's," Hollis Alpert declared that Irene left Jack for Jay Ward and then married Isman. But later Alpert wrote that Irene left Jack to marry Isman. Perhaps that discrepancy could be explained, but John Kobler added that the affair with Jack occurred around the time that Irene became a stage star. However, her stardom *followed* her divorce from Isman, which would relocate the affair from before 1906 to 1910. According to James Kotsilibas-Davis, Isman divorced Irene for adultery, but this is wrong because *Irene sued Isman for divorce*. Saying the same, Alpert added that Isman named Jack as one of the men in the divorce suit; the accounts by Margot Peters and Kobler followed Alpert, but all of this is factually wrong.[11]

The most likely timing of Irene's affair with Jack is after the 1909 divorce from Isman and before her marriage to Jay O'Brien in 1918. (*Variety* contradicted the often-repeated 1918 date by reporting that Irene married O'Brien on June 14, 1919.) According to Peters, Irene got involved with O'Brien after her divorce from Isman, but there is almost a ten-year gap between the Isman divorce and the O'Brien marriage. Asserting that Jack and Irene *resumed* a "youthful" affair in 1916, Kotsilibas-Davis also claimed that she was still married to Isman (whom she had divorced in 1909). Kobler wrote that Irene had an affair with Jack just before she married O'Brien in 1918.[12]

After eliminating assertions contradicted by facts (such as that Irene sued Isman for divorce) and by various dates, these assertions are what is left:

- Before the Isman marriage in 1906, Irene and Jack *may have had* a youthful affair, perhaps in 1904 or 1905 (according to Jack's biographer Terry Chester Shulman).
- She was married to Isman until she divorced him in 1909. She was between marriages for almost a decade, until she married O'Brien in 1918.
- Irene and Jack had a serious affair between 1909 and 1918. She *may have* left Jack to get involved with or marry O'Brien, but that is uncertain.

Moreover, the most likely point of connection between Jack and Irene is their professional association with playwright Ned Sheldon and producer Al Woods. Jack had appeared in Sheldon's *The Princess Zim-Zim* (1911–1912), and Irene starred in its film version, *A Coney Island Princess* (1916). Kotsilibas-Davis asserted that Irene and Jack had their serious affair when she was filming *A Coney Island Princess*, but Jack's biographer Terry Chester Shulman clarified that this date is impossible because the film's production date of November 1916 clashes with Jack's touring in *Justice* during November and December. However, while Irene was appearing onstage for Al Woods in Sheldon's *Song of Songs* (1914–1915), Woods was also promoting Jack in *Kick In*. Shulman thought that 1914–1915 was a possible date range for their serious affair, indeed pinpointing late 1914 to early 1915 as the most likely time, given their physical proximity; Jack's marital strife with his first wife, Katherine; and Katherine's angry departure for a vacation without Jack.[13]

Aside from the task of reanchoring the Jack-Irene affair in late 1914 to early 1915, another issue arises: Jack's extreme and permanent animosity toward Irene. Obviously, their affair had imploded, and consequently Jack chose to disparage Irene as a "whore." Gene Fowler wrote to Jack's physician

The Valley of Indecision, 1917–1925

Harold Thomas Hyman that Fowler's biography of Jack, *Good Night Sweet Prince*, had suppressed some details about Jack's affair with Irene to avoid distressing Lionel. An edited version of this letter in the biography of Gene Fowler written by his son Will excised the names of both Irene and Lionel. Margot Peters's *The House of Barrymore*, however, noted that Will Fowler had revealed the woman mentioned in the letter to be Irene.[14]

Searches in the three archives left by Gene Fowler and Will Fowler uncovered the unexpurgated letter to Hyman as well as further evidence. Gene Fowler wrote in his typewritten letter to Hyman of January 13, 1944, that "under no circumstances is this to be published until all of us have been dead for thirty years—and perhaps not even then." After revealing that "Jack was quite frank in discussing certain dark urges he had had," Gene Fowler characterized Jack's affair with Irene as "something Dostoyevsky could have cast into a great novel. . . . [But writing about Jack's 'dark urges'] would have crucified Lionel, a great person and my friend." A handwritten note in Gene Fowler's file of Lionel Barrymore material went into more detail about the matter referred to in the typewritten letter. During the Jack-Irene affair, when Irene left for the weekend with another man, Jack threatened suicide with a gun: "John + gun going to kill self because she went away for [the] weekend with another guy."[15]

During his various marriages and many affairs, Jack's extreme and obsessive jealousy periodically erupted. Although suspected incessantly, most of Jack's other ladies were probably guiltless of cheating. Being left triggered his deepest anxieties about sexual betrayal. A pathologically jealous person is hypervigilant for signs of betrayal and often imagines them. What could be more devastating to such a person than a real betrayal? All of his attempts to protect himself have failed. If Irene had given Jack cause or had simply defied his attempts to control her by getting involved with another man, this could be extremely upsetting, both as an experience in the present and, later, as a memory.

Nonetheless, in simple fairness, we can only speculate because we do not know Irene's account of her affair with Jack. Jack's views of Irene tell us nothing at all, one way or the other, about who she was, what her motives were for marrying Lionel, and whether she loved him. Calling Irene a "whore" seems like a red herring with which Jack tried to discourage Lionel from marrying Irene without disclosing a deeper, more disturbing issue. Fowler's note went on to record "put him to bed—still alive." This may mean that Irene responded to Jack's suicide threat by putting him to bed, drunken and depressed but unwounded, and then leaving for the weekend. Jack, who often drunkenly threatened suicide during his second marriage to Blanche but never actually injured himself, may have felt deeply humiliated by Irene's ignoring his attempted manipulation. Of course, this was also happening as his first marriage was breaking up, making him more vulnerable. His humiliation might have motivated both Jack's keeping this aspect a secret from Lionel and Jack's trying to discourage Lionel from marrying Irene. For his part, Fowler may have believed that Jack's revelation reflected poorly on Lionel's lost beloved and thus (in Fowler's words) that Lionel would feel "crucified" by disclosure of the story. Jack would not tell Lionel for Jack's own sake; Fowler would not tell Lionel for Lionel's sake. Absent, however, from Fowler's account is any attempt to consider how *Irene* experienced her relationship with Jack. Notably, after Irene died in 1936, Lionel sought comfort by visiting Ned Sheldon in New York and thanked him with these words: "Home has ceased to exist anywhere and New York with you in it is the best place I know." These do not seem like the words of a husband who felt unloved. "In love," explains a French proverb, "there is always one who kisses and one who offers the cheek." Even if this was true of Lionel and Irene, were they so very different from numerous other couples?[16]

In 1922, despite his passion for Irene, Lionel apparently resisted Doris's efforts to divorce him. As reported in the *New York Times* front-page story, his legal counsel emphasized that Lionel had contested the action. Two days later, according to the *New York Herald*, Lionel's attorney asserted that Lionel had not yet decided whether to appeal the decree of divorce. Doris's suit against Lionel for divorce, plus the comments of a friend, presents a fascinating contrast to the usual picture of Doris as a pitiable nonentity. Amy Fay Stone, who had acted as "Anne Faystone" with John Drew and whose longtime lover was theatrical producer John D. Williams (who had sued Lionel a few years earlier), had taken Doris in, first to visit and then to live with her. Stone informed her mother that Doris "is becoming so much gayer and seems to be getting so much enjoyment out of life that I shouldn't wonder if she finished up by being eternally grateful that her husband *did* get out and give her a chance to discover the joys of independence and being able to do exactly as she wants for the first time in her life." A month later, Stone expressed indignation that Doris has been "cast out on the world to shift for herself after having, for eighteen years, been kept isolated from the world as much as possible by that wretched husband of hers." She was very fond of Doris and enjoyed living with her but also realized that "the alternative would

The Valley of Indecision, 1917-1925

have been absolute solitude for her." After they attended a Halloween party with a reportedly "tight" Ethel Barrymore, Stone reported that she and Doris eventually left the party because Doris "did not want to stay and look on at Ethel making a spectacle of herself any longer!" (Around this time, Doris was supporting Ethel in Arthur Hopkins's production of *Rose Bernd.*) By early December, Stone lamented how, with the presence of this houseguest, she never seemed to get anything done but still considered Doris "very delightful society," which made up for it.[17]

Sixteen years old, almost seventeen, when she wed Lionel, Doris had invested more than half her life in their marriage by the time she sued for divorce. After the loss of their daughters, her loss of her husband must have been very painful. Yet Doris was still a relatively young woman. If at times she felt crushed by the situation, at other times she may have, as Stone remarked, seen the divorce as providing her with a new freedom. After their divorce in late December 1922, Doris resumed playing in vaudeville two months later, and she made a second marriage in June 1923 to Roger Mortimer. Described by *Variety* as a British actor and theater director, Mortimer played a supporting role when Doris costarred in a 1925 production, the vaudeville play *How Do You Know?* Also in 1925, the Mortimers had Doris's third but only living daughter, Pamela. Besides acting in more films, Doris in 1931 returned to the New York legitimate stage in Luigi Pirandello's *Six Characters in Search of an Author.* Doris and Lionel may have reconciled after Irene's 1936 death. She played uncredited roles in at least two of Lionel's films of the late thirties (*On Borrowed Time* and *You Can't Take It with You*). Viewers looking very hard may for a second glimpse Doris Rankin as the sheriff's wife in *On Borrowed Time* and, in *You Can't Take It with You*, as Mrs. Leach in the restaurant scene in which the Kirbys introduce Jean Arthur's and Jimmy Stewart's characters to Governor Leach and Mrs. Leach. *Photoplay* in 1938 spied Doris meeting Lionel near Stage 5 of the MGM lot: "They paused a moment and then spoke gently, eyes filled with blessings for each other . . . looking back together, in one brief moment, over a long span of years to other times and other places." Lionel outlived both of his wives, for Doris died in 1947.[18]

Irene received her own interlocutory degree of divorce from Jay O'Brien in April 1923, with the official filings seeking to disguise her identity by naming her as Irene O'Brien and not using her stage name. *Variety* reported that the court papers were sealed from press scrutiny and disclosed only to the attorneys involved. Nonetheless, *Variety* managed to scrounge up the details.

Irene, as plaintiff, alleged that she had become suspicious about O'Brien's infidelity when he stayed out all night and when she received a bill for jewelry that he had not given to her. Her hired private detective testified to seeing O'Brien meet for dinner at New York's Hotel McAlpin "an unknown woman . . . attired in a Hudson seal coat and picture hat." Following the guilty pair as they transferred themselves to 521 West 114th Street for further intimacies, the detective forced his way in and discovered them "en dishabille [sic]." Irene waived any application for alimony.[19]

Late in 1923, the production by David Belasco of *Laugh, Clown, Laugh* marked Lionel's last successful appearance on the New York stage. Expressing his reservations about the play itself, Sheppard Butler nevertheless declared that Lionel's "absorbing, infinitely varied, and, toward the end, terrific" acting amounted to "one of the most remarkable performances to be seen on the American stage." Butler found Lionel's intense performance "weirdly compelling." The critic for the *Rochester Times-Union* thought it "a remarkable piece of acting." Another reviewer noted that "his hair is of a carrot color, his eyes hauntingly sad and his eyebrows arranged on a strange slant. His face is full of contradictions, his smile whimsical and appealing and his expression often exceedingly comic. . . . [He] is never for a moment out of character. His own personality is completely covered by the part [of Tito Beppi]." (*Variety* reported that Lionel and Belasco eventually had a "disagreement," after which Belasco ordered the removal of Lionel's portrait from the lobbies of his Lyceum and Empire theaters.) As she would in two later stage productions, Irene also starred in *Laugh, Clown, Laugh*. However, she did not perform in the several films Lionel made for Samuel Goldwyn and UFA [Universum Film Aktiengesellschaft] in 1923 and 1924: for Goldwyn-Cosmopolitan (a Hearst production company), the box office smash *Enemies of Women* as well as *Unseeing Eyes*; for Goldwyn–First National, *The Eternal City*; and for UFA, *Decameron Nights* and *The Woman Who Did*. Some scenes of *Unseeing Eyes* were produced in the Canadian Rockies, ten thousand feet above sea level. Most of the other movies were filmed, at least in part, in Europe: *Enemies of Women* in Monte Carlo; *The Eternal City* in Rome; and *Decameron Nights* and *The Woman Who Did* in Germany. Travel to Europe in 1923 included Lionel's wedding to Irene in Rome on July 14. War hero Captain Ciamarra officiated, with other actors in *The Eternal City* in attendance as well as Benito Mussolini, prime minister of Italy, and the American ambassador to Italy, Richard Washburn Child. The film's director, George Fitzmaurice, and his wife, Ouida Bergère, were best man and matron of

The Valley of Indecision, 1917–1925

honor, and the ceremony took place in their hotel suite. Lionel and Irene then enjoyed a honeymoon in Venice before he returned to Rome to work. When Lionel traveled in the summer of 1924 to Germany for *Decameron Nights* and *The Woman Who Did*, a newspaper interview of him upon his return with Irene on the White Star *Majestic* quoted his opinion that "Berlin is a remarkable city for the making of motion pictures. It is nothing short of amazing the skill and ease with which the Germans build massive scenes."[20]

The year 1924 also saw Lionel's acting in some films produced by Chadwick Pictures Corporation (*Meddling Women, I Am the Man*). Chadwick promoted Lionel as "America's most distinguished actor." More importantly, 1924 reunited Lionel with D. W. Griffith, now directing his film *America* for his own production company and the distributor United Artists. A somewhat ponderous treatment of the Revolutionary War, *America* was filmed on location in Virginia in historic buildings, and local history enthusiasts lent artifacts. Griffith sought help from the Daughters of the American Revolution, Sons of the Revolution, the Smithsonian Institution, the New York Public Library, and several historical societies. Lionel excelled as a villain. While the movie's battle scenes were spectacular, the film's love scenes dragged, and it failed at the box office. Perhaps its appeal suffered from the dullness that afflicts overly reverential depictions of the American Revolution. Edward Wagenknecht and Anthony Slide, in *The Films of D.W. Griffith*, asserted that "Lionel Barrymore is excellent . . . as a thoroughly evil Walter Butler . . .; [however,] in the second half of *America*, the colonials seem to be fighting not England but Captain Butler." Robert M. Henderson's *D.W. Griffith: His Life and Work* explained this focus on the evil Captain Butler rather than on Great Britain as resulting from Griffith's Anglophilia.[21]

Three stage flops in a row in 1925 ended forever Lionel's willingness to expose himself to New York City theater audiences and theater critics. Two productions—*The Piker* (previously called *Four Knaves and a Joker*) and *Taps*—cast Irene as Lionel's costar, but Irene did not act in Lionel's last outing on the New York stage, *Man or Devil*. Percy Hammond appreciated *The Piker* by praising the "uncompromising fidelity" of Lionel's performance, which "made me believe that he was Bernie Kaplan, not Lionel Barrymore." *Variety* also was appreciative. Calling *The Piker* "absorbingly interesting," *Variety* asserted that "Mr. Barrymore adds Bernie Kaplan to his great characterizations." More typically, Burns Mantle sneered at the hapless protagonist of *The Piker*: "I sincerely hope no one writes an equally vivid piece about the towel man in the gentleman's rest room. Lionel might want to play him." A few months later, Mantle called *Man or Devil* "childish stuff." Reviewing *Taps* (like *Peter Ibbetson* and *Man or Devil*, a Shubert production), Stark Young had accused Lionel of "sniveling and sobbing"; Young had called Lionel's acting in *The Piker* "monotonous."[22]

Reacting badly to these failures, Lionel went so far as to compose an article for the *New York Herald Tribune* defending *The Piker*. Accusing the reviewers of believing that "nothing profound or moving or tragic or terrible or pathetic or grotesque can happen to a citizen of New York," he insisted that the story of *The Piker* included the elements of tragedy that the critics could appreciate in Shakespeare or Gorky but somehow failed to detect in an American drama. Lionel revealed that he had declared to producer Al Woods that he *must* play the part of Bernie Kaplan: "To me, it seemed a masterpiece. It still does." His defense of *The Piker* is interesting, not merely as a retort to bad reviews, but as a statement of his artistic values, his manifesto as an actor: "I came back the next day and said I must play that part. It wasn't a matter of money." Feeling that the play portrayed a human situation authentically, he had wanted to enact the role. His article in its defense was not simply a reaction of disappointment but his artistic manifesto, a cri de coeur.[23]

A comparison of this declaration with an interview of Lionel in Hollywood a few years later reveals the steadfastness with which Lionel upheld his artistic values. "He denies that the public wants good stuff," Cedric Belfrage reported; he quoted Lionel as saying that "the public today does not want sincere art and will not accept it." (Or, as the narrator of Thornton Wilder's *The Bridge of San Luis Rey* expresses it, "The public for which masterpieces are intended is not on this earth.") Lionel also decried movie censorship as "a horrible thing, forcing all reality out of pictures because it bans everything that would have any relation to life as it is." His artistic values did not change with the passage of years and his shift from theater to film. Nor did Lionel's love affair with Irene, his divorce from Doris, and his subsequent marriage to Irene indicate any alteration in his personal values. As his comments on his breakup with Doris emphasized, he judged his own behavior toward Doris as unworthy. To both of them, the marriage bond was a sacred contract, made no less so for actors than for other people. No one could think more poorly of Lionel's adultery than he himself did. As both an artist and a man, Lionel was remarkably consistent. He knew what he believed in, regardless of whether he himself, or Broadway, or Hollywood lived up to it. Jack understood his elder brother to be an idealist: "What I envy in Lionel is not only his mind but his ability to believe. If he never found love, he would still believe

The Valley of Indecision, 1917-1925

there was such a thing." Meanwhile, Lionel would head with Irene to California on the chance of acting in more movies produced by Chadwick Pictures Corporation, now filming on the West Coast. He was also talking about a road tour for *The Copperhead*. Fate, impersonated by Lionel's agent, Maury Small, had other intentions. Lionel's first exodus from the stage had taken him to Paris; his second had introduced him to Biograph and Metro; his third would transfer him to California and, eventually, commit him for the rest of his life to decades of work at MGM. Although he did act in California stage productions of *The Copperhead* and *Laugh, Clown, Laugh*, as well as in some East Coast vaudeville events, he never again starred in a New York City legitimate theater production.[24]

The period from 1917 through 1925 would prove crucial to the course of his entire life and career as the crucible in which his heightened dissatisfaction with his vocational options dissolved his long-standing and devoted marriage and ended his years as an actor on the New York stage. A new marriage began, and a committed career in film was in prospect. Yet by Lionel's own account, he had not intended to resume stage acting in 1917, nor did he expect to settle in Hollywood in 1925. He also apparently resisted, at least for a while, Doris Rankin's divorce suit against him for adultery with Irene Fenwick. Others were the agents of his resumed theater work (his friend the playwright Ned Sheldon), his divorce and remarriage (Doris and Irene), and his new status as a movie actor (his agent, Maury Small). Supporting this perception of Lionel's curious passivity in this valley of decision, he commented in later life, "All my successes were due to suggestions of others. I have never been too successful on any project of my own creation. This is the truth!" His own memories of these years stressed how conflicted he felt—a conflict that he inflicted on Doris by being disagreeable because he felt trapped in the theater yet unable to escape by working as a visual artist or a musical composer. So conflicted was Lionel that only the interventions of others and force of circumstance had cut the knot.[25]

Act Two
Chameleon

5

Silenced, Again, 1925–1928

By the end of his life and film career, Lionel had become an emblem of the MGM brand, as shown by his hosting and narrating two showcases for MGM films: *Some of the Best: 25 Years of Motion Picture Leadership* (1949) and *The Metro-Goldwyn-Mayer Story* (1951). His long association with MGM, however, did not begin immediately upon his uprooting himself from New York City and relocating to California in the mid-twenties. For a while, he acted in silent films for a miscellany of studios on both coasts, and he subsequently enjoyed a sensational success in a Los Angeles stage production of *The Copperhead*. His agent, Maury Small, had hooked up Lionel with B. P. Schulberg for *The Girl Who Wouldn't Work* and with MGM for *The Barrier*; Lionel's triumph in the Los Angeles *Copperhead* immediately preceded his Small-negotiated ongoing contract with MGM and his work with Greta Garbo in *The Temptress*. Even then, Lionel's full value to MGM had not yet become evident; it was not until the sound revolution that he was propelled to the studio's first rank of actors. The advent of sound also revived for a while his directorial ambitions.[1]

In this transitional phase, from 1925 into 1926, Lionel appeared in *Fifty-Fifty* (Associated Exhibitors/Encore), *The Wrongdoers* (Astor/Macfadden True Story Films), *The Girl Who Wouldn't Work* (B. P. Schulberg), *A Man of Iron/Iron Man* (Chadwick), *Children of the Whirlwind* (Arrow/Whitman Bennett Productions), *The Splendid Road* (Frank Lloyd Productions/First National), *Brooding Eyes* (Sterling/Ginsberg-Kahn), *Paris at Midnight* (PDC/Metropolitan Pictures), *The Lucky Lady* (Famous Players–Lasky), *The Bells* (Chadwick), and *Wife Tamers* (Hal Roach). For MGM, he made *The Barrier* (released in March 1926) and joined the cast of *The Temptress* in June 1926. About his work in *The Barrier*, *Variety* published the comment "What a dirty dog Lionel Barrymore can be in a picture. He is all that and then some." Other MGM silent films (1927) included *The Thirteenth Hour*, *Body and*

LIONEL BARRYMORE

Soul, The Show, and *Women Love Diamonds.* For United Artists, he acted in *Sadie Thompson,* as well as in *Drums of Love* (an adaptation of Dante's Paolo and Francesca story directed by D. W. Griffith). A study of Griffith's films by Edward Wagenknecht and Anthony Slide judged that, in *Drums of Love,* "Lionel Barrymore turns in a fine performance, giving a sympathy and a warmth to his role." Sympathy and warmth do not in any way describe Dante's villainous version of Lionel's character, so the film considerably alters the dynamics of the story, a staple of nineteenth-century theater whose tragic plot would upset twentieth-century movie audiences. According to Griffith's biographer, Robert M. Henderson in *D.W. Griffith: His Life and Work,* "A superb performance by Lionel Barrymore could not save the picture." (Jack in 1925 wanted to act in a film of *Paolo and Francesca* with Mary Astor, but that project never came off.) About this phase of his movie career, Lionel later humorously exclaimed to movie magazine reporter Gladys Hall, "I found myself playing the villain in a picture starring a police dog. I was supporting a dog!" He apparently referred to the star of *The Thirteenth Hour,* Napoleon the Wonder Dog. That accomplished canine was supposed to attack Lionel as the villain but liked him too well as a man to comply with the script; hungry after a studio-imposed fast, Napoleon then ferociously leapt on Lionel, whose wig now concealed a sirloin steak.[2]

As well as filming in California in 1926, Lionel led the cast of *The Copperhead* in a stage production hosted by The Playhouse in Los Angeles. An audience sensation, this production of his favorite role extended its planned run from March 3 until April 10, after which Lionel needed to assume his duties as a player under his ongoing contract at MGM. Although Lionel apparently forgot all about this triumph when he was working on his memoirs (he claimed to have forsaken the theater forever when he left New York), his acting won fervent audience and critical approval. He also starred in 1927 and 1928 California productions of *Laugh, Clown, Laugh* that were critically acclaimed and financially successful. Irene had journeyed east in April 1926 to discuss future stage appearances in New York, and a Los Angeles presentation of *The Claw* starring both Lionel and Irene was announced for late 1926; however, neither prospect materialized. As late as 1932, Sam Warshawsky was writing a never-produced play for Lionel, who also did not accept an offer from William Harris to appear in *The Anatomist* and who in 1933 rejected overtures from Crosby Gaige to return to the stage in *A Hat, a Glove, a Mantle.* Gaige then pursued Paul Muni for the role that Lionel had declined to play. A 1935 news item reported that Lionel had indeed experimented with a return to vaudeville in the east but quickly retreated to California: "People flocked to the theatres to see him. But once seated, they looked upon him as though he was a freak and displayed not the slightest interest in his stage performance." This may refer to a seventeen-minute vaudeville act staged by Lionel and Gene Ford in Baltimore that had presented ten minutes of *The Copperhead* following a seven-minute introductory trailer with Lionel and Jackie Cooper. While acknowledging that *The Copperhead* is "a time-worn bit of dramaturgy [that] under less brilliant treatment might appear ludicrous even to the most naive," *Variety*'s reviewer judged that Lionel "breathes life into a sluggish playlet" and recorded the observation that the vaudeville audience reacted with "dead-quiet eagerness," "rapt attention," and, at the finale, "tumultuous acclaim." A week later, *Variety*'s reviewer of the vaudeville act in New York City cited audience enthusiasm for Lionel and called him "the meat in the sandwich": "He grew up with the business and there's few who can tell him how to get his effects over. He knows the answers himself." Lionel's appearance in New York at the Capitol, a Loew's picture house, was part of an MGM arrangement to book some of its film stars for stage acts. Others from the MGM roster included Ramon Navarro, May Robson, and Clark Gable, whom Lionel had first met as a young member of the cast in the 1926 Los Angeles staging of *The Copperhead* and whose later film career at MGM owed much to Lionel's encouragement and practical support.[3]

Both Gable and Lionel would be famously associated with MGM in its prime. Lionel's on, off, and on again primary focus on his movie career intersected with three major phases of the development of the film industry: (1) the attempt by Thomas Edison's Motion Picture Patents Company (MPPC) to control the industry and independents' rebellion against the MPPC; (2) "vertical integration" of the independents; and (3) cooperation among the major studios. When Lionel had acted and directed during his first phase of movie life, he had worked for a member of the MPPC, Biograph, and then for an independent studio, Metro. After Lionel shook the dust of the New York legitimate theater from his shoes and moved to California for good, he eventually embraced a permanent film career during a succeeding phase during which the independent studios integrated film production, distribution, and exhibition to achieve industry dominance. Later, when their position was secure, these studios would not only compete but also cooperate, to their mutual advantage: "once the dust had cleared and a handful of major companies emerged who composed the industry, conditions would change again,

LIONEL BARRYMORE

moving from competition, which drove them toward vertical integration, to cooperation, which would result in oligopoly." One manifestation of cooperation was exhibition of a studio's product in another studio's theaters. Another manifestation was the "loan out" of star actors to the financial benefit of the home studio if not to the lent star. Anchored at Metro-Goldwyn-Mayer by his ongoing contract, Lionel would be loaned out to other studios at times but mostly act in MGM films until he died almost thirty years later.[4]

MGM publicist Walter Seltzer called MGM under Louis B. Mayer "the Tiffany's of the business." MGM was one result of the mergers of various film production companies, film distributors, and movie exhibitors that created and then winnowed the Hollywood studio system. The nineteen studios listed in a Hollywood directory in 1924 gave way to the eight studios listed in 1935.[5]

In the previous decade, in 1912, Independent Motion Pictures, Powers, Rex, Nestor Film Company, Champion, and Bison 101 (among other companies) had formed the production and distribution company Universal Film Manufacturing Company, reshaped as Universal Pictures Corporation in 1922, with Carl Laemmle in charge. Four years later, in 1916, the union of the distributor Paramount Picture Corporation with the producer Famous Players–Lasky (Adolph Zukor and Jesse Lasky) made Famous Players–Lasky a production and distribution company called Paramount-Artcraft, later renamed Paramount in 1935. United Artists, formed in 1919, was both a production and a distribution company. Two independent producers, Disney Brothers Cartoon Studio and Samuel Goldwyn Productions, both began in 1923. Louis B. Mayer, Irving Thalberg, and David O. Selznick would be associated with Metro-Goldwyn-Mayer, born from the 1924 merger of three production companies (Metro Pictures, Goldwyn Pictures, and Louis B. Mayer Productions) with the exhibitor Loew's. In that same year, Columbia began as a production and distribution company headed by Harry Cohn. Warner Brothers and Essanay, both film producers, merged with the exhibitor/distributor/producer First National and eventually, in 1928, evolved into Warner Brothers–First National, headed by Jack Warner. RKO–Radio Pictures in 1928 consolidated Radio Corporation of America, a producer, with the exhibitors Keith Theatres and Orpheum Theatres as well as with PDC Producers Distributors Corporation and Joseph Kennedy's FBO (Film Booking Office). David Sarnoff and David O. Selznick would be key figures for RKO. After the coming of sound to motion pictures, Monogram Picture Corporation–Rayart Pictures would become Monogram (1930), later the Allied Artists Picture Corporation. An exhibitor and producer, Fox Film

Silenced, Again, 1925-1928

Corporation united with 20th Century Pictures in 1935 to create Darryl F. Zanuck's 20th Century-Fox. In that same year, Consolidated Film Industries, Mascot, Monogram, and Liberty created Herbert Yates's Republic. Also in 1935, David O. Selznick formed Selznick International Pictures.[6]

Eventually, the "big five" studios were MGM, Paramount, 20th Century-Fox, Warner Brothers, and RKO. The "little three" studios were Universal, United Artists, and Columbia; their product was distributed by the big five. Monogram and Republic were among several other movie studios on "Poverty Row." Dominance in the industry was won by achieving vertical integration: "a single company controlling the means of film production, distribution, and exhibition."[7]

The creator of MGM was exhibitor Marcus Loew, the owner of the Loew's Theatres chain that showed both vaudeville acts and moving pictures. Not only did Loew want better, more reliable movie product, but distributors of Famous Players–Lasky product wanted to change from charging Loew's a flat rate for their movies to charging a percentage of the exhibitors' profit. Consequently, Loew needed his own production facility. The distribution company Metro that had worked with several production companies, including Rolfe, had reorganized itself as both a distributor and a production company and expanded its West Coast production facility, but Metro lacked its own theaters. Metro in 1920 sold itself to Loew's.[8]

In 1924, not long before Lionel's three stage flops in a row put paid to his career in the New York legitimate theater, Loew, still seeking more and better product, bought Goldwyn Pictures. The merger that created Metro-Goldwyn acquired for Loew's the extensive production facilities in Culver City, California, of Goldwyn Pictures as well as its theaters. As the distributor of William Randolph Hearst's Cosmopolitan movies, Goldwyn Pictures also benefited from favorable coverage in Hearst newspapers for the Goldwyn product. Needing a Hollywood-based manager for Metro-Goldwyn while Nicholas Schenck supervised the New York operation, Loew also acquired Louis B. Mayer Pictures. At one point company secretary at Metro, where he may have first met Lionel, Mayer had started as an exhibitor on the East Coast and then moved into distribution as well as into production in California on his own. Now he was vice president and general manager of Metro-Goldwyn, Irving Thalberg was head of production, and Nick Schenck and the New York office of Loew's retained financial control. In 1927, a somewhat luridly expressed account of Hollywood emphasized Nick Schenck's power and control:

All roads at United Artists lead to Joseph M. Schenck. All roads at Metro-Goldwyn-Mayer lead to Nicholas Schenck. There are no detours. At the terminal of each road is a Schenck with millions, power, a wife, a blinded tiny mother of eighty-five, a love of poker, and most important of all, each other. . . . The Schencks know everybody, the under-world and the upper, both mixing in politics, Nicholas in New York, Joseph in California, as the chairman of the Republican County Committee. Whatever it is, business or politics, the Schenck boys boss, Nick through a black telephone, Joseph through a gilded one.

Credits for films from the new studio could assert "produced by Louis B. Mayer for Metro-Goldwyn" or "produced by Metro-Goldwyn-Mayer"; Mayer opted eventually for the second designation. The corporate name changed from Metro-Goldwyn to Metro Goldwyn-Mayer in 1925.[9]

In *Hollywood East*, Diana Altman stressed that, throughout Mayer's quarter-century at MGM, his power was limited because he answered to the dictates of the New York office. Loew's owned, not only MGM, but 123 other subsidiaries. MGM's distribution company, like MGM itself, was one of those subsidiary companies. When Loew died in 1927, Nicholas Schenck took over Loew's; then, in 1929, with Schenck's help, William Fox tried but eventually failed to take over MGM. Mayer's relationship with Schenck decayed, as did his relationship with Thalberg. When Thalberg died in 1936, Mayer added to his own responsibilities the role of head of production. Lionel expressed his own sorrow about the premature death of Thalberg: "One of the greatest friends a man could have; one of the greatest creative minds the world has ever produced; the greatest leader our industry has ever had; no words can express my . . . own personal grief. . . . I can think of no one in our industry who does not owe Irving Thalberg a deep debt of gratitude." Lionel's friend Anita Loos shared her own assessments of both Thalberg and Mayer. Calling Mayer "the business brains of the studio," Loos remembered him as "the one you went to whenever you were in trouble and needed help. He always came through. He was a wonderful old boy." Impressed with Thalberg's creative genius, Loos revealed that "every moment I spent with Thalberg was like opening the door on the universe. You'd go into a story conference, and suddenly, in the midst of it, he'd open a door on a story that just illuminated the whole thing." Loos thought that Thalberg understood studio finances as well as Mayer did. David O. Selznick described Mayer and Thalberg as "an

Silenced, Again, 1925-1928

extraordinarily valuable team. They complemented each other very well. They were both men of great vision, both great showmen." In Selznick's judgment, neither man could have accomplished what he did without the other. Although George Cukor had befriended Mayer's two daughters, Cukor disliked their father, whom he nevertheless described as "a brilliant man," "a tough, ruthless man, but a very good showman." Yet Cukor doubted the practical wisdom of showmen and their pretensions to manipulate public taste: "A showman is an ardent animal and he must be respected. But he cannot prophesy things. . . . You talk to these professional people and your heart sinks. . . . Nothing to do with [artistic fidelity to] truth. . . . If they did one satirical picture the exhibitors were wise guys and say 'Well, that's what the public wants.' Well they never know what the public wants." Remembering poor previews of his film *Camille*, now considered a classic, Cukor judged that the "wise guys" were incapable of recognizing the brilliance of Greta Garbo's performance.[10]

Twelve years later, new head of production Dore Schary battled with Mayer about MGM films' content and focus, with Schenck using Schary to weaken Mayer's hold until Mayer's bitter departure from the studio in 1951. With the final settlement of the *United States v. Paramount* (1948) case, Loew's no longer controlled MGM. Because of this antitrust case, none of the movie studios could any longer merge production and distribution with exhibition. With a career at MGM that spanned the last three decades of his life, from 1926 to 1954, Lionel lived through all of these changes and controversies. Before Mayer was forced out in 1951, he seems to have protected Lionel, whom he esteemed as one of his few actor friends (like Lewis Stone and Marie Dressler). Lionel reportedly "fascinated" Mayer, whose own histrionic talents and closeness to Lionel gave rise to the nickname "Lionel B. Mayer." One of the stars to whom MGM reportedly gave a "lifetime contract" (another was Lewis Stone), Lionel may have become more expendable to the studio once Mayer had lost power.[11]

Back in the earlier decades of their association, during the sound revolution, MGM was the last major studio to transition into the production of talkies. In May 1929, Nicholas Schenck still expressed the view that "the silent film will never be eliminated, since certain stories are naturally suited for silent treatment." (Schenck also prophesized wrongly about the impact of television: "That'll never be much.") When the phenomenon of sound no longer could be resisted, Lionel would turn out to be one of MGM's assets— both as a star and as a director.[12]

6

Talkies Stardom and Detour into Direction, 1928–1931

Faced with the advent of sound in motion pictures, MGM dragged its industrial foot. Indeed, widespread dismay existed within the industry about the seismic consequences of a changeover to sound pictures. The movie industry was like a boa constrictor reluctantly swallowing a poisoned mouse.

For one thing, the term *silent movie* is misleading, for it implies a state of deficiency. As Kevin Brownlow put it, "The very word *silent* suggests that something is missing." This seems obvious, in the same way that deafness seems like an obvious state of deficiency to a person with normal hearing. However, just as members of the Deaf community who use sign languages would stress the beautiful utility of their signed speech, advocates of presound films (to use a less pejorative phrase) would argue for the virtues of a medium that conveyed meaning through the image and expected its audience to collaborate by using imagination. "As they could not speak, the spectator spoke for them," Arthur Hopkins explained. "Each spectator became his own author." Engaging a more active audience as well as minimizing the use of written and spoken language, the presound films held an international appeal that transcended barriers of nationality, ethnicity, and language. Film critic Cedric Belfrage, who like many others at the time predicted that the talkies would not last, lamented that "the international language was over.... And I still feel sad about it." When Lillian Gish accepted the 1984 American Film Institute Life Achievement Award, Gish still gamely argued for the superiority of films that relied less on divisive languages and more on unifying images: "when we went into words we lost 95 percent of our audience." In effect, the coming of sound to motion pictures rebuilt the Tower of Babel, for with the loss of silent film the world no longer had one language and a

Talkies Stardom and Detour into Direction, 1928–1931

common speech. George Cukor remembered that the industry lost faith in the artistry it had achieved in silent films in its anxious but rapt enthrallment with sound technology. "They abused it, they were fascinated by it the way they are by color or any new thing. They had a frying egg scene and the eggs made a big sound. . . . They panicked, so they gave up all the wonderful movement of cameras and all that. . . . [In my first picture] we had to shoot at night because there was no [distracting] sound [at night that would be recorded during filming]."[1]

Myrna Loy also recalled the resistance of the industry to sound: "The establishment for the most part cried: 'No, no talkies! The great form is the silent picture.'" Besides the artistic loss created by the switchover to sound, the talkie revolution created great fear. Loy, a survivor who went on to a long career in sound films, remembered the tension of the period. To an interviewer's question "You must have had some exciting times when sound came in?" Loy replied, "Really terrifying. . . . There were people on the lot who were just not going to make it—they absolutely were not going to. . . . This is how bad it was, at that time. It was a matter of survival to a lot of people."[2]

Mary Astor's comments about the sound revolution also concentrated on the dislocation it created within the industry. She herself lost her Fox contract because of the supposed unsuitability of her voice for talking pictures and her father's refusal to accept a lower salary for her. In episode 13 of the 1980 documentary *Hollywood* ("End of an Era"), Astor appeared twice. She stressed how sound seemed like a transitory phenomenon and how the now-silent sound stage inhibited the players because the director could no longer coach the actor during filming. Ironically, there was much noise during the filming of "silent" movies, but total silence was demanded during the filming of "talkies." Although Astor had certainly been a silent picture star, her pretalkie acting had never achieved anything like the quality of Lillian Gish's performances. Instead, the quality of her memoirs, *My Story* as well as *A Life on Film*, and of her 1967 *New York Times* feature "Talkies? 'They Can't Last'" made Astor an invaluable witness to the era. Everyone in the industry had dismissed sound as a fad, a gimmick, a flash in the pan. As Astor ruefully confessed, "I had no prescience of the end of an era." Most had thought that the audiences would be repelled by the noise, not attracted by it. There would be a loss of artistry. These predictions failed to envision the awful outcome: "Audiences loved it and we, the artists, shuddered. Or was it shivered?"[3]

Like Astor, Loy, and Gish, but unlike many other silent picture players, Lionel survived the transition to sound; indeed, he became, according to

LIONEL BARRYMORE

Belfrage, "the first outstanding success of the talkies." In an industry advertisement targeted "to the producers of talking pictures," the Edward Small Company trumpeted its representation of Lionel Barrymore "who gave the first OUTSTANDING performance" in American sound movies. "An actor whose career flourished precisely because of sound," Charles Affron asserted, "Lionel is one of the most significant figures in these extraordinary years, 1929 and 1930, when the movies go through the most radical change in their history." Reflecting MGM's queasiness about the new sound technology, Lionel acted in his first sound film when on loan-out in 1928 to Warner Brothers. Will Rogers reported in his column about *The Lion and the Mouse* "how the stage Actor does show up the Movie ones! Lionel Barrymore even as a Villian [sic] ... just made you wish the others hadn't talked." MGM responded to his success in *The Lion and the Mouse* by reshooting some scenes of *Alias Jimmy Valentine* to add dialogue spoken by Lionel and William Haines. *West of Zanzibar* and *The Mysterious Island*, as well as *Road House* and *River Woman*, maintained their silence or became part-talkies. In the talkie *The Hollywood Revue of 1929*, Lionel played himself directing Norma Shearer and John Gilbert in *Romeo and Juliet*. Other early sound pictures in which Lionel acted included *Free and Easy* (and its Spanish version, *Estrellados*), *Guilty Hands*, and *The Yellow Ticket*. Besides capitalizing on Lionel's theater-acquired mastery of his voice, MGM asked him to direct several early sound pictures as well. His experiences as an actor and a director of silent and sound pictures created for Lionel several strongly worded opinions about subpar quality and common industry practices. As MGM historian Bosley Crowther commented, "Marcus Loew was selling motion pictures in bulk and thought of motion pictures as bulk merchandise.... This was the way that [distributors] thought of films, as mass entertainment which they could possibly change every day.... Quality and so forth weren't as important as simply getting out a lot of pictures, a variety of pictures, with a lot of stars."[4]

Hollywood's industrialized and monetized approach to the film art manufactured in the "dream factory" produced prefabricated "product" that rolled off the studio assembly line as well as the illusions the "product" portrayed and sustained. Under the American studio system that was beginning to form in the twenties and reached its zenith during the thirties, forties, and fifties, both actors and the films in which they performed were primarily marketable commodities. Seeking to promote star actors as "types," studio publicity pretended that each star's type actually derived from the actor's real personality. Slotting actors into recognizable, popular types allowed movie

Talkies Stardom and Detour into Direction, 1928–1931

production to maximize studio output. Assembling a film by combining star types hastened the film's development and creation. David O. Selznick, for so long a successful producer within the studio system, later observed sourly and inconsistently, "There might have been good movies if there had been no movie industry." Lillian Gish commented that, with commercial success, "the formula story came into being. . . . Most films were just another product coming off the assembly line like cars." The convenience, speed, and cost-effectiveness of this approach to film production were all-important. Consequently, the studios often fictionalized the pasts and the current lives of their star actors, so that, even in "real life," the actors apparently embodied the desired types that they also portrayed on film. The exotic seductress Theda Bara, for instance, was a "prefabricated personality" created by William Fox. Supposedly, the star's type revealed something about the person. This was the essential illusion fostered and marketed by the star system. For its part, the moviegoing audience, by enthusing over or rejecting a film and its actors, chose the types that the studios then promoted back to the public. The discovery of a potential star, the screen test, the name change, the physical makeover, the vigorous publicity, the assignment to many films in order to cast to type—the whole process depended on the audience's enthusiasm for a particular actor and the studio's consequent identification of the actor's type. The audience indicated its preferred fantasies, and the studios manufactured them in great quantities. The actors served merely as raw materials for eventual manufacture into concrete fictions on the screen and in real life. Each star's image was standardized, made consistent and predictable, to meet and enhance the audience's expectations. This standardization included not merely casting by type but also generating (often false) publicity about who the actor supposedly was as a "real person." Acting ability was almost beside the point, for the star embodied a type rather than acted a role: "Once the public hailed them as stars, they ceased to be regarded as artists and became art objects. They were type-cast." David O. Selznick dismissed criticism of studio-era movies as deficient in artistic quality: "the concept of the commercial motion picture as an art form is ridiculous. It's entertainment, and it's business, and it's backed by individual stockholders, tens of thousands of them, who expect to get returns on their investment. . . . This is no art form." Substantiating Gish's account of the formula-born storyline, Selznick described how he had created *Duel in the Sun* by combining a formulaic western with a formulaic love affair while intensifying the sensationalism associated with each movie genre. "I just multiplied everything," Selznick explained. "Frankly, to a large extent I did it tongue-in-cheek." The critics trashed the film, but that did not matter, for artistic criteria have little to do with popularity. This approach to "the collaborative art" resembles the "can-opener cooking" recipes of the 1950s that relied on Frankenstein-style combinations of tinned soups.[5]

Lionel did not easily accept the rationale that a mass audience necessitated poor quality. Sometimes, he resigned himself cynically to the situation; sometimes, he shared an alternate vision of the wasted artistic potential of film. Over two decades, in several published articles and an interview with a sympathetic and astute reporter, Lionel recorded his aesthetic manifesto about movie acting and directing. Revealing a profound commitment to artistic quality, this manifesto resisted false depictions of reality embodied in cookie-cutter movie characterizations and plots as well as in the "star types" that governed casting. This emphasis remained consistent with his 1925 defense of *The Piker* as an underappreciated play that told the truth. His sarcastic note that "to the local play reviewer the only dramatic possibilities . . . are glorifiable girls and glamourous crooks and 'dicks' of the non-existent variety" would apply as well to the situations portrayed in Hollywood films. Lionel had failed in *The Piker*; three years later, the reporter who had called Lionel "the first outstanding success of the talkies" conveyed Lionel's profusely expressed contempt for movie product. The public, in his view, was uninterested in art as a reflection of life and simply wanted art as distraction from life. Claiming that his only motivation was a fat paycheck, Lionel nevertheless "never fails to deliver the knock-out performance of every picture he plays in. He does it in his sleep."[6]

A long article by Lionel published in 1926 had elaborately presented his perspective concerning the falsity of movies' presentation of life. Again sarcastic, Lionel acknowledged the function of "Girlie," the script doctor asked to "jazz up" a story for a film treatment. "If Nero were to be put upon the screen as an important character, it would be necessary to jazz him up a bit, even though centuries have looked upon Nero as quite a sensational figure." He expressed his sense of the squandered potential of films: "there is nothing wrong with the medium. There is no reason why it should not give great art and beauty to the public. . . . [But] it is as if the printing press were a recent invention, . . . and only detective stories and comic strips in newspapers were printed." Besides falseness in stories, he deplored falseness in acting. Reliance on actors who could portray many characters had given way to reliance on "star types." But an emphasis on stardom distorted the movies: "it would have been better for the industry if there had been no stars or very few of them." He cautioned that "an actor or director who continues to do the same type of work, picture after picture, is standing still, no matter how excellent and expert his work may be."[7]

Lionel's resistance to false depictions of life and false acting undoubtedly underwent considerable strain after MGM signed him on as a director. Perhaps he hoped to make more of a difference to quality as a film director than he could as an actor. Certainly, working as a director offered him an escape from his disliked profession of acting. He recorded further thoughts on movie acting and directing in the thirties. Himself a great success in the talkies because stage performing had trained his voice, he explained what the stage actor needed to know to adapt to films. Transitioning from an illusionistic to a realistic medium, the stage actor must recognize the need to discard stage conventions, such as the "stage whisper," to adjust to acting in scenes filmed out of sequence, and to avoid overacting. George Cukor, both a stage director and a film director, expressed this by saying "on the stage, people don't act with their eyes. They act with their voice. In movies, they act with their eyes. . . . the most perfect screen acting . . . [is] the combination of stage and screen acting." (Ironically, after their theater-trained voices deemed stage actors more "suitable" to the talkies than were many silent players, those very voices eventually made them *less* suitable to the film medium.) As a director, Lionel observed the artificiality of much movie acting. "[He] doesn't like affectation," according to a 1933 feature: "'It ruins good acting!' exclaimed Lionel, whose eminence as an actor is almost equaled in the film colony by his prowess as a director. 'It seems easy to be casual, but it isn't. Many actors are not good actors because they haven't mastered the art of being casual. I heard a group of players chatting around a breakfast table on the set the other day, waiting for the director's call *Action!* All they had to do was to sit there and continue chatting, but immediately they became affected. They used an exaggerated stage accent. They were tense. Their voices betrayed it. They began to *act!*'" To gain feedback, the stage actor must rely not only on the felt presence of the stage audience but also on the film director and the audience for daily "rushes." Lionel himself preferred film acting to the theater because "I find it an infinitely easier life, in the sense of physical strain." He may have found film direction preferable to film acting for a while, but eventually he experienced it as too stressful and returned to movie acting.[8]

Assigned by MGM to direct early talkies, he apparently took up the challenge with some aplomb and with more insight than Nick Schenk showed.

LIONEL BARRYMORE

Interviewed while waiting for a train from Chicago to New Bedford, Massachusetts, in 1928, Lionel expressed the opinion that sound and color would eventually characterize the movies and even the incredibly long-sighted view that television would eventually take over. "Pretty soon, they will have color, talking and the whole works in the movies. . . . I suppose they will be calling movies the talkies next. It won't be long now until movie actors will have to speak lines just as they do on the stage now. Then television will be the next thing." He explained to the *New York Times* (which reported that Lionel had "abandoned acting" for directing) that movie exhibitors would have to improve the acoustics in their theaters. While filming *Madame X* in 1929, he monitored the sound quality and vocal delivery while his assistant director guided the action. He thought that a two-director process would solve the quality difficulties of early sound pictures. Another tactic combined swift exchanges of short speeches with swift changes of scene. At a time when MGM was assigning "transmission units" to actors' voices—the average voice volume was 10 units; Lionel's voice rated 13.02 units—Lionel's interest in solving the technical problems was probably much valued. Eventually, he concluded that the studios had overemphasized the importance of voice quality: "Sound technicians have solved practically all problems of recording the most variable voices." Now that total silence was required during filming, he communicated with his actors by using an apparatus that delivered a tiny shock that signaled his direction. Lionel also applied a sympathetic and collaborative approach to directing actors: "The good director comes to the making of his picture with clear ideas of what he wants, but he does not want to deal with puppets, he wants intelligent and constructive contributions from all his players. He is eager to hear their ideas, and discuss his with them." He stressed the need for a collegial attitude: "the practical way to direct is to hold a round-robin conference about the story, give and exchange ideas and then allow the cast a great deal of latitude in working out ideas." His "phenomenal" patience as a director was emphasized. When irked by the "stupidity" of actors or crew, he would leave the set to expel whatever excitable feelings he was experiencing and then would return quietly to resume direction. Harold Bucquet, Lionel's assistant on *Madame X*, in later years directed him in some of the Dr. Kildare films and in *On Borrowed Time*. Lionel later reminisced, "I labored under the delusion that he was my assistant. I now often wonder, in the watches of the night, how much I directed of them and how much he did—and give it up and wind up reading a detective story." Ruth Chatterton appreciated Lionel's direction of *Madame X*: "Lionel, of

Talkies Stardom and Detour into Direction, 1928–1931

course, I knew on the stage, and it's wonderful to have him for a director. He's so much like his sister Ethel it sometimes amazes me." Chatterton recalled his forbearance with a shaky elderly actor as Lionel pretended to blame the sound equipment rather than discourage the foreign-born player: "He was a very great actor . . . but he couldn't get his lines. . . . The old fellow was agonized. His eyes were like a dog's eyes. . . . 'What do you mean you can no do,' [Lionel] roared, laughing. 'You were marvelous. Wonderful! We are only retaking this time because the lights went bad.' The result, the beautiful result, was that the old man had his confidence again. . . . He gave a magnificent piece of work. . . . The patience of Lionel Barrymore never faltered once, never failed. His enthusiasm was enormous. To me, he was Christ-like." A similar story was told in a feature about Lionel published a few years later: "In a recent picture a veteran stage actor, assigned to a moderately important part, was seized with an attack of nerves. He forgot his lines completely when the shooting started. The situation was growing decidedly uncomfortable when Lionel took the actor aside and said something in a low voice. No one heard what he said. It was probably to the effect that the movies were ridiculous, anyway, and certainly could not disconcert a veteran trouper. The actor grinned, pulled himself together and did very creditable work when the scene was taken again." Lionel's age-peer, friend, and frequent costar over their decades at MGM, Lewis Stone, named his own appearance in Lionel's *Madame X* as one of his favorite roles.[9]

Not everyone remembered Lionel as "a very great and good man" or regarded his directing days with fondness and praise. The first issue, dated June 13, 1929, of *Actors' Equity News of Hollywood* bitterly denounced his objections to the closed shop for the film industry. It attributed his opposition to self-interest: "Now that he is sitting back in a comfortable director's chair he opposes the very ideals which he favored when he was an actor." Pointedly entitled "Laugh, Clown, Laugh!," the editorial recalled Lionel's stirring support of the 1919 Actors' Equity theater strike, during which he had declared, "We're proud to be here. We'll be here forever, if necessary." In 1924, theater producer David Belasco had announced the nonrenewal of the contracts of several members of Actors' Equity, including Lionel, as a reaction to the imposition of the closed shop by the American Federation of Labor on Actors' Equity. Perhaps this episode during the last months of his New York stage career had soured Lionel on the closed shop requirement that, in 1929, he now opposed in Hollywood, to the disgust of *Actors' Equity News*. Going on to assert that, ten years later, "the cause is exactly the same," the editorial denounced Lionel in *very* personal terms: "We are ashamed of you, Lionel Barrymore; it is the first time in the history of the theatre that your brothers and sisters have been forced to blush because of the thoughtlessness of any member of their royal family." A sidebar to the issue exposed in embarrassing detail Lionel's chronic delinquency in paying Equity dues. Denouncing "disloyalty," the June 17 issue of *Actors' Equity News of Hollywood* advocated silence on the part of dissenters and scarified Lionel for statements he had released to newspapers "naming every single one of you as graspers." Lionel, as an MGM director, got to go home after a prolonged shoot, whereas his actors had to continue under another director. Countering the complaint of unreasonably long hours for players, Lionel had alleged that actors during their paid working hours had much free time on their hands.[10]

Equity's closed shop order had an effective date of June 5. An executive of Paramount–Famous Players reacted to Equity's demands with the dire prediction that "this Equity controversy will result either in the end of Equity or the end of the motion picture industry." Lionel retorted to Equity's order, "I see no necessity of performing a major operation on a perfectly healthy child. The motion picture business is a perfectly healthy youngster and the proposals of Equity are certainly a major operation. I do not see any fairness in having a small minority of people come into a new business and expect to change that business to conform with their own ideas." Equity president Frank Gillmore rebuked Lionel by telegraph: "before you placed yourself on record in this matter it would have been more courteous of you to have called at this office to investigate claims." Noting that Lionel's opposition would be widely publicized, Gillmore invited him for a parley. Gillmore offended Noah Beery by characterizing actors who opposed the order as "deserters" and "selfish egotists." "I'm seeing red," Beery declared. "I'd hate to voice the words that might be used to describe those who choose to come out here and threaten with a chaos a business upon which many thousands depend for their very livelihoods." Other actors who sided with Lionel and Beery against Equity included Marie Dressler, John Gilbert, and Norma Talmadge. Equity and its organized labor supporters responded by suspending performers who signed non-Equity contracts and threatening that its opponents would pay for their recalcitrance. Equity advocates included Lionel's good friend Louis Wolheim, Jean Hersholt, Conway Tearle, and Reginald Denny. "If I never play in pictures again," Wolheim commented, "I still want to be able to shave in the morning without a desire to vomit."[11]

Talkies Stardom and Detour into Direction, 1928-1931

In late July, the Los Angeles Central Labor Council, affiliated with the American Federation of Labor and the California federation, asked secretaries and members of affiliated local unions to bombard Lionel and other holdouts with letters protesting their lack of union solidarity. Although still "green recruits" to the cause of labor, the Actors' Equity organizers "are standing up like seasoned veterans" to industry pressure. Over 1,600 Actors' Equity members had been striking since the June 5 order. After praising the stalwarts, the council's letter bitterly condemned "the six or eight who have shown themselves in a niggardly fashion by breaking into print and denouncing Actors' Equity." Besides angry letters directed to the residences of Lionel, Conrad Nagel, Clara Bow, Louise Dresser, Marie Dressler, and Noah Beery, the council requested that the letters include official resolutions blasting their noncooperation. In addition, the council recommended pressure on local theaters not to show their movies, demonstrations of disapproval during their movies, and walkouts from their movies.[12]

A few weeks later, in mid-August, after what she described as a positive meeting with the movie producers, Ethel, vice president of Equity, severely criticized Gillmore for proposing to Equity members a measure that the producers had already rejected. Equity's demands had finally dwindled to just one: that 80 percent of the actors cast in each motion picture be Equity members. Ethel declared, however, that the producers had already rejected this proposition. By month's end, Gillmore notified Equity members to accept studio work. Cecil B. DeMille, president of the Association of Motion Picture Producers of Hollywood, chortled approval of the producers' victory: "[Equity's demands] meant virtual control of the motion picture business. This control was predicated on conditions unwise, impractical and unfair. The Equity movement did not have the approval or sympathy of a majority of the working actors and actresses in the motion picture studios." Gillmore had had to climb down from his earlier assertion that "we are going to win a clean-cut victory but without vindictiveness or even bitterness, if it can be avoided, for the producers and ourselves have ultimately to lie down together and it will be happier for both parties if neither feels that he must hide a gun under his pillow."[13]

Equity certainly did not have Lionel's approval or sympathy in 1929; nor did Lionel express solidarity with disaffected MGM employees in 1933 when Louis B. Mayer announced severe pay cuts after President Franklin D. Roosevelt instituted a bank holiday to rectify widespread bank failures in the wake of the Great Crash of 1929 and the ensuing Great Depression. The Association of Motion Picture Producers and the Academy of Motion Picture Arts and Sciences supported these studio-proposed industry-wide 50 percent pay cuts. Lionel vigorously lent his support to Mayer at an employee meeting: "Don't worry, L.B. We're with you." Wallace Beery stormed out of the room. To the courageous objections voiced by screenwriter Ernest Vajda, Lionel responded with ridicule: "Mr. Vajda is like a man on his way to the guillotine, wanting to stop for a manicure. The tumbrils are rolling. The guillotine is waiting outside, and we're haggling for pennies." Well, not pennies exactly. And the guillotine metaphor might seem strange to anyone who had not lived in France for a few years. MGM did have severe cash flow problems and difficulty meeting payroll, and after six weeks the pay cuts were gone. But the promised reimbursements of lost pay never occurred, and two groups had escaped the pay cuts altogether: studio executives and members of the International Alliance of Theatrical Stage employees.[14]

These drastic pay cuts, however, led directly to the formation in 1933 of the various film industry guilds, including the Screen Actors Guild (SAG). Writers organized within the Screen Writers Guild just before actors formed SAG, and directors would eventually create the Screen Directors Guild. Accounts of the founding of all of these guilds emphasize workers' grievances over severe pay cuts, layoffs, and excessively long working hours, including on weekends. In addition, the National Industrial Recovery Act had exempted the salaries of studio executives at the same time that it limited pay for actors, writers, and directors. SAG president Eddie Cantor would protest this to President Roosevelt, who then suspended salary caps. Denouncing the academy at the annual SAG meeting in May 1934 as an anti-employee "company union" that had "sold the actors down the river for the benefit of the producer," Cantor called for the academy's destruction. In 1935, the American Federation of Labor chartered SAG. Interpreting the intent of the 1935 studio-proposed contract as the destruction of members' trust in the guild, *Screen Guilds Magazine* expressed the confidence of SAG board members that "the freelance actor, with the memory of the past five years still fresh in his mind, would see through this very transparent attempt to destroy his only chance of getting a decent contract." Indeed, as *Screen Guilds Magazine* sarcastically commented, "with the exception of the actors on the Academy committee and Mr. Lionel Barrymore, no one was fooled." Eventually, threatened by a strike in 1937, the studios recognized SAG, and producers signed the National Labor Relations Act, the constitutionality of which the United States Supreme Court had just upheld in April.[15]

Talkies Stardom and Detour into Direction, 1928-1931

Actors' Equity in 1934 had ceded to SAG jurisdiction over the film industry's performers and in 1935 agreed that it would suspend Equity members doing film work who failed to join SAG. Suspension banned the actor from appearing with Equity casts. A year later, abiding by its agreement with SAG, Equity suspended Lionel for not joining SAG. When newly formed in 1933, SAG had telegraphed to Lionel, as well as to Jack and Wallace Beery, a plea that they join the union. Eddie Cantor, Fredric March, Adolphe Menjou, Ann Harding, Groucho Marx, and Kenneth Thomson signed the telegram: "We want you with us in the Screen Actors Guild. We need your help and your name. It will make all of us feel better to know that you are with us. If there is anything you want explained, call any of us and we will explain it. We are sending you an application for membership. Please sign it." *Screen Guilds Magazine* in November 1936 both noted that Actors' Equity had suspended Lionel and several other actors for balking at SAG membership and sarcastically listed Equity's and SAG's many attempts via five letters to recruit the holdouts. After reporting Lionel's (and Jack's) noncompliance with membership demands in September 1936, *Variety* headlined in October this airy rationalization for Lionel's delinquency: "The Barrymores Don't Read Mail": "'All the Barrymores are careless about their correspondence.' ... An Equityite added that he had seen one of the Barrymores dump a whole batch of letters into the wastebasket without glancing at the envelopes." Until 1938, Lionel held out. He then reluctantly became SAG member #14892. As *Variety* reported, Equity reinstated his membership after he paid a $250 fine; SAG recommended this resolution: "Actor gave various excuses, but evidently decided that membership in SAG organization was necessary for future screen engagements."[16]

By 1938, Lionel had forsaken directing for full-time acting, but, in 1929, *Variety* had reported that MGM had signed him to a contract to "direct exclusively." The popular *Madame X*, for which Lionel was considered for a Best Director Oscar and which film critics ranked third among the "10 Best Pictures of 1929," is one of his two best-remembered directorial efforts. The other is *His Glorious Night*, which some have viewed as Louis B. Mayer's vehicle for destroying the career of silent star John Gilbert by exposing the inadequacy of Gilbert's voice, aided by either Lionel's ineptitude or his collusion. Eve Golden, Gilbert's scholarly biographer, and Robert Gottlieb, in his book about Greta Garbo, both said that no one will ever know for sure. Scott Eyman, who expressed a very poor opinion of Lionel as a film director, thought that Lionel's incompetence contributed to Gilbert's decline but also cautioned that Schenck and Thalberg would never have allowed Mayer to destroy one of MGM's "most valuable commercial assets out of personal pique." Other films that Lionel directed or reshot, with or without credit, included *Confession, The Unholy Night, The Rogue Song, Redemption, Guilty Hands, The Sea Bat,* and *Ten Cents a Dance.* Acknowledging that the fifteen-minute short film *Confession* was "well-directed and acted," *Variety*'s tart review found "no apparent reason for its origin, finish or existence": "Technically this sketch is an excellent piece of work on direction and playing. In theme it's one of those one-acters the little theatre groups dote on to drive the local intelligentsia into ecstasies, and Barrymore has worked it out along this vein." Lionel's being a musician caused his selection as the director of Stan Laurel and Oliver Hardy in *The Rogue Song*, MGM's first "all-color feature sound musical," starring opera baritone Lawrence Tibbett. Thought lost for many decades and listed by the American Film Institute among its "10 most wanted lost films," *The Rogue Song* survives in a six-minute fragment whose recovery was reported in 1999. From a scholarly 1973 British film publication comes this rather snarky assessment of his career: "Latter-day Lionel specialized in hammed-up, gruff patriarchs, contrasting with his more rugged early Biograph roles, in which, of course, we were spared his irritating vocal mannerisms. . . . Perhaps he was trying to compensate for his physical immobility by accentuating his verbal presence. . . . Although his work as a director remains unknown to us, it would be interesting to see whether his slightly queasy acting persona came across from behind the camera." While none of these films is a great motion picture, Lionel as a film director made two more permanent contributions to the industry. One was creating a movable microphone to counteract the restrictions placed on actors in early sound pictures by heavy and static recording equipment. The other was encouraging the young stage actor Clark Gable to pursue a career in the movies.[17]

According to *Films in Review*, "Barrymore is reputed to have been the first director to use a moving microphone on a sound stage." Lionel explicitly claimed credit for bypassing the stationary microphone that inhibited actors' movements by attaching a microphone to a fishing pole hanging over the actors and moving with them. Not only did he repeat this claim in his memoirs, but Samuel Marx also asserted it in his biography of Mayer and Thalberg. Others frustrated by the heavy sound equipment may also have invented the sound boom, but Lionel (usually a self-deprecating storyteller) stuck to his tale that he did so as well. Scott Eyman in his history of the transition to

Talkies Stardom and Detour into Direction, 1928-1931

sound expressed the diplomatic view that several people came up with the solution: William Wellman, Eddie Mannix, Dorothy Arzner, and Lionel. At least one reviewer of *Madame X* appreciated Lionel's experiments: "Barrymore has introduced something new in talking screen technique, and the result is engrossing entertainment, minus the imperfections of the earlier offerings of the audible screen."

As for Gable, Lionel had headed the cast of *The Copperhead* stage production hosted in 1926 by The Playhouse in Los Angeles; Gable had a minor part. Lionel enjoyed recounting to Cameron Shipp how Gable had muffed his stage appearance: "He had dropped his hat in a prop well, supposedly forty feet deep, then calmly dipped in and picked it up while the audience howled . . . 'Did it all with the savoir-faire of a kid with a quarter.'" Assigned by MGM to direct *Never the Twain Shall Meet*, Lionel shot a screen test for Gable, still a stage actor in *The Last Mile*. "Lionel pressed buzzers on his desk and aid[e]s hopped out of drawers and wastepaper baskets," according to Ed Sullivan, then a newspaperman. "At the wardrobe department the startled Gable was handed a leopard skin, a knife, and a rose. . . . [Painted black in the makeup department, his leopard skin draped, his knife sheathed,] 'What's the rose for?' asked Gable, miserably. 'Mr. Barrymore wants you to wear that behind your ear.'" Thalberg viewed the screen test without enthusiasm and, according to Sullivan, checked out Lionel's breath. Although Thalberg also objected to Gable's "big, batlike ears," Gable, of course, soon became a sensational asset for MGM. Anita Loos remembered that Gable kidded about his heartthrob image: "Clark was a darling. He was less self-conscious than anyone I ever knew. . . . [Once] he was at a water faucet getting a drink, and he straightened up, looked at me and pulled out his teeth and said, 'Look, America's Sweetheart!'" Lionel never did direct *Never the Twain Shall Meet*, just as he had never directed the canceled MGM production of *Oliver Twist* that cast him as Fagin and Chatterton as Nancy or MGM's *Olympia* with John Gilbert or *Cheri Beri*, a "French pirate story" formerly considered a Lon Chaney vehicle. He reencountered Gable on the set of *A Free Soul*. As Cameron Shipp told it, "Gable, lean, hungry and unknown, was embracing Norma Shearer, who was then one of Hollywood's most glittering stars and the wife of Irving Thalberg, production head of MGM. Gable flipped Mr. Barrymore a casual salute, as if he swallowed great actresses before breakfast every morning."[18]

Gable gave vigorous support to Lionel and Shearer in *A Free Soul*, after which Lionel finally abandoned his directorial ambitions to revert to full-time acting in the talkies. A newspaper interview reported that he had intended to continue film direction but instead agreed to act in *Guilty Hands* after persuasion by his old friend Bayard Veiller, its scriptwriter, who wrote the screenplay with Lionel in mind. A very conscientious film director, Lionel worried himself into chronic stress and eventually decided that he had had enough of the responsibility. He later explained to a reporter, "It was too much for me, working all day and worrying all night, and making decisions at meal time. I returned to acting, and I have been sorry for movie directors ever since." To another reporter, he addressed a rhetorical question, "What's the point of it? You lie awake all night thinking about the next day's work and spend your lunch hour worrying instead of eating. And, anyhow, who wants to nurse a gang of actors? Let somebody nurse me." While he retained his kindliness toward his fellow actors, he preferred to express it as a first among equals rather than as their director. In addition, Lionel's chronic financial bafflement caused him much anxiety about movie budgets: "When an actor finishes his day's scenes, he's through until the next day; the director just goes home and worries about his schedule and his budget. It's an awful feeling to handle $1,000,000 or $2,000,000 of a company's money; to have the responsibility of losing it or sending it out to bring back another $2,000,000. Acting is easier on the nerves." Film acting, once his refuge from stage acting, now became his refuge from film directing: "They're paying me good, and I'm living in a house and I haven't seen a dressing-room cockroach in years." Yet he also felt ambivalent: "I'm often asked if I'd rather direct than act, and the answer is that it all depends on what it is necessary for me to express, I can express some things best by acting, some by directing—so the practical thing is to choose the tool best suited to the job in hand."[19]

Lionel's passage back to full-time film acting included his supporting Greta Garbo in *Mata Hari* and then Norma Shearer in *A Free Soul*. A newspaper account noted that "Barrymore, whose dislike for fuss and feathers is as well known as his histrionic talent, not only has to submit to cosmetic treatment in [*Mata Hari*], but also has his hair marcelled and pomaded, not to ignore a gorgeous uniform laden with gold braid and pompous trappings." But he acquiesced because he really wanted the part. Enjoyable hokum, *Mata Hari* is a highly fictionalized account of the "exotic dancer" shot by the French as a German spy in 1917. Greta Garbo gives a wonderful performance, especially when she uses the facial dexterity she had learned as a silent picture actress. Lionel and Ramon Navarro scamper in her wake as two of the beguiled men she fascinates. (Men react to Mata Hari like stunned bunny

Talkies Stardom and Detour into Direction, 1928-1931

rabbits.) Garbo evaded the strictures and demands of MGM and even responded to threats of deportation with cool aplomb; she brings those same negotiating skills to her characterization of Mata Hari. While Lionel does his best in the limited role of an enraptured Russian officer stuck in her sinuous coils, he surpasses himself in *A Free Soul* as an alcoholic criminal attorney who eventually denounces himself in a courtroom as a poor father. Six cameras filmed his rant in one take maintained over fourteen minutes. Lionel's flamboyant and extravagant performance won him the 1931 Oscar for Best Actor. Beating out for the Best Actor Oscar, among others, Fredric March playing a character based on Jack in *The Royal Family of Broadway*, Lionel had risen to the top of his inescapable profession.[20]

7

Scene Stealer, 1933–1935

Lionel's Oscar-winning turn in *A Free Soul* and his supporting role in *Mata Hari* foretold how MGM and the other studios to which MGM lent him out would cast him in the first half of the thirties. He would attract audiences as the leading actor in many films without ever being a romantic leading man or having a "star image" created for him. Long before, Lionel had expressed to Ashton Stevens his dubiousness about being the romantic lead: "being the whole table d'hôte instead of the entrée puts you hard against it for nervousness. . . . People don't know how hard leading business is. . . . The leading man is the most abused creature in the world. . . . He not only is, but he must tell, the whole story. . . . [In contrast,] the character man comes on with a selected situation and captures the works." Besides continuing in many parts in his preferred capacity as a character actor, Lionel would be in other films the leading male actor but not one with a "star image." Instead, when he acted the leading male role, he usually embodied the Father archetype, impersonating for a generation of Americans their concept of the wise and respected patriarch. Ironically, his unwise and disrespected patriarch in *A Free Soul*, whose award-winning self-denunciation bewailed his failings as a father, preceded many turns as a revered male authority figure. (His costar in *A Free Soul*, "daughter" Norma Shearer objected to the focus on Lionel in the fourteen-minute courtroom scene, but despite interventions on her behalf by her husband, MGM executive Irving Thalberg, the original passionate and "flawless" take was in the final cut.) For the rest of his film career, Lionel's archetypal Father would enliven many roles, eventually even that of Dr. Kildare's fatherly mentor, Dr. Gillespie, while Lionel's skill at character parts would make memorable such later roles as the villainous Mr. Potter in *It's a Wonderful Life*.[1]

In the twenty-eight films produced between 1932 and 1936 before Lionel's first experience of a broken hip threatened his livelihood, he made seven

Scene Stealer, 1933-1935

movies for other studios while on loan-out, and he acted in the other twenty-one movies for his home studio, MGM. Fox borrowed him for *Carolina* and *The Little Colonel*; Paramount for *Broken Lullaby*; Twentieth Century-Fox for *The Road to Glory*; and RKO for *Sweepings, One Man's Journey*, and *The Return of Peter Grimm*. Although Lionel worked with Howard Hawks (*The Road to Glory*) and Ernst Lubitsch (*Broken Lullaby*) only once, he worked in these twenty-eight films with several other directors and with a producer for whom, over the span of his film career, he performed more than once: King Vidor, W. S. Van Dyke, John Cromwell, and Edmund Goulding (twice each); George Cukor, Raoul Walsh, and Sam Wood (three times each); Tod Browning and Victor Fleming (four times each); Clarence Brown (five times); and Jack Conway (six times). David O. Selznick, who often wanted to cast the Barrymores, employed Lionel in six films. Not only were these earlier years of the thirties extremely busy ones for Lionel as an actor, but they were also consequential for his second marriage, for Irene's gradually deteriorating health created much worry and anguish for him.

As though Lionel was not busy enough, he was announced and/or sought after for some movies in which he never eventually appeared. MGM contemplated casting him for *It Can't Happen Here*, based on Sinclair Lewis's novel about American fascism, but the studio backed off from the controversial project. He refused the studio's proposal to remake his stage and silent hit *The Copperhead*. MGM recalled Lionel from RKO's project *Winterset*. Lionel never played in *Silas Marner* (like *A Yank at Oxford*, a project of MGM's British unit) or in *Skidding* or in *Valedictory*, an American version of *Goodbye, Mr. Chips* with Mickey Rooney and Judy Garland. Jack and Lionel never appeared in MGM's *The Paradine Case*, the brothers did not star as "Denver demons" in a film of their pal Gene Fowler's novel *Timber Line*, Lionel did not act with Jack in *Reunion in Vienna*, nor did Selznick ever achieve his ambition to cast the brothers, as well as Ethel, in his planned film for MGM of John Galsworthy's trilogy *The Forsyte Saga*—a most intriguing prospect. Would related actors have played related characters? Lionel as Old Jolyon, Jack as Young Jolyon, Ethel as Winifred? (Young Jolyon and Winifred are, of course, first cousins.) Or Jack as Soames? Presumably, Selznick would not have cast Ethel and Jack as lovers or spouses! This would rule out Ethel as Irene (if Jack was Soames) and Jack as Soames, Young Jolyon, or Bosinney (if Ethel was Irene). David Thomson's biography of Selznick seemed to imply that in 1933, he contemplated casting Lionel as the private detective who periodically updates Soames on his wife's infidelity with Young Jolyon. A story treatment from 1933 survives in a repository of MGM scripts but gives no clue as to prospective casting. George Cukor was very interested in directing this never-realized MGM production by Selznick. Perhaps motivated by Galsworthy's award of the 1932 Nobel Prize for Literature, RKO purchased *The Forsyte Saga* in 1934 for Katharine Hepburn, and a script apparently exists in RKO–Radio Pictures archives. In 1939, rumors alleged the casting of Myrna Loy in a production, but *That Forsyte Woman* did not make it to the silver screen until ten years later, with Errol Flynn and Greer Garson. The famed British television series starring Eric Porter in a masterly performance as Soames was in the far future.[2]

Among the movies in which Lionel embodied the benign Father archetype or positive male authority figure were some films in which he acted well and a few in which he acted superbly well. In the very likable King Vidor film *The Stranger's Return*, Lionel as an aged farmer takes a fancy to his granddaughter from the big city who has returned to her father's home for refuge even though she has never been there before. Miriam Hopkins plays the granddaughter with spirit, and Lionel puts the *c* in *cantankerous* but nevertheless is a benign figure. To play the part in a flowing beard yet still smoke his cigarettes, Lionel had to wear whiskers sprayed every morning with fire-retardant chemicals. Japanese master director Yasujiro Ozu watched *The Stranger's Return* four times; some even claim it was Ozu's favorite film. Partly made on location at a farm forty-five miles from the studio, the film required Lionel's reluctant presence so far from his usual haunts; however, he was so taken with the locale that he began to bring his etching equipment as well as befriended the farm's pigs. The *New York Times* reviewer asserted that Lionel's cranky but loving grandfather was a role "made in heaven for him" and assessed his acting as "hearty and brilliant" as well as "entirely delightful."[3]

From the cranky but loving grandfather in *The Stranger's Return* is but a step to the frustrated but loving father of *Sweepings*. Lionel builds a department store empire on the ashes of the Chicago Fire but fails to father children who are other than spoiled and entitled and disappointing. A good movie, *Sweepings* makes quite a statement about the effects of inherited wealth on character. Here Lionel is a failed but still loving father. Lionel as the entrepreneur and Gregory Ratoff as his underappreciated subordinate dominate the movie. Praising Ratoff's "beautiful performance," the *Coronado Eagle and Journal* declared that "it is becoming an established truth that Lionel Barrymore is the finest actor on the screen today," while, according to the *Madera Tribune*, "Lionel Barrymore finds a drama to suit his giant's stride." The *Wall*

Scene Stealer, 1933–1935

Street Journal and the *New York Times* noted how makeup wizards had transformed Lionel into a young man for the beginning of the movie. The author of *Sweepings*, Lester Cohen, later declared, "I have known three men of theatre who could do a scene right under your nose, any time of day and night, and with utmost reality: David Belasco, Lionel Barrymore, Gregory Ratoff."[4]

In Clarence Brown's *Looking Forward*, Lionel is very good as a loyal, long-serving clerk to Lewis Stone, department store owner, who reluctantly lays him off during the Depression. Stone is barely keeping the store open, and he is forced to contemplate selling it to a hated competitor. The movie focuses on the relationship between the two men and their families' responses to the crisis and threat. *Looking Forward* sought to encourage Depression-era audiences with a storyline about resilience after economic hardship and to dampen anticapitalist sentiment with a depiction of the loyalty and even the friendship between an employer and his longtime employee. Its title (previously *Service*, *Yesterday's Rich*, and *The New Deal*) exploited the sentiments of President Franklin D. Roosevelt's book of the same name, and its foreword showcased this quotation from FDR's book: "We need enthusiasm, imagination and ability to face facts—we need the courage of the young." Both employer and employee are fathers whose children support their efforts to survive and even to thrive amid severe economic stress. Their relationship with each other and their relationships with their children are central to the story.

One Man's Journey stars Lionel as a dedicated country doctor for whom medicine is both an art and a science. Lionel is very good as the overworked and underpaid physician, as is May Robson as his housekeeper. Lionel's country physician in *One Man's Journey* also acts as a benign patriarch to younger people, whether they are his own children or not, and indeed to all the people in his community. To serve them, he lets go by an opportunity to realize his private dream of becoming a specialist, for some crisis always prevents his departure. (In other words, he is George Bailey minus the bitterness.) More precisely, his paternal and professional devotion render him unable to leave those to whom he has dedicated his life and career.[5]

In Eugene O'Neill's atypical comedy, *Ah, Wilderness!*, Lionel plays the father of a rambunctious family, and Spring Byington plays the mother. Mickey Rooney and Bonita Granville, both very young here, play two of their children. This film adaptation is a charming portrayal of a long-vanished American way of life. *Ah, Wilderness!* director Clarence Brown had wanted to have Will Rogers repeat his stage role as the father, but failed negotiations with Rogers eventually resulted in Lionel's getting the film role. Facing some adolescent rebellion and acting-out by his elder son, Richard (Eric Linden), encouraged by his wastrel brother-in-law (Wallace Beery), patriarch Nat Miller responds with calm, restraint, and humor but also with careful reinforcement of traditional values and morals. Nat is Richard's father, not his pal. Brown lavished on the production details from his own schooldays gathered from his own high school yearbook, 1905 edition. He even included in the movie his high school class song, "Away to the Woods": "I wanted to get something representatively callow and in the spirit of this story, but I could remember only half the words. . . . Eventually [we] located one printed copy of 'Away to the Woods' in Cincinnati." The thirties adolescents brought to the studio as extras impersonating 1906 teenagers had to divest themselves of nail polish, makeup, anklets, costume jewelry, wristwatches, sports belts, and shoes as well as cigarette lighters. Alistair Cooke broadcast enthusiastically on the BBC: "About as charming film as we've had this year . . . the film [has] undeniable distinction. . . . The acting of, especially, Eric Linden and Lionel Barrymore saves Wallace Beery from the woeful emphasis he receives."[6]

Shirley Temple is *The Little Colonel*, a granddaughter who breaks down the resistance of her estranged grandfather, Colonel Lloyd, with Lionel playing another cranky but loving patriarch. About being an adult actress prompted by impatient children, Temple much later commented, "All I can think of is how I used to do the very same thing to Lionel Barrymore and of how he must have wanted to throttle me each and every time." Atypical fathers whom he played are the beleaguered characters in *Should Ladies Behave* and in *This Side of Heaven*. The *Wall Street Journal* sniffed about *Should Ladies Behave* that "Lionel Barrymore's opening snores seemed to echo faintly throughout the picture" and that "he seems to have an off day." The *New York Times* liked Lionel's weak and muddled father in *This Side of Heaven* rather better, saying, "The weakness of Martin Turner is not excused, but what serves to move the onlooker is the loyalty of his wife and children."[7]

While Lionel's performances in these roles are good, Lionel's superlative performances in the Father role came in Lubitsch's *Broken Lullaby*, Hawks's *The Road to Glory*, and Cukor's *Camille*.

Broken Lullaby, previously entitled *The Man I Killed* and then *The Fifth Commandment*, depicts a French veteran of World War I tormented by his memory of killing a German soldier. He eventually goes to meet the family of the man he killed but does not tell them of his guilt. Instead, he seeks relief

Scene Stealer, 1933-1935

by becoming a part of the family of his dead German opponent. The dead man's sweetheart discovers his secret but persuades him to continue his deception of the parents, for telling them the truth would rob them again of a son. Lionel as the German soldier's father passionately indicts his own generation as old men sending young men to die. Lionel's portrayal of the bereaved father moved a critic to assert that his was "the finest screen performance of 1932."[8]

In *The Road to Glory*, a mesmerizing depiction of life in the trenches, Lionel memorably portrays an elderly Frenchman who insists on serving in World War I under the command of his son even though his earlier army experience had occurred in 1870 during the Franco-Prussian War when he had signaled a cavalry charge with his bugle. As superannuated as his bugle, last sounded in war when he was a mere boy, he refuses to leave the front, and eventually heroic action causes him to die with his son. Expressing "resentful admiration," for this "stirring, dramatic and vivid picture," the *New York Times* deplored the movie's senseless heroics, which the reviewer felt the script should have probed and questioned more deeply. Expressing the opposite judgment, the *San Pedro News-Pilot* called *The Road to Glory* "this indictment of war" that "removes sentimentality from war as a surgeon's knife removes an ulcer." Howard Hawks directed the movie from a screenplay on which William Faulkner had worked.[9]

Camille features Greta Garbo and Robert Taylor as star-crossed lovers separated by her past and his future. Lionel in his supporting role as Taylor's disapproving father intervenes to persuade Camille to end the love affair for his son's sake. A less sympathetic part than his fathers in *Broken Lullaby* and in *The Road to Glory*, Lionel's father in Alexandre Dumas's *Camille* is determined to force a break between the lovers. Making very palpable the paternal concern of Monsieur Duval, Lionel's persuasiveness overcomes the aversion that a romantic audience enraptured by the film's two beautiful leads and that Camille herself might feel toward him. Originally, Jack was cast as Baron de Varville, Camille's patron and lover; illness caused Jack's replacement as the Baron by Lionel and then by Henry Daniell, whereas Lionel became Monsieur Duval instead. Years later, Lionel entertained Hedda Hopper with this eccentric anecdote about Dumas: "It came to me in the middle of the night. Dumas was the spitting image of the head waiter at the Burnett House in Cincinnati.... [Or] any bunch of waiters on the Canadian Pacific. If he'd been lucky, instead of writing *Camille*, he'd have been serving trout caught in Mexico on a train rocking towards Los Angeles."[10]

LIONEL BARRYMORE

Lionel's other portrayals during the first half of the thirties were character roles. The Barrymore brothers amuse each other by acting as antagonists (policeman and gentleman thief) in *Arsène Lupin*. Jack is at the center of *Grand Hotel* as a German baron with money woes who befriends a morose Russian ballerina (Greta Garbo), a snappy world-wise stenographer (Joan Crawford), and a dying man trying to squeeze a missed lifetime of sheer living into a few weeks (Lionel). Crawford is very good as the stenographer who understandably grimaces at her potentially intimate association with businessman Wallace Beery. Jack elegantly woos manic-depressive ballerina Garbo when he can spare time from chatting with his beloved dachshund, Max, as well as plotting to steal Garbo's jewels. For this engrossing movie, the Best Picture of 1932, the audience did not pay admission to see the real life that they desperately wanted to forget for a while. Taking *Grand Hotel* for what it is, a star vehicle meant to distract the masses from their economic burdens for two hours, it is enjoyable to see Garbo and Jack make love to each other's profiles, to see Crawford fall for Jack and detest her crude boss (Beery), and to see Lionel steal the movie as a lowly employee who believes he is dying and so intends to live it up at the Grand Hotel Berlin in his last days. Other films in which the Barrymore brothers challenged each other include the notorious *Rasputin and the Empress*, in which Jack vigorously tries to kill Lionel in an amazingly protracted murder scene, and *Night Flight*, a riveting aviation drama about the perils and challenges of night mail delivery in South America as well as a superior depiction of workplace and home tensions and conflicts over the dangers posed by terrain and weather. Although Ethel played the last Empress of All the Russias in *Rasputin*, she neglected to see the movie for a quarter century, but then she commented, "I thought it was pretty good, but what those two boys were up to, I'll never know. Wasn't Lionel *naughty*?" Recalling his own role as a court physician in *Rasputin*, Edward Arnold praised Ethel as "always a splendid trouper"; he had acted with her on the stage under Frohman management. Fixing his drooping makeup on a hot and humid day in his *Rasputin* dressing room, Arnold found himself hugged from behind by his "lovely leading lady" from the days when he had played her butler. After Arnold's father died during their stage engagement, Arnold found his father's casket blanketed with roses sent by Ethel. Lionel explained that he had prepared for the role of the Mad Monk by immersing himself in a dozen or more books as well as contemplating photographs and drawings: "I placed special reliance on personal memoirs and accounts of Rasputin's personal mannerisms coming from reliable sources." Reportedly, he also

Scene Stealer, 1933-1935

gleaned insights from his valet, Bill Cumner, a British soldier who claimed that before he had fought with the White Russians, he had seen Rasputin in action, and witnessed the recovery of Rasputin's body after his murder. Lionel summed up his impressions of Rasputin as "an ignorant peasant who had the strange faculty of making himself believe anything he set his mind to. This belief, plus an intense personal magnetism, won him many followers. Then came his lust for power. With all of it, his queer religious creed, his debaucheries, his intrigues, his hypnotic influence, there was an undercurrent of sincerity." Both Barrymore brothers are also in fine form in *Dinner at Eight*, which has stood up very well to time and features several excellent comic performances—especially by Marie Dressler, Jean Harlow, and Billie Burke.[11]

Despite the inspired and entertaining pairing of Lionel with Jack in *Arsène Lupin*, the studio had originally intended to cast Lionel and John Gilbert with Tod Browning assigned to direct. Instead, Gilbert dropped out, Browning directed *Freaks*, and Jack Conway ended up working with Lionel and Jack. Reviewer Tom Pettey noted the partiality of New York audiences for Lionel: "When he appears there is always a burst of handclapping in the neighborhood houses. John is received more quietly. . . . Lionel has been good regularly; John has frequently been bad." Featuring both brothers on the cover of its March 7, 1932, issue, *Time* recorded Lionel's revelation of his approach to his character: "Oh, I'll stumble around, growl a little, limp a little bit." The birthday cake given to Arsène Lupin in the movie was so large that it challenged the capacity of any available oven; the cake's bakers had to resort to a Southern California barbeque pit.[12]

Dissenting from the prevailing esteem for Lionel's Otto Kringelein in *Grand Hotel* (a part that the studio had previously considered offering to Buster Keaton), George Jean Nathan accused Lionel of viewing Hollywood "as a mere golden sewer from which to fish up some easy, if aesthetically tainted, manna." Rebuking this minority view, the *Chicago Daily Tribune* praised Lionel's performance as "the outstanding characterization of the group." Indeed, during a scene with Lionel, Crawford felt so moved that she burst into unscripted tears retained in the final cut: "She wilted completely when Lionel spoke the lines and burst into tears which were real instead of glycerin. This was not called for in the script, but the order to shoot the scene was hastily given and it became a high spot in the finished picture. To Lionel, though, this had been merely a sequence to be acted as well as possible. A few minutes later, he was profanely hunting for the mustache which was part of his makeup. It was constantly dropping off his lip and getting lost." Crawford liked Lionel as a person because he was kind to her on the set: "Every single day Mr. Lionel Barrymore would say something nice to me. He'd say, 'How are you, baby? I never saw you look so beautiful,' or he'd tell me that I had acted better than any other day that week. I know he didn't mean it, but it was nice to hear." Perhaps her on-screen tears reflected her off-screen vulnerability to Lionel's kindness. Spencer Tracy called Lionel's work in *Grand Hotel* "the finest thing an actor had accomplished on the screen."[13]

Rasputin and the Empress was the only major film in which all three Barrymore siblings appeared; the press and the studio took full advantage of the golden opportunity to sensationalize real and imaginary sibling conflicts. While this press coverage about the actors may have added to the film's appeal to the masses, a more consequential conflict emerged from an unfortunate feature of the script meant also to increase popular interest. The movie added a fictional love for Jack, the virginal Princess Natasha (the czar's niece), to its fictional account of the rise to power and the murder of Rasputin. Yet the movie also claimed at its beginning that most of the characters portrayed had died but a few remained alive: "This concerns the destruction of an empire, brought about by the mad ambition of one man. A few of the characters are still alive. The rest met death by violence." The film's relentless fictionalization contended with its bogus claims to authenticity—a ploy designed to promote its popularity and make money that instead exposed it to legal peril and great monetary loss. Jack's portrayal of Prince Paul Chegodieff prompted one of Rasputin's real assassins, Prince Felix Youssoupoff, to claim that some people identified him with Chegodieff. Youssoupoff later claimed that some viewers believed that Princess Natasha was his real-life wife, Princess Irina Romanoff Youssoupoff, the czar's niece, who actually had never met Rasputin but, in the uncut film, introduces him into the palace and later is seduced or raped by him. This intractable muddle of purported truth with purported fiction led to a libel action and a British court case, *Youssoupoff v. MGM*. If some people identified the character Princess Natasha with Princess Irina Romanoff Youssoupoff, any fictions attached to Princess Natasha further substantiated the evidence for libel. MGM lost both the case and its appeal. The costly damages exacted by the court led MGM and other studios to attach to future productions a fig-leaf disclaimer that these fictional movies had not intentionally portrayed any actual persons, living or dead.[14]

Night Flight, a box-office failure, disappointed some viewers who expected more interactions among its several stars (the Barrymore brothers,

Scene Stealer, 1933–1935

Clark Gable, Helen Hayes, Myrna Loy, and Robert Montgomery), but director Clarence Brown instead had used the film to express the awe, joy, and terror of pioneer aviators. Nevertheless, he impressed Howard Hawks, whose later film *Only Angels Have Wings* shows the influence of *Night Flight*. *Movienews* understood Brown's achievement: "There have been dozens of aviation pictures. This is the first picture of flying. Mark the distinction; it is tremendous." The *New York Times* called *Night Flight* "easily the outstanding screen contribution to aviation." The *Chicago Tribune*'s reviewer deplored how the movie afflicted Lionel's character with eczema, but Lionel used the opportunity to scratch himself incessantly and even stole a scene in which only Jack spoke any lines by exiting while casually rubbing his posterior. Admiring Lionel's resourcefulness, Jack thereby won a ten-dollar bet with Brown that Lionel would somehow find a way to upstage his younger brother: "He will snatch it if he has to hang from the chandelier." Not everyone found Lionel's scene stealing amusing—maybe not even Jack at times. Another player in *Night Flight*, William Gargan, also Lionel's son in *Sweepings*, claimed that Jack actually plotted with Gargan to counteract Lionel's moves: "Have you noticed that sweet sonofabitching brother of mine? . . . He's moving and scratching and mugging all over the place. . . . If you see him moving when I'm talking, you blow your line. If I see him move when you're talking, I'll blow." After many blown takes, Brown allegedly cautioned the offender, "Get the scratching over with before we shoot, Lionel." To which Lionel, according to Gargan, played dumb: "'Scratch?' he said, digging into an armpit. 'I haven't moved.'" Then, at the end of the next take, Lionel scratched his posterior anyway.[15]

While Lionel's part in *Dinner at Eight* is much less showy, it does pair him with Marie Dressler as a past love and Billie Burke as his wife. Featuring, like *Grand Hotel*, a glittering all-star ensemble, *Dinner at Eight* features Lionel in a role overshadowed by those played by Dressler, Burke, Jack, Wallace Beery, and Jean Harlow. Of Harlow, Lionel commented after her early death in 1937, "She won my heart by her courage and her humor, and, above all, by her dignity. I have known most of the stars of the theatre, and she deserved to be with the best of them." To Harlow's grave, Lionel reportedly sent white roses every day until his own death in 1954.[16]

Other character roles include Jefferson Keane who, like James Stewart's later Jefferson Smith, is an idealistic reformer and crusader for the people who becomes a US senator. Just as in *Mr. Smith Goes to Washington*, in *Washington Masquerade* the entrenched agents of corruption get to work to

LIONEL BARRYMORE

besmirch and thwart the idealists. Lionel does a good job as he repeats a role that he had played in the New York stage in *The Claw*, and Karen Morley also acts well her part of the betraying society hostess who becomes his wife. In Marie Dressler's last film, *Christopher Bean* (also called *Her Sweetheart*), Lionel and his wife, Beulah Bondi, try to cheat their maid, Dressler; with Lionel "in fine fettle," the *New York Times* declared, "he adds greatly to the general amusement." *Christopher Bean*'s director, Sam Wood, explained to newspaper readers how Lionel and Dressler "built" their scenes: "Lionel watched every detail of Marie's work and speech, and she his, as the business was worked out." (When Lionel had received his Best Actor Oscar, fellow nominee Jackie Cooper had napped on Dressler's lap.) *Carolina*, an early Shirley Temple vehicle, features Lionel as a crazed Confederate veteran. In the Jean Harlow comedy *The Girl from Missouri*, Lionel, Harlow, and Franchot Tone are all crooks trying to scam each other. The male characters respond to Harlow's presence like wilted plants that are suddenly hydrated. In *Public Hero No. 1*, a gangster and G-men picture from MGM, top-billed Lionel actually gives support to Joseph Calleia, Chester Morris, and Jean Arthur in a gaudy turn as a determinedly drunken physician long in service to the mob. Lionel's very entertaining performance goes way past scene stealing into grand larceny. Novelist and film critic Graham Greene judged Lionel's doctor "who bled gin" as "one of the best performances of his career." Shooting additional scenes of a blood transfusion required the previously filmed needle, which was missing until Lionel confessed that he had taken it and left it at home to use when applying acid to his etching plates. (Many years later, Chester Morris remembered "the same thrill, the same sharp enjoyment, . . . as in those early days when I had a supporting role with Lionel Barrymore.") Lionel enlivens *The Return of Peter Grimm* as he depicts a selfish man whose ghost returns to make amends for his failings. In *The Voice of Bugle Ann*, he plays a Missouri backwoodsman who kills a sheep farmer for shooting his beloved hunting dog. *The Devil-Doll* features a superlative performance by Lionel in his last Tod Browning picture. (Erich von Stroheim worked on its screenplay.) Minor contributions to movies include Lionel's very brief turn as Daniel Peggotty, the protector of Little Em'ly, in *David Copperfield*, as well as a vampire hunter in *Mark of the Vampire*. *Treasure Island* allows Lionel, in his exceedingly brief (although star-billed) appearance as Billy Bones, to be far more colorful. About *Mark of the Vampire*, Alistair Cooke recommended it "if you want to feel deliciously unwell."[17]

Scene Stealer, 1933–1935

Another minor role was President Andrew Jackson in *The Gorgeous Hussy*. The Hays Office suppressed in the film much of the colorful language favored by both Lionel and President Jackson, but Lionel made enough of an impression that he played Jackson again late in his career in *Lone Star*. Because of Lionel's long-standing interest in American history, he may well have felt intrigued by the controversy inspired by the fictionalization of Peggy Eaton's troubles in *The Gorgeous Hussy* and especially by his and Beulah Bondi's portrayals of Andrew Jackson and Rachel Jackson. Naturally circumscribed by MGM's screenplay, Lionel probably did not mistake the movie for an accurate historical account of the Petticoat Affair, but the board of the Ladies' Hermitage Association, worried that the public would so mistake it, voted to request that MGM affix a foreword clarifying "that the picture is fiction and not history." Most objectionable were the suggestions that the Jacksons, especially Rachel Jackson, were uncouth and poorly educated misfits in Washington. These characterizations seemed both disrespectful and inaccurate. Vigorously combating these misrepresentations, Ladies' Hermitage Association historian Mary French Caldwell wrote to the Associated Press as well as many women's clubs, sought to censor the movie in Tennessee, and succeeded in creating a great deal of adverse publicity for the movie. Caldwell also pointed out that, when President Franklin Delano Roosevelt had visited the Hermitage a few years before, he had received as a gift Rachel Jackson's personal copy of John Dryden's translation of Virgil, surely not a possession of an illiterate woman. Association regent Mrs. Reau E. Folk, condemning the movie as "wicked," scoffed at MGM assurances of historical accuracy, such as the alleged consultation of 218 books and a thousand pages of letters, and recalled that the association had refused permission to MGM for interior photography at the Hermitage "until more could be learned about how closely MGM proposed to follow history and facts." After much discussion, Mrs. Folk revealed, "we just decided to ignore it," but the class implications of Beulah Bondi's pipe smoking could not be ignored. Former regent Mrs. E. A. Lindsay offered the palliative that Rachel Jackson might have smoked herbs to soothe a respiratory complaint. Doubtless, the Ladies' Hermitage Association did not find soothing Bondi's nomination for the Best Supporting Actress Oscar for her turn as Rachel Jackson.[18]

The *New York Times* praised Lionel's performance as the previously uncompromising, eventually corrupted, but finally repentant senator in *Washington Masquerade*: "The role is a good one to begin with, and Mr. Barrymore ... has made it much better. He can even deliver the speeches about the Flag and the People so that they don't sound quite as bad as, say, in the Senate. His characterization . . . is excellent." Although The *Wall Street Journal* also liked Lionel's performance, it tartly dismissed the character he portrayed: the "man who decided against business development of natural resources stumbles over a first cup of Washington, D.C. tea and staggers towards the grave. . . . If the movie . . . is veracious, then of such is the kingdom of public ownership champions." So intense was Lionel's acting as Jefferson Keane that, when he pounded a table during a speech, he broke two bones in his hand.[19]

Peter Grimm persistently meddles in the affairs of his ward—before his death to Catherine's detriment and after his death to her gain. The *Chicago Tribune* admired the movie as a vehicle for Lionel, "for this master of characterization invests any role he plays with authenticity and humanness." The *New York Times* expressed boredom with this hoary stage piece from David Belasco but admitted that Lionel "is a thoughtful blend of dignity and septuagenarian coyness as he wanders about in the luminous haze which the photographers provide for him." After a week had passed, this reviewer irritably and pithily dismissed the film as an "ancient ghost story brought to the screen with unnecessary reverence" and "a funereal exhibit."[20]

Lauded as "the greatest tribute to the dog as a friend of man ever to be brought to the screen," *The Voice of Bugle Ann*, then and now, finds understanding viewers who sympathize with the grief and rage of a bereaved dog owner. To some people, mere death does not seem anything like punishment enough for killing a loved animal. Lionel defends his action during his trial:

> The only absolutely unselfish friend a man can have, one that will never be ungrateful or treacherous is his dog. Yes sir, a man's dog will stand by him rich or poor, sick or well. He'll sleep on the cold ground, don't make no difference. Wind or snow, all he asks is just to stand by him. He'll kiss the hand that ain't got no food to give him; he'll guard the sleep of a pauper just like he was a king. And when all his other friends is gone there you'll find his dog. A man might not have no roof to his head; he'd be friendless and homeless, and all the faithful dog asks is just to stand by him. Guard him agin any danger, that he kin. And when it's *all* over, a man can lay in Potter's Field in a grave that ain't got no headstone, there you'll find his dog. With his eyes sad, but open and watchin'. With his head between his paws, just waitin'.

Scene Stealer, 1933-1935

Some of the Missouri foxhounds used in the movie were promised to various actors—Lionel, Clark Gable, Jean Harlow, Spencer Tracy—but someone stole the dogs promised to Gable. Bugle Ann herself went home at night with Lionel and returned to the studio in the morning while seated beside him in the front seat of Lionel's car. This lucky pup had survived a month of competition with five other dogs who also had lived with Lionel to determine their compatibility with him.[21]

A major achievement in a character part is Lionel's performance in *The Devil-Doll*. While Tod Browning's *Mark of the Vampire* with its famous twist ending is a well-done riff on the subject of vampire hunting that makes the viewer feel the need to lay in a supply of prophylactic bat thorn, Browning's *The Devil-Doll* is not so much a horror film as a clever fantasy of elaborate revenge. Lionel, a French banker wrongly sent to prison for financial crimes, then escapes to avenge himself on the real criminals, associates who had framed him to exculpate themselves. In both movies, acting in roles that could hardly be more different from each other, Lionel disappears into the character. As the banker, he disappears even further when he disguises himself as an elderly Frenchwoman for most of the film. In drag, he speaks in a high-pitched voice. (An old acquaintance, Frances Preston, the widow of President Grover Cleveland, visited Lionel on the set of *The Devil-Doll*; in drag, Lionel tipped his granny's wig to her.) His fellow escaped prisoner and this man's mad scientist wife (whose horror-film hairstyle bears the obligatory skunk-stripe) have devised a miniaturization process that reduces people or animals to one-sixth their previous size. Then these "devil-dolls" obey the will of their creators. As the banker who seizes upon this method as a way to exact his revenge, Lionel outdoes himself.[22]

All of these professional challenges coincided with a domestic tragedy in which Lionel's second wife, Irene Fenwick, gradually lost her health and then, in 1936, her life. Gladys Hall recorded that the health troubles had worsened in 1928, when doctors diagnosed Irene with "tubercular" illness. Lionel routinely called his wife from the set of whatever movie he was filming, then sent her on a trip around the world, and then sought medical treatment and rest for her in New York and Phoenix, Arizona. When Irene was hospitalized, he filled her room with flowers. Amused by Walt Disney's *Three Little Pigs*, Lionel asked Marie Dressler to loan him her film projector so that he could run the cartoon for Irene in her hospital room. Much as he would have denied it, the countdown to her early death was inexorable, as Fortune decreed.[23]

LIONEL BARRYMORE

With regard to Fortune and the careers of film actors, Lionel's costar in *The Road to Glory*, Warner Baxter, in 1936 openly discussed with a reporter how he then was transitioning from being a romantic lead actor, the hero who gets the girl, to being a character actor. In *The Road to Glory*, Fredric March handles being the romantic leading man while Baxter and Lionel play character roles. "The romantic role has a limited time to live in the career of any one actor," Baxter assessed. "Now I have been able to bridge the gap between romantic and character parts without the slightest interruption and without an intermediary loss of status." It is important to make this transition at the height of romantic stardom, Baxter explained. "Once one had descended to obscurity, or is even threatened with such a state, there is almost no use in trying, The time to change is while success is still with you for you thus save several years of heartbreaking attempt[s] that may result in nothing."[24]

Thus Baxter described the successful metamorphosis of some Hollywood male movie stars with a "star image" into character actors. In contrast, Lionel's path in Hollywood was atypical. Even at the time, many others at MGM saw him as an anomaly:

> But the man who believed enough in films to join them when they were scorned by the artistic world, who has proved himself as great an actor as he is a director, is anything but inscrutable or enigmatic. . . . In blatant, loud-talking Hollywood Barrymore sticks out like a sore thumb. His monk-like studio-dressing room retreat is completely at variance with the gilded dressing rooms of most of the stars. He hates interviews as much as he does cameras. Had he been born in another age he would probably have been an obscure craftsman or artist. But so long as acting is his forte he wants to be judged on the merit of his work, not on what he has to say about it.

Others in the industry liked and teased him, as when the cast and crew of *Carolina* affectionately mocked his penchant for napping between scenes: after Lionel had delayed a scene's filming by showing a friend some etchings in his dressing room, he finally showed up only to find every person on the set "prostrate on the floor, curling over benches, slumped into chairs, or leaning at tables." Noticing his diffidence at industry events, one wise guy joked after the Academy Awards that Lionel acted more as if he were going to be hanged than as if he were going to win the Best Actor Oscar. In his isolated dressing room, he would sit at his makeup table, his grand piano, or his printing press in a solitary contentment incomprehensible to many. Oddball Lionel anticipated the later development of the "neo-star" in the seventies, "the actor who floats between typecasting and character acting" rather than embodying a "star image." Never ever having had a "star image" nor ever having wanted to be the romantic lead, he nevertheless took the leading male part in many films by embodying the (usually) benign Father. So popular a draw was he that he even sometimes received star billing with or above the leads for his preferred character parts. Yet even though many spectators regarded Lionel as "the greatest actor on the screen today," Lionel never seemed to believe much in his own talent. The self-doubt that he had shared with Ashton Stevens in 1905 characterized his self-evaluation of his work as both a stage and screen actor. Besides expressing his preference for character acting over romantic leading parts, Lionel had declared, "I have no hope of attaining to greatness," to Stevens, who called him even then "the foremost American character actor of his years," but Lionel added in derision, "I don't think it matters much who plays the character part." Stevens commented, "I had to laugh. For here was a man who had worked, had invented, for every success of his life." "I suppose I have worked," Lionel admitted. "I am not as clever as my brother Jack. . . . But my work has been largely subconscious. I've never had that good and proper feeling that comes from a good day's work—that is to say, I can't nail anything."[25]

Act Three

After Life

8

Year of Disaster, 1936

Two devastating events in 1936 overshadowed the rest of Lionel's career and personal life: the death of his beloved second wife, Irene Fenwick, after years of illness, and the accident that broke his hip for the first time, threatened his livelihood, and eventually resulted in constant pain and reliance on a wheelchair.

Lionel's pride in Irene is evident in his account in his memoirs of her professional achievements. Calling Irene Fenwick an accomplished light comedienne who had graduated to dramatic roles, Lionel quoted Alexander Woollcott's praise for her acting in *The Claw*, "Irene Fenwick acquits herself handsomely as the wife," and characterized this as prophetic of her real-life performance as Lionel's spouse. Although some biographical accounts of the Barrymore family disparage her career, Irene had in fact drawn considerable acclaim.[1]

The prevailing image of Irene Fenwick as an opportunistic floozy has erased her professional accomplishments, just as the image of Doris Rankin as a pitiable nonentity has obscured her own record as a good actress. Each woman has been seen primarily in her relation to Lionel rather than as a person with her own aspirations and achievements. Reviewing the vaudeville performances in California of Doris, Lionel, and her father, McKee Rankin, the *San Francisco Call* headlined them as a "noted trio," while the *Los Angeles Herald* in 1910 had lauded each as "a star in his own right," and in 1911 pointedly praised Doris's beauty as "far more alluring to look upon" than her sisters' appearance. Performing in Lionel's vaudeville sketch *The White Slaver*, "all three actors won praise from the very demanding vaudeville audiences" in Atlantic City, on tour, and at the close in New Orleans. Then, in 1918, when Lionel's opening night performance on Broadway in *The Copperhead* inspired fifteen minutes of cheering by the audience, "the greatest ovation for an individual in the history of the American theater," Doris also won national fame for her double performance in the roles of Milt Shanks's wife and granddaughter. *Variety* in 1920 reported that Whitman Bennett/First National had signed Lionel after his departure from Famous Players and would foster the ambition of "the Barrymore family [which] intend[s] to make a star of Doris Rankin."[2]

As with Doris, Lionel was quite correct in his assessment that Irene had been an accomplished actress. While Irene had played minor parts before her 1906 marriage to and 1909 divorce from Felix Isman, her career as a major stage performer and then film actress followed her divorce from Isman in 1909. A chorus girl before she retired to marry Isman, the now-divorced Irene returned to the stage to perform for Charles Frohman in four productions in a single New York season. She credited Frohman with changing her surname from Frizelle to Fenwick—derived, he explained, from the name of a famous English court beauty. (Irene pronounced her new surname with a silent *w*.) Irene had starred in a very successful production of Ned Sheldon's *Song of Songs*—her favorite role—and had signed with George Kleine to act in films. Before that, five prominent theater producers had featured her, she had toured in England in *The Importance of Being Earnest*, and she had worked with Douglas Fairbanks Sr. in a very successful national tour of *Hawthorne of the U.S.A.* The *New York Times* critic lauded her work in *Song of Songs* as "outstanding." By 1915, the press was describing Irene as "magnetic" and as the "present sensation of Broadway." Simultaneously, Irene was being puffed as a film star. *Photoplay Review* devoted the cover of its August 28, 1915, issue to her, as did *The Theatre* in October 1916. In its April–June 1917 issue, *Motion Picture News* featured an advertisement that called Irene "All America's Stage Idol." Famous Players engaged Irene to act in the movie version of *The Princess Zim-Zim, A Coney Island Princess*, upon the recommendation of the Princess's creator, Edward Sheldon, who admired her work in his other play *Song of Songs*. Reporting the completion of Doris's suit of divorce from Lionel, the *Washington Times* described Irene as "one of the most beautiful actresses on the stage." After Irene's death, the *New York Times* even commented that "she was for many years one of America's outstanding actresses." An unrealized ambition of hers was to play Nora in Henrik Ibsen's *A Doll's House*.[3]

After Irene's 1923 marriage to Lionel, she had appeared with him in some of his final New York stage performances, but she retired from acting after they moved permanently to California. For the next decade, press coverage of Irene's life stressed her participation in Hollywood and New York

Year of Disaster, 1936

City society, various accidents and illnesses, and lawsuits filed against her. (Lionel himself attracted lawsuits for nonpayment of bills for physicians' services and for personal apparel.) The most serious lawsuit concerned a long-ago transaction.

Irene's first husband, Felix Isman, whom she divorced in 1909 after three years of wedlock, defaulted in 1912 on the mortgage for the Stewart Building that they both had signed in 1908. The plaintiff, the Central Union Trust Company of New York, a trustee suing for the late Henry Hilton, sought in 1928, five years after Irene married Lionel, to recover over $3.5 million from Irene. Isman was the original defendant when the suit was filed in 1912, and the court issued a foreclosure judgment, but Isman's death, according to the *New York Times* and the *Chicago Tribune*, rendered Irene the technical defendant because she also had signed the documents in litigation. (The newspapers' report of Isman's death was erroneous, for he outlived Irene by several years and died in 1943.) Understandably "stunned," Irene retained counsel who pointed out that she had been under eighteen years old at the time she signed the papers: "This heavy judgment against Miss Fenwick 'is cruel and unusual' and to our minds decidedly unfair. At the time she was not eighteen, she did not participate in the real estate deal, nor did she profit from it." Her affidavit declared that she had not understood that she was obligated to repay this vast sum: "My signing a mortgage for $3,700,000 would be laughable were it not so tragical in my life. If the judgment is allowed to stand I may as well be put in chains." Her attorneys filed for a reconsideration, and Isman's continued earthly existence was recognized. "Why [the plaintiff's attorneys] are suing Mrs. Barrymore solely and not Isman is problematic to her attorneys," *Variety* reported. "She has no estate or property of any consequence, and her husband [Lionel], of course, cannot be assessed for any liability." Nevertheless, her plea was denied, although the judge allowed her to renew her plea on other grounds, such as having been misled, if she could prove her claim. Although Ethel had signed an affidavit that she had known Irene as a very young girl married to Isman, Irene had not submitted to the court the precise documentation of her age that it required. (Having shaved off a few years from her age, she could not document her pruned age with legal proof.) A further hearing some days later resulted in Irene's having "lost [her] application to set aside the default judgement." The final outcome of this lawsuit is unknown, as is the effect on the household finances of the cost of defending it. Maybe Irene's decision to retire permanently from acting derived from the threat to her earnings posed by the case: "unless some higher court intervenes, she will have to turn over all her theaterical [sic] earnings for the rest of her life toward paying the judgment." If Lionel could not be held liable and Irene had no assets or earnings to satisfy the judgment, perhaps it was a pointless exercise, or perhaps the plaintiff's attorneys had intended to use the lawsuit as leverage to get Irene to pressure Isman to pay up. The episode contrasted sharply with a farcical lawsuit filed by Isman himself in 1907 during his short marriage to Irene the chorus girl: "Mrs. Felix Isman . . . has sued Wallach laundry . . . to recover $100, the price of two Parisian shirtwaists, which she alleges were lost. The laundry offered her $6.50, which excited the ire of her husband, the Philadelphia real estate man, who said that he would recover the full amount and convince the laundry people that his wife wore a $50 shirtwaist if it cost him $1,000,000." Doubtless, the 1928–1929 lawsuit added considerable stress that undermined Irene's health.[4]

Documentation in the general news media and the industry press as well as in Barrymore group biographies referred to illnesses, accidents, operations, and hospitalizations that attest to what Lionel called many years of poor health. Irene seems to have suffered from an eating disorder, variously described in terms that suggest anorexia nervosa or bulimia nervosa. Nevertheless, she vigorously pursued Hollywood and New York City social life as well as her portrayal in movie magazines as a woman of cultivated taste. Socially active when her health permitted, Irene was close friends with, among others, actress Lilyan Tashman and her husband Edmund Lowe. Irene was among the mourners when Tashman died suddenly in 1934 and "hundreds of women screamed and fought . . . trying to attend the funeral rites." Irene's own recurrent illnesses and hospitalizations often made the news. The *Chicago Tribune* reported in 1930 that Irene was to "go under [the] knife" for "a delicate operation, the exact nature of which was not disclosed." According to *Variety* in 1933, "after a long illness" at Good Samaritan Hospital, Irene was "greatly improved." A 1933 magazine spread on former movie actor Bill Haines's interior decorating business included Irene as a Haines celebrity client along with Claudette Colbert, Franchot Tone, and Joan Crawford. As late as 1934, a *Hollywood Reporter* news item reported that "Irene Barrymore, who arrived in town [New York City] the other day with her husband and under the care of a nurse, dashed from her suite right over to the hairdressers for a permanent, came back, had a large luncheon party followed by a cocktail party that she gave for Tallulah Bankhead [and others] . . ., went out to dinner and stayed out until four in the morning. The next day, Mrs. Barrymore suffered a very serious relapse. So serious, indeed, that even

Year of Disaster, 1936

Lionel is not allowed to see her." *Motion Picture* reported in 1934 that her "delicate health has not kept her from becoming famous as a hostess—particularly at the small, intimate gatherings that her husband so much enjoys." The article quoted Tashman as saying that she traced her friendship with "Irenee" and Lionel to their being neighbors living just a block away and detailed Lowe's memory of Lionel playing Chopin and Brahms while Lionel and Irene waited for Tashman and Lowe to dress for a party. While on vacation in Hawaii in 1934, Irene was admitted to the hospital. A 1935 report asserted that the same painful stomach complaint that caused her Hawaii hospital admission had returned and necessitated another hospitalization in Hollywood. After being ill for months in 1936, Irene died suddenly at home on Christmas Eve. Widely reporting her fatal illnesses as influenza and pneumonia, the national press also repeated the refrain "Their marriage had been considered among the more successful ones of Hollywood." While the Hollywood reference might render this the faintest and most ironic of compliments, it nevertheless recalls what the national press had asserted about Lionel's marriage with Doris: "Their marriage was considered a happy one."[5]

Throughout it all, as others observed, Lionel remained as devoted a husband to Irene as he once had been to Doris. Mainstream press reports, as well as movie magazines, continually stressed how unusually successful their marriage was. Gladys Hall even termed Lionel, rather tartly, as "without much competition, the most devoted husband in Hollywood." When Irene died suddenly at their home, Lionel was devastated. Although recently hospitalized, Irene had seemed better, and her unexpected and shocking passing at the age of forty-nine crushed him utterly. Jack visited his grieving brother, but their encounter apparently exploded into an argument, after which Lionel asked Jack to leave. In Elaine Barrie's strange account of Jack's disastrous visit to Lionel, Jack explained to her, "I used to know Irene, long before he married her. We had a little romance. He's never forgotten it. He said the filthiest things." This seems to flip the truth, probably because Jack lied to Elaine by giving his wife a heavily redacted version of the quarrel that erased his full history with Irene and his hatred of her. Jack made it appear to Elaine that Lionel, not Jack, was carrying the full load of bad feelings about this long-ago affair that Lionel had actually disregarded when he married Irene. Jack may have clumsily comforted his brother by suggesting that Lionel would soon recover from his loss of Irene—a tactless intervention that would have enraged a husband who never, in fact, "got over it." Or maybe Jack even revived his 1923 characterization of Irene as a "whore." Distraught, Lionel could not bear to live any longer in the Beverly Hills home they had shared, 802 North Roxbury Drive, but preserved it as a shrine that he periodically visited in memory of his lost love. The need to pay back taxes finally forced him to sell the house in 1949. In 1937, he needed to work for financial reasons, but according to Gladys Hall, "he was in a daze, a bottomless dream of pain. Irene had just passed away." His remarkable acting seems even more remarkable, given that he was sunk in profound grief.[6]

While Irene had been ill for much of 1936, Lionel's own health had suffered late that year when he broke his left hip for the first time, perhaps during the filming of *Camille*, in which his scenes show him relying on a cane. Embellishing a drawing on a drafting board in his home studio, Lionel overturned the drafting board and then tripped over it. Hospitalized and immobilized, Lionel feared the end of his film career and the loss of his livelihood. His later account of this crisis humorously emphasized his lack of fortitude and stoicism, while it also stressed the support he received from Louis B. Mayer, who tried to reassure him about his continued employment by MGM. Lionel hinted that the New York office had contemplated releasing him but also recorded that Mayer objected, "Tell everybody that if Lionel is out I am through too." While some may doubt any story of kindliness on Mayer's part, his advocacy of Lionel satisfied the demands of both business and friendship. If the welfare of MGM was Mayer's paramount objective, preserving Lionel's ability to act in MGM films met that objective. Lionel's hip mended well enough that he was able to adapt during filming to the studio's needs. But then, in 1937, during the filming of the ill-fated *Saratoga*, Lionel tripped over a cable on the set and broke his left hip for the second time. By his account, the damage was now worse, but Mayer again rescued him by casting him in the *Dr. Kildare* film series as the brilliant diagnostician Dr. Gillespie, who uses a wheelchair. Audience acceptance of this expedient relieved the anxieties of MGM about casting Lionel, and he appeared in many more films. He also underwent more medical treatment, including six weeks in the hospital in 1939, three years after the first accident. Two months after discharge, although somewhat better, he could still walk for only short distances. He did emphasize, however, that despite numerous repetitions of the story (then and even now) that his need for a wheelchair resulted from arthritis, he did not suffer from this condition.[7]

Regarding the often-repeated assertion that arthritis necessitated Lionel's use of a wheelchair, a neurologist elucidated, "Arthritis is a very unlikely cause for needing a wheelchair, since it is almost always a relapsing-remitting

Year of Disaster, 1936

disease. You have joint inflammation and pain for a few days; then, typically, it remits. I doubt very much that arthritis accounts for his need for a wheelchair. There is no evidence for any degenerative disease, like multiple sclerosis, to account for the wheelchair. So I think someone is engaging in rank speculation to try to say why he required a wheelchair." Granted that his broken/rebroken hip resulted from falls in 1936 and 1937, Lionel could not have had hip replacement surgery (introduced in 1940 but not widely used until 1950). "Depending where the hip was fractured, pins could have been used surgically to repair it. There would be a clear record if that happened. Barring that type of surgery, pain medication and rest were the only treatments. It is a pretty scant record, and I think it is pure speculation to try to explain his medical condition with the available evidence. I think it would be very hard to argue a medical etiology." It is difficult to see why Lionel would deny having arthritis if he actually had it, so we are left with his accounts of two falls and the supposition that his treatment options from 1936 to 1954 for the broken hip and chronic pain were very limited. Indeed, Lionel told an interviewer as much in 1948: "For 10 years Barrymore's done all his acting on wheels. And kept up with the best of 'em, too. There were times, he says, when it wasn't too hard to be a grumpy old man who hollered at people. Everybody, says Barrymore with a wag of his white mane, thinks he was crippled up with arthritis. 'No truth to it,' he harrumphed. 'I fell off a blankety-blank horse back in 1915 and broke my left leg. After that I always limped a little. Then in 1936, I was doing a scene with Jean Harlow. I tripped over a cable and fractured the other side of me—my right hip [sic]. It didn't heal right.' Not long after, he said, walking became almost too painful to bear. Crutches helped a little, but not for long. That's when he took to his wheelchair." While not conclusive, the available evidence suggests that many years of inadequate pain relief necessitated the wheelchair.[8]

9

Mike and Jake
Exit Jack, 1942

At age seventeen, during the filming of *Beau Brummel* (1924), Mary Astor had engaged in what she later portrayed as a mutually enraptured love affair with the much older John Barrymore. Despite declarations of passion and discussions of plans for marriage, she lost Jack in 1926 to a rival who became his third wife, Dolores Costello. The Barrymore-Costello union finally collapsed, and Elaine Barrie eventually became the fourth Mrs. John Barrymore in a tumultuous and highly publicized marriage. Astor herself went on to marry four unlucky times. Yet her enchantment by Jack never quite died. Cast as his wife in the comedy *Midnight* (1939), Astor encountered a much-diminished, rather moldy-looking John Barrymore, who is fun to watch as he parodies himself. At times, he looks more like his older brother, Lionel, than he does the Great Profile of twenties fame. Despite being plagued with health problems, Jack delivers an amusing, self-amused performance, although "he drank coffee endlessly and nothing could keep him from urinating into the potted plants on the set." Barrie was also in the cast; Mitchell Leisen, the director of *Midnight*, explained that he included Barrie "because only she could keep her husband from drinking." Astor's memoirs recorded a poignant remembrance from the filming of *Midnight* of her last conversation with Jack. Pregnant by her third husband, Manuel Del Campo, with their son, Tono, Astor felt saddened by Jack's premature aging and inability to deliver his lines without prompt cards. Jack kept aloof from her. While they were waiting to play a scene as husband and wife (a painful scenario in itself), she lovingly touched his hand, but he jerked it away from her and protested, "My wife—ah—Miss Barrie is very jealous." The hurt Astor felt, although unexpressed, is palpable, yet she loyally wrote, long after Jack's death, "even with cue cards and only a faint idea of what the picture was all about, he had enough years of experience behind him to be able to act rings around anyone else." Astor also remembered her final glimpse of her lost lover as Jack wearily trudged down a radio studio hallway. Wanting to preserve his dignity, she anxiously watched from behind but did not approach him: "I saw a man who was catching his breath before doing battle, and quite a battle it was, with death." Indignant about the coarse jokes made about his decline, she never lost her esteem for Jack or, indeed, recovered from her loss of his love. Yet she did not counter his rejection with contempt or hatred but only with compassion. He had tears in his eyes when he pulled his hand away from her touch; perhaps he felt moved by her expression of undying affection. Having reviewed Astor's memoirs, Stephen Longstreet sent her a revelatory letter responding to her thank-you note for his review. Longstreet had written radio scripts for Jack, "when the poor man was drifting into a far from amusing senility, but he did talk of you often, but never by name, and so until I read your book I never knew who the girl was." Astor's anecdotes capture all the facets of Jack's prolonged decline: the memory lapses that compromised and derailed his film career; his conflicted marriage to and professional relationship with Elaine Barrie; his use of radio while his health declined to rake in an income and to settle debts; his power, in spite of everything, to compel devotion and friendship and respect.[1]

Despite his ravaged health, decayed memory, and a trajectory into decline from his elegant earlier film stardom, Jack nevertheless somehow managed to deliver some of his best performances in these last years: *Counsellor-at-Law, Topaze, Twentieth Century, Romeo and Juliet* (as Mercutio), *True Confession, Marie Antoinette, The Great Man Votes,* and *Midnight.* Sensing that both the press and the public battened on his engagement in self-parody, self-mockery, general outrageousness, recurrent bankruptcies, and the seesaw of his last marriage between reconciliation and inevitable implosion, Jack capitalized on these elements of notoriety by starring with Elaine Barrie in the stage show *My Dear Children.* Portraying a famous Shakespearean ham reminiscent of himself, Jack battled with his real-life wife (who played his daughter) as well as battled with the script and producers by ad-libbing and guying the part. After months on a riotous tour in 1939, the production reached Chicago, where its scheduled two-week run mutated into a thirty-four-week audience sensation and spectacle. Jack and Elaine zigzagged between contentious marriage and impending divorce, and she left the company. Ned Sheldon, who had tried to discourage the *My Dear Children* project, recruited Orson Welles to check up on Jack; with Lionel and Ethel, Welles eventually found Jack "pie-eyed in a cathouse" from which they extracted him. As Welles told it, "The three great Barrymores, who hadn't seen each other since *Rasputin*, were reunited in a bordello and there followed a great warm weekend." (While Lionel was hospitalized in 1943 with "acute indigestion," Welles impersonated Lionel in his radio series *Mayor of the Town*; *Variety* commented, "Welles' maintenance of the Barrymore rasp throughout the sketch was in itself no little feat." Welles himself remarked, "Understudying Barrymores is old stuff with me, and that goes for Ethel, too.") In early 1940, *My Dear Children* ran for four months in New York City, its sensationalism driving ticket sales and prices and gleeful pleasure in watching Jack's self-immolation. As Brooks Atkinson commented, "[The public] looked as if they hoped to be present at the final degradation of Icarus. Standing behind police barriers, they looked sinister. The crowds that watched the tumbrils pass in the French Revolution could not have been more pitiless or morbid." Yet Atkinson defended Jack: "He can still act like a man whom the gods have generously endowed. . . . He is nobody's fool in *My Dear Children* but a superbly gifted actor in a tired holiday." Atkinson detected in Jack's performance "an alert sense of mischief." Ideally, Jack would act in more suitable material, but "a superb actor, now in reduced artistic circumstances, is capering as buoyantly as his health permits. The important thing is that he is a superb actor."[2]

Radio offered yet another way in which Jack could exploit his notoriety and conscious self-degradation. In 1941, his association with Rudy Vallee on radio made his decline into the stuff of comedy: "He is pictured as an aging ham, physically debilitated. Sometimes he derides himself with the preposterous snorts and inflections of an old-time ranting actor; more often he is the butt of jokes made by others." Jack's biographer Terry Chester Shulman noted that, well aware of the public appeal of this characterization, he deliberately used it to his own advantage: "He ran with the drunk character that he was pigeonholed into becoming by the vampiric press and the scandal-hungry public; it became his métier. He was smart enough to understand what it was that was selling him to the public in his last years. And turned it into a way to keep working and pay his bills." The inevitable collapse occurred when, only sixty years old, Jack died on May 29, 1942.

In the difficult spring of 1942, his recurring medical crises had involved cirrhosis, chronic gastritis, bleeding ulcers, arteriosclerosis, and hypostatic pneumonia. Jack's final collapse came on May 19 while he was rehearsing a Rudy Vallee radio series episode. (During this emergency, Lionel substituted

Mike and Jake

for Jack on the air.) Diagnosed at Hollywood Presbyterian Hospital with myocarditis and chronic nephritis, Jack wavered between episodes of jokey consciousness, serious moments of penitence and confession to a Catholic priest, and periodic oblivion during which Lionel and Jack's cronies kept anxious watch. During this last hospitalization, Lionel rescued Viola, Jack's Afghan hound, who now patiently awaited her master's return in the house Lionel had once shared with Irene; Viola eventually eloped with a Great Dane, and their embraces produced an impressive litter of seven females. Among Jack's last exchanges was one in which the brothers used their ancient nicknames for each other. Lionel questioned his younger brother, "What did you say, Jake?" and Jack replied, "You heard me, Mike." Elaine, whose calls to the hospital had been ignored, came to the funeral. Lionel and Jack's daughter Diana by his second wife, Blanche, came together. No other ex-wife or child attended. Mark Nishimura, Jack's gardener for fifteen years, had been a victim of the internment in Manzanar of Japanese Americans after Pearl Harbor; Lionel secured permission for "Nishi" to attend Jack's funeral. Jack's will gave Viola to Nishi. Instead, Lionel bought Viola at auction and visited her every weekend at Jack Oakie's ranch because Lionel's dog resented Viola's residing with Lionel. As for Nishi, Lionel clearly felt saddened both by Nishi's unjust detention and by the hostility Nishi would encounter were he to return home. Lionel commented to Louella Parsons, "I wouldn't think of bringing him back now when it would only bring grief to him."[3]

Lionel's recorded afterthoughts about Jack, his expressions of helplessness and sadness, attempted to explain but admitted that he did not really understand his brother's self-destruction. His rueful comments on Jack's marriage to Dolores Costello expressed chagrin that this marriage had faltered in spite of its idyllic beginnings. Dolores apparently recounted to Lionel how her marriage had disintegrated, to which he replied, "You're his last chance, Dolores. If he goes through with this, if he breaks up with you, I'll never see my brother again." Although Lionel in fact broke this vow, his making it reveals his distress over the end of what he saw as a good marriage and his hopelessness about his brother's prospects. The advent of Elaine Barrie did not seem a good omen to Lionel (or to Ethel). He also noted Jack's recurrent boredom with his acting accomplishments on the screen and in the theater but defended Jack's radio work by insisting that Jack took it to satisfy his debts of honor. Analyzing Jack's marital and professional record, Lionel linked Jack's restlessness in his acting to his restlessness in his relationships: "My brother was a strange fellow," he commented in later years. "He'd try to make friends, but as soon as people liked him he would withdraw from them. . . . Jack couldn't stand monotony and he had a dread of being possessed by people. . . . [The poet Lord Byron] was a strange, unhappy fellow. He reminds me of my brother Jack." When Jack died, Arthur Hopkins had telegraphed his condolences to Lionel: "Jack could never bear a part after he grew tired of it. Am sure he has been weary of the last one for a long time. Am glad he has found a new one."[4]

10

Radio Days and the Taxman Cometh, 1934–1954

DIANA BARRYMORE: *"What do you do, Uncle Lionel?"*
LIONEL: *"Do? I do what your father does!"*
JOHN: *"Why, Lionel!"*

Capitalizing on public enjoyment of fraternal jousting, *Variety* in 1941 even concocted front-page news out of the tiny item "John and Lionel Barrymore tilt verbal lances on the Seal Test airer [*sic*] May 1. No holds are barred." Fans of classic radio may have enjoyed these scripted exchanges with Jack from the *Rudy Vallee Sealtest* show, or have heard Lionel hosting the *Hallmark Hall of Fame* radio program, or have listened to him play Dr. Gillespie in an episode of the radio version of *Dr. Kildare*, yet they may still not realize the wide range of Lionel's radio appearances or know about his Hollywood Walk of Fame star at 1651 Vine Street for radio broadcasting or about his Speech Arts Medal for his radio work.[1]

For an actor who often mocked his own alleged laziness, Lionel actually racked up an impressive roster of credits on radio shows to complement his extensive work in the movies. After MGM had registered its reluctance to allow Lionel to perform on radio, he did eventually, in 1936, become one of the first contract players to win a contract that freed him for radio work. After his 1936 hip injury and its later exacerbation by a second fall, radio presented him with physically undemanding acting roles and with a physical invisibility to the radio audience that protected the livelihood that his disability threatened in films for a while. For *Maxwell House Good News of 1938*, Lionel resurrected his roles in the films *A Free Soul* and *The Copperhead*. He also appeared on *Cavalcade of America, Command Performance, Doctor Kildare, The Edgar Bergen and Charlie McCarthy Show, Encore Theatre, Family Theatre, Hear It*

LIONEL BARRYMORE

Now, Kraft Music Hall, Magic Key of RCA, Mail Call, One Night Stand, Orson Welles Almanac, Radio Almanac, Radio City Playhouse, Radio Hall of Fame, Request Performance, Screen Guild Players/Screen Guild Theatre, Shirley Temple Time, Symphonies under the Stars, Treasury Star Parade, Up for Parole, and *Vanished without a Trace*. Lionel did reject overtures from CBS in 1937 to portray King Lear on radio. A 1946 broadcast by *Screen Guild Players* costarred Lionel with Ethel and Douglas Fairbanks Jr. in *The Old Lady Shows Her Medals*. Both Lionel and Jack also had paid tribute to Ethel on the fortieth anniversary of her stage stardom in a 1941 NBC Blue Network radio show billed as the first to feature all three siblings. Having overcome MGM's reluctance to let him appear, Lionel had to endure the censorship of one of his best digs at Jack, yet he still managed to slip in other gags that perhaps were more cryptic and over the heads/under the radar of the censorious. Referring to Ethel's current stage appearance in *The Corn Is Green*, Lionel wheezed, "The corn is green. The corn is green. How green is the corn? I don't know, but I bet Jack will." (Ethel wittily expressed her reservations about such anniversaries to her friend and former stage director George Cukor. After L. B. Mayer saluted her at a seventieth birthday lunch in 1949, Ethel commented to Cukor, "Mayer made a speech. He just lowered me into the grave.") In *Motion Picture Daily*'s annual poll of radio news editors, Lionel in 1946 won the accolade of "The Best Film Player on the Air."[2]

Not long after Pearl Harbor, Lionel participated in the *We Hold These Truths* radio broadcast that commemorated the 150th anniversary of the ratification of the Bill of Rights. For the Armed Forces Radio Service, from 1944 to 1949, each program of his *Lionel Barrymore Concert Hall* featured a vocalist and an instrumentalist. Eventually, he was honored as one of the three civilians who had done the most to support the morale of the armed forces during wartime. Often a guest on *Lux Radio Theater*, he hosted the series twice in 1945. He also hosted *Hollywood Playhouse*, as well as *Hallmark Hall of Fame*'s series of "biographical" radio plays aired on over 190 CBS Radio stations.

Lionel probably especially enjoyed one of these, *Hallmark Hall of Fame*'s "The Long Boyhood of Mark Twain" (broadcast on January 17, 1954), because of his own memorable boyhood encounter with Samuel Clemens. Situated in Hannibal, Missouri; on a steamboat in the Mississippi; in the gold fields of California; on board the *Quaker City*, the ship that escorted Clemens to Europe for the trip immortalized in *Innocents Abroad*; and in Olivia Langdon's home in Elmira, New York, the radio play portrays Clemens's long

Radio Days and the Taxman Cometh, 1934-1954

search for adventure and vocation, as well as for an understanding sweetheart. On June 6, 1954, mere months before Lionel's death in November, *Hallmark Hall of Fame*, by popular request, broadcast a program based on Lionel's own anecdotes about his misbegotten career as an actor. Its theme concerned how "finally, after every effort to halt its inception, the fabulous career of Lionel Barrymore, America's most beloved character actor, was born." The preparatory interview with Lionel included some blue language, much protest by Lionel that the audience would not be interested in his life story ("I'm really kind of nervous about this thing because . . . these people . . . they're used to Victoria Regina and General Crappo . . . [but not] in some ham that wants to eat"), his usual refrain that he hated acting ("I never liked acting. Never, never liked it. . . . My dislike of it has grown through the ages. I don't like it now, but I don't like laying off either"), and an eventually unused tall tale about a bear that Lionel supposedly won in a crap game in a Denver saloon. "I didn't want the bloody thing," Lionel dubiously claimed. "Only I was more afraid of the bartender than I was of the fucking bear." The allegedly full-grown beast and Lionel traveled to Lionel's room at the Brown Palace Hotel via taxicab and hotel elevator. "I was stinking and fell on the bed and I guess the bear did too. . . . [In the morning,] the bear had my breakfast and he ate everything in sight. Oh Jesus! And then he got kind of mean, you know." The hotel waiter referred Lionel to a local bear pit to which he delivered the bear, and then he had to pay an annual fee for maintenance for a few years. Part scripted interview, part dramatization by radio actors, the broadcasted episode began with Lionel's pretend-snarling, "I was raised in the finest traditions of the theatre. From the day I was born I had theatre rammed down my throat. . . . I was driven to acting by the fact that I had to eat. And how this unwanted career came to be—well, that's a long story." The program roamed from his farcical failure in *The Rivals* to the cherished bad review in 1898 by Frank Butler to his happy years in Paris to his triumph in *The Mummy and the Humming Bird* to his stint in Griffith's films at Biograph. Especially amusing was Lionel's account of how George Barnum and Ralph Delmore determinedly coached him through his part in *The Mummy and the Humming Bird* as the Sicilian organ grinder: "We're going to do this right. First stop: Plavano's Restaurant. We're going to stuff you with spaghetti, garlic, chianti, and tortoni. And while you're eating, you're going to study the waiters!" Newspaper obituaries announced that his friend and frequent costar Edward Arnold would substitute for Lionel as host of *Hallmark Hall of Fame* on the Sunday after Lionel died. Within a week of his death, *Hallmark Hall of Fame*

LIONEL BARRYMORE

broadcast a tribute to him on November 21, 1954. Among others, Gene Fowler, Edward Arnold, Lew Ayres, Louis Calhern, Bing Crosby, Agnes Moorehead, James Stewart, and Helen Hayes participated. Another special program on Lionel Barrymore's music aired on April 25, 1955, on NBC's *Best of All*. Although Arnold assumed Lionel's place as host/narrator of *Hallmark Hall of Fame*, Arnold's stint on the radio show did not long survive Lionel's passing.[3]

In 1949, *Billboard* had reviewed MGM's thrice-weekly, fifteen-minute radio program *At Home with Lionel Barrymore* as having a "home-spun folksy quality," praised Lionel's "masterly reading" of his scripts, and mentioned his "relaxed assurance and artful timing." On his imaginary front porch, Lionel gossiped with his costar Richard Simmons about imaginary neighbors. The program pretended that he was actually speaking from his real home in Hollywood. Simmons recalled, "Barrymore was like a father to me. He was fantastic. We had great, wonderful fun." As part of MGM Radio Attractions, *At Home with Lionel Barrymore* accompanied such offerings as *The Story of Dr. Kildare* (with Lionel and Lew Ayres), *MGM Theatre of the Air*, as well as Mickey Rooney and Lewis Stone in *The Hardy Family*. The buildup to a broadcast in early 1949 described Lionel as "the screen's most beloved star and everyone's treasured friend." Discussing a 1944 newspaper clipping, Lionel recounted the story of how a sailor jumped off a battleship on its way to the Pacific theater to save the battleship's mascot bulldog. The rest of the broadcast rambled through several topics, including the young Lionel's disillusionment with holiday resorts and his consequent determination to stay at home dreaming of perfect (because imaginary) trips to Cuba or India. He ended with a bizarre but humorous "recipe for living" that alleges that a woman cooking roast beef approaches her culinary task by thinking about her sweetheart: "For she knows that a roast beef is indeed like the man of her dreams—tanned and handsome on the outside, but on the inside *tender*."

Perhaps MGM was building on the success of one of Lionel's most significant radio productions, his long-running radio serial, *Mayor of the Town* (1942–1949), and on the audience's feeling of comfort with him as a recognizable personality. By permitting Lionel to be the eponymous mayor, MGM had departed from its long-standing objection to its movie stars appearing on radio in what *Variety* termed "a sharp reversal of a long-held Metro policy," and his radio show had then secured an audience. The federal government had encouraged the program as a booster of civilian morale during wartime. Lionel remembered that the advertising agency that proposed the

Radio Days and the Taxman Cometh, 1934-1954

radio series to MGM had intended to mask war propaganda as entertainment. *Variety* judged that the program fulfilled this intention: "It is pitched, completely, vividly and incisively to the war. It moves determinedly and courageously away from the orbit of escapism and into the psychological path of a realism that Americans must become inured to sooner or later." The program, in *Variety's* view, was lucky to have Lionel, "bound to receive a warm response in millions of American homes." Consequently, in the postwar period, MGM tried to benefit directly from Lionel's wartime radio success by producing another radio show, *At Home with Lionel Barrymore*, that highlighted his personality.[4]

For most of the forties, in *Mayor of the Town* (broadcast in different seasons by NBC, CBS, ABC, and Mutual Radio and for four years by *both* ABC and CBS), Lionel had impersonated the mayor of the midwestern town of Springdale as he dealt with his gossipy housekeeper, Marilly (Agnes Moorehead), and with Butch, a motherless boy in whom the mayor took an interest (Conrad Binyon). Claire Trevor, for a short while, played the mayor's secretary. The serial episodes addressed both wartime concerns and everyday problems. "The character of Butch didn't stem from the show's beginning," Binyon remembered. "I seem to recall about three years or so playing the character, who was introduced as a boy who lost both his parents in an auto accident. Prior to that, the story line involved the mayor in city administration plots, police investigations, and fraud schemes against citizens. The Butch character became the mayor's ward and turned the plot line more into a family-like situation." Moorehead respected Lionel: "He's one of the finest actors and personalities I know. . . . He's generous of spirit and [has] a rare sense of humor." In the 1943 season, after appearing with such guest stars as Bob Hope, Marlene Dietrich, and James Cagney, Lionel was honored by *Movie-Radio Guide* as "Favorite Radio Actor on the Air." *Variety* praised the attempts by *Mayor of the Town* to acclimate its listeners to the realities of total war: "[the series] raised its initial curtain on the grimmest theme of all, the casualty list. . . . Barrymore fashioned a characterization that grips hard on the heart and the mind."[5]

Besides dramatizing the tragic aspects of wartime, *Mayor of the Town* also amused its listeners by dramatizing petty conflicts between the mayor, Marilly, and Butch. In the episode aired on February 4, 1948, for example, the mayor is trying to do his income tax return, Marilly is preparing to visit an elderly neighbor who is considering selling her house and moving away because her household chores have become too burdensome, and Butch is avoiding his algebra homework. Marilly wants to protect her goldfish and her rubber plant from the winter cold by moving them to the mayor's desk.

"Will you tell me how I can work with that rubber tree cutting off the light and a goldfish splashing water like a stern-wheeler?" . . . "Mr. Weismuller, my goldfish, is not a stern-wheeler. His stern, as you call it, is what is known as a fan-tail." "Okay—fine—but let him fan it over yonder."

Sarcastic teasing and enjoyable bickering follow.

"Do you think this hat is too old for me?" "No—not at all. From the back, I'd say you looked about sixteen. . . . Front view, I'd just reverse that figure."

Discovering that teenagers are trespassing in an uninhabited house because they have nowhere to meet, the mayor avoids getting them in trouble by suggesting that they volunteer to do the elderly neighbor's chores if she will allow them to meet in her house instead. For the sleepy Butch, the Mayor ends up finishing Butch's algebra homework: "I'll bet dollars to doughnuts that the guy who wrote this book is the same son-of-a-gun who made up those income tax reports!"[6]

During the run of *Mayor of the Town*, a disastrous interview for *Radio Life* roamed among Lionel's many professional and avocational activities. The intimidated reporter in vain tried to extract from Lionel any anecdotes or opinions of interest: "Gulping noisily, we plunged determinedly into prospective subject matter, gaining courage in the certainty that, of all people, a Barrymore must have something to say. One by one, we introduced what seemed to us likely topics for fluent conversation, as Barrymore surveyed us under gesticulating eyebrows and made replies graciously though not generously wordy nor ever without his 'Gillespie grunt.'" The reporter cleverly built an entire article around her desperate but futile attempts that elicited only Lionel's repeated response "There's nothing to tell. I'm sorry. I wish I could think of something." Lionel did briefly come alive when asked about the stage: "'Don't miss it in the least!' Barrymore grunted emphatically. 'Don't have any desire whatsoever to go to New York again. . . . Horrible town! Don't know why anyone wants to go there.'" The reporter's humorous account went on: "He then reverted to noncommunicative communication: 'Well—lll, I wish I could have helped you,' Mr. Barrymore said again, with the 'sweetness' his friends had told us was there. 'I tell you!' he exclaimed eagerly, as we reluctantly brought the 'interview' to a close. 'I'll try to think of something. I will! I'll go home and try to think of something to tell you.'" (Undoubtedly, Lionel shared Alan Rickman's wittily expressed frustration and boredom with answering the same perpetual questions from different interviewers: "They are like tired dogs with a very old slipper.") The reporter prefaced this hilarious account of frustration with her "unwavering fascination" while she watched as Lionel, Moorehead, and Binyon twice went through a *Mayor of the Town* script—once for practice and once for a preview audience. Lionel in another interview did express discontent with having to perform for a studio audience, dismissed as "the very bane of a broadcaster's existence." "I don't see any sense in people wanting to peep behind the scenes during a broadcast," he protested. "There is no more point to it than in the public witnessing the rehearsals of a play or a motion picture. To me it is like watching a suit being made. . . . It is particularly exasperating to the actor to be spied upon and caught in the act of reading his lines from a script."[7]

A decade earlier, Lionel had given to Gladys Hall for *Radio Life* another grumpy interview about his radio career, but he was then more forthcoming. He claimed to believe that radio acting was more difficult than stage or movie acting because the medium deprived the actor of any tool but her or his voice. "Actors need greasepaint," he explained to Hall on the movie set of *The Devil-Doll*. "I am an actor, if anything. I am not a monologist, not a ventriloquist, not an off-stage voice. I dislike being an off-stage voice. . . . I don't know what to do when I am disembodied." Because the stage or screen actor employs the voice in concert with the body, the challenges posed by radio performances disconcert the experienced actor: "Into the voice on the air must go, then, all of the makeup, the costumes, the props, the scenery, the gestures to which we have been accustomed. . . . To give drama on the air is doubly, trebly difficult a feat as giving it on stage or screen could ever be." Compounding these difficulties, the Barrymore voice is too distinctive and particularized. "On the air," Lionel asserted grimly, "the Barrymore voice is a curse."[8]

One testament to Lionel's reluctant eminence as a radio actor was his engagement to narrate the 1944 movie *Dragon Seed*, directed by his longtime associates in many other films, Jack Conway and Harold Bucquet. A more substantial tribute to Lionel's radio celebrity and to the familiarity of his voice was his invitation to participate in an immense live event. Originally meant to occur during two nights in the Coliseum, it eventually spanned five nights in the Hollywood Bowl; free admission attracted 25,000 spectators on the event's final night and a total of over 125,000 spectators over the five evenings. From his perch in a sound booth in the Hollywood Bowl, Lionel narrated California's official state centennial show, *The California Story*, which ran for five performances on September 8–12, 1950. The production removed the shell of the Hollywood Bowl, expanded the stage, and even included the surrounding landscape. Written by Ed Ainsworth and Jack Moffitt, the first act of the elaborate script ranged from a 1506 discussion of California by Christopher Columbus in a Spanish university to gold rush settlers in 1849; the second act began with John C. Frémont near his gold mine in 1849 and ended with events of the present day. In at least one version of the script, a San Francisco scene set in 1906 featured John Barrymore, Rudyard Kipling, and Henry George's celebrating after an evening's inebriation and Jack's waking up to the famous earthquake and being drafted to fight the fires: "I wish my uncle John Drew could see this. He always said it would take an earthquake to get me out of bed and the army to put me to work." Theater director Vladimir Rosing was general director for the production, while Meredith Willson, who composed the score, was music director and conductor for the eighty-five-piece Centennial Symphony Orchestra as well as a chorus of 150 singers. Hundreds of actors portrayed the various historical personages included in the pageant. Lionel's narration, synchronized with Willson's score, began by introducing the scene in which Columbus visited the University of Salamanca and ended by praising the valor of Californians during World War II and the Korean War. As the *Los Angeles Times* reported, the spectators, responding to Lionel's final paean to freedom, gave him and the pageant a standing ovation: "Enthralled as it spontaneously rose to its feet, the crowd had heard his voice rise with the music to the final peak." Responding to popular request, the *Los Angeles Times* soon printed an abridged version of Lionel's celebrated narration. This personal triumph for Lionel may have been marred by the death of another participant, Lionel's fellow actor in *Enemies of Women* and *The Devil-Doll*, Pedro de Cordoba. Found dead in his home on September 17, he had felt ill during the pageant's performance. A stage and screen actor, he had differed from Lionel by being the first Actors' Equity member in New York to refuse film work in 1929 during the Actors' Equity struggle to establish a closed shop in Hollywood.[9]

Annually, taking time out from domestic, local, and national crises, the mayor of Springdale played Scrooge in a local production at the Bijou

Radio Days and the Taxman Cometh, 1934-1954

Theatre of *A Christmas Carol*. This inside joke obviously riffed on Lionel's longtime identification with the role of Scrooge on American radio. Charles Dickens never created two more dissimilar characters than the skinflint, rapacious, merciless creditor Ebenezer Scrooge and the hapless, good-natured, hopelessly indebted Wilkins Micawber. Yet, although Lionel impersonated the avaricious Scrooge for almost twenty years on American radio, in real life Lionel resembled most closely the improvident Mr. Micawber. Not only does this enjoyable irony add to our appreciation of Lionel's achievement as an actor, but it also lends insight into his character as a man and his process as an artist.[10]

Money woes were chronic, not only for Lionel but for both of his siblings and for their parents, Maurice and Georgie. As Ethel recalled about their youth, except from revenue earned by their maternal grandmother's management of a Philadelphia theater, the only income came from acting gigs, and the family survived financially from week to precarious week. The theme of severe financial stress recurred, as Ethel put it, over many years of worrying about where to earn money and wondering why it then simply vanished. Ethel as an adult commented further, "for Lionel and myself, it does not matter how much we earn; it all goes. We spend every cent, and gracious knows where it disappears." Twice bankrupted at his death, Jack left an estate that had to be liquidated to satisfy the claims of his many creditors. His finances were "over-extended by a luxurious lifestyle as well as medical and tax debt." Indeed, most of Jack's debts were to the California and federal departments of revenue. This even forced Jack back into better-paid motion picture acting under orders from Ernest R. Utley, bankruptcy commissioner, to which Jack responded, "My God, I'm nothing but a slave. A mere puppet to be tossed about willy nilly wherever my creditors want me to go." There was some uncertainty about the ability of Jack's estate to pay for his funeral, and the Pierce Brothers funeral home claimed that Lionel would make up any shortfall. This oddly confident assertion seems ignorant of Lionel's long history of improvidence, shared at times with his brother in their adulthood as stage troupers. Lionel recalled a dismal Christmas Eve on the road in the Midwest: "I was down to about a dime and so was Jack. We ... didn't know where we were going to get anything to eat, and the manager couldn't advance us a cent on our small salaries because the company was only a very small jump ahead of the sheriff.... With another fellow in the company as lonesome and broke as we, ... [we] heated a can of beans over the gaslight. That, with some crackers and milk, was our Christmas dinner."[11]

Lionel's own account of his personal financial ineptitude engagingly admitted his lifelong inability to manage money. With the self-deprecating humor characteristic of his memoir, Lionel confessed to being bewildered in school by sums: "I went to Seton Hall . . . from the age of ten to fifteen, setting an all-time record, as yet unapproached, for resistance to knowledge. . . . In arithmetic I remained with the small boys from the day I arrived until the day I departed. . . . The mysteries of simple addition and subtraction were too deep for me." Compounding his financial difficulties in later life, he never understood how to put money aside even when he prospered, at least on paper: "I managed without any effort at all to spend almost every cent of it. How I accomplished this I am bewildered to explain, just as I am still bewildered of anything that smacks of a decimal point." Lionel mocked himself for dissuading his colleague and friend Harry Carey from investing in what later proved to be some exceedingly valuable real estate. (Carey's friend Frank Scully did report in *Variety* that he founded the town of Carey, California, after he bought four thousand acres forty miles northwest of Hollywood. Despite once having a trading post and its own post office, the town of Carey had disappeared by 1947, submerged by sand after its destruction by a busted dam.) Lionel also reported humorously his own naivete in salary negotiations. By his own reckoning, he was saved from financial disaster while on contract with MGM only because the studio (and a consistently benevolent L. B. Mayer) often bailed him out. MGM's M. E. Greenwood noted in a 1930s studio memo, "He just manages to keep his head above water and some day I expect a small wave to hit him and knock him completely under."[12]

Lionel perched on the precipice of financial ruin largely because of his income tax woes. Several sources offer different explanations of how his income tax problems developed. Apparently, he took a deduction on his federal taxes in the thirties that reduced his taxable income but that the Internal Revenue Service (IRS) rejected. Lionel's MGM salary in 1935 was reportedly $100,000 or more. In that same year, Lionel filed with the Board of Tax Appeals a request that the board reverse an IRS rejection of his deduction for the 1932 tax year of a real estate loss of $18,041 as a "bad debt"; recategorizing it as a capital loss that he could deduct only from net capital gains, the IRS thereby increased his tax bill. Concerning Lionel's 1934 taxes, the IRS filed a lien of $9,649. In 1936, the federal government sent Lionel and Irene a bill for almost $15,000 in additional taxes on their 1935 income—yet another reason, besides Lionel's hip injury and Irene's death, why 1936 was a year of disaster. California state income taxes also led Lionel to consider commuting to work from Arizona. George Murphy, a fellow movie actor turned senator from California, gave a different origin story for Lionel's tax troubles. Murphy told his Senate colleagues that, when the federal income tax was new, Lionel did not realize that it applied to traveling actors and unintentionally dodged his tax obligations. As an old actor, Lionel reportedly paid 85 percent of his shrunken income to the IRS. He pleaded with Murphy, "I wonder if you can arrange somehow to get the tax people to let me keep enough money to buy two tires for my automobile; otherwise, I won't be able to get to work."[13]

These fragmentary explanations suggest incompetent or misunderstood investment and tax advice given to a financial naïf, plus the detrimental consequences of penalties and compounded interest. Perhaps the IRS delved further into Lionel's tax history after denying his inappropriate deduction against income. Cameron Shipp, who coauthored Lionel's memoirs a few years before Lionel's death and remained his friend, remembered, "He was dead broke and in debt to the government for more than $100,000 in back taxes. No one knows where all the money went. . . . Financially, he was as casual as a child with a handful of sunlight." Shipp recorded Lionel's fear of imprisonment. After a fraught trip east to the Treasury Department, Lionel exhaled, "They're not going to put me in the calaboose after all! Why, those are *splendid* fellows in Washington! They're just doing their wretched job." He had agreed to turn over almost everything he earned, except for "a mere pittance." When less than a year before he died Hedda Hopper asked him when he planned to retire, Lionel reverted to his haunting fear of prison: "I can't. I'd land right in San Quentin prison. I've got to earn at least the pittance I got last year to pay my blankety-blank income tax." Suffering from a mild heart attack and pneumonia in his last years, Lionel declined hospital care to avoid the cost. He claimed that his creditors "prayed so hard, I got well."[14]

Death negated Lionel's apprehensions about San Quentin but not his tax debt to the federal government that still amounted to $40,000. Even before he died, the Beverly Hills house on Roxbury Drive in which he had lived with his second wife had been sold to pay a tax lien. (When in 1939, Lionel purchased his next and last residence in the San Fernando Valley, his twenty-two-acre ranch in Chatsworth, he put the property in the names of his caretakers.) Attorney Gordon Levoy, the executor of Lionel's estate, hoped that an estate sale would net $25,000 to satisfy the IRS and explained that Lionel had sunk more deeply into a tax mire as his tax rate zoomed, as did penalties and interest. The auctioneer predicted that his sale would bring about twice as much. Lionel's and Jack's friend Gene Fowler, in a radio tribute after Lionel's death, deplored the emotional toll that Lionel's tax indebtedness had exacted on him: "As is the case with many creative or interpretive artists, Lionel was no bookkeeper.... He had no head for the kind of records that businessmen find essential in dealing with the tax collector.... Lionel somehow fell behind with the prosaic diary of his expenditures and his income." Fowler protested that the federal government should have instead shown leniency to this national treasure.[15]

Over twenty years, these tax difficulties created chronic fear, stress, and financial strain on a man who claimed to never have mastered basic arithmetic; during the same time period, they also informed his stunning and esteemed portrayal of Scrooge on American radio. In 1934 and 1935, in 1937, and from 1939 to 1953, American audiences delightedly tuned in during Christmas week to hear Lionel growlingly menace Bob Cratchit.

Lionel's chronic financial messes had a contradictory effect on his portrayal of Scrooge (and, in 1946, of Mr. Potter in Frank Capra's film *It's a Wonderful Life*). Lionel's experiences as a chronic debtor envenomed his portrayals of these merciless creditors as diabolical; yet, at the same time, his resentment of taxes enlivened his expression of Scrooge's and Potter's sentiments. His impossible situation generated anger—both a debtor's indignation *at* Scrooge and *Scrooge's* anger at the meddling do-gooders who want to pick his pocket to benefit the poor. Animated by his financial captivity by a federal tax system designed to pay for extensive government services, Lionel could voice Scrooge's sentiments with gusto yet (as a man sunk neck-deep in debt) also portray Scrooge the creditor as evil, almost subhuman. Witness Lionel's comments on liberal social policies: "[My] talent for throwing away money is not a unique or even novel thing.... A number of gentlemen close to the White House... seem to possess comparable capacities for tossing dollars at birds." And he grimly predicted, "These curious economic theories which we have borne since approximately 1913 are the forerunners of disaster.... The harbingers of the destruction of all the great civilizations before us were strangulating taxes."[16]

Lionel's introduction to a 1938 edition of Dickens's *A Christmas Carol* both shared his perceptions of Scrooge and revealed his process as an actor of immersing himself in the character. The imagery Lionel used is strong. First, he called Scrooge "a human termite... in subterranean darkness." Continuing with the termite metaphor, he pictured Scrooge as "gouging deeper, bolstering up his tunnel's walls with his usurious gains." Next, in an odd comparison, Scrooge pokes his pen into the starved bodies of his debtors, thereby

Radio Days and the Taxman Cometh, 1934–1954

transfusing their scanty blood into his moneybox. The diabolical reference becomes clear: Scrooge's moneybags "sink under their pendulous weight down to the slough of hell." Besides being a devil, Scrooge is "a carrion-flecked buzzard, a wolf, a vampire, a rat, a snake, or a leech." Reverting to diabolical metaphors, "One cloven foot scrapes impatiently to track down his debtors." Not content with a mere cloven foot, Lionel also mentioned "his thin serpent-tongue." With the eventual redemption gained through Jacob Marley's intercession, Scrooge is "a devil who has turned traitor to hell!"[17]

Having thus depicted his understanding of Scrooge, Lionel then described his process of preparing to act the role on radio. Immersing himself in the character, Lionel felt himself stooping like Scrooge and perceiving with Scrooge's twisted vision: "I seem to shrink, and an unnatural meanness of disposition comes upon me." Nastily threatening and self-seeking, Lionel-as-Scrooge resented having accepted the insufficient payment offered for this job. He should have driven a harder bargain. He thought about ruining his debtors. He snarled at the radio studio's doorman. After the performance, Lionel recovered his normal kindliness: "Scrooge is no more: his pinched-thin, miserly stoop has left my body; I breathe more easily, less stingily; my step is lighter and my heart is lifted." Lionel's imagination of Scrooge's subjective world, his expression of Scrooge's sentiments, and his condemnation of Scrooge all benefited from his unfortunate and permanent entrapment in a financial bog.[18]

Except for 1936, when Jack substituted for Lionel because Lionel's wife, Irene, had suddenly died in their Roxbury Drive garden, and for 1938, when Lionel promoted MGM's film of *A Christmas Carol* by insisting that its Scrooge, Reginald Owen, should lead the radio broadcast, Lionel impersonated Ebenezer Scrooge on the radio for almost twenty years, from 1934 to 1953. With the audience's response being described as "rapturous," only Lionel's own death in November 1954 ended his run as Scrooge. A recorded performance was aired on radio in December 1954, and his passing ended plans to televise his performance. (Appearing on February 14, 1954, on Ed Sullivan's TV program *Toast of the Town*, Lionel revealed his anxieties about his continued employability: "After 30 years of living and working with the Metro family, I'm still going strong. So don't any of you gentlemen offer me a gold watch.") Identified strongly in the public mind with the character, Lionel was MGM's first choice to play Scrooge in its film, but his being in a wheelchair by the late thirties seemed to rule out his casting. Instead, he went to the set to advise on the film, and he recorded a trailer for it, *A Fireside Chat with*

LIONEL BARRYMORE

Lionel Barrymore. Radio audiences, in a national poll, elected him "Best Actor of 1942–1943." Perhaps their being devoted to Lionel's annual broadcast resulted from their sensing the motivation behind his acting the part of Scrooge. As he expressed it in 1949,

> human beings are all inherently kind, and inherently generous. But in the turmoil of modern times people are likely to forget. Their true instincts are prone to be buried under trying individual problems and rushing events of the day. Then a message like that of *A Christmas Carol* reminds them of what they really are, deep down in their souls. . . . I don't do it for any money that's in it—I don't care a hoot about the money. It is because it gives me a feeling that I have, perhaps, performed a slight service in reminding people of their own selves, helping them to remember that when a man lays aside all extraneous matters that cloud an issue, he is kind.

"Of all the roles I've done," Lionel declared in 1947, "the one I'd like best to be remembered for is Scrooge."[19]

In 1828, Louisa Lane at eight years old played five characters in *Twelve Precisely*. American Antiquarian Society.

Maternal uncle John Drew, in 1894, played Petruchio in Shakespeare's *The Taming of the Shrew*. Philip H. Ward Collection of Theatrical Images, Ms. Coll. 331, Kislak Center for Special Collections, University of Pennsylvania.

Maurice Barrymore was not only an actor but also a playwright. P. W. Costello and Family Art Collection, University of Scranton Digital Collections.

Georgiana Drew excelled as a comic actress. P. W. Costello and Family Art Collection, University of Scranton Digital Collections.

Louisa Lane Drew called the death of her daughter Georgiana Drew Barrymore in 1893 the greatest grief of her life. John Henry James Collection, Billy Rose Theatre Division, New York Public Library.

Lionel, appearing in *The Fires of Fate*, 1909, showed the effects of a few years of eating French cooking. Free Library of Philadelphia, Theatre Collection.

Lionel and Ethel Barrymore appeared in *Camille* in 1919 to support fellow players during the Actors' Equity strike. Photograph by Charlotte Fairchild. Museum of the City of New York.

Doris Rankin married Lionel in 1904 and divorced him in 1922. *Philadelphia Record* Photograph Morgue Collection [V07]. Box 732, Collection of Historical Society of Pennsylvania.

Irene Fenwick was Lionel's wife from 1923 until her early death in 1936. *Philadelphia Record* Photograph Morgue Collection [V07]. Box 299, Collection of Historical Society of Pennsylvania.

Lionel and Jack Barrymore appeared together at the premiere of *Don Juan*, 1926. Image ID 159350, Wisconsin Center for Film and Theater Research.

Lionel directed Ruth Chatterton in *Madame X*, 1929. Here they posed with Ralph Forbes, Chatterton's husband at the time. Motion Picture Stills Collection [Box 2, Folder 40], Hanna Holborn Gray Special Collections Research Center, University of Chicago.

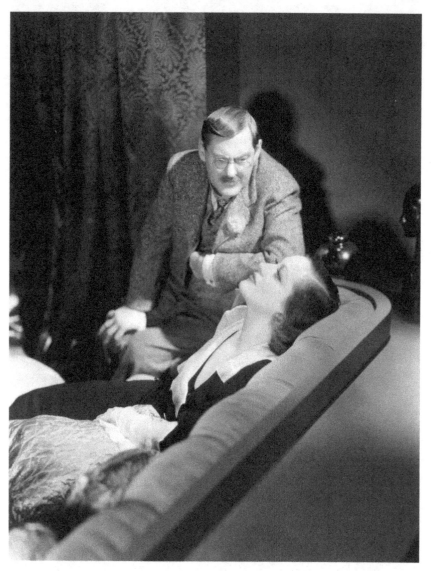

Lionel won Joan Crawford's esteem during the filming of *Grand Hotel*, 1932. Motion Picture Stills Collection [Box 2, Folder 40], Hanna Holborn Gray Special Collections Research Center, University of Chicago.

Lionel was memorable as a supporting player in *Captains Courageous*, 1937. Free Library of Philadelphia, Theatre Collection.

Laraine Day enjoyed working with Lionel in the Dr. Kildare films, 1939–1941. L. Tom Perry Special Collections, Harold B. Lee Library, Brigham Young University.

Lionel and Agnes Moorehead engaged in feisty exchanges during radio broadcasts of *Mayor of the Town*, 1942–1949. Image ID 159351, Wisconsin Center for Film and Theater Research.

In 1954, Richard Powell kidded Lionel as he enjoyed a cake during his last birthday. Free Library of Philadelphia, Theatre Collection.

Lionel's friend Ernest Blumenschein painted Lionel, Doris, and baby Ethel in Paris in 1909. The two men remained friends for many decades after their return to America. Pennsylvania Academy of the Fine Arts, Philadelphia. *Allegory in Honor of a Barrymore Child.* PC0104_1910_031.

Lionel narrated *The California Story* commemorating the state's centenary in September 1950. *Los Angeles Times* Photographic Archive, Library Special Collections, Charles E. Young Research Library, University of California at Los Angeles.

11

Brilliant Grouch
Dr. Gillespie and Other Roles, 1937–1951

In the strange, half-hidden genealogy of the icons of popular culture, Mickey Rooney's Andy Hardy is the cousin of Lew Ayres's Dr. James Kildare, and Kildare's fatherly mentor, Lionel Barrymore's Dr. Leonard Gillespie, is the brother of Lionel's Judge Hardy. The great popular success of the Andy Hardy films had inspired MGM's interest in creating another film series that replicated the father-son relationship between Andy and the judge. Although Lionel had played Judge Hardy in the original 1937 movie, *A Family Affair*, he was unavailable to appear in its sequels while filming *A Yank at Oxford* in England, so MGM cast Lewis Stone instead. Interviewed on the *Queen Mary* as he returned to America with the star of *A Yank at Oxford*, Robert Taylor, mocked by reporters as "America's sweetheart," Lionel defended Taylor as "a great kid with no vanity." The article noted that Lionel, after his hip fracture, limped and walked with a cane. Asked if he was now going to retire from screen acting, Lionel retorted, "I'll never quit until they push me off." After Lionel's return to Hollywood, the studio assigned him the role of Dr. Gillespie, despite qualms felt by some MGM executives about Lionel's need for a wheelchair. In 1936, Lionel's annus horribilis, he had experienced both the disability and the widowerhood that defined his remaining eighteen years. His wife Irene's sudden death after years of illness robbed him of much of his joy in life, and the accidental injuries that would necessitate a wheelchair frightened him with the prospect of unemployment. By using crutches, he navigates the role of the patriarch of the *You Can't Take It with You* household, and after managing to avert MGM's planned replacement of him with Frank Morgan in *On Borrowed Time*, he plays the grandpa role from his wheelchair. When Death rescues him from his stigmatized disability at the end of the film, Lionel stands and seems to walk in an illusion created by rear projection. He did lose the roles of Scrooge in *A Christmas Carol* and of Dr. Meade in *Gone with the Wind*, although he was still definitely cast as Meade on November 26, 1937. His former brother-in-law Harry Davenport eventually played Dr. Meade. (Davenport's wife and Doris Rankin's sister, Phyllis Rankin, had died in 1934.) About Davenport, who appeared with Lionel in *You Can't Take It with You*, Lionel asserted that he "gave everybody a lesson every time he stepped on a stage or before a camera." Reginald Owen, Lionel's candidate, took the role of Scrooge in MGM's 1938 film, for which Lionel recorded an introduction. With L. B. Mayer's support and the studio's discovery that Dr. Gillespie's wheelchair was a useful audience attraction rather than a detriment, Lionel eventually portrayed the brilliant diagnostician in fifteen MGM films and, later, in a radio series. Living and working in a wheelchair that he needed because of mysteriously long-lasting cancer, Dr. Gillespie enlivens the *Dr. Kildare* films (1938–1942), the *Dr. Gillespie* films (1942–1947), and the postwar *Dr. Kildare* radio episodes (1949–1951). (Hedda Hopper teased Lionel in print that "I can't wait to hear [him] sing *Rockabye Baby* for *The Personal Touch* [the last Dr. Gillespie movie, released as *Dark Delusion*]. That should either kill or cure.") Acting as Dr. Gillespie not only gave Lionel one of his signature roles but ensured his assignment to other acting jobs once the movie audience had reassured his nervous studio that it would accept an actor in a wheelchair. Presumably because of his impersonation of Dr. Gillespie, the National Council of Rehabilitation in 1949 gave him an award "for activities in behalf of the disabled." So adept was Lionel both in his acting of his part and in his maneuvering of the wheelchair, that other actors perceived the wheelchair as his means of stealing scenes. Former movie actor Ronald Reagan later reminisced about "the Barrymore wheelchair [that] had become Hollywood's most larcenous prop": "He could whip that contrivance around on a dime."[1]

Before following up the well-received *A Family Affair* with its fifteen sequels, unit production head Joe Cohn had decided to focus the movies on the relationship between Andy Hardy and his upright father. Eventually, MGM executives became enthused about the Andy Hardy series because its entries won back three to four times their production expenses. L. B. Mayer in particular took the series to his heart. *Love Finds Andy Hardy* made more money than other 1938 MGM films that had cost ten times more. Both the Andy Hardy series and the Doctor Kildare series, as well as the succeeding Dr. Gillespie series, were financed on B picture budgets. Nonetheless, Mayer insisted on quality, stressing that "if it's an MGM film, it has to look like an

Brilliant Grouch

MGM film." Mayer, too, realized that the father-son bond was key to the movies' appeal. "Don't go crazy because you have an oil-well in this boy," Mayer warned his subordinates. "Be careful. If you let Andy's relationships with the girls predominate, you'll lose your audience." The studio sought to discover other suitable material with which to repeat this successful formula. It found it in Max Brand's Doctor Kildare stories featuring a young intern and his experienced, fatherly mentor. After some hesitation about Lionel's ability to continue acting while using a wheelchair, MGM executives allowed his casting as Dr. Gillespie, who now also needed a wheelchair. Mayer, who obsessed about the Hardy family as an American ideal and about Dr. Kildare because of Mayer's personal fixation on medicine, was also very supportive of Lionel, who reciprocated his friendship. "His loyalty to me never wanes," Lionel stressed, "and that is why I remain loyal to him." Margaret O'Brien much later in life asserted that, despite Mayer's reputation for being "difficult to deal with," "he was wonderful to Lionel Barrymore. . . . The studio did very well with the Kildare series, so it showed that [the wheelchair] didn't inhibit their moneymaking ability at all. . . . That didn't hurt the film one bit and the audience didn't even notice that he was in a wheelchair." Although Mayer was Lionel's boss, Lionel was also Mayer's friend, perhaps because they may have known each other in the old days at Metro on the East Coast and because Lionel was Mayer's elder by several years. Mayer's younger daughter, Irene Mayer Selznick, noted that her father as an adolescent had "developed a habit that lasted most of his life, that of seeking out older people because he could learn from them." The success of both the Hardy and the Kildare series inspired MGM wits to outrage Mayer by joking that Andy should consult Dr. Kildare about a venereal infection contracted at Carvel High School.[2]

Just as Lionel Barrymore, not Lewis Stone, was the first actor to play Judge Hardy, Joel McCrea, not Lew Ayres, was the first to play Dr. James Kildare. Paramount's *Internes Can't Take Money* (1937) did not include Dr. Leonard Gillespie. At first, Ayres was reluctant to play Kildare and reacted to his casting "[by] biting and scratching. . . . I didn't want to do it because actors don't like to be typed. . . . I didn't want to have to play the same character all the time." Ayres recalled being "very disappointed" by feeling trapped by the great success of his first Kildare film. In the nine films in MGM's subsequent *Dr. Kildare* series, Ayres proved to be an excellent foil to Lionel, who later praised Ayres's low-key, offhand acting style. Ayres calmly acts his part of a determined young idealist, while Lionel impersonates an experienced mentor trying to save Kildare from the practical consequences of his idealism.

Often, Dr. Gillespie resembles an exasperated dog owner shooing his eager puppy away from danger. In *The Secret of Dr. Kildare*, Gillespie even exclaims to Kildare, "I've been leading you like a pug dog on a string!" Molly Byrd, the director of nursing, goes so far as to tell Kildare that he was born to be hanged. Ayres found that he had many artistic, literary, and musical interests in common with Lionel, they enjoyed debating their differing politics, and they developed a warm off-screen friendship. Ayres's ability to convey idealism had motivated MGM's decision to cast him as Dr. Kildare; his real-life idealism exceeded even that of his character, as Ayres's pacifism led to his declaring himself a conscientious objector during World War II. Fear of public disapproval caused MGM to remove Ayres from the series; the studio continued with Dr. Gillespie and cast as interns other younger actors, such as Van Johnson. For the first installment, Mayer ordered the deletion of Ayres's scenes in *Born to Be Bad*, now retitled *Calling Dr. Gillespie*, and had them reshot with Philip Dorn. Public support for Ayres came from such disparate sources as Hedda Hopper and Humphrey Bogart, while Studs Terkel denounced him. Wartime service in the medical corps, however, revived Ayres's popularity, and he eventually reunited with Lionel in a postwar radio version of the series. Considered for the role as a middle-aged Kildare in a 1953 pilot episode for television, Ayres, continuing his record of risky idealistic stands, had objected to cigarette advertising for the proposed TV series. The later famous TV series reverted to the familiar formula of a young Kildare (Richard Chamberlain) and a middle-aged Gillespie (Raymond Massey).[3]

The radio version of *Dr. Kildare* was one of the programs marketed as MGM Radio Attractions and broadcast from Loew's-owned radio station WMGM. Others included radio versions of additional MGM film stalwarts such as *The Adventures of Maisie*, *Crime Does Not Pay*, and *The Hardy Family*. MGM Radio Attractions's ultimate purpose was to achieve national and Canadian syndication. In the summer of 1949, MGM offered eight programs: *M-G-M Theatre of the Air*, *At Home with Lionel Barrymore*, *Hollywood, U.S.A.*, *Good News from Hollywood*, *Crime Does Not Pay*, *The Hardy Family*, *Maisie*, and *The Story of Dr. Kildare*.[4]

Ayres fondly remembered his enjoyable personal and professional relationship with Lionel: "we had a lot in common and I enjoyed conversations with him. Of course, he was an erudite man, but quite set in his ways, and I might say quite conservative in his attitude toward culture, cultural ideas. And, in fact, toward almost everything, he was quite conservative. I might

Brilliant Grouch

say I even think politically to some extent. And I have always been more or less—well, I don't know. A little more liberal, let's say. But for the purpose of enjoying our relationship, I would always take the side—even the radical side—to whatever it might be. (LAUGHS) I think just to hear him completely annihilate me, you know. He would be so vehement in his rejection of some of the propositions that I would put forward, that would be more or less considered to be radical. So we had a great time." Calling Lionel "a brilliant man," Ayres explained that they had bonded over their shared passions for art and music: "I went to art school for about four years. We both played and composed music." (Lionel composed the music for his and Ayres's film *Dr. Kildare's Wedding Day*.) Emma Dunn, who played Dr. Kildare's mother, and Laraine Day, who played Dr. Kildare's favorite nurse and sweetheart, also recorded their admiration for Lionel, with Day thanking him for his supportive friendship and Dunn declaring, "I have seen all kinds of courage through the years, but nothing excels the quality of courage shown by Barrymore." Remembering Lionel as "so wonderful," Day stressed Lionel's coping with "terrible pain" during the shooting of the Dr. Kildare films in which she appeared until MGM killed off her character in *Dr. Kildare's Wedding Day*. MGM would accommodate Lionel by filming his scenes at the end of the day. In Day's opinion, putting Dr. Gillespie in a wheelchair enhanced the series by adding an interesting facet, as did Lionel's flamboyant acting of the character. Like Ayres, Day felt dismayed by being cast in the *Dr. Kildare* series; although happy to work with Ayres, Lionel, the directors, and the other regular players, Day felt that her career had stalled.[5]

"He loved woman—not women, woman," remembered Lionel's music teacher Eugene Zádor; Lionel's appreciation of the female gender extended beyond adult women like Dunn and Day to little girls like Margaret O'Brien. Indeed, Lionel felt so smitten by O'Brien that she was the only actress his memoirs discussed at length besides Greta Garbo. (Lionel thought that Garbo was shy. His friend Anita Loos commented, "You could no more get close to Garbo than you could get close to a wild deer . . . if you reach out your hand, it will go away, but if you pay it no attention at all, the first thing you know it's coming around and getting friendly. . . . She's more like a wild doe than anything I can think of. . . . She is so fey, that's the only word I know that can describe her." Ayres judged Garbo to be "a very nice, gentle lady who was not outgoing. She was introverted.") Lionel made rag dolls for Margaret, his five-year-old costar in *Dr. Gillespie's Criminal Case* (1943), whom he declared to be "the only actress besides Ethel who's made me take out my handkerchief in thirty years." Admiring O'Brien's achievements in her later films, Lionel presented his friend Margaret with Mum Mum's sapphire-and-pearl pin because she was a "magnificent actress" worthy of the heirloom. As late as 1952, Lionel was still promoting O'Brien's career by lobbying for an MGM film of Dickens's *Little Dorrit* that would star both of them.[6]

Besides enjoying his personal and professional relationships with O'Brien, Ayres, and other costars, Lionel appreciated working with the first director of the Dr. Kildare/Dr. Gillespie film series, Harold Bucquet, Lionel's assistant director during his filming of *Madame X* (1929). After winning an Oscar in 1938 for the short subject *Torture Money* (an entry in the *Crime Does Not Pay* series), Bucquet made his debut as a director of MGM features with *Young Dr. Kildare*. Unfortunately, he died suddenly in 1946 at the age of fifty-four. Indeed, one account credits Bucquet with choosing Lionel, over studio resistance, to play Dr. Gillespie and quotes Lionel as saying, "Harry did a lot for me. I'll play that part for him if I have to do it in a wheel chair."[7]

Lionel reveled in the role of Dr. Leonard Gillespie so much that he read medical journals and joked that he now was "a second-class quack and a first-class hypochondriac." (Ayres remembered that, during the shooting of the *Dr. Kildare* films, a medical doctor was always available as a technical advisor.) Much enjoyed by audiences in this role that he himself so much enjoyed, Lionel even inspired Bugs Bunny to impersonate Dr. Gillespie in the 1948 Warner Brothers cartoon *Hot Cross Bunny*. Dr. Gillespie would inspire as well other grouchy but brilliant physicians in such future long-running mass entertainment series as *Doc Martin* and *House, M.D.*[8]

Like "Doc Martin" Ellingham and Greg House, Dr. Gillespie is a crack diagnostician whose social skills are suspended or absent. Welding the physician with the scientist, the role of diagnostician requires superior intelligence as well as acute observation and a logical bent. Mass entertainment dilutes this overwhelming degree of rationality with social awkwardness or even with chronic misanthropy. The diagnostician's intellectual superiority is balanced by his social inferiority. Dazzled by his gifts, the audience can feel reassured in its self-esteem by his character deficits. Far from being outraged by Gillespie's habits of yelling at and insulting his medical team members, the audience is apt to feel superior to and amused by a man whom Kildare's nurse and sweetheart Mary Lamont calls "a rambunctious old fossil." Adding a disability to this mixture of brilliance and grouchiness only adds to the characters' appeal and fascination. The chronic pain of House's wounded leg and his drug addiction, Doc Martin's blood phobia as well as possible high-functioning autism,

Brilliant Grouch

and Dr. Gillespie's use of a wheelchair lessen the threat that their intelligence poses to the nonmedical mass audience. While they may have superior minds, they are not supermen but wounded healers.

Besides starring as Dr. Gillespie in fifteen MGM movies, Lionel enlivened several other films during this time of adjustment to great personal loss and then of world war. These included *Captains Courageous*, a very enjoyable film about fishermen that the passage of time has not touched. The story about a spoiled but neglected boy (Freddie Bartholomew), his father (Melvyn Douglas), and his fisherman friend (Spencer Tracy, who won the Oscar for Best Actor) also features Lionel as the captain of the vessel. As Judge Hardy, Lionel guides Mickey Rooney in the initial feature of the Andy Hardy series, *A Family Affair*. (Rooney later did spot-on impersonations of Lionel and Gable in *Babes in Arms* and in *Thousands Cheer* as well as before live audiences. One of the several other popular entertainers who often impersonated Lionel was the young Art Carney, later famous as Ed Norton in TV's *The Honeymooners*.) The *New York Times* noted that Lionel as the dutiful patriarch "wears the mantle of justice and the crown of thorns with his usual dignity and patience.... Mr. Barrymore knows how to handle these things." *Saratoga* paired Lionel with Jean Harlow in her last movie, somewhat clumsily patched together by the studio after Harlow's death. Lionel's second accident occurred during the filming of *Saratoga*, breaking his hip again and necessitating the two canes he uses to walk in *Navy Blue and Gold*. This depiction of the experiences of three roommates at the Annapolis Naval Academy culminates with an Army-Navy football game. Lionel has a minor role. Billie Burke is in her usual fine form. Fans of James Stewart and Robert Young get to see them early in their careers. Lionel also appears in minor supporting roles in *A Yank at Oxford, Test Pilot, Let Freedom Ring, The Penalty, Lady Be Good*, and *Since You Went Away*, David O. Selznick's home front drama (directed by John Cromwell) that depicts a mother and her two daughters as they miss the husband and father who has gone away to war. Although some moments are excruciating, Claudette Colbert is fine as the mother, and several character actors give excellent support: Hattie McDaniel, Robert Walker, Joseph Cotten, Agnes Moorehead, and Monty Woolley. Bizarrely, Lionel gets sixth billing, just above Walker at number seven, even though Lionel appears for only a few minutes (as a clergyman giving a sermon) and Walker has a much more important part. It's sad to view Jennifer Jones in her love scenes with estranged husband Walker (her lover was the film's producer). Jones and

Shirley Temple are just adequate, inspiring the unkind thought that the dog does a better job than either.[9]

Meatier supporting parts for Lionel during this period of adjustment include *The Bad Man, Tennessee Johnson,* and *A Guy Named Joe.* A western tale that portrays an outlaw and cattle rustler as a fairy godmother intent on rectifying wrongs done to a man who once saved his life, *The Bad Man* stars Wallace Beery in outrageous flamboyance as the bandit. Lionel is great fun as the grandfather of the bandit's friend, and Ronald Reagan renders a pallid performance as the grandson. In this film, Lionel anticipates the characters played in later life by Walter Brennan. Although a minor and largely forgotten film, *The Bad Man* is very amusing, mostly because the viewer can't decide whether it is playing its absurd fairy godmother story straight or is deliberately campy. *Tennessee Johnson* portrays President Andrew Johnson from the perspective of the forties. In *Black Reconstruction*, a counternarrative published in 1935, W. E. B. DuBois decried the fictionalization of history in the history books: "The magnificent figures of Charles Sumner and Thaddeus Stevens have been besmirched almost beyond recognition.... This may be fine romance, but it is not science. It may be inspiring, but it is certainly not the truth.... [Instead, it is] a cheap and false myth.... Suppose the slaves of 1860 had been white folk. Stevens would have been a great statesman, Sumner a great democrat . . . in a mighty revolution of rising humanity." Adhering to this falsification of the historical record, *Tennessee Johnson*, a fictionalized account of Johnson's life, career, and survival of impeachment (he was impeached by the House of Representatives but acquitted at his Senate trial), demonizes Representative Thaddeus Stevens of Pennsylvania, Johnson's nemesis and the force behind his impeachment. Although *Tennessee Johnson* gives a very slanted account of Reconstruction and in general portrays Stevens negatively, Van Heflin and Lionel Barrymore do credible jobs as Johnson and Stevens. *Time* magazine's review actually reported that some scenes were reshot to make the "unscrupulous," "fanatical," and vindictive Stevens "more sympathetic." *Variety* also confirmed the alteration of the script ("almost a complete rewrite"), although it misreported that Lionel played Johnson rather than Stevens. Then, a week later, *Variety* reported influence from Washington to correct Lionel's portrayal of Stevens, to erase "aspersions on a man who today would be recognized as a true liberal, perhaps a New Dealer." *Variety*'s eventual review noted "the switch in facts necessary in the film biography to get it past audiences in the South." This either means continued misunderstanding of what alterations occurred or suggests

Brilliant Grouch

countervailing pressures to change the depictions of both Johnson and Stevens. Reflecting all of this controversy, the studio dropped the movie's original title, *The Man on America's Conscience*. Barrymore as Stevens protests sacrificing the interests of the oppressed former slaves to the interests of traitorous white men. After Stevens makes the point, Johnson ignores it, saying the harmony between North and South will benefit the former slaves as well. Stevens does not buy this argument. An interesting focus of the film in the beginning is the rebellion of "poor whites" against the state's ruling class. A more perceptive treatment might have made more of the failure of poor whites to make common cause with Blacks. Also, the film ignores the disenfranchisement of all women. Much more could have been done with these blind spots. Still, this fictional treatment does create curiosity about who Thaddeus Stevens was and about what he advocated. Finally, in *A Guy Named Joe*, Lionel gets to play God in uniform. This fantasy film features Spencer Tracy as a daredevil, lone-wolf fighter pilot who after death in combat serves as a grumpy and jealous guardian angel to the pilot who falls for his girl. Ward Bond is memorable in this movie, as he is in *The Maltese Falcon*. Tracy, Irene Dunne, and Van Johnson are good. Lionel has a small but effective part as Tracy's commanding officer in Heaven.[10]

Amid these supporting roles, Lionel led the cast in Frank Capra's comedy *You Can't Take It with You* and in the fantasy *On Borrowed Time*. In what may be Lionel's most likable role, he brilliantly portrays for Capra the patriarch of a clan in which the members "follow their bliss." The irony, of course, is that Lionel was very much *not* "following his bliss" by acting in *any* movie. Grandpa Vanderhof long ago gave up the corporate success that made him unhappy and, like Lionel himself, has attracted the attention of the tax authorities. The scene in which the IRS agent tries to make Vanderhof aware of his income tax arrears has the audience in stitches: "I wouldn't mind paying for something sensible," Vanderhof asserts. When the agent then asks him, "Who's going to pay for the Constitution?" he scoffs, "The Constitution's been paid for years ago." Lionel convinced Capra that he could play his role in *You Can't Take It with You* on crutches; for *On Borrowed Time*, the studio had planned to replace him with Frank Morgan, but he managed to persuade studio executives to let him work. He plays from his wheelchair throughout the film until the end when he stands and seems to walk (an illusion created by rear projection). Lionel formed a warm attachment to the child actor who played his grandson, Bobs Watson, denigrating himself at age seven in comparison to Bobs: "Why, when I was seven I couldn't even read the funny papers. And here I am working with a youngster just a year older than that who can read a complete motion picture script. You can practically see the thoughts take shape in that boy's mind. He is that responsive. He goes over the script with his father before the scene is rehearsed and you can watch him decide how it should be played."[11]

Unlike the actors who played Doc Martin and Gregory House, Lionel actually had a disability, and as we have seen, it threatened his career prospects while his studio worried about audience aversion to an actor in a wheelchair. Audience acceptance of Dr. Gillespie negated that worry, and Lionel continued to act while using his wheelchair until he died. For an actor with a disability to play a character with a disability is still remarkable, however, so the question arises whether Lionel's personal success actually improved opportunities for other actors with disabilities.

Several issues come to mind. A character's disability can be incidental or integral to the story—either essential to the plot or as incidental as eye color. For Lionel's characters, including Dr. Gillespie, the wheelchair (or, earlier, the crutch) tends to be incidental to the story, as in *You Can't Take It with You* and *On Borrowed Time*. This is an ideal situation—that a person with a disability is not defined by it but seen as a whole person, like the other characters. Moreover, Dr. Gillespie functions brilliantly in his role as diagnostician, so he is not perceived as "unable."

For many people, disability connotes *in*ability. A person with a disability who functions well may be misperceived as having little or no difficulty; therefore, the person's successful functioning does not alter the stereotype, for such a high-functioning person is misperceived as not *really* disabled. This misperception perpetuates the stigma. So, Lionel's impersonating characters whose disability is incidental to the plot is a good precedent, while his being perceived as extremely able does not alter the prejudice. Moreover, Lionel's disability was not lifelong but acquired, so he was perceived as an unfortunate but previously able-bodied actor, in a category different from actors disabled from birth. His success as a late-disabled actor would not improve the prospects of actors whose disabilities are lifelong. Perhaps Lionel's not being defined by his disability, not being seen as "unable," and not being stigmatized as much because he "acquired" his disability all mark him as an outlier still within the boundaries of normalcy, whereas actors with lifelong disabilities exist outside those boundaries, would be defined by their disabilities, would be misperceived as inherently "unable," and would be stigmatized. The stigma and misperceptions reflect, not the reality of people with disabilities, but fantasies derived from the fears and ignorance of the able-bodied. One of "us" rather than "them," Lionel survived on the right side of the line. *Variety* early in 1939 reported that he had "discarded his wheel chair for a cane." A 1939 news item in *Silver Screen* stressed how, with medical treatment and exercise, Lionel had recovered his mobility: "He moved to a farm in the San Fernando Valley, and added sunshine and strenuous farm work to his itinerary. He built fences, planted flowers, shrubs and trees, and gradually overcame the handicap. He walked before the camera recently for the first time and from now on has no use for crutch or wheel chair." *Current Biography* in 1943 even included a quote asserting that Lionel could now get around without help and that the wheelchair was for Dr. Gillespie's sake, not Lionel's!: "The studio plans to keep him in his wheel chair during future *Dr. Kildares* unless the medical profession discovers a plausible cure for his cinema cancer." A 1941 interview categorized Lionel's wheelchair as "a prop, not a necessity" and stressed its acting utility: "as a scene-stealing device (Barrymore, of course, would never dream of turning it to so base a use) it is the biggest thing since the winning chariot in *Ben Hur*." Besides being misleading and untrue, this information shows how Lionel was defined as "one of us," a person who would, by force of will, become able-bodied again. Because he overcame his studio's assumption of incapacity and acted in many roles in which his wheelchair was incidental to the main plot, he disproved David O. Selznick's assumption in 1938 that "such appearances as the poor fellow is going to make in the future are going to have to be in a wheel chair . . . which naturally limits the number of things he can do." Had he been born with a disability, however, it would, in the minds of many able-bodied people, "naturally limit the number of things he can do."[12]

Entertainment executives are still slow to offer roles to actors with disabilities—whether the roles depict the disabilities as integral or incidental to the story. Actors with disabilities are still "other." In addition, stories about people with disabilities continue to reflect the prejudices, fears, and hopes of their able-bodied creators and audiences rather than the realities of people with disabilities. This brings up a related issue of acting authenticity. Can an actor who does not have a disability portray, as so many able-bodied actors have done, a character with a disability, especially a disability central to the story? If the actor is able to convey the real situation, feelings, and strivings of the character, one would say that the best actor should get the part—but how can we know that the best actor is cast if actors with disabilities are continually overlooked? And, without the input of actors, writers, directors, and producers with disabilities, how can we ensure that the story accurately reflects the lives of people with disabilities instead of an able-bodied perspective?

As for Lionel's own off-screen life with his disability, several anecdotes depicted Lionel's possible addiction to painkillers. Without citing any sources, James Kotsilibas-Davis alleged that the MGM infirmary regularly supplied him with cocaine, even in excess of legal restrictions, and also reported that he had conquered that addiction. More detailed discussion by Margot Peters included the supposition that Lionel had acquired a morphine habit as far back as 1925 in order to lessen arthritis discomfort associated with a venereal infection. Peters cited John Barrymore's biographer Gene Fowler as her source; Fowler had discussed Lionel's alleged drug habit with Barrymore expert Spencer Berger. By the thirties, according to Peters, Lionel was addicted to both morphine and cocaine. Paying Lionel back for his contemptuous rejection of her as John's fourth wife, Elaine Barrie alluded obliquely to the story that Lionel had suffered from syphilis by accusing Lionel of being a hypocrite, of being "guilty of excesses that revolted even John," and of being "in a wheelchair from his own excesses which by comparison made John a model of virtue and moderation." Barrie offered no sources for her allegations. (Naturally omitting any discussion of venereal disease or painkillers, Lionel's own memoir explicitly denied that he ever had arthritis.) James Bacon in his very nasty chapter on Mayer in *Hollywood Is a Four Letter Town* claimed that Lionel had once declared to him that Lionel would have killed himself long ago had Mayer not supplied $400 worth of cocaine every day. This claim (in the last paragraph of his chapter) follows a rhetorical question about whether Mayer ever did anything good for anyone, surely a highly prejudiced statement. The allegation assumes that Mayer operated outside of the control of the New York office to benefit a personal friend at great expense to the studio, a most dubious assumption—as dubious as the often-repeated allegation that Mayer deliberately destroyed, for personal reasons, the career of moneymaking star John Gilbert. We are left therefore with remarks Lionel reportedly made to Gene Fowler and James Bacon. Without access to records, we can neither prove nor disprove the allegations.[13]

Of course, it is possible that Lionel kept himself working by obtaining morphine or cocaine. Absent, however, from all of these accounts are any sense of the agony of living with severe chronic pain, any assessment of the efficacy of contemporary pain management, and any awareness of how much good work Lionel completed even if he was actually addicted to morphine or

Brilliant Grouch

cocaine or both. Use of painkillers to alleviate severe chronic pain is very different from recreational use of drugs and calls for understanding rather than judgment. Regarding the availability, legality, and effectiveness of pain relievers, Nancy Campbell, PhD, editor of the University of Chicago Press journal *Social History of Alcohol and Drugs*, offered this explanation:

> Then, as now, many chronic pain patients were effectively maintained on morphine, which was synthesized in the early nineteenth century and was widely used prior to the Harrison Act (1914) and the closure of the morphine maintenance clinics in the early 1920s. Prior to criminalization—and the resulting prosecution of physicians who wrote prescriptions to maintain their chronic pain patients on morphine—there was quite widespread use of morphine, laudanum (tincture of opium in alcohol), paregoric, and other opiates. Occupational injuries and railway accidents were common, and there was much popular knowledge of this practice. During World War II, however, opiates, including morphine, were stockpiled for the war effort, so it would have been more difficult to obtain a supply unless through a physician. Cocaine was also available during the period of Lionel's need for pain management, and it is an excellent topical anesthetic although of not much use in alleviating pain per se. However, many used it on occasion for energy, and often injectors mixed it with morphine.

Campbell added, "Cocaine, in particular, was not understood as 'addictive,' even into the 1970s. . . . It was generally an occasional-use drug, and of course it was more expensive than gold until the marketing innovation that was crack-cocaine in the mid-1980s. That meant that wealthier people might well have had access to it to a greater degree than many," although Lionel's perpetual money woes probably did not keep him in this category. Campbell agreed with the assertion that, if pain relief makes a person more productive (as Lionel certainly was), judgments based on the assumption that it will render the person nonfunctional do not make much sense. "Opiate use was associated with productivity," she clarified. "Many people used it to maintain function. In the nineteenth and early twentieth centuries, most of what we would call 'addiction,' a term that was not used until the turn of the twentieth century, was 'iatrogenic' in etiology—meaning that physicians caused it and often maintained it because opiates were therapeutically effective."[14]

Lionel surmounted the threat posed to his movie career so well that, in 1939, *Variety*'s analysis of "top films and stars" listed him among MGM's best draws and commented, "Lionel Barrymore, the old warhorse, was impressed into service aplenty, and, although not an outstanding magnet with the buyers, always proves to be potent enough to attract attention to the pictures he works in." A 1942 discussion in the article "Males Outlast Pix Femmes" listed Lionel among the durable male actors. This seemed to invalidate studio concerns about Lionel's continued appeal to audiences after his acquisition of a wheelchair, as well as a long-ago (1932) classification of both Lionel and Jack as belonging to the lesser B category of box-office moneymakers at Metro, trailing Joan Crawford, Norma Shearer, Marie Dressler, Wallace Beery, and Clark Gable in the A category.[15]

12

The Best Wine for Last, 1945–1953

Lionel's recurrent performances as Scrooge and Dr. Gillespie foreshadowed his late-career appearances as avaricious banker Henry F. Potter in *It's a Wonderful Life*, spiteful rancher Senator Jackson McCanles in *Duel in the Sun*, and embittered and bereaved father James Temple in *Key Largo*. By accident, these three roles have made him the Barrymore sibling most recognized by the general movie-watching public in the early twenty-first century: Henry Potter, because an oversight in copyright renewal led to the extraordinary afterlife that Frank Capra's film enjoyed on television; Senator McCanles, because David O. Selznick's overheated and ludicrous movie became notorious; and James Temple, because Humphrey Bogart evolved into a cult favorite after his untimely death. In these, his best-remembered roles, as well as in the less-famous *Three Wise Fools* and *Down to the Sea in Ships*, Lionel perfected his impersonation of a cantankerous elder and became identified with it—much as Gladys Cooper had patented the role of disagreeable matron and as Maggie Smith was to do decades later. In his less prominent performances in this postwar decade, Lionel often sat in bed, in a wheelchair, or behind a desk to serve as acting support, yet it is noticeable how often his minor characters are nevertheless pivotal to the action as they exert either a sage or a malign influence on the leads.

In *The Valley of Decision* (1945), Lionel—injured years before by an industrial accident—angrily derails the romance between his daughter, Greer Garson, and her employer's son, Gregory Peck, as well as ignites labor strife. Seeing Lionel flinch as a studio hairdresser performed his daily curling, Garson teased him, "She won't hurt you," to which Lionel retorted, "She won't hurt a beautiful woman. But how about a nasty old man?" In *The Secret Heart* (1946), Lionel the psychiatrist advises Claudette Colbert about how to help her emotionally disturbed stepdaughter, June Allyson. Lionel's part was filmed a month after production had ended because resolving the entangled plot required a psychiatrist's intervention! In *Malaya* (1949), James Stewart finds the help of Lionel the newspaper publisher crucial as Stewart plans to smuggle rubber out of Japanese-occupied territory. Saloon owner Sydney Greenstreet's pairing with a pet bird in Greenstreet's last film stirs up memories of *Casablanca*. In the boxing melodrama *Right Cross* (1950), Lionel is the fight promoter betrayed by his longtime client. In *Bannerline* (1951), Lionel the dying history teacher exhorts a reporter to expose corruption. In *Lone Star* (1952), Lionel, in his second filmed impersonation of Andrew Jackson, counsels Clark Gable about securing the support of Sam Houston for Texan statehood rather than for Texan independence. Beulah Bondi, who as Rachel Jackson in *The Gorgeous Hussy* (1936) had felt surprised by finding herself shooting a scene with Lionel in a double bed, here plays an "old friend" of Jackson's. Newcomer Keefe Brasselle, while filming the lead role in *Bannerline*, humorously complained about the screen dominance exhibited by Lionel and his fellow movie veterans: "You get a little sick feeling about it, because they're so great. I'm waving my hands, hopping around and booming the lines out. And they're behind me, quietly stealing the scenes away. I ask you!" Lionel certainly makes the most of his few lines. Asked if he fears dying, he replies, "A teacher's reward must be in the next world, but it certainly can't be in this one." He asks for paper and his glasses to write his own obituary, "assuming of course in the place I am about to go warmth won't be gilding the lily." Urging reform but expressing cynicism about any positive effects of a newspaper exposé in a town "where the corrupt lead the corrupted," he snorts, "Land where our fathers died. Died for what?" He tells the villain that he has "all the charm of a plague epidemic": "you pose as a lovable person, but you're really filth incarnate."[1]

Besides these several minor yet consequential roles, Lionel appears with his sister as themselves in *Main Street to Broadway* (1953), a production intended to benefit the Council of the Living Theatre, as well as narrates two documentaries promoting MGM: *Some of the Best: 25 Years of Motion Picture Leadership* (1949) and *The Metro-Goldwyn-Mayer Story* (1951). For a while, he was hoping that MGM would revive the Dr. Gillespie film series. "Those were good little pictures—moneymakers, too. And look at the stars who came out of them—Van Johnson, Red Skelton, Laraine Day, Lana Turner, Donna Reed and many others." These lesser contributions in Lionel's last years of movie acting accompany his five major appearances: *Three Wise Fools* (1946), *It's a Wonderful Life* (1946), *Duel in the Sun* (1946), *Key Largo* (1948), and *Down to the Sea in Ships* (1949).[2]

The Best Wine for Last, 1945–1953

In *Three Wise Fools*, Lionel, Lewis Stone, and Edward Arnold portray three embittered elderly bachelors who unexpectedly encounter the granddaughter of their long-ago sweetheart when the girl comes from Ireland to her ancestral home in America. Stuffed with whimsy and often achingly arch, not to mention full of hoary stereotypes about Irish people, *Three Wise Fools* could have reunited all of Ireland in outrage at its nonsensical portrayal. The movie nevertheless showcases Margaret O'Brien's extraordinary acting skills. Even if, as Oscar Wilde wrote about the troubles of another beleaguered heroine, one would have to have a heart of stone not to laugh, O'Brien creates some touching and pathetic moments as the loving poppet who shames three nasty old men who seek to exploit her. During a celebration on the set, O'Brien delivered the first piece of cake to Lionel "because I love you"; this is the occasion that prompted him to reciprocate by giving her Mum Mum's sapphire-and-pearl brooch as a tribute to her fine acting. Their personal relationship as grandfather and granddaughter was important to both of them. At seventy-four, O'Brien remembered her affection for Lionel: "He became the grandfather that I never had because I never knew my real grandfather. Lionel Barrymore and I became very close, and he would make me rag dolls. He was very respectful of me and treated me as an actress. I became very fascinated with the Barrymore family, and Lionel would tell me stories of his family's life in the theater. At the wrap party for *Three Wise Fools*, Lionel gave me his mother's [sic] pin that had been worn by all the Drew women on opening night. He had been looking for someone to give this pin to, which he called one of the crown jewels of the theater. So, he gave it to me. It was a great honor." Asked if Lionel really was a grouch, O'Brien recalled, "He'd pretend to be sometimes, but he wasn't at all. Not at all. All you'd have to do is get a sad look, and he'd try to do something for you." In 1948, Lionel wrote the appreciative foreword to O'Brien's published diary, and as late as 1952, Lionel was still trying to boost O'Brien's career by pitching to MGM a movie version of Dickens's *Little Dorrit* with O'Brien in the title role and himself as William Dorrit, but he sensed a politely hidden lack of interest in his suggestion.[3]

Henry Potter in Frank Capra's *It's a Wonderful Life* has become Lionel's most remembered role, so powerfully enacted that the FBI worried that his portrayal of an avaricious banker amounted to communistic propaganda—a fear contradicted by testimony before the House Un-American Activities Committee that James Stewart's benign businessman offset Potter's negative image of American commerce. Nonetheless, seven of the nine screenwriters who worked on the film got into trouble during the postwar blacklisting period—including Capra himself. A less political contemporary review labeled the film as skillfully made but sentimental with "impossible parts" and called Potter a "hobgoblin." Although very different rejections of the movie, these two reactions shared the common mistake of judging Capra's films in terms of their degree of realism. Capra was not a sophisticated thinker but a filmmaking genius whose apparently political themes are really allegorical and symbolic. This appeared clearly, for example, when Capra horrified Gore Vidal by suggesting the addition to Vidal's *The Best Man* a scene in which a presidential candidate dresses up as Lincoln to visit delegates on the convention floor. Henry Potter himself is not merely the town banker of Bedford Falls but Mephistopheles of old offering George Bailey a Faustian swap of riches and success for George's soul. Although George initially succumbs but then quickly rejects the bargain, he subsequently descends into a hell of his own making by committing the worst sin of all, despair, and wishing that he had never been born at all. George Bailey could turn into Henry Potter, for they are not opposites but mirror images of the same bitter and thwarted man at the beginning and end of his self-degradation. Yet George rejects his demonic self and allies himself with his guardian angel instead. The events in *It's a Wonderful Life* amount to a drama of a human soul's crisis and redemption, not to an episode in the history of American savings and loan associations.[4]

James Stewart remembered that, when Capra was casting the actors, Stewart was taken with Capra's incoherent account of the story: "I didn't know what the hell he was talking about. But he went on and on and it just grew on me." He responded, "Frank, if you want to make a movie about a fella who wants to commit suicide and an angel with no wings, I'm your boy!" Having been absent from Hollywood during his wartime military service, Stewart also remembered Lionel's encouragement when he felt insecure about his rusty acting skills: "[Don't] apologize for not being in town the last four years. He told me to just do it, not to make excuses or feel sorry for myself. It was wonderful for me. I'll always be grateful." Capra had asked Lionel to counsel Stewart, and Lionel obliged: "Jimmy, don't ever forget that acting is the greatest profession ever invented. When you act you move millions of people, shape their lives, give them a sense of exaltation. No other profession has that power." Stewart later commented, "I was terribly influenced by what he said." Capra also recalled that Barrymore challenged Stewart about whether acting was "decent" by asking whether it is more "decent" to bomb people: "Stewart told me that Lionel's barbs had knocked him flat on his ass and that now acting was going to be his life's work."[5]

When reminiscing about Lionel for his memoirs, Capra declared that he "revered" Lionel: "LB's name deserves top billing among the immortals. Yet he was the humblest, most cooperative actor I've ever known." He declared that he had targeted Lionel for Potter because "no one else would do" and that Lionel then signed on without even reading the script. Capra's account seems to be untrue, for a typed list of prospective actors includes almost 30 men considered for Potter, including Thomas Mitchell and Edward Arnold. Regardless of this discrepancy, once Lionel was chosen, Capra focused on the demonization of Potter, partly by requesting makeup inspired by Grant Wood's *American Gothic* that included a tight plastic cap over Lionel's skull. So successful was this diabolical portrayal that a newspaperman joked in 1949 about Potter's being "so mean he'll cross the street in his wheelchair just to run over a centipede who's minding it's [sic] own business." Potter's misdeeds disturbed audiences, and over the years viewers troubled that Potter was not punished for stealing $8,000 from George Bailey's savings and loan wrote to Capra about this more often than about any other issue. Almost sixty years later, participants in an American Film Institute poll in 2003 voted Potter among the top ten most popular movie villains. Although Capra claimed that his own wartime experiences had taught him that there was "much more to the world than what we did here for each other in Hollywood," he used the talents of Lionel and his other stars to turn resolutely away from realistic depictions of real-world evil and toward spiritual allegory. Dissenting from the American Film Institute's inclusion of the film in its poll of the 100 best American films ever, Russell Baker chortled, "it first appeared in 1946 when a generation hardened to reality by Depression and war let it pass without saluting. They knew from bitter experience that the whole town never shows up to slather its George Baileys in money and love. . . . Mean old Lionel Barrymore, you told it like it was."[6]

Regardless of whether Mr. Potter "told it like it was," Capra's creation of Potter as a stereotypical villain absent from the original story and from earlier scripts showed no growth in Capra's political or social awareness after his wartime service. This was true even though Capra had formed his own postwar production company, Liberty Films, with fellow directors George Stevens and William Wyler, who echoed the sentiment that Hollywood movies are "divorced from the main currents of our time" and do "not reflect the world in which we live." Capra retreated into allegory and nostalgia as a relief from wartime stresses; yet *It's a Wonderful Life* is nevertheless a very dark film. Greatly affected by his own wartime experiences and dislocated in postwar Hollywood, Stevens—invited with Capra to view David O. Selznick's *Duel in the Sun* in production—commented that the movies were "not made from life, but made from old films."[7]

Certainly, *Duel in the Sun* was a product of Hollywood unreality as well as a manifestation of the lurid fantasies of its producer rather than a movie that showed any awareness hard-earned during wartime. Eventually, reacting to the panning reviews, Selznick would realize that the film had destroyed his reputation. Seeking to build on the popularity of Jennifer Jones, Joseph Cotton, and newcomer Gregory Peck, Selznick fashioned a story of obsessive passion and hate; yet he sought to indulge baser instincts while still preserving a veneer of morality. Selznick wrote to a concerned Sister Ursula, Jones's "former spiritual advisor" in Tulsa, that the film "preaches a very moral lesson ... that 'the wages of sin are death'"; yet Selznick also badgered Dimitri Tiomkin to compose "orgasm music" for the rape sequence: "It's not *shtup*. It's not the way I fuck." Tiomkin responded: "Mr. Selznick, you fuck your way. I fuck my way. To *me* that is fucking music."[8]

Selznick's thumbprints are all over this garish production; he had wanted it to be his signature achievement. Its ridiculous plot notwithstanding, most of the character actors (Herbert Marshall, Lionel Barrymore, Lillian Gish, Charles Bickford, Walter Huston) are fine. Jennifer Jones substitutes for acting a snarl, a sneer, and an elevated hipbone, and she wears full makeup (eyeshadow!) to the fatal rendezvous. Gregory Peck has a grand time as the baddie. But in spite of the valiant efforts of several excellent character actors—Lionel among them—"Lust in the Dust," as it is jokingly referred to, is a terrible movie choked with racial and gender stereotypes and sexual hysteria that render it unintentionally hilarious.

Working on *Duel in the Sun* did reunite Lionel with his esteemed Biograph colleague Lillian Gish, and their old boss from the Biograph years, D. W. Griffith, even visited them on the set. Their characters' wedding photo, displayed in the sitting room in which their acerbic exchanges occur, actually came from an old Biograph film of theirs. Charles Affron, a film and theater historian, asserted that Griffith was on set by request to advise on *Duel in the Sun* but being in Griffith's presence paralyzed both Gish and Lionel. Having just watched these two veteran actors in a 1913 two-reeler, Affron found it very moving to see them together again in the 1946 film. Although this seems unlikely, Lionel reportedly consented to director King Vidor's request that his character fall from his horse, get entangled in the reins, and be dragged, bounced, and rolled. This recalls a similar feat in his next important film, *Key Largo*, in which Lionel's enraged character rises from his wheelchair and stumbles toward the evildoer. Lionel insisted on swinging at his taunting enemy, Edward G. Robinson, and falling to the ground. As a contemporary account told the story, "His body turned completely around and dropped to the floor. There was a moment of anguished silence. Then, instinctively, Robinson leaned down to help him up. 'Stop it, you fool!' yelped Barrymore. 'You've ruined the take.' He had. They had to shoot it three times. And everyone but Lionel had the screaming meemies by the time they finished." Here we see, not only Lionel's professionalism, his willingness to do whatever a role required, but also his determined refusal of the pity with which good-hearted people often burden others with disabilities. His late-life interviewer Daniel Blum noted on Lionel's questionnaire that he "dislikes sympathy." *Variety*, possibly referring to this episode, misreported that Lionel "fell out of his wheelchair during a scene in *Key Largo* and sustained bruises."[9]

Key Largo seems to have been a happy set for its stars, even if its production marked John Huston's angry departure from Warner Brothers. Huston was unhappy because the studio had refused his project of filming Eugene O'Neill's *A Moon for the Misbegotten*. Nonetheless, Huston later emphasized how much he had enjoyed working with Lionel and even recalled Lionel's claim that his brother Jack's troubles had begun when Jack brought back an Alaskan totem pole and disrespectfully erected it in his garden. Edward G. Robinson, so vividly ungentlemanly as Johnny Rocco, remembered Bogart's gentlemanly deference to him, despite Robinson's second billing. Bogart would routinely inquire as to whether Robinson was ready for a take and then escort him to the set. Robinson stressed his and Bogart's respect for Lionel: "Lionel Barrymore was in the picture, and we both gave *him* the deference he deserved." Lauren Bacall similarly recalled her husband's and her own esteem for Lionel. "Bogie enjoyed the company of all those actors so much," she remembered. "Lionel Barrymore, you know, and Claire [Trevor]." About Lionel, Bacall stressed, "I adored him. He was wonderful—*wonderful* . . . so thoughtful, so kind." She perceived his constant physical discomfort manifested in his constant but unconscious moans: "Lionel pretended to be a grouch who needed no one. . . . His legs pained him almost unceasingly." An enthusiastic attendant at Bacall's daily serving of tea and cookies in her dressing room, Lionel always expressed anxiety that there might not be any cookies left for him. Ardent Democrat Bacall amusedly recounted the story that Huston filmed a scene, later cut, that required Lionel to praise Franklin Delano Roosevelt. Although Lionel gritted his teeth, he complied—a true manifestation of the actor's art! Claire Trevor was grateful for Lionel's encouragement when she had to sing *Moanin' Low* without the rehearsal Huston had misled her to expect.[10]

Lionel's last major film appearance was in Henry Hathaway's *Down to the Sea in Ships*, a revived prewar project that, in its current state, had previously envisioned Tyrone Power as the lead in a remake of a popular silent film. (Twentieth Century–Fox in 1942 had sent a camera crew to the Antarctic to film whaling expeditions.) This postwar production was troubled by Hathaway's unhappiness with the casting by producer Darryl F. Zanuck of Richard Widmark in the other major adult role. Both producer and actor wanted to variegate Widmark's villainous image by adding to his résumé the part of the upstanding first mate to Lionel's sea captain. Even so, the premiere of *Down to the Sea in Ships* in New York's Roxy Theatre and the movie's associated publicity still featured Widmark as the wicked Tommy Udo of *Kiss of Death*. Lionel at first only added to Hathaway's frustrations. According to a contemporary account, "he forgot the lines, muffed the lines, blew up on the lines, stumbled over the lines" for two days. Out of condition and somnolent during the earlier weeks of the shoot, Lionel then absented himself for two weeks to divest himself of some excess weight, and he returned to the set invigorated and better prepared: "Scenes that had formerly been exercises in elocution suddenly took on atomic force." Taking off some weight also made Lionel more mobile; he disclosed to a reporter that his physician recommended a leather girdle: "if he can just get up enough gumption to wear the thing." After the film's release, Lionel apologized to Hathaway: "I know the grief I caused you. I wish we could do it again and it might be a different story." In later years, Lionel often visited Hathaway, seemingly to discuss the improbable filming of Lionel's vivid but eccentric novel *Mr. Cantonwine* but more probably (according to Hathaway) to ease Lionel's loneliness.[11]

Other people besides Hathaway may have perceived Lionel as a lonely man (one article's headline even called him "the loneliest man in America"), but this judgment seems to misunderstand his introversion as well as to discount the many warm remembrances of him by his friends. He himself scoffed at the notion that he was lonely: "Don't listen to that! I have my own way of being happy. I have my own friends. If my way and those friends happen to be a little different . . ., that still doesn't alter the fact that I'm happy." The late-life questionnaire that Lionel filled out contains these annotations

The Best Wine for Last, 1945-1953

by his interviewer, Daniel Blum: "he appears gruff and hard but he really is a gentle and kindly man—soft under the surface ... a quiet man—prefers solitude." Gene Fowler recorded his opinion that Lionel was "a great person and my friend." Lionel's physician described him as "a cultured personality with the rare gifts of simplicity, humility and naiveté." Besides friendship, he offered encouragement to other actors, such as James Stewart and Claire Trevor, as well as his example as a great performer. Gregory Peck remembered Lionel's professionalism from the shooting of *The Valley of Decision*: "he delivered a tirade to striking steelworkers. The minute we started filming that scene at 8:30 in the morning, Lionel gave it everything he had. He was going all out in the long shots and in the crowd-reaction shots when the camera wasn't even on him. Finally, the director, Tay Garnett, said, 'Lionel, I may not get to your close-ups until late this afternoon. Take it easy. You'll give yourself a heart attack.' And Lionel looked up from his wheelchair and snarled, 'Well, who gives a goddamn?' Because he was loving going all out; he was loving giving a bravura performance. Nothing could hold him back. You can't not learn from old pros like that!" Peck also recalled the importance to his own career of observing Lionel, Lillian Gish, and Walter Huston during the protracted shooting of *Duel in the Sun*: "In the end, [Peck] says, he always followed the philosophy he had learned from such old-timers . . .: 'Be prepared and get on with it.'" This example could be both inspirational and daunting. Stewart commented on acting with Lionel: "I go charging into a scene with Barrymore, get my ears pinned back, the scene stolen right out of my hand. Then I wonder if, in arguing that I'll be a whiz of an actor by eighty, if I'm giving myself enough time."[12]

Lionel discussed none of these last major roles in *We Barrymores*, but he did devote a few pages to a now-forgotten film in which he did not appear, *The Beginning or the End*. After testing successfully for the role of Franklin Delano Roosevelt in this movie about the atomic bomb, Lionel had already acted in some scenes when Eleanor Roosevelt discovered his casting as her late husband. The Roosevelt family then made its displeasure known, creating what Bob Considine called "the oddest political squabble to ever hit this or any other drama mecca." At MGM's invitation, James Roosevelt and two other family members viewed Lionel's scenes; James Roosevelt then suggested that a personal letter to his mother might change her mind, Lionel wrote it, and Loew's executive Nick Schenck delivered it in person. Although Lionel's conciliatory letter had tried to mollify Eleanor Roosevelt by disavowing personal hostility to the man he was portraying, it failed to sway her.

Contemporary accounts seemed to suggest a division between James Roosevelt and his mother on the issue. Asked if Lionel's opposition to FDR's fourth term motivated the family's displeasure, James Roosevelt in Beverly Hills redirected the reporter to Eleanor Roosevelt in New York. Hedda Hopper went so far as to characterize the family drama as Eleanor's "sternly" vetoing permission to cast Lionel that James already had granted. MGM removed Lionel from the movie's cast. (Raymond Massey was considered after Lionel's removal; then Godfrey Tearle was chosen to replace Lionel. Not only did Lionel's scenes need to be reshot, but Harry S. Truman later asked that scenes depicting Truman be reshot to convey his "long deliberation and mental anguish" before deciding to drop the bombs on Japan.) Attempting to excavate and then bury this controversy graciously, Lionel's account noted that he had indeed spoken against Roosevelt's reelection in 1944 at a Los Angeles rally. He admitted that, during this Republican demonstration of support for New York governor Thomas E. Dewey, he probably had used powerful and colorful language to express his opposition to FDR. Yet he countered these admissions by asserting that, despite deep political disagreement, he admired President Roosevelt as a man and even wished that he had known him personally. He then exculpated Eleanor Roosevelt from blame by praising her loyalty to her spouse even if she was mistaken in Lionel as a guilty target for her wrath.[13]

Lionel, in this apologia, also included a passing reference to Roosevelt ally Harold Ickes as a vigorous slinger of mud from Eleanor's own battlements. Westbrook Pegler had reported that Ickes, during a radio address after the Dewey rally, had mocked Lionel's support for Dewey from a wheelchair. This mean-spirited ridicule will not surprise anyone who has dealt with her or his own disability or that of a loved person, but surely the insult was rich, coming from the partisan of a president who himself used a wheelchair. After Pegler stressed this incongruity, he went on to comment that "all men and women above that ethical sub-stratum which may be termed the Ickes level instinctively forebear to mock the lame or halt or blind for their impairments. . . . This leering was authentic Ickes humor." According to Pegler, Gene Fowler, on hearing Ickes express these sentiments, said to his pal W. C. Fields, "If this fellow keeps on talking, Dewey is going to lick Roosevelt with the jawbone of an ass." In a further show of intemperate rhetoric, Harold Ickes also had called Dewey "a miniature fascist." Thanking Hedda Hopper in a letter for an on-air tribute to himself on October 16, 1944, Lionel jokingly described himself, "I am, bar Ickes, the meanest old bastard that ever lived."[14]

The Best Wine for Last, 1945-1953

Although Lionel's autobiography did not discuss his political views at great length, it made clear his opposition to the policies of FDR as embodied in the New Deal and to those of Harry S. Truman and his Fair Deal. (Louis B. Mayer, a friend of Herbert Hoover, had orchestrated the 1932 Republican convention that renominated Hoover and sent Ethel and Lionel to Hoover rallies. During the twenties and thirties, Mayer had sponsored visits by prominent politicians to the MGM studio for luncheon conversations with the stars, including Lionel.) Well aware of his own monetary ineptitude, Lionel joked that Truman ought to turn to him as an experienced advisor on unhealthy budgets. Pessimistic about the present and future of free enterprise under these presidential caretakers, Lionel traced the trouble back further, to 1913 and the imposition of a federal income tax by constitutional amendment. Strangling taxes would doom economic freedom and initiative. These comments seem to indicate that Lionel's permanent submersion in an income tax bog had opened his ears to the anti-Sixteenth Amendment views espoused by Frank Chodorov or similar proto-libertarian thinkers. According to Richard Hofstadter, the right wing deplored what it characterized as attempts "to undermine free capitalism, to bring the economy under the direction of the federal government, and to pave the way for socialism or communism.... Many would agree with Frank Chodorov, the author of *The Income Tax: The Root of All Evil*, that this campaign began with the passage of the income tax amendment to the Constitution in 1913." Advocating repeal of the Sixteenth Amendment, Chodorov denounced it as beginning a war against individualism and freedom. Although *The Income Tax: The Root of All Evil* did not appear until 1954, Chodorov had been sharing his views for some years. Apparently, when speaking for Dewey, Lionel was angry about FDR's position about the graduated income tax.[15]

If Lionel by 1944 held what we would now term libertarian views, he could not have taken much encouragement from the Republican Party platform of 1944 nor from the positions of Governor Dewey as the Republican presidential candidate. Lionel burst out with exclamations that Election Day would be "the day we are liberated from the New Deal." An advertisement signed by Lionel expressed these contradictions, with Lionel's cry for liberation from the New Deal just below the central statement's paragraph "We acknowledge and endorse the progress made in social legislation in the past decade and believe that it is essential that it be extended and better administered." Winning the election clearly would require soft-pedaling doctrinal objections to federal government interference and instead promising a more effective and efficient delivery of government programs. It would require hopping into bed with newfound friends with benefits, such as organized labor. Mocking this expediency, FDR laughed about how the devisers of the 1944 GOP platform would "discover that they really love labor and that they are anxious to protect labor from its own friends." The *St. Louis Post-Dispatch* would criticize the Republicans for having "little to offer except an acceptance of the New Deal philosophy and the promise 'we can do it better.'" Yet the GOP was hopeful that the 1944 election could put paid to the presidential run of FDR. The Democrats had not done well in the 1942 midterm elections; FDR did not announce his own intentions for quite a while; the Democratic Party was in its customary state of disarray; and Dewey enjoyed a stellar reputation as a prosecutor of racketeers. To the Democratic argument that the voters should not change horses in midstream, California governor Earl Warren replied in the GOP convention keynote address, "For eleven long years we have been in the middle of the stream. We are not amphibious. We want to get across. We want to feel dry and solid ground under our feet again."

At a meeting at the home of David O. Selznick to organize Hollywood for Dewey, Lionel was elected chairman, and Ginger Rogers was elected vice-chairman. Although Lionel never starred with Rogers in a movie, she was married to Lew Ayres during most of his work with Lionel in the *Dr. Kildare* film series. Cecil B. DeMille oversaw the planning for the Dewey rally on September 22 in the Los Angeles Coliseum, Selznick chaired the steering committee, and Adolphe Menjou ran the finance committee. DeMille and Selznick had served as California delegates to the Republican National Convention that nominated Dewey. Edward Arnold's two-page, single-spaced statement enunciated the group's credo that "the America we love is being seriously jeopardized by the New Deal and the philosophy of the indispensible [sic] man," and Lionel himself declared that "we want to make November 7 our American D-Day: Dewey Day." DeMille in October would continue to invoke freedom from oppression by tastelessly comparing 1944 Republicans to George Washington's barefoot soldiers bleeding in the snow: "We are at Valley Forge again in our history." On September 22, before the rally, Dewey conferred with DeMille, Walt Disney, Arnold, and George Murphy (the current president of the Screen Actors Guild) and then enjoyed a reception hosted by Selznick at the Ambassador Hotel. Lillian Gish was among many Hollywood celebrities present at this tea. Other guests invited to the reception included Joan Blondell, Irene Dunne, Ruth Hussey, Hedda Hopper,

The Best Wine for Last, 1945–1953

Norma Shearer, Barbara Stanwyck, Gene Tierney, Claire Trevor, and Jeanette MacDonald. The Coliseum crowds included ninety-three thousand spectators who assembled to glimpse Don Ameche, George Burns and Gracie Allen, Gary Cooper, Irene Dunne, Clark Gable, Cary Grant, Fred MacMurray, George Murphy, Raymond Massey, Adolphe Menjou, Ray Milland, William Powell, Ginger Rogers, and Barbara Stanwyck. Ethel did not like Dewey, so she declared her allegiance to FDR in answer to a newspaper reporter's question, which outraged the staunchly Republican Alice Roosevelt Longworth. Longtime friends, Alice and Ethel very soon made up. Although the *Los Angeles Times* reported that the Coliseum crowd gave Lionel "an impressive reception" as Lionel claimed that Dewey's was "the voice of America," *Time* denied that Lionel was even there. The typed program in DeMille's archives does include Lionel as one of the presenters in the 7:30 to 7:44 p.m. time slot. Regardless of whether he actually spoke at the Coliseum rally, Lionel participated in radio appeals for Dewey as Election Day approached. He and Ginger Rogers also sent telegrams about a mass meeting of Hollywood for Dewey workers at the Beverly Wilshire Hotel on October 5 to plan strategy and assess prospects. It is unfortunate that Lionel's support of FDR's opponent embittered Eleanor Roosevelt into forbidding what might have been a fascinating impersonation. Yet her veto of his appearance as her late husband in *The Beginning or the End* was consistent with her self-proclaimed credo, "I forgive but I *never* forget."[16]

13

Compensations, 1937–1954

Two stars on the Hollywood Walk of Fame honor Lionel: one for movie acting and one for radio acting. In addition, he was inducted into the American Theater Hall of Fame. Yet more than likely, Lionel prized above his acting honors his being elected to the American Society of Etchers and to the American Society of Composers, Authors, and Publishers. Besides his etchings and engravings, as well as his many musical compositions that won him these memberships, Lionel wrote (with Cameron Shipp) his engaging memoir, *We Barrymores*, as well as a published novel, *Mr. Cantonwine*, and other unpublished fiction, *The Shakespeare Club*. His nonfiction pieces are also notable. Lionel's avocational pursuits of art, music, and writing satisfied his deepest creative impulses and gave him joy that offset his permanent grief over the loss of his wives and daughters and perhaps distracted him from his chronic physical pain.

After the year of catastrophe, 1936, Lionel sought refuge with members of Irene's family, the Wheelers, a mother and her three daughters, related to Irene on their father's side. While Irene still lived and endured periodic illness, the Wheelers had helped Lionel cope, and they had been present when Irene died suddenly. Keeping his Beverly Hills home with Irene on Roxbury Drive as a shrine that he visited at intervals but never lived in again, Lionel moved in with Mary Ellen Wheeler, as well as with Florence, Violet (called Benson), and Murdie, at their Pacific Palisades residence. A registered nurse (as was Murdie), Florence had also worked for Lionel as his secretary. In the spring of 1939, Lionel, Mary Ellen, Florence, and Benson moved to a twenty-two-acre San Fernando Valley ranch at 11050 Independence Avenue, Sycamore Woods, in the Browns Canyon area of Chatsworth. Murdie Wheeler and her husband, Stanley Campbell, lived close by in Studio City. A makeup artist for Lionel and Jack at MGM, Campbell also worked as Lionel's driver and served as one of Jack's pallbearers. (Other Chatsworth residents at

Compensations, 1937–1954

various times included Mae Marsh, Lucille Ball, Desi Arnaz, Roy Rogers, Dale Evans, Veronica Lake, and Barbara Stanwyck.) Lionel's crescent-shaped, rambling house encircled a giant sycamore tree on three sides. To minimize his chronic tax problems, Lionel had bought the farm acreage in 1938 but put the property in the Wheelers' names. There, he lived with his new family, as well as well-beloved cats and dogs; he raised razor-backed hogs and cultivated roses, orange trees, and Indian corn. The hogs' job description was to unearth rattlesnakes. A late-life letter mentioned Lionel's love for his roses, but he withheld praise from his gardener: "I thought for several days that he was a statue—but he scratched his ear this morning, so I realized that he is the gardener." Neighboring farmers once rescued him when his car sank into floodwaters: "Barrymore was in a dangerous spot a while back, and it wasn't one of those things that are part of a scenario, when the actor knows he'll be rescued. Driving home, he miscalculated the depth of flood water near his ranch, and found himself sitting in his stalled car in water up to his neck. The swift current started moving the car toward deeper water. But neighboring farmers came along with chains and hauled the car back onto the highway. The car was ruined, but the famous Barrymore wasn't damaged."[1]

The Wheelers displaced the Barrymores in Lionel's emotional life. In his later life, Lionel seems to have kept his distance from his birth family and their descendants. Perhaps, over the years, Lionel had become tired of the Barrymores' personal dramas. He may have preferred the Wheelers, not for the sinister or salacious reasons others hinted at, but because he felt more at home with them and more cared about. Jack's three children may have reminded Lionel too painfully of his lost brother, and Lionel and Ethel seem to have fallen out at times in later life. (At the end of her memoirs, Ethel noted the news of Lionel's unexpected death, and she expressed the hope that, after her own death, her brothers would welcome her spirit. Her tone seems rather tentative.) Her daughter, Ethel Barrymore Colt, once characterized Lionel as a "misanthrope" who had "very few human contacts," surely more an expression of Barrymore family resentment than any accurate depiction of her uncle. In contrast, Ethel Colt's cousin John Barrymore called their Uncle Lionel "the sweetest man who ever lived." A less troubled family from whom Lionel actually may have received more emotional sustenance, the Wheelers were also Irene's relatives, which was another attraction. Perhaps revealingly, Gene Fowler did comment in a handwritten note that "L.'s nurse looks like I[rene] except for [Irene's] red hair—Wears furs and jewels also keeps thin like I[rene]." Red-headed Irene lookalike Florence Wheeler eventually became Lionel's sole heir. One news item about Lionel's will mentioned the hope that his small estate of $25,000 would be balanced by royalties from his books and his artwork; another account mentioned royalties from Lionel's music. Reportedly, Florence Wheeler did not benefit from these bequests because of the Internal Revenue Service's prior claims against Lionel's estate, but the Wheelers did continue to live for many years in the Independence Avenue home. Five years after Lionel's death, Benson Wheeler dedicated a children's book to him; illustrated by Lionel, *I, Becky Barrymore* portrayed him affectionately as a protector and cherisher of cats.[2]

Lionel's lifelong interest in visual art had led him from the paintings and illustrations created in his youth in New York and Paris to his later interest in etchings. To design his dry-point etchings, he used tools to engrave lines on copper. "A fellow [who is] etching has to cut every line slowly with painstaking exactness—or he'll lose a plate," he explained. "It's a lot like etching—acting is. In both cases, you create a picture, on copper with tools, in a characterization by words, gestures, and adherence to the character you are playing. . . . You have to study the character saying the lines, then rehearse them to yourself, work out every gesture, every piece of business, until all are perfectly timed." As early as 1933, as a feature on William Haines's home decoration business explained, Lionel both collected and made etchings. To complement Haines's decorative placement of his bamboo-framed etchings, Lionel painted a screen copied from a six-hundred-year-old original that he carefully researched in order to enhance his copy's fidelity. Haines praised Lionel's "great courtesy, appreciation and taste . . . generosity and simplicity of spirit" and remarked that he was "very sweet to work with." Azusa Pacific University's "Barrymore Collection" includes sixteen of Lionel's etchings. Artnet lists the following institutions as holding some of Lionel's artwork: the Carnegie Museum of Art in Pittsburgh, the Metropolitan Museum of Art in New York, and the Walker Art Center in Minneapolis. Other owners are the Phoenix Art Museum, the Delaware Art Museum, and the University of Wyoming Art Museum. During his lifetime, New York City's Milch Gallery and Dallas's Print Center showed some of his artwork. The *New York World Telegraph* review of Lionel's four etchings at the Milch Gallery show described them as "commendable if unpretentious . . . well-drawn, decorative renderings of picturesque locales, done with no provocative originality of design, texture or linear pattern, but nevertheless possessing a definite, rather romantic charm." Lionel became a member of the Society of American Etchers, which in 1938 selected his *Boatyard in Venice* as one of its

Compensations, 1937–1954

Hundred Prints of the Year; the society also exhibited his etching *San Pedro*. Rex Rivolo of Roving Sands Fine Arts has commented, "He was very proud of his etchings, rightly so, as he was a master at it. In all the films he acted in, he demanded that the director/producer include some of his etchings in the scenery. If you watch his films, you will always see in an interior scene his etchings on the wall. I love his work, but his prints don't come up often at auction. I have only one, *Shoreside Farm*." Attentive viewers of the Dr. Gillespie series can detect an etching press in the master diagnostician's office. Twenty years after Lionel's death, his niece Ethel Barrymore Colt exhibited some of his work in a show based on the memorabilia collection of her cousin John Drew Devereux. Colt deplored the mass reproduction of Lionel's artwork: "Reproductions of those things are a dime a dozen. Not that his paintings weren't lovely, but some foundation or charity now gives them out on gold foil if you donate a dollar to their cause. They look so tacky on that foil."[3]

A late-life encounter demonstrated Lionel's enjoyment both of painting and of other people's appreciation of his talents as a visual artist. The Keystone Literary Club of Rock Hill, South Carolina, had created for its members a project focused on "Great Families." Choosing the Barrymores, Eva Moore White, a retired English teacher, wrote to Lionel for information. He responded with a personal letter and a telegram. Keystone Literary Club members then inundated Lionel with hundreds of seventy-fifth birthday greetings. Touched by their remembrance, Lionel answered most of the messages with personal notes ("I do want all you folks to know that it has made me very happy that you have wished me well on the threshold of the last quarter of a Century of life!") and also sent to Rock Hill's mayor a gift to the city: a watercolor painting he called *Holiday Time in the South*. "It is the first time in my experience that a city has taken me to its ever-loving heart," he explained. "And I am proud indeed of the honor." Lionel's painting was displayed at the city's public library from 1953 to 2007. More birthday greetings followed in 1954. As Lionel wrote to the town librarian, "I think it so very nice of the folks in Rock Hill to have taken me to their hearts as they have done. . . . I have done nothing to deserve their wonderful loyalty, but I love it and them." When he died in 1954, the *Evening Herald*'s obituary commented that he was "almost the patron saint of the Keystone Club which 'adopted' him nearly two years ago" and reported that "Mrs. White said that his wire of felicitation to the club threw club members into a swoon similar to that of a teenager over Perry Como."[4]

LIONEL BARRYMORE

Like Lionel's passion for visual art, his interest in music was of long standing. He recalled first enjoying Bach's music at the home of one of his father's acquaintances. "I didn't have to acquire a taste for Bach or other fine music any more than I had to acquire a taste for plum jam," Lionel explained. "But [my host's] personal enthusiasm for Bach made me glad that my musical perceptions were accurate." Deciding to learn how to play the piano so that he could play Bach, the eighteen-year-old had then studied with teacher Agnes Morgan for several years. This led to further studies in composition with Henry Hadley. *Pacific Coast Musician* noted in 1946 that Hadley had "held out hope for the young matinee idol to become an important composer.... [Lionel] never let go of his desire to compose music.... He composes music that satisfies him as being sound and of good workmanship simply because he loves doing it."

Lionel's MGM dressing room included a studio where he could create copperplate etchings and play his piano and compose music. Formerly a loft situated over a sound stage, this isolated haven also served as a perch within which to review movie scripts. Disguised by a screen was a jumble of papers, wardrobe miscellany, and artistic detritus. One interviewer described Lionel's dressing room thus: "A slanting skylight floods the room with a steady north light. A long pine table is littered with sketches, on the wall beyond are etchings and on another wall oil paintings—all done by the actor. In one corner is an easel, paints and brushes. A piano is on the opposite side of the room. No trace of lighted dressing table or make-up box—they're in another room, a very small one.... You can't help thinking, 'This doesn't suggest an actor.'" As he experienced increased difficulties with mobility, these furnishings were moved to the ground floor of his Chatsworth home.

Instead of frequenting Hollywood night spots on the way home from the studio, Lionel at one time would drop by a Sunset Boulevard hot dog stand almost every night to chat about music with the owner, a former musician. In the early forties, he started to invest more energy and time on musical composition than on painting or etching. Recently emigrated from Hungary, composer and orchestrator Eugene Zádor first met Lionel in 1940 at MGM. Calling Lionel "the most remarkable" person he encountered in Hollywood, Zádor described him as "above all, in his last years, a passionate amateur musician." By Zádor's count, Lionel studied music with him for a decade, for five days per week, for four or five hours each day. Besides the intense joy that Lionel experienced from music, "the fascination of music distracted him from pain and worry and eased the necessity of medication." An adorer of

Compensations, 1937–1954

Brahms, a hater of the later Schoenberg, Lionel collected thousands of records and remembered music so vividly that he could accurately name a composer after hearing two bars. Nevertheless, Lionel reinforced his modesty about his musical accomplishments by joking "about what would happen if any of my music came to the attention of Brahms in a bad mood."

When the Japanese Broadcasting Company in 1952 aired a performance by singers of the Tokyo Broadcasting chorus and musicians of the Tokyo Philharmonic orchestra of Zádor's opera *Christopher Columbus*, Lionel narrated the program. A "highly talented amateur professional," according to Zádor, Lionel enjoyed having some of his own compositions played by orchestras. In 1940, the Los Angeles WPA Symphony Orchestra conducted by James Sample presented his symphonic suite *Tableau Russe*, as the San Francisco Symphony Orchestra led by Pierre Monteux did later. In 1944, the Philadelphia Orchestra under Eugene Ormandy performed *In Memoriam*, Lionel's tribute to Jack, and CBS Radio broadcast it nationwide. Also in 1944, Fabien Sevitzky twice conducted Lionel's *Partita*—first with the Indianapolis Symphony Orchestra and later with the New York Philharmonic. Sevitzky also conducted Lionel's *Preludium and Fugue* in 1944 and a piano concerto in 1946. George Szell of the Metropolitan Opera in 1944 conducted the Cleveland Symphony Orchestra in renditions of Lionel's *Fugue Fantasia*; also in 1944, Vladimir Bakaleinikoff led the Pittsburgh Symphony Orchestra in Lionel's *Valse Fantasia*. The 1946 nationwide broadcast of *Partita* by the New York Philharmonic under Artur Rodzinski inspired an overwhelmed Lionel to imbibe a full bottle of sherry. Acknowledging the outstanding success of Lionel's appeal to the general public to support the New York Philharmonic, a 1945 letter to Rodzinski from orchestra management had gingerly begged Rodzinski to conduct *Partita* as a thank-you to Lionel: "If this will hurt your artistic feelings, let the matter drop right now, but if you can do it, you will oblige us tremendously." "More than delighted," Rodzinski assented and even (after talking with Sevitzky) suggested performing a newer composition by Lionel. Besides making a new appeal to the public to support the orchestra in 1946, Lionel revised *Partita* for this performance and expressed confidence that any further changes Rodzinski added would only improve it. The Burbank Symphony Orchestra under Leo Damiani in 1947 performed Lionel's *Halloween* ("written after a story told to Mr. Barrymore by Miss Florence Wheeler") and in 1949 performed Lionel's *Opera Buffa*. The collection of Lionel Barrymore's musical manuscripts held by the University of California at Los Angeles Special Collections Library consists of thirteen boxes containing fugues, works for orchestra and solo, orchestral works, solo pieces, and miscellaneous compositions. A colleague of Zádor, Mario Castelnuovo-Tedesco, assessed Lionel as a man "who possessed a certain musical culture, and studied music seriously . . . a refined and cultured spirit . . . a courtly person and a true artist. . . . He had a curious fascination for Russian music and had memorized Tchaikovsky's entire thematic catalogue."[5]

One consequence of Lionel's intense passion for great music was his invitation to German composer Richard Strauss to live in the Roxbury Drive home that Lionel had once shared with Irene and had maintained for many years as a shrine to her memory. Feeling guilty about owning an unoccupied house during a postwar housing shortage, Lionel offered his old residence as a haven in the United States to Strauss, who reserved berths on the *Queen Mary* for himself and his wife and asked Lionel for help with the affidavits to the American consul in Switzerland that obtaining a visa for Strauss would require. However, Lionel's attorney believed the allegations about Strauss's Nazi sympathies (allegations that Lionel had never heard) and warned him off. Despite all of Lionel's efforts to retrieve the situation, he was forced by disapproval to withdraw his invitation. Strauss responded to Lionel's reluctant withdrawal with sadness and understanding in a reply that Lionel found courteous. Writing from his hotel in Switzerland on January 1, 1947, Strauss adamantly denied any membership in, sympathy with, or propaganda for the Nazi Party, asserted that the Nazis had treated him with hostility and harassment, and even mentioned his letter to Stefan Zweig that the Gestapo had intercepted and denounced. Strauss then expressed his gratitude to Lionel for the kind offer of a place to live. According to one later account,

> [Strauss] certainly had many strikes against him when it came to accusations of collaboration. . . . Nonetheless, he also suffered increasingly at the hands of the Nazis. This suffering was not only professional but also personal. Strauss's daughter-in-law Alice was Jewish, as were (according to Nazi racial law) his grandchildren. He was able to use personal connections to prevent his family from the full force of harassment during Kristallnacht in November 1938, and in 1942, he moved with them to Vienna, where they benefited from the protection of Hitler Youth leader and Vienna Gauleiter Baldur von Schirach. Toward the end of the war, however, while Strauss was away, Nazis arrested Alice and held her for several days; Strauss was barely able to secure her release, moving her and

Compensations, 1937–1954

the family to Garmisch, where they were kept under house arrest until the War's end. In addition, many members of Alice's immediate family were deported to Theresienstadt. When Strauss's letters asking for their release were unsuccessful, the composer drove to the camp personally, but to no avail; all died or were murdered, in Theresienstadt and other camps. Richard Strauss died on 8 September 1949, absolved of any Nazi affiliations.

Strauss and Lionel both expressed the opinion that politics has no place in the great arts.[6]

Besides creating music and visual art, Lionel also explored the literary genres of the play, the novel, and the memoir. Early in his life, Lionel had worked as a newspaper reporter for the *New York Telegraph*, whose city editor had deflated his writing ambitions: "I would go out to cover a big fire in Brooklyn and come back and write a big story. Two lines would turn up in the paper. Then I'd cover a murder in the Bronx, and I'd expect at least a column. The paper would carry two paragraphs. I hated that city editor's guts." Not permanently deterred from realizing his literary dreams, in the early forties, for example, he collaborated with old acquaintance Anita Loos on *Old Buddha*, a play for his sister about a Chinese empress and her dentist; regrettably, this irresistible subject never made it to actual performance. *Old Buddha* was pitched as a vehicle for Ethel in 1943. Apparently a long-standing enthusiasm for Lionel, *Old Buddha* in an earlier form cowritten with K. Schmidt had been copyrighted in 1928 as a two-act play. A script described as from the 1930s—perhaps the collaboration with Schmidt or a revision of it—turned up among the many items from Debbie Reynolds's collection of Hollywood artifacts auctioned after her death. Producer Arthur Hopkins did accept the forties version by Loos in which the empress plans to reward the dentist for any failure to relieve her toothache with her specialty, poisoned apricot cream, but Ethel passed on the project, and eventually Hopkins dropped it. Regarding *Mr. Cantonwine*, Lionel's allegorical fiction about the troubles of Uncle Sam, the *New York Times* reviewer admitted its oddity but graciously allowed that "this unusual book has added literary laurels to one of the nat[i]on's favorite Thespians." More openly baffled, the *Chicago Tribune* reviewer called *Mr. Cantonwine* "strange," yet recorded some astute perceptions: he noticed that it is anti-realistic, formal, well-unified in its tone, offbeat, yet winning to the receptive reader. The Washington *Evening Star* found the novel "diverting," "quaint," and "archaic." Abraham Lincoln is central to the narrative, for Mr. Cantonwine prevents the anguished young Lincoln from killing himself over the death of his sweetheart. Indeed, the novel showcases Lionel's long interest in American history and especially in the Civil War, a preoccupation that dated back at least to his playing Milt Shanks in *The Copperhead*. He, of course, played Andrew Jackson twice, in *The Gorgeous Hussy* and in *Lone Star*, and he impersonated Thaddeus Stevens in *Tennessee Johnson*. Lionel told Bob Thomas that, many years before, his ideas for this novel had failed to attract the interest of Zoe Akins and Edgar Lee Masters, but then Cameron Shipp, his collaborator on his memoir, had encouraged him to complete *Mr. Cantonwine*. Lionel forged ahead, armed with "a chewed-up pencil." After its publication, Lionel composed the unpublished "novel" *The Shakespeare Club*, a hodgepodge of his historical knowledge and real-life anecdotes gathered from his varied experiences of the stage and screen. In addition, in his final years, he reportedly was working on a history of the theater and/or a book about the motion picture industry called *The Passion Flower*. Both of these projects possibly are garbled recollections by others of Lionel's descriptions of *The Shakespeare Club*, but Lionel did report to the Rock Hill, South Carolina, librarian in 1954 that "I am writing a book with a theatrical background not reminiscing really."

Although Lionel participated less enthusiastically in the creation of his memoir than in his other literary projects, *We Barrymores* stands on its own as an engaging ramble through Lionel's past with dutiful stops to recount some theatrical and cinematic milestones punctuated with much more lively accounts of his artistic and musical enthusiasms. As Shipp amusedly remembered, *We Barrymores* "got done, begrudgingly, between snatches about Ludwig von Beethoven, James McNeill Whistler, a confusion of baseball players and prize fighters (he knew them all), and a number of current enthusiasms, including Lucille Ball and the dog Lassie." For weeks, he evaded painful queries posed by Shipp, especially those concerning Doris Rankin, by proposing that they work together instead on an opera. A long-ago interviewer had noticed Lionel's difficulty with dredging up memories of the past, about which Lionel had explained, "I have always lived in the present; never in the past, nor in the future. What's over is over; and what's to come is to come." Although it dodges and omits, *We Barrymores* is Lionel's most readable literary work, primarily because of its prevailing tone of self-deprecatory humor. Besides much documentation of interest in Ethel's own memoirs from book and serial magazine publishers, the preserved correspondence about Ethel's *Memories* contains some sidelights on *We Barrymores*. Ethel's determination

Compensations, 1937–1954

to write her autobiography by herself created anxiety for the publisher about possibly delayed delivery of her manuscript and precipitated the publisher's suggestions about assistance from a coauthor like Shipp. Trying to discover whether Ethel did intend to commit to compiling her memoirs, *The Ladies Home Journal* shared with Ethel its perceptions of the *We Barrymores* project: "We were able, in conjunction with Cameron Shipp, to persuade your brother Lionel to write his autobiography. . . . As we read it, our admiration—if possible—increased for your brother as an actor and as a man, to say nothing of our admiration for his autobiographical job." The *Saturday Evening Post*, which eventually serialized publication of *We Barrymores* because the *Ladies Home Journal* considered Lionel's memoir more interesting to men, paid $50,000 for the rights to publish installments in six issues. Shipp himself, eventually reviewing Ethel's "delightful" and "charming" *Memories*, noted that one does not advise a Barrymore about how to do something. Shipp emphasized that the various members of the Drew and Barrymore clans "appear briefly off-stage, never front and center": "As Lionel used to tell me, and as Miss Ethel relates here, the Drews and Barrymores were diffident persons who never managed to know their own kin very well. . . . This oddness is itself a fascinating commentary on a fascinating family."[7]

The world did not lose a great composer or a groundbreaking novelist or an innovative painter when Lionel bound himself to MGM for life. Well aware of his limitations, he was grateful for others' appreciation of his efforts and overwhelmed when orchestras presented his compositions. While not works of genius, his music, visual art, and writing were often striking and sometimes original. It is important to recognize both his weaknesses and his strengths because he tended to be very self-deprecatory, and some might dismiss his music and visual art as the work of a mere actor. John Barrymore's biographer Terry Chester Shulman, who began his career by writing about music, asked whether Lionel found his own voice in his musical compositions or merely rewrote works of the great composers whom he loved. Agreeing with orchestral conductor and historical musicologist Bar Haimov that Lionel's music was not original but imitative, Shulman detected strong influence by Russian composers. Haimov noted, "He could imitate any style he set out to re-create—particularly late nineteenth-century Viennese salon music and midthirties to midforties film music, especially that of Korngold. He most definitely was a very skillful composer." Shulman expressed some reservations and qualified praise: "Theme piled on theme, each jamming hard up against each other, some of which are almost good. His orchestral homage to Jack comes the closest to being thematically memorable. Little in the way of nuance, quiet contemplative passages that don't have to roar to get their point across. Most everything is trapped between mezzo forte and fortissimo. A couple of beautiful, sixty-fourth note passages in the concerto, however."[8]

Whether talking about his avocations or his vocation, Lionel habitually, even compulsively, denied his talents, deplored their results, and even stressed his own laziness. One must retort that seldom has an allegedly lazy person accomplished so much. Lionel also groused all of his life about the abhorred necessity of being an actor. There is no doubt that he vastly preferred his cherished avocations of painting, etching, illustrating, composing music, and writing to his necessary vocation of stage and screen acting. To an early interviewer, he explained that he had felt the imperative to choose a path for himself away from the well-trodden roads of family tradition but admitted that "my ambition to be a painter was a great deal like the monkey's ambition to pass for a biped." Acting was a more natural vocation, yet it interested him so little that he barely remembered the roles he had played. In 1943, he shared with a reporter his aspirations for his future: "After this war is over there's going to be a flivver plane you can fly off your back porch and land on the roof. I aim to fly one of 'em. I want to compose a piece of music I can be proud of. There's an etching or two I have in mind. And a lot of just plain living on my farm with my roses, Indian corn and razorback hogs." None of his stated aspirations mentioned acting. He spoke of his music and art as providing a necessary escape from acting. And yet, without the fame and friends that his acting won for him, he likely would not have secured the opportunities to draw, compose, and write that he eventually did. While praise for his art, music, and writing greatly pleased him, he mocked his acting accomplishments. Yet Lionel quoted a private letter by theatrical producer Arthur Hopkins who in 1949 had expressed his view that Lionel was the most gifted and accomplished of character actors. Lionel clearly felt pleased by Hopkins's recognition. Perhaps including Hopkins's praise for his acting in his memoir revealed an awareness, concealed even from himself, that he had excelled as an actor far more than as a practitioner of his other arts. Lionel's compulsive self-deprecatory humor kept insisting that he had failed at art, music, and acting. We know that he in fact excelled at the form of art he least enjoyed. Because he had the conscience of an artist, he acted brilliantly even though he hated acting. Perhaps he hated acting because he felt oppressed by the glories of his family's past, which had convinced him at an early age that he could never measure up. Composing music, creating visual art, and writing—besides Lionel's fiction and nonfiction, Laraine Day remembered that he even wrote poetry—allowed him to express his individuality and escape the straitjacket, his compelled destiny, of being a Great Actor as a member of the Royal Family of Broadway.[9]

14

Down the Valley of the Shadow, 1954

Fatally stricken with heart-related illness at the Chatsworth home that he had shared with the Wheeler mother and daughters for fifteen years, Lionel died at Valley Presbyterian Hospital in Van Nuys, California, on November 15, 1954. While watching television at home with the Wheelers, Lionel had become short of breath, Florence Wheeler and another nurse had helped him to the door for fresh air, but nothing had eased his suffering. As his physician, John Paul Ewing, MD, explained, upon Lionel's arrival at the hospital, he had been placed in an oxygen tent but had lapsed into unconsciousness and failed to respond to treatment. After witnessing Lionel's death in the presence of the Wheelers, Ewing signed the death certificate that listed chronic myocarditis, chronic nephritis, and acute lung edema. Two thousand fans, "a hushed but pushing throng," crowded into his funeral service on November 18 at Calvary Cemetery Mausoleum Chapel: "The onlookers pushed past studio and cemetery aides and overflowed into the massive Spanish-type chapel." Some of his movie industry friends and colleagues in attendance included James Stewart, Red Skelton, Jimmy Durante, Buster Keaton, Lew Ayres, Laraine Day, Gene Fowler, Edward Arnold, and director David Butler. Clark Gable, Francis X. Bushman, Bob Hope, Darryl Zanuck, David O. Selznick, and Louis B. Mayer were honorary pallbearers, as were Dore Schary, Clarence Brown, Frank Capra, Gene Fowler, Spencer Tracy, and the three Schenck brothers. The actual pallbearers were Lionel's old pals. After a requiem Mass at which Reverend John J. Hurley of Our Lady of the Valley Church in Canoga Park officiated, Lionel's remains were interred in a crypt at the side of the chapel near the graves of Irene and Jack, that uneasy triumvirate together again after death.[1]

In a *Hallmark Hall of Fame* radio tribute to Lionel, who had hosted the program since September 1952, Edward Arnold, Helen Hayes, James

Down the Valley of the Shadow, 1954

Stewart, Bing Crosby, Gene Fowler, and Dore Schary spoke, with an additional eulogy by Norman Vincent Peale. Tallulah Bankhead led another radio tribute in which Schary spoke again, as did John Hodiak, reading the words of Gene Fowler. Among the miscellany of memories shared by Fowler were accounts of Lionel's coping with his many bereavements and losses: "With the good manners learned in the Victorian era that have almost disappeared, Lionel met his tragedies without a whimper for the public to hear." He loved children intensely; his daughters' early deaths had turned him to music as a consolation. When, in 1935, Irene underwent surgery, "he seemed like a madman that night." Lionel then said to Fowler, "I feel as if I have dived under a raft and can't come up," and when Irene died in 1936, Lionel "went into a shell"—"a great piece of him died then." A few weeks before Lionel finally collapsed in 1954, he had declared to Fowler, "I don't care to go on any longer."[2]

Many others expressed their high regard for Lionel's character and accomplishments. Some hoped to inherit the types of parts he had made his own. Many years later, Edward Everett Horton confided to another character actor, Hans Conried (who had appeared in *On Borrowed Time*), "Hans, you know when the Old Boy died, I thought I'd inherit his crown and wheelchair, and get all those parts—and a few months later the whole industry died!" With the deaths of Lionel, Lewis Stone, and Wallace Beery, *Image* mourned, "it is quite certain that American films have lost forever a considerable portion of their quality that defined them internationally. The acting career of Lionel Barrymore was prodigious.... Lionel Barrymore acted with an ease and style that completely outclassed many an award winner.... It is extremely doubtful whether widening screens will in any measure make up the loss motion pictures suffered with the departure of the last and most beloved of the old school titans: Lionel Barrymore." Bob Thomas had interviewed Lionel about his seventy-sixth birthday in April; Lionel had then expressed an enthusiastic interest in several offers of television gigs, pending MGM permission. During Hedda Hopper's interview just before Christmas 1953, they had discussed MGM's reluctance to allow Lionel to appear on TV. Seeking to allay his fears that MGM might fire him, Hopper replied, "You'd be snapped up the next day for TV and you'd be wonderful on television.... You'd get the goddamnest best television show anybody ever had. You'd be marvelous." Now that Lionel was gone, Bob Thomas recalled "that exterior toughness [that] was only to hide a soft-hearted gentleman who was sincerely interested in people.... *Lionel carried the secret of his real self to the grave* [italics added].

LIONEL BARRYMORE

But a member of the family once told me of the tragedy of his life.... The family member recalled Lionel's weeping one time as he recalled what might have happened if his daughters had lived.... And no one ever filled the void in his life" after Irene died. Just a few years before, in 1949, the tragedy of Kathy Fiscus had disinterred Lionel's buried grief for his baby girls. In San Marino, the three-year-old ran across a field and fell ninety-five feet into an abandoned well left unused but also unsealed for thirty years. Although Kathy drowned shortly after she entered the fourteen-inch pipe two hundred yards from her home, an intensive search and rescue operation lasting for two days and nights and featuring floods and cave-ins riveted the attention of millions reading their newspapers or following updates on radio or television. Thousands of people congregated nearby: "They couldn't bear to leave, although the estimate [of time until resolution] was wrong again and again. As the rescue operations went on, feverishly reported by radio, more watchers kept arriving to stand in the hot sun and hope. And almost none went away." Jeepers, the child's fox terrier, also kept "dejected and bewildered" watch with the girl's parents. Riveted by the tragic spectacle like millions of other people, Lionel sent a five-foot cross of white sweet peas and white roses to the funeral service in an Alhambra chapel.[3]

Ethel commented in her memoirs, published after Lionel's death, that she believed that a "dark star" had governed the fates of Lionel, Jack, and Ethel herself and deprived all three of any lasting joy. From his neglected childhood onward, through the hated days of stage performances, until the loss of his wives, his daughters, and his brother, as well as of his own health and mobility, Lionel had indeed endured much. As a character in Iris Murdoch's *The Green Knight* says, "The theatre is a tragic place, full of endings and partings and heartbreak. . . . Suddenly it's over, it's perpetual destruction, perpetual divorce, perpetual adieu. . . . It's like falling in love and being smashed over and over again." Lionel's whole life was a study in endurance—both the endurance of pain and grief and the endurance of lasting artistic accomplishment. And yet Lionel's own sense of his achievement always remained very fragile. An uxorious husband, Lionel was devoted to both of his wives; an adorer of little girls, he was devastated by the early deaths of his children. Thwarted in his desire to be a husband and father by the loss of his wives and his young daughters, Lionel found in his artistic avocations—his etchings and engravings, his musical compositions, his writing of fiction—some compensation for his experience of devastating loss. As with his acting, his other artistic pursuits inspired his perfectionism. When his friend

Down the Valley of the Shadow, 1954

and physician, Dr. Kalavros, assured the elderly Lionel, "You have accomplished much; you have done so much. People admire and love you," a tear dropped down Lionel's face as he expressed his perennial sense of inadequacy and failure. After smuggling into his memoir Arthur Hopkins's praise of Lionel as a superlative character actor, Lionel basked for a second in this tribute, then promptly disavowed its truth. Hopkins was far from alone in his high esteem for Lionel's acting. Noting that "Lionel's the real one," Ethel considered Lionel "the genius of the family." Yet, he never thought of himself in that way.[4]

Given Lionel's often-expressed dislike of and contempt for acting, how did he become a great character actor? The answer seems to be that he had an artist's conscience, that he felt the obligation to excel as much as possible as a visual artist, as a musician, as a writer, and *even* as an actor—although it was his least-favored means of expression. Over the decades, his most perceptive interviewers and friends realized that he combined great sensitivity to beauty, much kindness, unusual intelligence, a voracious hunger for knowledge, immense curiosity, and high standards for art as a means to attain and probe the truth of human experience. His perfectionism both helped him achieve a staggering amount of excellent work and prevented him from feeling satisfied with his attainments. Moreover, the star system in which he worked in Hollywood devalued character acting, and the traditions of the theater so important to his family devalued movie acting. As a line in the George S. Kaufman and Edna Ferber satire on the Barrymores, *The Royal Family*, expresses it, "You can't call pictures acting." And of the three Barrymore siblings, only Jack (to his amusement) and Ethel (to her outrage) are depicted in this play. Jack commented, "Ethel never did like the play. Parts of it, she thought, libeled even me. . . . Fredric March made me an utterly worthless, conceited hound, and he had my mannerisms, exaggerated but true to life. . . . 'That's the greatest and funniest performance I ever saw,' I said [to March]." But Lionel is not portrayed in *The Royal Family* at all.[5]

Lionel extended his perfectionism to movie "product" as he fled to Hollywood and analyzed the American film industry's prefabricated, market-tested approach to its stories. "It is an optimistic world that is pictured upon the screen, and one in which success is ever and always the chief consideration," he noted in 1926. "But with the enduring books of the world . . ., and with the literature of retrospection, the screen can do little or nothing. So it seems." Lionel joked, "Directors and producers often feel the necessity of jazzing up a classic. . . . If Nero were to be put upon the screen . . ., it would be necessary to jazz him up a bit." He clearly distinguished between the wonderful medium of film and the often-tawdry use made of its potential. The public, for its part, contributed to the problem as it neglected films of greater worth and import, of higher fidelity to life, like *Abraham Lincoln* or *The Last Laugh*. Popular success translated into monetary profit was the overriding criterion. As the narrator of Saul Bellow's novel *Humboldt's Gift* puts it, "To make capitalists out of artists was a humorous idea of some depth. America decided to test the pretensions of the esthetic by applying the dollar measure."[6]

Two more years in Hollywood deepened Lionel's disappointment as he expressed all the cynicism typical of a jilted romantic. "His opinion of the movies is fifty degrees below zero," revealed Cedric Belfrage. "He doesn't believe they are getting more intelligent. He doesn't believe they ever will. He denies that the public wants good stuff." Hollywood understandably avoided higher-quality product that lost money. Defending Lionel against the charge of ingratitude to the industry, Belfrage asserted, "He has given thought to its artistic problems and found them insoluble." Characterizing Lionel "as one of the world's naturally brilliant men" who does not take seriously either himself as an actor or Hollywood movies as an art form, Belfrage pointed out that, nevertheless, "he never fails to deliver the knockout performance of every picture he plays in. He does it in his sleep." "The first outstanding success of the talkies," asked to comment on the quality of sound pictures, replied, "I doubt if they can be any worse than the silent kind."[7]

His subsequent service to MGM as a film director moderated this criticism of American movies, at least on the surface and in public. Stressing the collaborative nature of film production, Lionel praised the industry for its "concentration on the subject at hand, . . . clarity about what is wanted, and swift efficiency in setting about getting it." Dismissing the scorn expressed for movie acting by theater folk, Lionel argued that stage acting and film acting are essentially unalike and that stage actors could benefit from learning to act in films: bringing valuable skills from the theater, in the movies "they undoubtedly broadened and deepened their all-around artistic and dramatic ability." He emphasized that switching to the movies had given him "an infinitely easier life, in the sense of physical strain, than the theatre."[8]

His conflicts about the stage resolved by his resolute abdication from the Royal Family of the American Theatre, Lionel continued to believe in art as

Down the Valley of the Shadow, 1954

revelatory of deep human truths. His consistent excellence as a film actor demonstrated his personal application of high standards of artistry. Yet this did not diminish his unease with acting as his unchosen vocation, nor did it properly increase his self-awareness of his very real superiority. He also channeled his creativity into his preferred avocations of writing, composing, etching, and painting. Yet even in these more enjoyable pursuits, his perfectionism tormented him with a sense of goals missed and dreams deferred. Admitting in 1941 that "I . . . use music to get away from acting. Sometimes I will sit down at the piano and soon forget my weariness. . . . In studying music and painting, I believe I have made myself a better actor, for all art has common fundamentals." He asserted, "Art is inexhaustible; it leads you on and on. It's a constant challenge." Eugene Zádor commented in 1948, "He is definitely good. He works very hard and very slowly. Time means nothing to him: he goes on until three or four in the morning, working with a piano. He has studied a lot and is never satisfied with what he has done." Lionel's physician in his last years sketched a similar portrait of a greatly gifted, restlessly curious man tortured by his unrelenting perfectionism. Sharing with Dr. Kalavros that he worked very late at night, mostly on his writing, Lionel explained, "A personality must function according to the way it is made. Only then will it be in harmony with itself, the world and the universe." Yet, one day, in frustration, Lionel exclaimed, "Foolishness! What is all this, what's the meaning of all this?" Kalavros tried to comfort him, "You have accomplished much; you have done so much. People admire and love you." "I know, I know but don't you see?" Lionel replied, "I am not better than when I started." His sense of inadequacy had haunted him even during his greatest triumphs, as when, during *The Jest*, he told himself he was sure to be found out at long last as an acting fraud. Lionel openly libeled himself as a fraud on the very first page of his memoirs.[9]

Ironically, when he advised others about the way to create satisfying lives for themselves, Lionel counseled *against* perfectionism. First, he explained the importance of observing the successful lives of others and setting goals: "this is the way a person must plan his life. Adopting, borrowing, and adapting a little here and a little there from his predecessors and his contemporaries, then adding a few touches until he's created himself." Then, he warned, "if you keep aiming at an attainable target, you can always raise your sights on another and more difficult one. But if you start off for the impossible, you're foredoomed to eternal failure." He emphasized, "Don't aim too high for your capacity." Maybe he was unaware of the irony, or maybe he was only too aware of it but simply unable to apply his own advice. As a character in Oscar Wilde's *An Ideal Husband* explains, "I always pass on good advice. It is the only thing to do with it. It is never of any use to oneself."[10]

Lionel stuck a favorite quote from Immanuel Kant into both his odd memoirs and his even odder novel: "Time passeth not, but in it passeth the existence of the mutable." The fascination Lionel felt with this observation by Kant suggests that he experienced strongly the pull of absolute values and ideals, yet he always sensed their distinction from mere earthly life and human effort. Nothing human ever measured up to them. Yet human beings must, Lionel must, go on trying, yet forever failing, to attain beauty, truth, goodness, and integrity: "But if [God] knows I'm weak in flesh and spirit, why does He put obstacles in my way that are unsurmountable? Then I fail, I hurt myself, and at the end He punishes me." Yet he endured, and his achievement endures. As S. J. Perelman wrote in "Moonstruck at Sunset," "immortality is a chancy matter, subject to the caprice of the unborn. Not every notable wins his niche in the hall of fame on precisely the terms he would have chosen."[11]

Gaily bedight,
A gallant knight,
In sunshine and in shadow,
Had journeyed long,
Singing a song,
In search of Eldorado.

But he grew old—
This knight so bold—
And o'er his heart a shadow—
Fell as he found
No spot of ground
That looked like Eldorado.

And, as his strength
Failed him at length,
He met a pilgrim shadow—
"Shadow," said he,
"Where can it be—
This land of Eldorado?"

Down the Valley of the Shadow, 1954

"Over the Mountains
Of the Moon,
Down the Valley of the Shadow,
Ride, boldly ride,"
The shade replied,—
"If you seek for Eldorado!"

—"Eldorado" by Edgar Allan Poe

Acknowledgments

The professional expertise and dedicated service of librarians and archivists, editors and writers, as well as the thoughts of film scholars and enthusiasts, have provided crucial assistance to this enterprise. This is especially true because Lionel Barrymore left no collection of his papers, and the MGM archives are closed to researchers. Veteran biographers Joseph McBride, Carl Rollyson, and Patrick McGilligan served as much-appreciated mentors. Ashley S. Runyon of the University Press of Kentucky gave support and served as a sounding board. Margaret Kelly of the University Press of Kentucky offered ever-prompt help. Ila McEntire and the copyediting team headed by Kousalya Krishnamoorthy provided editorial expertise. Editor of *Illinois Heritage*, William Furry, encouraged the publication of material later used here. Terry Chester Shulman, an esteemed and ever-generous colleague in Barrymore research, was an invaluable fellow researcher and writer without whose friendship this project would have been much less fulfilling.

Genevieve Maxwell, reference librarian, Academy of Motion Picture Arts and Sciences, Margaret Herrick Library, responded patiently and conscientiously to several requests for documentation. Sandra Garcia-Myers, University of Southern California Library, forwarded valuable material. Mary K. Huelsbeck, Wisconsin Center for Film and Theater Research, was always prompt and resourceful. Valerie Yaros, historian/archivist, Screen Actors Guild–American Federation of Television and Radio Artists, generously went out of her way to find sources. Karin Suni and Karen Kirsheman, Free Library of Philadelphia, Theatre Collection, Rare Book Department, were exceptionally thoughtful. The staff members at Brigham Young University Library, L. Tom Perry Special Collections, went out of their way to be extraordinarily helpful: Maren Hatch, Hannah Daines, Haley Nelson, and Kayla Peless. Hannah Daines put forth much-appreciated extra effort to aid me.

Acknowledgments

Angie Baugher, Woodstock (Illinois) Public Library, gave me dedicated and admirable support in locating hard-to-find books, articles, and films, as did her colleagues Martha Hansen, Matt Wier, and Kirk Dawdy. Tim Riordan offered kindly help. Martin F. Norden, University of Massachusetts Amherst, shared some articles as well as offered insights into disability studies, and Gerry Slater, MD, explained the limited options for treating broken hips in the 1936 to 1954 period. Nancy Campbell, PhD, editor of the journal *Social History of Alcohol and Drugs*, advised about the availability and efficacy of relief from severe chronic pain during Lionel's time of trial, 1936 to 1954, as well as the effect of opiates on productivity. Jonathan D. Moreno, PhD, and Laura Kolbe, MD, also guided me. Richard Hugunine provided expertise about images.

Guy Moffitt employed his detective skills in trying to find Ernest Blumenschein's painting of Lionel, Doris, and Ethel Barrymore. Sammy Lopez's blog on Lionel Barrymore was invaluable, as were the thoughts and practical assistance of Lionel enthusiasts Amanda Wells and Brenda Cantrell. Stacey Kirsch made connections to a French genealogy group. Alicia Mayer provided context and perspective. Brian Neve kindly answered queries about *Key Largo*. Dennis Carlisle, vice president of real estate acquisition, OCF Realty, who had himself written about Felix Isman, also probed for details of the lawsuit against Irene Fenwick prompted by Isman's real estate dealings and very generously shared his findings. Steve Aavang and Steve Krause retrieved specific information, as did Sammy Jones. Jon Burlingame supplied some musical references. Orchestral conductor and historical musicologist Bar Haimov offered his expertise.

For help with specific queries, I thank Brianne Barrett, American Antiquarian Society, Library; Robert Kelly, archives specialist, American Heritage Center, University of Wyoming; Etan Rosenbloom, American Society of Composers, Authors, and Publishers; Jennifer Schmidt, collections manager, Andrew Jackson Foundation | Andrew Jackson's Hermitage; Stephanie Cassidy, Art Students League of New York; Galina Mardilovich, Association of Print Scholars; Lorna Kirwan, Bancroft Library, University of California at Berkeley; Richard Koszarski, Barrymore Film Center, Fort Lee, New Jersey; Naomi Saito, Mary Ellen Budney, and Jessica Tubis, Beinecke Rare Book and Manuscript Library, Yale University; John Calhoun, Billy Rose Theatre Division, New York Public Library; Mel Johnson, British Library, Humanities Reference Team; Kevin Schlottmann and Tara Craig, Butler Library, Rare Book and Manuscript Library, Columbia University Library; Michael

Acknowledgments

Dolgushkin, California State Library; Ray Vincent, Chatsworth Historical Society; Steve Chapman, former columnist at the *Chicago Tribune*; Kathryn Ercole, Episcopal Academy; Virginia Lewick, Franklin D. Roosevelt Presidential Library; Michael Allen, Kerry Masteller, Zahra Garrett, and Emily Walhout, Houghton Library, Harvard University; Andrew Williams and Justine Kessler, Historical Society of Pennsylvania, Digital Services; Matthew Gengler and Rebecca Tousley, Ingalls Library and Museum Archives, Cleveland Museum of Art; Toby Dana and Ralph Drew, *Los Angeles Times*; Michael Laney, Suzanne Teghtmeyer, and James Voges, Michigan State University Libraries; Nicole M. Quaranto, Mount Saint Vincent; John Martino, Newberry Library; Mary Jones and colleagues, New York Public Library; Meredith Self, New York Philharmonic; Malia Guyer-Stevens, New York University Library, Special Collections; Rebecca Jewett and Orville Martin, Ohio State University Libraries, Special Collections; Hoang Tran, director of Archives & Collections, Pennsylvania Academy of the Fine Arts; Amelia Bathke, Players Club; Teresa Garner, Rogersville (Alabama) Public Library; Rex Rivolo, Roving Sands Fine Arts; Courtney Davis, San Luis Obispo Museum of Art; Laurie S. Ellis and Teddy Schneider, Schlesinger Library, Harvard University; Anthony D. Bellucci and Alan Delozier, Seton Hall; Sylvia Wang, Shubert Archive; Katelyn M. Miller, Syracuse University Libraries; Matthew Ainslie and colleagues, Temple University Library; Dale Stinchcomb, Theatre Library Association; David Sigler, University Library, California State University at Northridge; Sangeet Gill, University of California at Davis Library, Archives and Special Collections; Hanako Redrick, University of California at Irvine Library, Special Collections and Archives; Maxwell Zupke, Simon Elliott, Molly Haigh, and Julianna Jenkins, University of California at Los Angeles Library, Special Collections, with additional gratitude to Simon Elliott for his help in obtaining a photograph; Jordan Wright, University of Chicago, Hanna Holborn Gray Special Collections Research Center; David M. Hays and Ashlyn Velte, University of Colorado at Boulder Libraries; Eric Dillalogue and Rebecca Stuhr, Franklin Library, University of Pennsylvania Library; Michael Knies, University of Scranton, Special Collections; Claude Zachary, University of Southern California Library; Peter Lawrence-Wehrle, University of Wisconsin–Madison Library; and Shannon H. Wilson and Christopher Girgenti, Winthrop University Library.

Notable Films and Radio Performances of Lionel Barrymore

Films in Review (April 1962) included Bert Gray's "A Lionel Barrymore Index," 220–29.

In a late-life interview by Hedda Hopper, Lionel Barrymore quoted the great stage actor Joseph Jefferson as saying, "There's nothing deader than a dead actor." Characterizing this comment as "the greatest line that was ever said," Lionel appended the wisecrack, "All he's gotta do is come to Hollywood." Notwithstanding this and numerous other self-deprecatory remarks uttered by Lionel about his stage, screen, and radio careers as an actor, the memory and accomplishments of Lionel Barrymore will not die so long as viewers can watch his silent and talking motion pictures and listeners can hear his radio broadcasts. The following list seeks to select the best of his acting work.

As Silent Film Actor
1912
The New York Hat [Biograph, D. W. Griffith]
The Burglar's Dilemma [Biograph, D. W. Griffith]

1913
The House of Darkness [Biograph, D. W. Griffith]
Death's Marathon [Biograph, D. W. Griffith]

1920
The Copperhead [Paramount, Charles Maigne]

Notable Films and Radio Performances of Lionel Barrymore

1924
America [United Artists, D. W. Griffith]

1926
The Temptress [MGM, Fred Niblo]
The Bells [Chadwick, James Young]

1928
Drums of Love [United Artists, D. W. Griffith]
Sadie Thompson [United Artists, Raoul Walsh]

As Sound Film Actor
1931
Guilty Hands [MGM, W. S. Van Dyke]
A Free Soul [MGM, Clarence Brown; winner of Academy Award for Best Actor]
Mata Hari [MGM, George Fitzmaurice]

1932
Grand Hotel [MGM, Edmund Goulding]
Arsène Lupin [MGM, Jack Conway]
The Washington Masquerade [MGM, Charles Brabin]
Broken Lullaby/The Man I Killed [Paramount, Ernst Lubitsch]
Rasputin and the Empress [MGM, Richard Boleslawski]

1933
The Stranger's Return [MGM, King Vidor]
Looking Forward [MGM, Clarence Brown]
Sweepings [RKO, John Cromwell]
Dinner at Eight [MGM, George Cukor]
One Man's Journey [RKO, John Robertson]
Night Flight [MGM, Clarence Brown]

1934
Treasure Island [MGM, Victor Fleming]

1935
Ah, Wilderness! [MGM, Clarence Brown]
Public Hero No. 1 [MGM, J. Walter Ruben]

Notable Films and Radio Performances of Lionel Barrymore

1936
The Voice of Bugle Ann [MGM, Richard Thorpe]
The Devil-Doll [MGM, Tod Browning]
The Road to Glory [Twentieth Century–Fox, Howard Hawks]
The Gorgeous Hussy [MGM, Clarence Brown]
Camille [MGM, George Cukor]

1937
A Family Affair [MGM, George Seitz]
Captains Courageous [MGM, Victor Fleming]

1938
You Can't Take It with You [Columbia, Frank Capra]
Young Dr. Kildare [MGM, Harold S. Bucquet]

1939
The Secret of Dr. Kildare [MGM, Harold S. Bucquet]
Calling Dr. Kildare [MGM, Harold S. Bucquet]
On Borrowed Time [MGM, Harold S. Bucquet]

1940
Dr. Kildare Goes Home [MGM, Harold S. Bucquet]
Dr. Kildare's Strange Case [MGM, Harold S. Bucquet]
Dr. Kildare's Crisis [MGM, Harold S. Bucquet]

1941
The Bad Man [MGM, Richard Thorpe]
Dr. Kildare's Wedding Day [MGM, Harold S. Bucquet]
The People vs. Dr. Kildare [MGM, Harold S. Bucquet]
Dr. Kildare's Victory [MGM, W. S. Van Dyke]

1942
Tennessee Johnson [MGM, William Dieterle]
Calling Dr. Gillespie [MGM, Willis Goldbeck]
Dr. Gillespie's New Assistant [MGM, Willis Goldbeck]

1943
Dr. Gillespie's Criminal Case [MGM, Willis Goldbeck]
A Guy Named Joe [MGM, Victor Fleming]

Notable Films and Radio Performances of Lionel Barrymore

1944
Three Men in White [MGM, Willis Goldbeck]

1945
Between Two Women [MGM, Willis Goldbeck]
The Valley of Decision [MGM, Tay Garnett]

1946
Three Wise Fools [MGM, Edward Buzzell]
It's a Wonderful Life [Liberty Films/RKO, Frank Capra]

1947
Dark Delusion [MGM, Willis Goldbeck]
Duel in the Sun [Selznick, King Vidor, and William Dieterle]

1948
Key Largo [Warner Brothers, John Huston]

1949
Down to the Sea in Ships [Twentieth Century–Fox, Henry Hathaway]

As Sound Film Director
1929
Madame X [MGM; considered for Academy Award for Best Director]
His Glorious Night [MGM]

1931
Guilty Hands [MGM; uncredited]

As Radio Star
Episodes uploaded at Internet Archive website, archive.org
A Christmas Carol (1934–1935, 1937, and 1939–1953)
Mayor of the Town (1942–1949)
Dr. Kildare (1949–1951)

Further Reading

Articles by Lionel Barrymore on Stage and Screen, 1925, 1926, 1938, and 1948

"The Actor—II." In *Behind the Screen: How Films Are Made*, edited by Stephen Watts, 93–101. London: Arthur Barker, 1938. Reprinted in *Playing to the Camera*, edited by Bert Cardullo, Harry Geduld, Ronald Gottesman, and Leigh Woods, 79–82. New Haven, CT: Yale University Press, 1998.

"David Ward Griffith." *Screen Writer*, August 1948, 2. Available on archive.org.

"On *The Piker* and the Reviewers." *New York Herald Tribune*, January 25, 1925, C13.

"The Present State of the Movies." *Ladies Home Journal*, September 1926, 25, 205–206.

The Most Perceptive Interviews of Lionel Barrymore, 1905, 1922, and 1928

Belfrage, Cedric. "He's in Pictures for the Money." *Motion Picture Classic*, November 1928, 58, 87.

Mullett, Mary B. "Lionel Barrymore Tells How People Show Their Age." *American*, February 1922, 37–39, 84, 86.

Stevens, Ashton. "Lionel: The Big Brother of the Barrymores." April 16, 1905. Ashton Stevens Papers, Newberry Library.

Notes

Introduction

1. *Closeup on Lionel Barrymore* (Tucson, AZ: Motivational Programming, 1969), cassette recording of 1954 radio broadcast.

2. Lionel Barrymore and Cameron Shipp, *We Barrymores* (New York: Appleton-Century-Crofts, 1951), 35; Carol Stein Hoffman, *The Barrymores: Hollywood's First Family* (Lexington: University Press of Kentucky, 2001), 34, 37; Jeanine Basinger, *The Star Machine* (New York: Knopf, 2007), 11; Lionel Barrymore, "The Present State of the Movies," *Ladies Home Journal*, September 1926, 206. John thought it was "cruel": "It was a cruel thing to do to Lionel, who was only thirteen and sensitive. My grandmother's favoritism had built a wall between us. It was years before he forgot" (quoted in Hollis Alpert, *The Barrymores* [New York: Dial Press, 1964], 37).

3. Basinger, *Star Machine*, 49, 79, 523; Alexander Walker, *Stardom: The Hollywood Phenomenon* (New York: Stein and Day, 1970), 54, 127, 253, 254, 303, 307, 361.

4. Basinger, *Star Machine*, 458.

5. Stark Young, *Theatre Practice* (New York: Charles Scribner's Sons, 1926), 73–74, 76–77, 80, 86; Rudolph Arnheim, "In Praise of Character Actors," in *Movie Acting: The Film Reader*, ed. Pamela Robertson Wojcik (New York: Routledge, 2004), 205–206.

6. Leonard Maltin, ed., *The Real Stars* (New York: Curtis Books, 1973), 115.

7. John Drew, *My Years on the Stage* (New York: E. P. Dutton, 1922), 202; Alpert, *Barrymores*, 95; Philip Kalavros, "I Remember Lionel," *Fortnight*, February 2, 1955, 17; Barrymore and Shipp, *We Barrymores*, 212; Ashton Stevens, "John, The Youngest of the Barrymores," interview, February 5, 1905, Ashton Stevens Papers, Newberry Library, 6; Margot Peters, *The House of Barrymore* (New York: Knopf, 1990), 135, 173, 174, 216, 228, 294, 363, 437; Lillian Gish and Ann Pinchot, *The Movies, Mr. Griffith, and Me* (Englewood Cliffs, NJ: Prentice-Hall, 1969), 88; P. G. Wodehouse, "The Barrymores, and Others," *Vanity Fair*, April 1918, 51.

8. Gladys Hall, "The Barrymore Voice Is a Curse on the Air," Gladys Hall Papers, Special Collections, Margaret Herrick Library, Academy of Motion Picture Arts and Sciences, Beverly Hills, CA, 4; Mary B. Mullett, "Lionel Barrymore Tells How People Show Their Age," *American*, February 1922, 37, 86.

9. Ashton Stevens, "Lionel: The Big Brother of the Barrymores," April 16, 1905, Ashton Stevens Papers, Newberry Library, 1, 2, 5, 6.

10. Lionel Barrymore, "On *The Piker* and the Reviewers," *New York Herald Tribune*, January 25, 1925, C13.

I. Disorder and Early Sorrow

1. Ethel Barrymore, *Memories* (New York: Harper and Brothers, 1955), 7, 8, 42, 272; Elaine Barrie and Sandford Dody, *All My Sins Remembered* (New York: Appleton-Century, 1964), 154; Ashton Stevens, "Ethel Barrymore Will Leave the Dramatic Stage to Become a Prima Donna," July 14, 1907; Stevens, "John, The Youngest of the Barrymores," 8, both from Ashton Stevens Papers, Newberry Library.

2. Barrymore, *Memories*, 5, 37, 38, 46; Episcopal Academy records; Peters, *House of Barrymore*, 20, 22, 27–28, 35, 37, 39, 44–45; James Kotsilibas-Davis, *Great Times, Good Times: The Odyssey of Maurice Barrymore* (Garden City, NY: Doubleday, 1977), 251, 252, 279, 353, 461, 466; Seton Hall records; "Posing for Pictures," *Philadelphia Times*, reprinted in *St. Paul Daily Globe*, December 25, 1882, 5; Barrymore and Shipp, *We Barrymores*, 14; Louisa Lane Drew, *Autobiographical Sketch of Mrs. John Drew* (London: Chapman and Hall, 1900), 138, 141.

3. John Barrymore, *Confessions of an Actor* (Indianapolis: Bobbs-Merrill, 1926), n.p. [end of Part One]; Barrymore, "Those Incredible Barrymores," *American*, March 1933, 21, 22 and *American*, May 1933, 58.

4. Barrymore and Shipp, *We Barrymores*, 22, 35, 44, 85; "Maurice Barrymore's Son Arrested," *New York Times*, August 23, 1895, 1.

5. Kotsilibas-Davis, *Great Times, Good Times*, 156, 185, 192, 254, 271, 286, 307, 346; "Royal Family," *Wisconsin State Journal*, June 20, 1933, 16.

6. Kotsilibas-Davis, *Great Times, Good Times*, 337; Barrymore, *Memories*, 16.

2. Twenty Years, Two Apprenticeships

1. Barrymore and Shipp, *We Barrymores*, 116.

2. Kotsilibas-Davis, *Great Times, Good Times*, 364–65, 471–72; Stephanie Cassidy, head of Research & Archives, Art Students League of New York, email to Kathleen Spaltro, July 26, 2021; Barrymore and Shipp, *We Barrymores*, 63, 66–69.

3. Barrymore and Shipp, *We Barrymores*, 43–46.

4. Kotsilibas-Davis, *Great Times, Good Times*, 181, 255; *Current Biography*, 1943, 28–29; John Barrymore, "Those Incredible Barrymores," *American*, March 1933, 20, 21; James Kotsilibas-Davis, *The Barrymores: The Royal Family in Hollywood* (New York: Crown, 1981), 18.

5. *Los Angeles Herald*, March 11, 1904, 11; Hedda Hopper, interview with Lionel Barrymore, December 21, 1953, Hedda Hopper Papers, Special Collections, Margaret Herrick Library, Academy of Motion Picture Arts and Sciences, Beverly Hills, CA, 1, 2; "Lionel Barrymore" Folder, Box 9, Collection 878, James Poe Papers, 1940–, University of California at Los Angeles Library, Special Collections, 22, 23, 24, 25.

Notes to Pages 20–25

6. Barrymore and Shipp, *We Barrymores*, 37–40, 46–48, 52–55; Lionel Barrymore Clippings, Theatre Collection, Free Library of Philadelphia.

7. Barrymore and Shipp, *We Barrymores*, 61–63, 95, 102; *Indianapolis Journal*, February 15, 1903; *Inter-Ocean*, September 14, 1902, 35; *Inter-Ocean*, September 28, 1902, 36; Barrymore, *Memories*, 127; Kotsilibas-Davis, *Great Times, Good Times*, 486–487; *San Francisco Call*, March 30, 1905, 9.

8. Stevens, "Lionel: The Big Brother of the Barrymores," 1–7; *Marshall County Democrat*, April 3, 1902, 4.

9. Alpert, *Barrymores*, 102.

10. David Beasley, *McKee Rankin and the Heyday of the American Theater* (Waterloo: Wilfrid Laurier University Press, 2002), 240–44, 268–69, 278, 295, 367–68, 439; Terry Chester Shulman, text communication to Kathleen Spaltro, April 8, 2022; "Lionel Barrymore Marries in Rome," *New York Times*, July 15, 1923, 24; *Los Angeles Herald*, April 3, 1898, 13; *Los Angeles Herald*, May 24, 1903, 1; Johnson Briscoe, *The Actors' Birthday Book*, 3rd series (New York: Moffat, Yard, 1909), 79.

11. Sources regarding the daughters of Lionel Barrymore and Doris Rankin include the following. Ethel Barrymore: Paris, France, Births, Marriages, and Deaths, 1792–1930; Passenger manifest for the SS *Pennsylvania*, arriving August 6, 1909; Philadelphia, Pennsylvania; US, Death Certificates Index, 1803–1915; New York State Undertaker's Certificate; Pennsylvania and New Jersey, US, Church and Town Records, 1669–2013. Mary Barrymore: New York, New York, US, Birth Index, 1910–1965; New York, US, Death Index, 1852–1956; cemetery record for Mary Barrymore, buried March 21, 1917; Daniel Blum, Questionnaire, Clipping File, Lionel Barrymore Folder 1, Wisconsin Center for Film and Theater Research; Cameron Shipp, "The Most Unforgettable Character I've Met," *Reader's Digest*, August 1957, 120; Barrymore, "My Reminiscences," *Delineator*, December 1923, 81.

12. Michael Strange [Blanche Oelrichs], *Who Tells Me True* (New York: Charles Scribner's Sons, 1940), 161; Robert W. Larson and Carole B. Larson, *Ernest L. Blumenschein: The Life of an American Artist* (Norman: University of Oklahoma Press, 2013), 176.

13. Larson and Larson, *Ernest L. Blumenschein*, 30, 35, 41–44, 49, 73, 175; Passenger manifest for the SS *Pennsylvania*, arriving August 6, 1909.

14. Hopper, interview with Lionel Barrymore, 2, 4; Alice L. Tildesley, interview with Lionel Barrymore, Lionel Barrymore Clippings, Theatre Collection, Free Library of Philadelphia.

15. *Los Angeles Herald*, January 2, 1910, 2; Peters, *House of Barrymore*, 121; McKee Rankin, *Confusion*, D-179 Davenport, Folder 18, Box 16, Edward L. Davenport Collection, University of California at Davis Library, Special Collections; Barrymore, *Memories*, 176, 177; *Variety*, September 16, 1911, 18; *Variety*, September 30, 1911, 26.

16. Beasley, *McKee Rankin*, 418; *Variety*, March 12, 1910, 16; *Variety*, March 19, 1910, 18; *San Francisco Dramatic Review*, October 29, 1910, 16; *San Francisco Dramatic Review*, November 5, 1910, 10; *San Francisco Dramatic Review*, December 3, 1910, 5.

17. Beasley, *McKee Rankin*, 417–19. Peters, *House of Barrymore*, 135. Ethel came to appreciate vaudeville and made many recurrent appearances herself (Barrymore, *Memories*, 176, 177).

Notes to Pages 26–32

3. Escape into Films

1. Peter Kobel and the Library of Congress, *Silent Movies: The Birth of Film and the Triumph of Movie Culture* (New York: Little, Brown, 2009), 40, 46; Kevin Brownlow, *Hollywood: The Pioneers* (New York: Knopf, 1979), 90–91; Tim Dirks, "The History of Film: The Pre-1920s; Early Cinematic Origins and the Infancy of Film," part 3, Filmsite, accessed January 9, 2024, https://www.filmsite.org/pre20sintro3.html.

2. Kobel and the Library of Congress, *Silent Movies*, 44, 151; Brownlow, *Hollywood*, 157, 158.

3. *Variety*, January 4, 1939, 55; September 20, 1944, 2; October 1, 1947, 53; September 3, 1958, 61.

4. *Moving Picture World*, November 9, 1912, 541; Elizabeth Dixon, interview of George Cukor (1963), Center for Oral History Research, University of California at Los Angeles Library, Special Collections, 110.

5. Gish and Pinchot, *The Movies, Mr. Griffith, and Me*, 66, 88.

6. Kobel and the Library of Congress, *Silent Movies*, 94. Beasley, *McKee Rankin*, 385, 488n334; Robert M. Henderson, *D.W. Griffith: His Life and Work* (New York: Oxford University Press, 1972), 115; Chatsworth Historical Society, "1914 Feature Films in Chatsworth," Chatsworth History website, February 27, 2022, https://www.chatsworthhistory.com/Program%20Downloads/1914%20Feature%20Films%20in%20Chatsworth.pdf; interview with Anita Loos, July 14, 1971, Oral History Research Office, Columbia Center for Oral History Archives, Rare Book and Manuscript Library, Columbia University, New York, 5, 21, 28.

7. Frederick James Smith, "The Loneliest Man in America," *New York Herald Tribune*, May 4, 1941, 10; Frederick C. Othman, "Hollywood Isn't Any Fun, Says Barrymore at 65," *New York World-Telegram*, April 28, 1943, 23; *San Pedro News–Pilot*, June 12, 1934, 6. Gish and Pinchot, *The Movies, Mr. Griffith, and Me*, 65. Kotsilibas-Davis, *Barrymores*, 10; Gish and Pinchot, *The Movies, Mr. Griffith, and Me*, 76; Anthony Slide, ed., *D.W. Griffith: Interviews* (Jackson: University Press of Mississippi, 2012), 182, 215; "Lionel Barrymore" Folder, James Poe Papers, 1940–, 30.

8. Kotsilibas-Davis, *Barrymores*, 10; Gish and Pinchot, *The Movies, Mr. Griffith, and Me*, 76; Slide, *D.W. Griffith: Interviews*, 182, 215; "Lionel Barrymore" Folder, James Poe Papers, 1940–, 30.

9. Ed Sullivan, "Looking at Hollywood: Portrait of an Actor," *Chicago Daily Tribune*, May 4, 1940, 15; *Variety*, March 5, 1915, 20.

10. Kotsilibas-Davis, *Barrymores*, 16–19; Peters, *House of Barrymore*, 172, 567. Peters reported that in 1916 Ethel signed a contract with Metro-Rolfe for four movies (*House of Barrymore*, 148).

11. *Los Angeles Herald*, October 20, 1917, 15; *[Santa Rosa, CA] Press-Democrat*, June 2, 1918, 2; *Variety*, October 12, 1917, 40; *Chicago Daily Tribune*, October 1, 1917, 20; *Sacramento Union*, October 14, 1917; Kotsilibas-Davis, *Barrymores*, 19.

12. Lionel Barrymore, "David Ward Griffith," *Screen Writer*, August 1948, 2.

13. Kevin Brownlow, *The Parade's Gone By* (Berkeley: University of California Press, 1968), 124; Lionel Barrymore, "The Actor—II," in *Behind the Screen: How Films*

186

Are Made, ed. Stephen Watts (London: Arthur Barker, 1938), 93, 94, 96, 98, 100, 101. Frederick C. Othman, "Hollywood Isn't Any Fun, Says Barrymore at 65," *New York World-Telegram*, April 28, 1943, 23.

14. Cedric Belfrage, "He's in Pictures for the Money," *Motion Picture Classic*, November 1928, 58, 87; Brownlow, *Parade's Gone By*, 22; *Los Angeles Herald*, June 17, 1916, 15.

4. The Valley of Indecision

1. Cemetery record for Mary Barrymore, buried March 21, 1917.

2. Lionel Barrymore, Letter to Marion Meigs Woods, July 27, 1951, Edward Sheldon correspondence, Houghton Library, Harvard University; Kotsilibas-Davis, *Great Times, Good Times*, 485; Kathleen Spaltro, "Who Was Ned Sheldon?," *Illinois Heritage* 24, no. 4 (2021): 33–37. Online at https://www.wellesnet.com/who-was-ned-sheldon/.

3. Barrymore and Shipp, *We Barrymores*, 178–81, 193–94; Barrymore, *Confessions of an Actor*, 145; Loren K. Ruff, *Edward Sheldon* (Boston: Twayne, 1982), 128–30, 133–34; Alpert, *Barrymores*, 172, 175, 178, 179, 180–81, 190, 193; Burns Mantle, "*The Copperhead* in New York," *Chicago Daily Tribune*, February 28, 1918, C1; "'Milt Shanks': A Masterpiece," *Chicago Daily Tribune*, December 5, 1918, 6; Alexander Woollcott, "*The Jest* Resumes," *New York Times*, September 20, 1919, 18; *Morning Press*, May 6, 1920, 6; *Los Angeles Herald*, February 18, 1919, 28; John Barrymore, "Those Incredible Barrymores," *American*, February 1933, 12; Spencer Berger, Letter to Margot Peters, November 3, 1987, in the Spencer Berger Collection on Film, Theater, and Music, *House of Barrymore* folders, Yale Collection of American Literature, Beinecke Rare Book and Manuscript Library; Constance Collier, *Harlequinade* (London: John Lane/The Bodley Head, 1920), 252; Colgate Baker, "Lionel Barrymore and *The Copperhead*," Lionel Barrymore Clippings, Free Library of Philadelphia; *Variety*, January 31, 1920, 22; July 16, 1924, 21; April 18, 1933, 42; June 3, 1942, 14.

4. Blum questionnaire; Barrymore, *Memories*, 116, 118, 152, 211, 259; Mullett, "Lionel Barrymore Tells How People Show Their Age," 86; Barrymore and Shipp, *We Barrymores*, 189, 196, 217; Lionel Barrymore Clippings, Free Library of Philadelphia.

5. https://t2conline.com/the-lambs-club-remembering-the-1919-actors-strike/?fbclid =IwAR2yT9SEOSJLQl0t1nNo59PCjWUnracgFJxfazK5-vNid_92jxtEbcZb6vQ; https://www.americantheatre.org/2013/03/01/when-actors-equity-staged-its-first -strike/; Peters, House of *Barrymore*, 190; Barrymore, *Memories*, 225; *Shadowland*, November 1919, 71; Heywood Broun, *New York Tribune*, September 7, 1919, 7; Dorothy Parker, "The New Plays—If Any: The Actors' Strike Has Seriously Cut In on the Theatrical Season," *Vanity Fair*, October 1919, https://archive.vanityfair.com/article /1919/10/01/the-new-plays-if-any; Kotsilibas-Davis, *Barrymores*, 22; Edward Arnold, *Lorenzo Goes to Hollywood* (New York: Liveright, 1940), 194, 195.

6. Alexander Woollcott, "Second Thoughts on First Nights," *New York Times*, February 29, 1920, X5 and March 14, 1920, BR5; "The Screen," *New York Times*, February 9, 1920, 10; *Los Angeles Herald*, February 9, 1920, B5; "Barrymore as Traitor Patriot Does Great Work," *Chicago Daily Tribune*, February 9, 1920, 20; "You Have Here a Fine Actor in a Fair Picture," September 14, 1920, 18; "Say 'Barrymore' and

Notes to Pages 43–48

You Have Said Everything," November 10, 1920, 20; "Mr. Bennett and Mr. Barrymore Prove Fine Team," March 19, 1921, 14; "Lionel and Mack Seem to Please Us," April 3, 1921, F3; Kotsilibas-Davis, *Barrymores*, 28, 341; *Press Democrat*, June 21, 1921, 3; *Riverside Daily Press*, March 17, 1922, 3; *San Luis Obispo Tribune*, July 10, 1923, 1; *San Pedro News–Pilot*, October 11, 1921, 8; *Boomerang Bill* Clippings. Collection of Scrapbooks, Stills, and Ephemera about the Barrymore family, 1900s–1960s, University of California at Los Angeles, Special Collections, Collection 2145. Box 5, Folder 22 [Clippings about Lionel Barrymore. (ca. 1920s–1930s)].

7. Alpert, *Barrymores*, 211; "Fails to Hold Barrymore," *New York Times*, February 15, 1921, 8; Gene Fowler, *Minutes of the Last Meeting* (New York: Viking, 1954), 63; Edmund Wilson, *The New Republic*, March 9, 1921, 47; Alexander Woollcott, "Second Thoughts on First Nights," *New York Times*, February 20, 1921, X1; James Whittaker, "Give Us Drama, Me Lords! Scenic Art. Howe'er Gorgeous, Is Not Shakespeare," *Chicago Daily Tribune*, February 27, 1921, F1; *Variety*, February 2, 1921, 13; February 25, 1921, 12, 16, 22; March 4, 1921, 14, 15; Barrymore and Shipp, *We Barrymores*, 206, 209, 212; Lionel Barrymore Clippings, Free Library of Philadelphia; *Variety*, July 26, 1918, 15; February 18, 1921, 16; September 8, 1922, 16; October 6, 1922, 12; May 24, 1923, 13; Blum questionnaire.

8. Mullett, "Lionel Barrymore Tells How People Show Their Age," 36, 37, 38, 39, 84; Alexander Woollcott, "Barrymore and Bernstein," *New York Times*, October 18, 1921, 27; Lionel Barrymore Clippings, Free Library of Philadelphia; *Variety*, September 23, 1921, 17.

9. Alpert, *Barrymores*, 241.

10. Strange, *Who Tells Me True*, 185; John Kobler, *Damned in Paradise: The Life of John Barrymore* (New York: Atheneum, 1977), 189; Kotsilibas-Davis, *Barrymores*, 41.

11. Kotsilibas-Davis, *Barrymores*, 12, 39, 41–42; Alpert, *Barrymores*, 133, 239, 241; Kobler, *Damned in Paradise*, 95, 189; Peters, *House of Barrymore*, 125, 554. Kobler and Peters largely follow Alpert in their accounts of Irene.

12. *Variety*, May 10, 1923, 1, 47.

13. Kotsilibas-Davis, *Barrymores*, p. 12; AFI [American Film Institute] Catalog of Feature Films: The First 100 Years, 1893–1993, "*A Coney Island Princess*, 1916," catalog. afi.com; Terry Chester Shulman, text communication to Kathleen Spaltro, December 14, 2021, August 17, 2022, and April 19, 2023.

14. Will Fowler, *The Young Man from Denver* (Garden City, NY: Doubleday, 1962), 209; Peters, *House of Barrymore*, 554.

15. Gene Fowler to Harold Thomas Hyman, January 13, 1944, 5, in Folder Hyman, Harold Thomas—Correspondence re John Barrymore and Ben Hecht, 1944, Series II: Gene Fowler Files, 1915–1963, Subseries B: Office Files, 1915–1963, Box 32, Folder 30, Hy, William Randolph Fowler Collection, California State University, Northridge, Library Special Collections; Gene Fowler Papers, COU:4381, *Good Night Sweet Prince*, Part 2, Folder 6, Box 2, Special Collections & Archives, University of Colorado Boulder Libraries.

16. Terry Chester Shulman, text communication to Kathleen Spaltro, August 18 and 19, 2022; Eric Barnes, *The Man Who Lived Twice* (New York: Charles Scribner's Sons, 1956), 233.

Notes to Pages 49–58

17. "Lionel Barrymore Divorced in 14 Days; Name of Correspondent Is Not Disclosed," *New York Times*, December 22, 1922, 1; *San Francisco Call*, December 23, 1922, 1; "Lionel Barrymore to Wed Irene Fenwick, Is Rumor," *New York Herald*, December 24, 1922, 12; Amy Fay Stone to Katherine Fay Stone, September 30, 1922 (2), October 24, 1922 (3–4), October 30, 1922 (4), December 5, 1922 (1), Fay Family Papers, 1800–1967, 78-M105–96-M100, Schlesinger Library, Radcliffe Institute, Harvard University, Cambridge, Massachusetts; *Variety*, September 29, 1922, 18.

18. "Cal York's Gossip of Hollywood," *Photoplay*, September 1938, 76; *Variety*, April 26, 1939, 5; Gladys Hall, "Hollywood's Greatest Love Story," 6, Gladys Hall Papers, Special Collections, Margaret Herrick Library, Academy of Motion Picture Arts and Sciences, Beverly Hills, CA; *Variety*, June 28, 1923, 3; *Variety*, October 7, 1925, 5.

19. *Variety*, May 10, 1923, 1, 47; *Chicago Daily Tribune*, May 11, 1923, 1.

20. Sheppard Butler, "Mr. Barrymore's New Adventure in Madness," *Chicago Daily Tribune*, November 4, 1923, E1; A. J. Warner, quoted in "New Plays Out of Town," *New York Times*, October 28, 1923, X2; "Picture Plays and People," *New York Times*, May 27, 1923, X2; "Lionel Barrymore Marries In Rome," *New York Times*, July 15, 1923, 24; "Film Folks at Wedding of Barrymore, Fenwick," *Exhibitors Herald*, June–August 1923, 27; "Lionel Barrymore Home," *New York Times*, September 24, 1924, 19; Lionel Barrymore Clippings, Free Library of Philadelphia; *Variety*, September 30, 1925, 18.

21. Brownlow, *The Parade's Gone By*, 80–81; Iris Barry, *D.W. Griffith* (New York: MOMA, 1965), 71–73; Edward Wagenknecht and Anthony Slide, *The Films of D.W. Griffith* (New York: Crown, 1975), 204; Henderson, *D.W. Griffith: His Life and Work*, 249.

22. Percy Hammond, "Eight Good Actors," *[Omaha] Sunday Bee*, January 25, 1925, 6-C; Burns Mantle, "*The Piker* Swells Sordid Drama List," *Chicago Daily Tribune*, January 25, 1925, G1; Mantle, *Chicago Daily Tribune*, May 31, 1925, D1; Stark Young, *New York Times*, April 15, 1925, 16; Young, *New York Times*, January 16, 1925, 14; *Variety*, January 14, 1925, 19; January 21, 1925, 24.

23. Lionel Barrymore, "On *The Piker* and the Reviewers," *New York Herald Tribune*, January 25, 1925, C13.

24. Belfrage, "He's in Pictures for the Money," 58. Barrymore and Shipp, *We Barrymores*, 218. Alpert, *Barrymores*, 190.

25. Blum questionnaire. Barrymore and Shipp, *We Barrymores*, 217.

5. Silenced, Again

1. Kotsilibas-Davis, *Barrymores*, 59–60; Alpert, *Barrymores*, 245–246; Barrymore and Shipp, *We Barrymores*, 223–26.

2. AFI [American Film Institute] Catalog of Feature Films: The First 100 Years, 1893–1993, "*The Temptress* (1926)," accessed January 9, 2024, https://catalog.afi.com/Film/12568-THE-TEMPTRESS?sid=3022191f-672d-4689-97db-107c2617f78f&sr=8.387391&cp=1&pos=0; Edward Wagenknecht and Anthony Slide, *The Films of D.W. Griffith* (New York: Crown, 1975), 230; Hall, "Hollywood's Greatest Love Story," 7; Barrymore and Shipp, *We Barrymores*, 259; Henderson, *D.W. Griffith: His Life and Work*, 268–69; *Variety*, March 31, 1926, 14.

3. Barrymore and Shipp, *We Barrymores*, 224; *Los Angeles Daily News* reviews of *The Copperhead* on March 4, 1926 (21), March 13, 1926 (19), March 14, 1926 (34), March 28, 1926 (26), April 4, 1926 (52); notices about *Laugh, Clown, Laugh* in *San Pedro Daily News*, November 30, 1927, 5 and December 31, 1927, 7; in *San Bernardino Daily Sun*, February 12, 1928, 10, and February 16, 1928, 7; in *Lompoc Review*, February 14, 1928, 8; *Variety*, September 12, 1933, 2; Lionel Barrymore Clippings, Free Library of Philadelphia; *Variety*, April 21, 1926, 12; *Variety*, October 6, 1926, 78; *Variety*, January 18, 1928, 49; *Variety*, February 16, 1932, 62; *Variety*, September 12, 1933, 2; *Variety*, February 6, 1934, 49; *Variety*, February 13, 1934, 17; *Variety*, February 27, 1934, 48.

4. Jackson Schmidt, "On the Road to MGM: A History of Metro Pictures Corporation, 1915–1920," *Velvet Light Trap* 19 (1982): 51; Peter Hay, *MGM: When the Lion Roars* (New York: Turner, 1991), 100, 296; Diana Altman, *Hollywood East* (New York: Carol Publishing Group, 1992), 191.

5. Scott Eyman, *Lion of Hollywood: The Life and Legend of L.B. Mayer* (New York: Simon and Schuster, 2005), 286; Walker, *Stardom*, 121–22.

6. Silent Era, "Progressive Silent Film List: Production and Distribution Companies," accessed January 9, 2024, https://www.silentera.com/PSFL/companies/index.html.

7. Kobel and the Library of Congress, *Silent Movies*, 47.

8. Bosley Crowther, *The Lion's Share* (New York: E. P. Dutton, 1957), 42; Schmidt, "On the Road to MGM," 46–52.

9. Crowther, *Lion's Share*, 80–81; Eyman, *Lion of Hollywood*, 85; Allene Talmey, *Doug and Mary and Others* (New York: Macy-Masius, 1927), 149, 150.

10. *Los Angeles Daily News*, September 15, 1936, 12; interview with Anita Loos, June 1959, Columbia Center for Oral History Archives, 24, 29, 30; interview with David O. Selznick, September 1958, Columbia Center for Oral History Archives, 7, 8; Dixon, interview of George Cukor, 40, 107, 109, 111, 112, 115.

11. Altman, *Hollywood East*, xii, 111, 117, 235; Hay, *MGM: When the Lion Roars*, 121, 277, 279, 282; Charles Higham, *Merchant of Dreams: Louis B. Mayer, MGM, and the Real Hollywood* (New York: Donald I. Fine, 1993), 104, 123; Peters, *House of Barrymore*, 495, 605; Hay, *MGM*, 100, 296.

12. Eyman, *Lion of Hollywood*, 142, 381.

6. Talkies Stardom and Detour into Direction

1. Kevin Brownlow, introduction to Kobel and the Library of Congress, *Silent Movies*, x; Arthur Hopkins, "Hollywood Takes Over the Theatre," *Screen Guild Magazine*, April 1937, 6–8, 10, 23–28, reprint, in *Celebrity Articles from the "Screen Guild Magazine*," ed. Anna Kate Sterling (Metuchen, NJ: Scarecrow Press, 1987), 152; Brownlow, *Hollywood*, 266; American Film Institute, "Lillian Gish Accepts the AFI Life Achievement Award in 1984," accessed January 9, 2024, https://www.youtube.com/watch?v=CG7-t_hxIoU; Genesis 11:1–9; Stephen Farber, interview of George Cukor (1969), Center for Oral History Research, University of California at Los Angeles Library, Special Collections, 2, 3, 13.

2. James Kotsilibas-Davis and Myrna Loy, *Myrna Loy: Being and Becoming* (New York: Knopf, 1987), 52; interview with Myrna Loy, June 1959, Columbia Center for Oral History Archives, 10–11. Loy was interviewed by Joan Franklin and Robert C. Franklin.

3. David Gill and Kevin Brownlow, dir., "End of an Era," episode 13 in *Hollywood*, Thames Television, broadcast April 1, 1980 (New York: HBO Video, 1980); Mary Astor, "Talkies? 'They Can't Last': That's When Talkies Were Born," *New York Times*, October 15, 1967, 1, 15, included in Mary Astor, *A Life on Film* (New York: Delacorte Press, 1971), 72–78.

4. Belfrage, "He's in Pictures for the Money," 58, 87; Scott Eyman, *The Speed of Sound* (New York: Simon and Schuster, 1997), 176; Kotsilibas-Davis, *Barrymores*, 78, 80; Alpert, *Barrymores*, 248–249; interview with Bosley Crowther, May 1958, Columbia Center for Oral History Archives, 26–27; Charles Affron, "The Barrymores and Screen Acting," *Performing Arts Resources* 13 (1988): 79; *Variety*, August 22, 1928, 98.

5. Basinger, *Star Machine*, 18, 49–50, 72, 73, 75, 76, 79, 523; David Thomson, *The Big Screen: The Story of the Movies* (New York: Farrar, Straus and Giroux, 2012), 243; Gish and Pinchot, *The Movies, Mr. Griffith, and Me*, 158; Walker, *Stardom*, 51, 54, 127, 253, 254, 303, 307, 361; interview with David O. Selznick, September 1958, Columbia Center for Oral History Archives, 6, 15, 16.

6. Barrymore, "On *The Piker* and the Reviewers," C13; Belfrage, "He's in Pictures for the Money," 58, 87.

7. Barrymore, "The Present State of the Movies," 205–206; Lionel Barrymore Clippings, Free Library of Philadelphia.

8. Barrymore, "Actor—II," 6; Dixon, interview of George Cukor, 36.

9. "Sees Theatres Scrapped: Lionel Barrymore Predicts Television Will Displace Them," *New York Times*, May 11, 1928, 33; Mordaunt Hall, "Greta Garbo Explains Her Picture," *New York Times*, July 28, 1929, 101; "Making Scenes for a Talking Film: So Different," *New York Times*, April 7, 1929, X8; Wade Werner, "Screen Life in Hollywood," *Alton Evening Telegraph*, October 9, 1928, 7; Eyman, *Speed of Sound*, 282; Barrymore, "Actor—II," 100; Karl Schriftgiesser, *Families* (New York: Howell, Soskin, 1940), 228–29; Ed Sullivan, "Looking at Hollywood: Portrait of an Actor," *Chicago Daily Tribune*, May 4, 1940, 15; Scott O'Brien, *Ruth Chatterton* (Albany, GA: BearManor Media, 2013), 133; Gladys Hall, "I Am a Renegade in Hollywood: Ruth Chatterton," *Motion Picture*, July 1929, 97; Henry Pringle, "Late-Blooming Barrymore," *Collier's*, October 1, 1932, 27; John H. Rothwell, "Lewis Stone: Perennial 'Prisoner of Zenda,'" *New York Times*, June 1, 1952, X3; Lionel Barrymore Clippings, Free Library of Philadelphia.

10. "Actors' Equity Attacks Hearst," *San Pedro News–Pilot*, June 13, 1929, 13; Dorothy Parker, "The New Plays—If Any: The Actors' Strike Has Seriously Cut In on the Theatrical Season," *Vanity Fair*, October 1, 1919, https://archive.vanityfair.com/article/1919/10/01/the-new-plays-if-any; *Stockton Independent*, March 4, 1924, 6.

11. *Exhibitors Herald–World*, June 15, 1929, 97, 115; June 29, 1929, 104, 105.

12. J. W. Buzzell, secretary-treasurer, Los Angeles Central Labor Council, to City Central Bodies and State Federations of Labor, July 22, 1929, provided by Valerie Yaros, email communication to Kathleen Spaltro, August 26, 2020.

13. *Exhibitors Herald-World*, August 17, 1929, 27, 34; August 31, 1929, 40; *Actors' Equity News of Hollywood*, June 13 (2 and 3) and June 17, 1929 (3), Actors' Equity Collection, Box 5, Folder 31, Wagner Labor Archives, New York University Library.

14. Kotsilibas-Davis, *Barrymores*, 145–46; Miranda J. Banks, "Hollywood in the Depression," Delanceyplace, February 17, 2015. Governor's Woods Foundation, An excerpt from *The Writers: A History of American Screenwriters and Their Guild*, by Miranda J. Banks (New Brunswick, NJ: Rutgers University Press, 2015).

15. Scott O'Brien, *Ann Harding: Cinema's Gallant Lady* (Albany, GA: BearManor Media, 2010), 256, 257; "'Academy Must Go'—Cantor," *Hollywood Reporter*, May 14, 1934, 1, also see 4; Valerie Yaros, "Hollywood Organizing," Los Angeles Archivists Collective, accessed January 9, 2024, http://www.laacollective.org/work/hollywood-organizing-valerie-yaros; *Screen Guilds Magazine*, March 1935, 8, 15.

16. Keith Collins, "Screen Actors Guild Timeline," *Variety*, January 24, 2008, https://variety.com/2008/film/awards/screen-actors-guild-timeline-1117979576; *San Pedro News-Pilot*, October 15, 1936, 8; Valerie Yaros, Screen Actors Guild board minutes, email communication to Kathleen Spaltro, August 10, 2020; *Screen Guilds Magazine*, November 1936, 4, 13, 23; *Variety*, September 16, 1936, 3; October 21, 1936, 61; August 11, 1937, 21; May 4, 1938, 27.

17. O'Brien, *Ruth Chatterton*, 130; Eve Golden, *John Gilbert* (Lexington: University Press of Kentucky, 2013), 204, 207–208; Robert Gottlieb, *Garbo* (New York: Farrar, Straus and Giroux, 2021), 78. Eyman, *Speed of Sound*, 300; Affron, "Barrymores and Screen Acting," 79; "Bringing 'Song' to Light," *Moving Image Review*, Winter 1999, 9; Markku Salmi, "Lionel Barrymore," *Film Dope*, March 1973, 98; *Variety*, January 22, 1930, 14.

18. Robert Downing, "Lionel Barrymore, 1878–1954," *Films in Review*, January 1955, 10; Lionel Barrymore, "Lionel Barrymore Looks Back to Days of 'Leaping Tintypes,'" undated newspaper clipping from the Museum of the City of New York; Samuel Marx, *Mayer and Thalberg: The Make-Believe Saints* (New York: Random House, 1975), 111; Barrymore and Shipp, *We Barrymores*, 238–40, 244–45; Eyman, *Speed of Sound*, 227n; *Madera Tribune*, January 2, 1930, 2; Sullivan, "Looking at Hollywood: Column on Gable," 23; Kotsilibas-Davis, *Barrymores*, 86; O'Brien, *Ruth Chatterton*, 160; interview with Anita Loos, July 14, 1971, Columbia Center for Oral History Archives, 28; Cameron Shipp, "1954: The Gable Saga," *Cosmopolitan*, June 1954, https://dearmrgable.com/?page_id=3488; *Variety*, February 13, 1929, 13; *Variety*, May 15, 1929, 5; *Variety*, August 28, 1929, 54; *Variety*, February 26, 1930, 10; *Variety*, September 24, 1930, 2.

19. Othman, "Hollywood Isn't Any Fun," 23; "As Lionel Barrymore Would Say," *New York Times*, November 24, 1935, X4; Kyle Crichton, "Barrymore the Lionhearted," *Collier's*, March 26, 1949, 36, 37; Tildesley, Lionel Barrymore Clippings, Free Library of Philadelphia (and other clippings).

20. Herb Gordon, "Royal Trio, Part Two," *Classic Images*, no. 84 (June 1982): 36–37; Lionel Barrymore Clippings, Free Library of Philadelphia.

7. Scene Stealer

1. Stevens, "Lionel," 4, 5; Gwenda Young, *Clarence Brown* (Lexington: University Press of Kentucky, 2018), 126–27.

Notes to Pages 82–85

2. Jacqueline T. Lynch, "It Can't Happen Here—The Movie That Was Never Made," *Another Old Movie Blog*, April 12, 2018, https://anotheroldmovieblog.blogspot.com/2018/04/it-cant-happen-here-movie-that-was.html; Peters, *House of Barrymore*, 365; "Barrymore Out of Winterset," *New York Times*, July 23, 1936, 24; "Before the Cameras and Microphones," *New York Times*, July 16, 1933, X3; Kotsilibas-Davis, *Barrymores*, 146, 151; David O. Selznick, *Memo from David O. Selznick*, ed. Rudy Behlmer (New York: Viking, 1972), 62; *Variety*, December 12, 1933, 26; *Variety*, November 27, 1935, 2; *Variety*, December 9, 1936, 4; *Variety*, February 10, 1937, 2; *Variety*, December 23, 1936, 5; *Variety*, June 28, 1939, 5; *Variety*, November 30, 1960, 17; David Thomson, *Showman: The Life of David O. Selznick* (New York: Knopf, 1992), 159; "English Family," File T-623, *That Forsyte Woman*, Turner/MGM scripts, Margaret Herrick Library, Academy of Motion Picture Arts and Sciences, Beverly Hills, CA; Emanuel Levy, "Cukor, George: A Life—1933–1935, First Peak," Emanuel Levy: Cinema 24/7, April 2, 2014, https://emanuellevy.com/profile/cukor-george-a-life-1933-1936-first-peak/; *Motion Picture Herald*, September 8, 1934, 32; https://viennasclassichollywood.com/2021/08/04/rumours-and-speculation/. At https://oac.cdlib.org/findaid/ark:/13030/kt267nd72c/entire_text/, the Finding Aid for the RKO Radio Pictures, Inc. Studio Records PASC.0003 lists the Forsyte material at Box 341S.

3. "*The Stranger's Return* 1933 Directed by King Vidor," accessed January 9, 2024, https://letterboxd.com/film/the-strangers-return/; George Shaffer, "Easy to Keep a Barrymore Down on Farm," *Chicago Daily Tribune*, May 19, 1933, 19; "Lionel Barrymore and Miriam Hopkins in 'The Stranger's Return,'" *New York Times*, July 28, 1933, 18.

4. *Coronado Eagle and Journal*, May 18, 1933, 2; *Madera Tribune*, June 28, 1933, 2; "Merchant Prince," *Wall Street Journal*, March 25, 1933, 3; Mordaunt Hall, "Lionel Barrymore and Gregory Ratoff in a Film Version of a Novel by Lester Cohen," *New York Times*, March 24, 1933, 22; *Variety*, January 4, 1961, 10.

5. AFI [American Film Institute] Catalog of Feature Films: The First 100 Years, 1893–1993, "*Looking Forward* (1933)," accessed January 9, 2024, https://catalog.afi.com/Film/7203-LOOKING-FORWARD?sid=397c88d8-686d-4b3c-a073-b9c9b7db0341&sr=12.124932&cp=1&pos=0.

6. AFI [American Film Institute] Catalog of Feature Films: The First 100 Years, 1893–1993, "*Ah, Wilderness!* (1935)," accessed January 9, 2024, https://catalog.afi.com/Film/7096-AH-WILDERNESS?sid=ec8565dd-f408-4b3f-93e0-73f3878764ce&sr=11.629963&cp=1&pos=0; George Shaffer, "Knoxville '05 Gets Big Play in New Movie: 'Ah Wilderness' Sets Taken from High School," *Chicago Daily Tribune*, October 4, 1935, 28; "Film Reproduces Small Village in New England," *Daily Herald*, May 1, 1936, 8; Alistair Cooke, *The Cinema*, BBC, April 27, 1936, reprinted in *Alistair Cooke at the Movies* (New York: Open Road, n.d.).

7. "From The Vinegar Tree," *Wall Street Journal*, December 18, 1933, 3; Mordaunt Hall, "Loyalty of a Family: Lionel Barrymore's Stirring Acting," *New York Times*, February 18, 1934, X5; Lionel Barrymore Clippings, Free Library of Philadelphia; *Variety*, December 14, 1960, 33.

8. "Broken Lullaby, Superb Drama," *San Pedro News-Pilot*, March 16, 1932, 4.

9. Frank S. Nugent, "An Objective War Film," *New York Times*, August 6, 1936, 22; Estelle Lawton Lindsey, "Mob, War Films Teach Children Valuable Lesson," *San Pedro*

Notes to Pages 85–92

News-Pilot, July 20, 1936, 6; Carl Rollyson, *The Life of William Faulkner,* vol. 2 (Charlottesville: University of Virginia Press, 2020), 31.

10. Hedda Hopper, "Lionel Barrymore Tells Important Events of Life," *Chicago Daily Tribune,* December 25, 1953, A2.

11. Kotsilibas-Davis, *Barrymores,* 140; Lionel Barrymore Clippings, Free Library of Philadelphia; Edward Arnold, *Lorenzo Goes to Hollywood* (New York: Liveright, 1940), 117–19.

12. Cliff Aliperti, "Arsène Lupin (1932) Starring John and Lionel Barrymore," Immortal Ephemera, December 28, 2014, https://immortalephemera.com/56027/arsene-lupin-1932/; Tom Pettey, "The Barrymores Vie for First Screen Honors," *Chicago Daily Tribune,* March 13, 1932, C8; https://content.time.com/time/subscriber/printout/0,8816,743272,00.html; "Arsène Lupin Has Biggest Cake That Was Ever Baked," *Eagle Rock Sentinel,* April 22, 1932, 4.

13. AFI [American Film Institute] Catalog of Feature Films: The First 100 Years, 1893–1993, "*Grand Hotel* (1932)," accessed January 9, 2024, https://catalog.afi.com; Burns Mantle, "First Night of *Grand Hotel* on Silver Screen Draws Crowd," *Chicago Daily Tribune,* April 24, 1932, F1; Alpert, *Barrymores,* 293. Kotsilibas-Davis, *Barrymores,* 123; Pringle, "Late-Blooming Barrymore," 27, 28.

14. David Napley, *Rasputin in Hollywood* (London: Weidenfeld & Nicolson, 1989), 171.

15. Philip K. Scheuer, "A Town Called Hollywood," *Movienews,* August 25, 1933, 5; Mordaunt Hall, "*Night Flight* an Absorbing Film," *New York Times,* October 15, 1933, X3; Mae Tinee, "*Night Flight* Offers Thrills for Air Fans," *Chicago Daily Tribune,* October 7, 1933, 17; Barrymore and Shipp, *We Barrymores,* 233–34; William Gargan, *Why Me?: An Autobiography* (Garden City, NY: Doubleday, 1969), 99.

16. Marcella Rabwin, "Harlow: This Lady Was No Tramp," *National City Star-News,* March 3, 1977, B1.

17. Mordaunt Hall, "Marie Dressler and Lionel Barrymore," *New York Times,* November 25, 1933, 10; "Marie Dressler and Barrymore Praised," *San Pedro News-Pilot,* December 19, 1933, 2; *Madera Tribune,* April 14, 1964, 3; Graham Greene, *The Pleasure-Dome* (New York: Oxford University Press, 1980), 8; George Shaffer, "Mary Pickford Will Speak at Easter Service," *Chicago Daily Tribune,* April 6, 1935, 19; AFI [American Film Institute] Catalog of Feature Films: The First 100 Years, 1893–1993, "*The Gorgeous Hussy* (1936)," accessed January 9, 2024, https://catalog.afi.com; Cooke, *Cinema,* September 30, 1935; *Variety,* March 12, 1958, 74.

18. Ladies' Hermitage Association Board minutes for September 1936, provided by Jennifer Schmidt, collections manager, Andrew Jackson Foundation, Andrew Jackson's Hermitage, email communication to Kathleen Spaltro, August 15, 2022; *Nashville Banner,* September 1, 1936, 15; *Commercial Appeal,* September 6, 1936, 38; *Commercial Appeal,* August 30, 1936, 41; *Knoxville Journal,* September 21, 1936, 6; *New York Times,* September 13, 1936, X3.

19. "A Senator from Kansas," *New York Times,* July 22, 1932, 18; "For Public Ownership," *Wall Street Journal,* August 3, 1932, 3; "Hollywood Film Shop," *Calexico Chronicle,* October 14, 1936, 3.

Notes to Pages 92–103

20. Mae Tinee, "Peter Grimm Well Done in Film Version: Lionel Barrymore Scores," *Chicago Tribune*, October 22, 1935, 13; Andre Sennwald, "Lionel Barrymore and a New Screen Version of The Return of Peter Grimm," *New York Times*, October 4, 1935, 25; "Morning after a Dream," *New York Times*, October 13, 1935, X5.

21. *Adin Argus*, June 25, 1936, 3; "Director Thorpe Seeks Aid in Missing Dog Mystery," *Bureau County Democrat*, March 27, 1936, 7; Rosalind Shaffer, "Actor Calls Hollywood a Prosaic Town," *Chicago Daily Tribune*, January 12, 1936, D4; George Shaffer, "Six Foxhounds Being Tested for Film Lead," *Chicago Daily Tribune*, November 8, 1935, 32.

22. George Shaffer, "Ginger Rogers Given Rating of Full Star: Studio Buys Story for Her First Solo Lead," *Chicago Daily Tribune*, June 4, 1936, 18.

23. Hall, "Hollywood's Greatest Love Story," 8–10.

24. "Hollywood Film Shop," *Calexico Chronicle*, November 20, 1936, 3.

25. *Madera Tribune*, January 26, 1934, 2; *San Pedro News-Pilot*, February 23, 1934, 10; Ivan St. Johns, "The Barrymore Mystery," *New Movie Magazine*, July 1932, 50; Elza Schallert, "Who Else Is a Man of Mystery? Lionel Barrymore!," *Motion Picture*, August 1934, 86; Basinger, *Star Machine*, 537, 538; "At the Theatres," *Coronado Eagle and Journal*, February 24, 1932, 7; Stevens, "Lionel," 1, 4, 5–6.

8. Year of Disaster

1. Barrymore and Shipp, *We Barrymores*, 218, 219, 260, 262.

2. *San Francisco Call*, October 27, 1910, 7; *Los Angeles Herald*, September 15, 1910, 5; August 27, 1911, 7; Beasley, *McKee Rankin and the Heyday of the American Theater*, 418, 419; *Variety*, March 19, 1920, 58.

3. *Photo-Play Review*, August 28, 1915, cover, 7; *New York Times*, September 7, 1913, X3; June 20, 1915, X4; "Irene Fenwick Buried," *New York Times*, December 29, 1936, 21; *Movie Pictorial*, March 1915, 17; *Moving Picture World*, March 13, 1915, 1621; *Moving Picture World*, October 28, 1916, 533; *Theatre*, October 1916, cover; *Motion Picture News*, April–June 1917; *Washington Times*, December 23, 1922, 1; Lionel Barrymore Clippings, Theatre Collection, Free Library of Philadelphia.

4. "Wife of Lionel Barrymore Sued for $3,641,452," *Chicago Daily Tribune*, June 27, 1928, 16; "Actress Contests $2,500,000 Claim," *New York Times*, September 28, 1928, 14; "$3,641,452 Suit Lost by Irene Fenwick," *New York Times*, March 10, 1929, 20; "Irene Fenwick Fails to Reopen Big Suit," *Evening Star*, March 10, 1929, 23; "Irene Fenwick Buried," *New York Times*, December 29, 1936, 21; "Felix Isman Married," *New York Times*, May 5, 1906, 9; *New York Times*, June 27, 1928, 25; *New York Times*, September 13, 1943, 19; "Irene Frizelle A Divorcee," *Chicago Daily Tribune*, October 26, 1909, 6; *Variety*, July 4, 1928, 42; September 15, 1943, 4; October 3, 1928, 50; *Richmond Palladium and Sun-Telegram*, December 14, 1907, 5; *Buffalo Courier-Express*, September 28, 1928, 1; *Seward Daily Gateway*, March 20, 1929, 5; *Variety*, April 12, 1932, 42; *Variety*, January 22, 1935, 60.

5. *Chicago Daily Tribune*, September 22, 1930, 5; July 19, 1931, C6; March 24, 1934, 16; Harriet Parsons, "He Hitches His Houses to a Star," *Movie Mirror*, November 1933, 44–46, 84; "Yesterday in New York," *Hollywood Reporter*, February 2, 1934, 3; *San Pedro*

Notes to Pages 104–112

News–Pilot, November 21, 1934, 1; *Calexico Chronicle*, February 12, 1935, 3; *New York Times*, July 15, 1923, 24; *New York Times*, February 9, 1935, 11; *New York Times*, December 25, 1936, 23; Elza Schallert, "Who Else Is a Man of Mystery? Lionel Barrymore!," *Motion Picture*, August 1934, 86; *Variety*, October 10, 1933, 2.

6. Hall, "Barrymore Voice Is a Curse on the Air," 3; Hall, "Hollywood's Greatest Love Story," 5; "Irene Fenwick, Wife of Lionel Barrymore, Dies: Actor at Bedside," *Chicago Daily Tribune*, December 25, 1936, 20; Barrie and Dody, *All My Sins Remembered*, 153; Barrymore and Shipp, *We Barrymores*, 262; Burbankbob, "The Barrymore Family Tour, Part One, 1878–1925," NitrateVille, posted October 16, 2010, https://www.nitrateville.com/viewtopic.php?t=7421.

7. Kotsilibas-Davis, *Barrymores*, 212, 222, 224–25; Barrymore and Shipp, *We Barrymores*, 285–88; "Barrymore Recovers from Hip Injuries," *San Bernardino Sun*, September 15, 1939, 14; *Variety*, September 20, 1939, 54; *Variety*, November 22, 1939, 55.

8. Gerry Slater, MD, personal communications to Kathleen Spaltro, August 2, 2022, and August 18, 2022. *Madera Tribune*, November 1, 1948, 4.

9. Mike and Jake

1. David Chierichetti, "Mitchell Leisen, Charles Brackett, and Billy Wilder: A Strained and Successful Collaboration," *Films of the Golden Age*, Spring 2013, 25; Astor, *Life on Film*, 143–145; Stephen Longstreet to Mary Astor, October 1, 1958, Boxes 5 and 6 (*My Story*), Mary Astor Collection, Boston University Library.

2. Kobler, *Damned in Paradise*, 353, 357; Barnes, *Man Who Lived Twice*, 239–42; Patrick McGilligan, *Young Orson* (New York: HarperCollins, 2015), 544; Todd Tarbox, *Orson Welles and Roger Hill* (Albany, GA: BearManor Media, 2013), 126; Brooks Atkinson, "John Barrymore Returns to New York after 17 Years," *New York Times*, February 1, 1940, 25; Atkinson, "Barrymore Comes to Town," *New York Times*, February 11, 1940, 127; *Variety*, May 26, 1943, 36, 38, 55.

3. Terry Shulman, personal communication to Kathleen Spaltro, May 1, 2022; Alpert, *Barrymores*, 359; Kotsilibas-Davis, *Barrymores*, 195, 197, 199; Gene Fowler, *Minutes of the Last Meeting* (New York: Viking, 1954), 216; Gregory Mank, *Hollywood's Hellfire Club* (Los Angeles: Feral House, 2007), 259; Pacific Coast Committee on American Principles and Fair Play, Japanese Americans—Evacuation and relocation, 1942–1945, folder k63b65kr-FID1, Clippings File, University of California at Berkeley Library, 74; Steve Tillotson, "1942 John Barrymore Afghan Hound," *Afghan Hound Times*, December 2015, https://afghanhoundtimes.com/barrymor.htm.

4. Alpert, *Barrymores*, 338; Barrymore and Shipp, *We Barrymores*, 12, 34, 85, 87, 227–28, 230, 276–77, 281–82; Kalavros, "I Remember Lionel," 18–19, 20; Fowler, *Minutes of the Last Meeting*, 220.

10. Radio Days and the Taxman Cometh

1. *Variety*, April 23, 1941, 1; November 17, 1954, 70.

2. *Variety*, June 26, 1934, 41; July 3, 1934, 47; April 8, 1936, 35; June 23, 1937, 44; January 29, 1941, 3, 54; December 18, 1946, 43; June 22, 1949, 26; *Time*, "The Theatre:

Notes to Pages 114–118

Ethel's 40th," February 17, 1941, http://content.time.com/time/subscriber/article/0,33009,851030,00.html; Dixon, interview of George Cukor, 1, 24.

3. *We Hold These Truths*, aired December 15, 1941, downloaded from Old Time Radio Downloads, https://www.oldtimeradiodownloads.com/historical/we-hold-these-truths/we-hold-these-truths-1941-12-15; Brett Kiser, "Ginny Simms," in *The Pin-Up Girls of World War II* (Duncan, OK: BearManor Media, 2013), unpaginated; *Lionel Barrymore*, aired November 21, 1954, downloaded from Old Time Radio Downloads, https://www.oldtimeradiodownloads.com/drama/the-hallmark-hall-of-fame/lionel-barrymore-1954-11-21; Martin Grams Jr., "The Mystery of Greta Garbo," *Martin Grams Blog*, September 16, 2011, http://martingrams.blogspot.com/2011/09/mystery-of-greta-garbo.html; "Lionel Barrymore" folder, James Poe Papers, 1940–, 16, 22, 31, 32, 36; James Poe, "Lionel Barrymore," *Hallmark Hall of Fame*, radio show for CBS, June 6, 1954, 1–2, 15; E. Jack Neuman, "The Long Boyhood of Mark Twain," *Hallmark Hall of Fame*, radio show for CBS, January 17, 1954, Hallmark Hall of Fame Scripts and Production Information, Collection PASC 71, University of California at Los Angeles Library, Special Collections; *Evening Bulletin*, November 16, 1954, Lionel Barrymore Clippings, Free Library of Philadelphia; *Variety*, April 8, 1953, 26; March 2, 1955, 25; September 21, 1955, 32.

4. *Billboard*, November 12, 1949, 9; Tom Goldrup and Jim Goldrup, "Richard Simmons," in *The Encyclopedia of Feature Players of Hollywood*, vol. 3 (Duncan, OK: BearManor Media, 2012), unpaginated; *Billboard*, September 12, 1942, 6; *Variety*, September 2, 1942, 35; September 9, 1942, 28; Barrymore and Shipp, *We Barrymores*, 275; *At Home with Lionel Barrymore*, Script written in April 1949, MGM Radio Scripts, Collection 2411, box 5, script 28, University of Southern California Special Collections, 7.

5. Ivan G. Shreve Jr., "Friendship, Friendship . . . Just a Perfect Blendship," Radio-Spirits, April 11, 2020, http://www.radiospirits.info/page/7/; Charles Tranberg, *I Love the Illusion: The Life and Career of Agnes Moorehead* (Albany, GA: BearManor Media, 2007), 89; Ronald L. Smith, *Horror Stars on the Radio: The Broadcast Histories of 29 Chilling Hollywood Voices* (Jefferson, NC: McFarland, 2010), 220; *Variety*, September 9, 1942, 28; May 19, 1948, 21.

6. "John Alden Had a Word for It," script for *Mayor of the Town* (ABC), February 4, 1948, Agnes Moorehead Papers, Wisconsin Center for Film and Theater Research.

7. Shirley Gordon, "We Beard Lionel in His Den," *Radio Life*, July 28, 1946, 30–31, 35; Fiona Sturges, "Madly, Deeply: The Alan Rickman Diaries Review—Inside the Actor's World," *Guardian*, October 12, 2022, https://www.theguardian.com/books/2022/oct/12/madly-deeply-the-alan-rickman-diaries-review-inside-the-actors-world; Lionel Barrymore Clippings, Free Library of Philadelphia.

8. Hall, "Barrymore Voice Is a Curse on the Air," 2–7.

9. "Dragon Seed," *Radio Times*, accessed January 9, 2024, https://www.radiotimes.com/movie-guide/b-jee4jk/dragon-seed/; *Desert Sun*, July 28, 1950, 6; *Palos Verdes Peninsula News*, August 24, 1950, 9; Ed Ainsworth, *The California Story* (Los Angeles: California Centennials Commission and the Los Angeles County Centennial Celebrations, 1950); Meredith Willson's script for *The California Story* by Jack Moffitt, Meredith Willson Papers Collection, Great American Songbook Foundation, https://indianamemory.contentdm.oclc.org/digital/collection/p16066coll91/id/1788; Ed

Ainsworth Papers, 1945–1968, box 61, 50–52 and box 80, folder 8, 2, Collection 405, Special Collections, University of California at Los Angeles Library; Alpert, *Barrymores*, 375; Kotsilibas-Davis, *Barrymores*, 235; *New York Times*, September 18, 1950, 23.

10. "The Mayor of the Town," Old Time Radio Catalog, accessed January 9, 2024, ttps://www.otrcat.com/p/mayor-of-the-town.

11. Barrymore, *Memories*, 7, 43; Barrymore and Shipp, *We Barrymores*, 33 (also see 81, 91); Kotsilibas-Davis, *Barrymores*, 16; "Final Act: The Bankruptcy of John Barrymore," *National Archives at Kansas City Newsletter*, October 2018, 4, 7; Florabel Muir, "Profile Must Produce—Quick—Stage Is Out," *New York Daily News*, October 10, 1940, 26; Smith, "Loneliest Man in America," 17. In *We Barrymores* (33), Lionel spoke of their father's "sure instinct against the hoarding and compounding of money."

12. Barrymore and Shipp, *We Barrymores*, 22, 114, 157, 224, 255–57; Peters, *House of Barrymore*, 365; *Variety*, September 20, 1944, 2; *Variety*, October 1, 1947, 53.

13. "1935 Garbo Salary Totaled $332,500: Treasury Report Shows More Film and Industrial Salaries in High Figures," *New York Times*, January 28, 1937, 23. "Movie Stars Fight Income Tax Levies," *New York Times*, August 20, 1935, 24; "L. Barrymore, Beery Appeal on Income Tax," *Chicago Daily Tribune*, August 20, 1935, 6; "Lionel Barrymore and Wife Named in Income Tax Lien," *Chicago Daily Tribune*, August 16, 1935, 5; *San Pedro News–Pilot*, August 6, 1936, 1; "Lionel Barrymore Sent to Arizona by Tax Rate," *Illustrated Daily News* [Los Angeles], January 18, 1936, 10; *Tax Treatment of Single Persons and Married Persons Where Both Spouses Are Working: Hearings before the Committee on Ways and Means, House of Representatives, Ninety-Second Congress, Second Session . . . April 10 and May 1, 1972*, Washington, DC: US Government Printing Office, 1972, 33. *Variety*, August 21, 1935, 2. On August 18, 2021, the Internal Revenue Service declined a Freedom of Information Act (FOIA) request for any information about the income tax situation of Lionel Barrymore. Alpert in *Barrymores* (367) reported a *New York Times* story that Lionel's 1938 salary was more than $138,000.

14. Shipp, "The Most Unforgettable Character I've Met," 121; Hopper, "Lionel Barrymore Tells Important Events of Life," A2; Peters, *House of Barrymore*, 495.

15. "Late Actor Owed $40,000 in Taxes at Time of Death," *Valley News*, July 21, 1955; Alpert, *Barrymores*, 366; Kotsilibas-Davis, *Barrymores*, 216, 229; Peters, *House of Barrymore*, 440–41, 495, 504; "Lionel Barrymore's Art Treasures to Be Sold," *Los Angeles Times*, October 28, 1955; *Closeup on Lionel Barrymore*.

16. Barrymore and Shipp, *We Barrymores*, 256, 295.

17. Lionel Barrymore, introduction to *A Christmas Carol*, by Charles Dickens (New York: Garden City Publishing Company, 1938), xiii, xiv, xvii.

18. Barrymore, introduction, xvii, xix, xx, xxi.

19. Alpert, *Barrymores*, 364–65; Kotsilibas-Davis, *Barrymores*, 213, 215–16, 224; DLF Music Transfer, "Lionel Barrymore as Ebenezer Scrooge in Dickens' 'Christmas Carol,'" Unforgettable Christmas Music, posted October 17, 2011, https://unforgettablechristmasmusic.blogspot.com/2011/10/lionel-barrymore-as-ebenezer-scrooge-in.html; Lionel Barrymore, "Guideposts Classics: Lionel Barrymore on '*A Christmas Carol*,'" *Guideposts*, December 1949, https://www.guideposts.org/better

Notes to Pages 126–129

-living/entertainment/books/guideposts-classics-lionel-barrymore-a-christmas
-carol; Frank J. Taylor, "A Christmas Message from America's Scrooge," *Better Homes and Gardens*, December 1940, 15–17, 98; Dorothy O'Leary, "Barrymore's Scrooge," *New York Times*, December 21, 1947, X13; Downing, "Lionel Barrymore," 8; *Variety*, February 17, 1954, 18; *Variety*, December 1, 1954, 27. "Christmas in the Air" details the various radio network programs on which the annual broadcast appeared: http://www.jimramsburg.com/christmasintheair.html. The trailer for the film, *A Fireside Chat with Lionel Barrymore*, is available for viewing at https://www.youtube.com/watch?v=1uXf_bTwpic. MGM records sold a 1947 performance on disc with great success. It was rereleased five times from 1950 to 1981. ABC Radio broadcast this recording from 1954 to 1965.

11. Brilliant Grouch

1. Kotsilibas-Davis, *Barrymores*, 223; Alpert, *Barrymores*, 369; Peters, *House of Barrymore*, 597; Robert Wilder, "On the Sun Deck: Gasping Comment on a Breathless Moment—Miss America's Boy Friend," *New York Sun*, December 14, 1937, 28; Selznick, *Memo from David O. Selznick*, 158; Cynthia Brideson and Sara Brideson, "Harry Davenport," in *Also Starring* (Duncan, OK: BearManor Media, 2012), 147; *Variety*, April 27, 1949, 62; *New York Times*, April 22, 1949, 20; *Chicago Daily Tribune*, October 24, 1946, 32; *Variety*, November 23, 1938, 4; December 14, 1938, 14.

2. Crowther, *Lion's Share*, 254–59; Hay, *MGM*, 268; Bosley Crowther, *Hollywood Rajah: The Life and Times of Louis B. Mayer* (New York: Holt, Rinehart, and Winston, 1960), 240; Martin F. Norden, *The Cinema of Isolation: A History of Physical Disability in the Movies* (New Brunswick, NJ: Rutgers University Press, 1994), 145; Manny Pacheco, interview with Margaret O'Brien, in *Forgotten Hollywood* short film, premiered April 13, 2022, Los Angeles, https://www.youtube.com/watch?v=JO26F1nWCFA; Irene Mayer Selznick, *A Private View* (New York: Knopf, 1983), 5.

3. Barrymore and Shipp, *We Barrymores*, 251; Eyman, *Lion of Hollywood*, 304; Leslie L. Coffin, *Lew Ayres: Hollywood's Conscientious Objector* (Jackson: University Press of Mississippi, 2012), 72–115, 151–52, 157; James D'Arc, Lew Ayres Oral History Interview (1978), folder 1, MSS OH 852, Brigham Young University Oral History Project, L. Tom Perry Special Collections Library, Harold B. Lee Library, Brigham Young University, 10, 11. "Dr. Kildare Unaired Pilot," accessed January 9, 2024, https://www.imdb.com/title/tt24322074/.

4. See "Radio Days" chapter.

5. "Reminiscences of Lew Ayres," interview by Charles Higham, June 29, 1971, Hollywood Film Industry Oral History Project. Columbia University: Oral History Research Office, 1988; Kotsilibas-Davis, *Barrymores*, 218–219. D'Arc, Lew Ayres Oral History Interview, 11; ASCAP Verification of Lionel Barrymore's Musical Score for *Dr. Kildare's Wedding Day*, Clifford McCarty Collection, file 29, Special Collections, Margaret Herrick Library, Academy of Motion Picture Arts and Sciences, Beverly Hills, CA; Barbara Hall, Laraine Day Oral History Interview (1998), MSS OH 1900, Academy of Motion Picture Arts and Sciences, Oral History Program, L. Tom Perry

Notes to Pages 130–142

Special Collections Library, Harold B. Lee Library, Brigham Young University, 42, 49, 88, 89, 101.

6. Kotsilibas-Davis, *Barrymores*, 219, 224; Barrymore and Shipp, *We Barrymores*, 248–50. Hay, *MGM*, 213; Lionel Barrymore, foreword to Margaret O'Brien, *My Diary* (Philadelphia: J.B. Lippincott, 1948), vii–ix; Lionel Barrymore to Edward Wagenknecht, April 4, 1952, Pierpont Morgan Library, Wagenknecht Collection; interview with Anita Loos, July 14, 1971, Columbia Center for Oral History Archives, 21; D'Arc, Lew Ayres Oral History Interview, 4.

7. "H.S. Bucquet Dead; Film Director, 54," *New York Times*, February 15, 1946, 22; Ed Lawrence, "Hollywood's Jacks of All Trades," *New York Times*, November 17, 1940, 140.

8. Barrymore and Shipp, *We Barrymores*, 286; "Reminiscences of Lew Ayres," 30.

9. *New York Times*, April 20, 1937, 29; *Variety*, August 24, 1938, 45; November 9, 1938, 55; November 23, 1938, 45; August 23, 1939, 18.

10. *Time*, "Cinema: The New Pictures," January 11, 1943, https://content.time.com/time/subscriber/printout/0,8816,884767,00.html; W. E. B. Du Bois, *Black Reconstruction* (New York: Library of America, 2021), 868, 872; *Variety*, September 23, 1942, 2; *Variety*, September 30, 1942, 27; *Variety*, December 16, 1942, 16.

11. *Calexico Chronicle*, May 9, 1939, 3.

12. *Variety*, January 18, 1939, 54; *Silver Screen*, October 1939, 12; *Current Biography*, 1943, 31; Selznick, *Memo from David O. Selznick*, 129; Lionel Barrymore Clippings, Free Library of Philadelphia.

13. James Bacon, *Hollywood Is a Four Letter Town* (Chicago: Henry Regnery, 1976), 126; Barrie and Dody, *All My Sins Remembered*, 153, 183; Kotsilibas-Davis, *Barrymores*, 212, 222, 224–25; Peters, *House of Barrymore*, 248, 337, 356, 482, 523, 571, 603.

14. Nancy Campbell, email communication to Kathleen Spaltro, October 27 and 28, 2022.

15. *Variety*, August 23, 1932, 3; January 4, 1939, 10; August 12, 1942, 3.

12. The Best Wine for Last

1. Erskine Johnson, *Los Angeles Daily News*, February 2, 1945, 31; AFI [American Film Institute] Catalog of Feature Films: The First 100 Years, 1893–1993, "The Secret Heart (1946)," accessed January 9, 2024, https://catalog.afi.com/Film/24943-THE-SECRETHEART?sid=57c74f2e-cfef-4741-8a99-a5eb64268cc3&sr=7.459296&cp=1&pos=0; Sheilah Graham, "Hollywood Today," *Citizen–News*, October 2, 1946, 7; Stephen Cox, *"It's A Wonderful Life": A Memory Book* (Nashville: Cumberland House, 2003), 67; Erskine Johnson, *Los Angeles Daily News*, May 11, 1951, 35.

2. *San Bernardino Sun–Telegram*, February 15, 1948, 25.

3. Kotsilibas-Davis, *Barrymores*, 227; Allan R. Ellenberger, *Margaret O'Brien: A Career Chronicle and Biography* (Jefferson, NC: McFarland, 2000), 11, 60, 63, 97, 123, 124; Lionel Barrymore, foreword to Margaret O'Brien, *My Diary*; Lionel Barrymore to Edward Wagenknecht, April 4, 1952.

4. Joseph McBride, *Frankly: Unmasking Frank Capra* (Berkeley, CA: Hightower, 2019), 229–30, 280; Manny Farber, *Farber on Film* (New York: Library of America, 2009), 308; Gore Vidal, *Palimpsest* (New York: Random House, 1995), 396.

5. Scott Eyman, *Hank and Jim* (New York: Simon and Schuster, 2017), 167–168; Joseph McBride, *Frank Capra: The Catastrophe of Success* (New York: Simon and Schuster, 1992), 525–26.

6. Frank Capra, *The Name above the Title* (New York: Macmillan, 1971), 242, 377; Jeanine Basinger, *The "It's a Wonderful Life" Book* (New York: Knopf, 1986), 8, 31, 41, 351; Cox, *"It's a Wonderful Life,"* 124; Russell Baker, "What! No Buster Keaton?," *New York Times*, June 19, 1998, A29; *Variety*, January 5, 1949, 42.

7. McBride, *Frank Capra*, 521–22; Mark Harris, *Five Came Back* (New York: Penguin, 2014), 415, 419, 421, 423.

8. Selznick, *Memo from David O. Selznick*, 362, 373; Thomson, *Showman*, 461, 465.

9. Kotsilibas-Davis, *Barrymores*, 226–27; Kate Holliday, "The Old Man," *McLean's*, May 1, 1948; Blum, Questionnaire, 4; Affron, "Barrymores and Screen Acting," 70.

10. John Huston, *An Open Book* (New York: Knopf, 1980), 150–52; Edward G. Robinson, *All My Yesterdays* (New York: Hawthorn, 1973), 254; Lauren Bacall, *By Myself and Then Some* (New York: Harper Entertainment, 1978), 186; Peters, *House of Barrymore*, 487, 488; Dennis McLellan, "A Hollywood Reputation," *Los Angeles Times*, May 28, 1995, 1; interview with Lauren Bacall, June 1971, Columbia Center for Oral History Archives, 22.

11. "Craig to Replace Johnson in Role," *New York Times*, October 11, 1946, 37; Kim Holston, *Richard Widmark: A Bio-Bibliography* (New York: Greenwood Press, 1990), 5, 40, 112, 134; Peters, *House of Barrymore*, 493–94; Kotsilibas-Davis, *Barrymores*, 234–35; Crichton, "Barrymore the Lionhearted," 36; *Madera Tribune*, November 1, 1948, 4; Harold M. Pomainville, *Henry Hathaway* (Lanham, MD: Rowman and Littlefield, 2016), 138.

12. Smith, "Loneliest Man in America," 10, 17; Blum Questionnaire, 4; Fowler to Hyman, January 13, 1944, 5; Kalavros, "I Remember Lionel," 17; Jim McClelland, "The Barrymores of Philadelphia: America's Royal Family of Theatre," *Pennsylvania Heritage*, Summer 2008, https://paheritage.wpengine.com/article/barrymores-philadelphia-americas-royal-family-theatre; Michael J. Bandler, "Gregory Peck: A Look Back at an American Icon," *Santa Cruz Sentinel*, June 13, 2003, B-5; Cox, *"It's A Wonderful Life,"* 68; Tildesley, Lionel Barrymore Clippings, Free Library of Philadelphia.

13. Greg Mitchell, *The Beginning or the End* (New York: New Press, 2020), 131–33; *New York Times*, June 7, 1946, 16; Hedda Hopper, "Eleanor Forbids Barrymore in Role of FDR in Movie," *Chicago Daily Tribune*, June 7, 1946, 1; Barrymore and Shipp, *We Barrymores*, 288–91; *Variety*, November 27, 1946, 3.

14. Barrymore and Shipp, *We Barrymores*, 288–89; Sammy Lopez, "Politics, Manana, and Lionel Barrymore: An Actor Makes Political Hay in Spite of Himself," in *Barrymuch, Barrymore, Barrymost: Lionel Barrymore, Obsessively*, March 24, 2017, https://lionelbarrymore.blogspot.com/2017/03/politics-manana-and-lionel-barrymore.html; Hollywood for Dewey Scrapbook, Special Collections, University of California at Los Angeles, A Collection of Scrapbooks, 1830–1960, Collection 155, Box 91, Scrapbook 68, 42; David M. Jordan, *FDR, Dewey, and the Election of 1944* (Bloomington: Indiana University Press, 2013), 64; Lionel Barrymore to Hedda Hopper, October 17, 1944, Hedda Hopper Papers, Special Collections, Margaret Herrick Library, Academy of Motion Picture Arts and Sciences, Beverly Hills, CA.

Notes to Pages 149–158

15. Barrymore and Shipp, *We Barrymores*, 256, 295; Steven J. Ross, *Hollywood Left and Right* (New York: Oxford University Press, 2011), 69, 78; Richard Hofstadter, *Hofstadter*, ed. Sean Wilentz (New York: Library of America, 2020), 521–22, 960–61; Mitchell, *Beginning or the End*, 132.
16. Hollywood for Dewey Scrapbook, 6, 7, 8, 9, 15, 16, 23, 27, 30, 34, 37, 45; Cecil B. DeMille Papers, Folders 10 and 12, Box 111, Special Collections, Brigham Young University Library, 20, 71, 81; Jordan, *FDR, Dewey, and the Election of 1944*, 3, 15, 16, 20, 22, 25, 43, 57, 111, 230, 231, 232, 326, 329; Donald T. Critchlow, *When Hollywood Was Right* (Cambridge: Cambridge University Press, 2013), 67; Barrymore, *Memories*, 132.

13. Compensations

1. Alpert, *Barrymores*, 365. Peters, *House of Barrymore*, 440–41; "Lionel Barrymore," PowerPoint presented at the Chatsworth Historical Society, November 20, 2018; *Healdsburg Tribune, Enterprise and Scimitar*, April 9, 1943, 3; Lionel Barrymore Collection, Accession 1716 M828 (885), Louise Pettus Archives and Special Collections, Winthrop University Library.
2. Terry Chester Shulman, text communication to Kathleen Spaltro, April 6, 2022; Peters, *House of Barrymore*, 498; "Ethel Barrymore Colt, 65, of Noted Acting Dynasty," *Washington Post*, May 26, 1977, https://www.washingtonpost.com/archive/local/1977/05/26/ethel-barrymore-colt-65-of-noted-acting-dynasty/5b54b2e9-c4d6-4ebe-bae0-5e2612dfb572/; Gene Fowler, Papers; "Lionel Barrymore's Nurse Sole Heir to Actor's Estate," *Los Angeles Daily News*, December 2, 1954, 3; "Barrymore Estate Willed to Nurse," *Napa Register*, December 31, 1954, 3; Kotsilibas-Davis, *Barrymores*, 238; Benson Wheeler, *I, Becky Barrymore* (New York: Robert Speller, 1959).
3. Lionel Barrymore Clippings, Free Library of Philadelphia; Parsons, "He Hitches His Houses to a Star," 45, 93; "Barrymore Collection," accessed January 9, 2024, https://www.apu.edu/library/specialcollections/art/; "Lionel Barrymore," accessed January 9, 2024, https://www.artnet.com/artists/lionel-barrymore/; "Lionel Barrymore (1878–1954) collection, Art Fluens," accessed January 9, 2024, https://artfluens.com/en/artists/lionel-barrymore/profile; "Artist Auction Records: Lionel Barrymore," accessed January 9, 2024, https://www.askart.com/auction_records/Lionel_Barrymore/10002951/Lionel_Barrymore.aspx; Kotsilibas-Davis, *Barrymores*, 219, 228; Barrymore and Shipp, *We Barrymores*, illustration facing page 249; Rex Rivolo, email communication to Kathleen Spaltro, February 24, 2022; *New York World Telegraph*, November 13, 1937, Ingalls Library–Cleveland Museum of Art, Lionel Barrymore file; "Lionel Barrymore Revealed as Expert Etcher," *Chicago Tribune*, November 6, 1937, Ingalls Library–Cleveland Museum of Art, Lionel Barrymore file; Agnes Clark, "Ethel Barrymore Colt Holds a 'Family Reunion,'" *Women's Wear Daily*, May 6, 1974, 32.
4. Lionel Barrymore Collection, Winthrop University Library.
5. Lionel Barrymore, "Music in Hollywood," *Picturegoer*, January 5, 1946, 9; Barrymore, "How Music Has Helped in My Life," *Etude*, December 1941, 805, 848, 859; Alpert, *Barrymores*, 369–70; *Calexico Chronicle*, March 18, 1938, 3; Eugene Zádor, "The Musical Barrymore," *Music Journal*, March 1967, 59; Bruno Zirato to Artur Rodzinski, October 10, 1945, "Radio Membership Speeches 1945–46: Membership Appeals;

Notes to Pages 159–163

Zirato Correspondence," October 10, 1945–March 31, 1946 (ID: 027-01-15), NY Philharmonic Shelby White & Leon Levy Digital Archives, https://archives.nyphil.org/index.php/artifact/ea3240e7-9cbd-4251-9519-135e93525fbf-0.1/fullview#page/1/mode/1up; Artur Rodzinski to Bruno Zirato, October 15, 1945, "Radio Membership Speeches"; and Lionel Barrymore to Bruno Zirato, December 31, 1945, "Radio Membership Speeches"; Clarissa Saunders, "Dear Mr. Mayer," *Stars and Letters* (blog), January 31, 2023, https://starsandletters.blogspot.com/search/label/Lionel Barrymore; Finding Aid for the Lionel Barrymore Music Manuscripts, ca. 1920–1954, UCLA Special Collections; Peters, *House of Barrymore*, 469–70, 603; R. Vernon Steele, "The Squire of Chatsworth," *Pacific Coast Musician*, March 16, 1946, 3, 14; "Lionel Barrymore and His Films," *Picture Show*, March 14, 1936, 20; Lionel Barrymore Clippings, Free Library of Philadelphia.

6. Barrymore and Shipp, *We Barrymores*, 263–65; Richard Strauss to Lionel Barrymore, January 1, 1947, Miklós Rózsa Collection of Music Letters, Photographs, and Other Material, Collection 0329, University of Southern California Library Special Collections; "Richard Strauss," ORT: Music and the Holocaust, accessed January 9, 2024, https://holocaustmusic.ort.org/politics-and-propaganda/third-reich/strauss-richard/.

7. Bob Thomas, "Hollywood," *Santa Cruz Sentinel*, April 24, 1953, 15; Sally Speller, "Cast of Thousands: The Life, Wit, and Work of Anita Loos," New York Public Library blog, March 18, 2021, https://www.nypl.org/blog/2021/03/18/anita-loos-life-wit-work; Henry Cavendish, "Medicine-Man on the Wilderness Trail," *New York Times*, May 24, 1953, BR24; Alfred C. Ames, "Lionel Barrymore's 'Moral Tale,'" *Chicago Daily Tribune*, May 24, 1953, H4; *Evening Star*, May 24, 1953, E-7; Shipp, "The Most Unforgettable Character I've Met," 118, 119; Lionel Barrymore, *The Shakespeare Club*, Samuel Colt Collection, University of Southern California Archives; Bob Thomas, "Hollywood," *Santa Cruz Sentinel*, April 29, 1954, 9; "Lionel Barrymore, Stage Great, Dies," *Los Angeles Daily News*, November 16, 1954, 10; Kotsilibas-Davis, *Barrymores*, 237, reported that Lionel in old age was preparing to write a syndicated newspaper column. Library of Congress, Copyright Office, *Catalog of Copyright Entries, 1928 Dramatic Compositions . . .*, vol. 1, part 1 (Washington, DC: Government Printing Office, 1928), 3567; Ethel Barrymore Papers, File 7, *Memories*, Special Collections, Margaret Herrick Library, Academy of Motion Picture Arts and Sciences, Beverly Hills, CA, 10, 11, 40, 63, 64, 70; Profiles in History, "Debbie Reynolds: The Auction Finale, May 17–18, 2014," Catalog, 2014, 46, accessed January 9, 2024, https://profilesinhistory.com/wp-content/uploads/2014/05/DR64_Catalog_Small.pdf; *Evening Star*, October 4, 1943, B–12; Lionel Barrymore Collection, Winthrop University Library; *Variety*, May 10, 1950, 53; Mullett, "Lionel Barrymore Tells How People Show Their Age," 86; Gary Carey, *Anita Loos* (New York: Knopf, 1988), 203–7.

8. Bar Haimov, text communication to Kathleen Spaltro, August 10, 2022; Terry Chester Shulman, email communication to Kathleen Spaltro, March 2, 2022.

9. Barrymore and Shipp, *We Barrymores*, 212–13, 268, 274, 294; Mullett, "Lionel Barrymore Tells How People Show Their Age," 84, 86; Edward Lawrence, "A Golden Jubilee for Lionel Barrymore," *New York Times*, May 16, 1943, X3; Lionel Barrymore, "How Music Has Helped in My Life," 859; Hall, Laraine Day Oral History Interview, 42.

Notes to Pages 164–170

14. Down the Valley of the Shadow

1. M. F. Steen, comp., "Lionel Barrymore," in *Celebrity Death Certificates* (Jefferson, NC: McFarland, 2003), 21. *New York Times*, November 16, 1954, 1; *New York Times*, November 19, 1954, 32; *New York Times*, November 17, 1954, 32; Peters, *House of Barrymore*, 605, 606; Lionel Barrymore Clippings, Free Library of Philadelphia.

2. *Closeup on Lionel Barrymore*.

3. *Image*, December 1954, 63; Bob Thomas, "Hollywood Roundup," *Belvidere Daily Republican*, April 28, 1954, 2 and November 20, 1954, 2; Hopper, interview with Lionel Barrymore, 5; *New York Times*, April 11, 1949, 3; *Los Angeles Evening Citizen News*, April 13, 1949, 1; *Press Democrat*, April 14, 1949, 4; Maltin, *Real Stars*, 75.

4. Kalavros, "I Remember Lionel," 20.

5. George S. Kaufman and Edna Ferber, *The Royal Family*, in *Kaufman & Co.: Broadway Comedies* (New York: Library of America, 2004), 16; John Barrymore, "Those Incredible Barrymores," *American*, February 1933, 74.

6. Barrymore, "Present State of the Movies," 25, 205–6.

7. Belfrage, "He's in Pictures for the Money," 58, 87.

8. Barrymore, "The Actor—II," 93, 94, 96, 99.

9. Barrymore, "How Music Has Helped in My Life," 859; Holliday, "The Old Man"; Kalavros, "I Remember Lionel," 17, 20; Barrymore and Shipp, *We Barrymores*, 1, 196.

10. For Edward R. Murrow's series *This I Believe*, see "Does Anybody Believe an Actor?," https://thisibelieve.org/essay/16351/.

11. Barrymore and Shipp, *We Barrymores*, 13; Lionel Barrymore, *Mr. Cantonwine* (Boston: Little, Brown, 1953), 148; Kalavros, "I Remember Lionel," 20.

Bibliography

"187 Productions Here This Season." *New York Times*, June 20, 1915, X4.
"1935 Garbo Salary Totaled $332,500: Treasury Report Shows More Film and Industrial Salaries in High Figures." *New York Times*, January 28, 1937, 23.
"$3,641,452 Suit Lost by Irene Fenwick." *New York Times*, March 10, 1929, 20.
"Actors' Equity Attacks Hearst." *San Pedro News–Pilot*, June 13, 1929, 13.
Actors' Equity News of Hollywood, June 13 (2 and 3) and June 17, 1929 (3). Box 5, Folder 31, Actors' Equity Collection, Wagner Labor Archives, Special Collections, New York University Library.
"Actress Contests $2,500,000 Claim." *New York Times*, September 28, 1928, 14.
Adin Argus, June 25, 1936, 3.
Affron, Charles. "The Barrymores and Screen Acting." *Performing Arts Resources* 13 (1988): 77–85.
Ainsworth, Ed. *The California Story*. Los Angeles: California Centennials Commission and the Los Angeles County Centennial Celebrations, 1950.
———. Papers, 1945–1968. Folders 2 and 8, Boxes 50–52, 61, 80. Collection 405. University of California at Los Angeles Library, Special Collections.
Alpert, Hollis. *The Barrymores*. New York: Dial Press, 1964.
Altman, Diana. *Hollywood East*. New York: Carol Publishing Group, 1992.
Ames, Alfred C. "Lionel Barrymore's 'Moral Tale.'" *Chicago Daily Tribune*, May 24, 1953, H4.
Arnheim, Rudolf. "In Praise of Character Actors." In *Movie Acting: The Film Reader*, edited by Pamela Robertson Wojcik, 205–206. New York: Routledge, 2004.
Arnold, Edward. *Lorenzo Goes to Hollywood*. New York: Liveright, 1940.
"*Arsène Lupin* Has Biggest Cake That Was Ever Baked." *Eagle Rock Sentinel*, April 22, 1932, 4.
ASCAP Verification of Lionel Barrymore's Musical Score for *Dr. Kildare's Wedding Day*. File 29, Clifford McCarty Collection, Special Collections, Margaret Herrick Library, Academy of Motion Picture Arts and Sciences, Beverly Hills, CA.
Astor, Mary. *A Life on Film*. New York: Delacorte Press, 1971.
———. "Talkies? 'They Can't Last': That's When Talkies Were Born." *New York Times*, October 15, 1967, 1, 15. Included in Astor, *Life on Film*, 72–78.
Atkinson, Brooks. "Barrymore Comes to Town." *New York Times*, February 11, 1940, 127.

Bibliography

——. "John Barrymore Returns to New York after 17 Years." *New York Times*, February 1, 1940, 25.
Bacall, Lauren. *By Myself and Then Some*. New York: Harper Entertainment, 1978.
Bacon, James. *Hollywood Is a Four Letter Town*. Chicago: Henry Regnery, 1976.
Baker, Russell. "What! No Buster Keaton?" *New York Times*, June 19, 1998, A29.
Bandler, Michael J. "Gregory Peck: A Look Back at an American Icon." *Santa Cruz Sentinel*, June 13, 2003, B-5.
Banks, Miranda J. "Hollywood in the Depression." Delanceyplace, February 17, 2015. Governor's Woods Foundation. An excerpt from *The Writers: A History of American Screenwriters and Their Guild*, by Miranda J. Banks. New Brunswick, NJ: Rutgers University Press, 2015.
Barnes, Eric. *The Man Who Lived Twice*. New York: Charles Scribner's Sons, 1956.
Barrie, Elaine, and Sandford Dody. *All My Sins Remembered*. New York: Appleton-Century, 1964.
Barry, Iris. *D. W. Griffith*. New York: MOMA, 1965.
Barrymore, Ethel. *Memories*. New York: Harper and Brothers, 1955.
——. "My Reminiscences." *Delineator*, December 1923, 81.
——. Papers. File 7, *Memories*, Special Collections, Margaret Herrick Library, Academy of Motion Picture Arts and Sciences, Beverly Hills, CA.
"Barrymore Estate Willed to Nurse." *Napa Register*, December 31, 1954, 3.
Barrymore, John. *Confessions of an Actor*. Indianapolis: Bobbs-Merrill, 1926.
——. "Those Incredible Barrymores." *American*, February 1933, 11–15, 70, 72, 74; March 1933, 20–23, 114–119; April 1933, 26–29, 77–78; May 1933, 58–61, 78, 80, 82.
Barrymore, Lionel. "The Actor—II." In *Behind the Screen: How Films Are Made*, edited by Stephen Watts, 93–101. London: Arthur Barker, 1938. Reprinted in *Playing to the Camera*, edited by Bert Cardullo, Harry Geduld, Ronald Gottesman, and Leigh Woods, 79–82. New Haven: Yale University Press, 1998.
——. "David Ward Griffith." *Screen Writer*, August 1948, 2.
——. "Does Anybody Believe an Actor?" *This I Believe*, hosted by Edward R. Murrow. https://thisibelieve.org/essay/16351/.
——. Foreword to *My Diary* by Margaret O'Brien, vii–ix. Philadelphia: J. B. Lippincott, 1948.
——. "How Music Has Helped in My Life." *Etude*, December 1941, 805, 848, 859.
——. Introduction to *A Christmas Carol* by Charles Dickens, xiii–xxi. New York: Garden City Publishing Company, 1938.
——. Letter to Edward Wagenknecht, April 4, 1952, Pierpont Morgan Library, Wagenknecht Collection.
——. Letter to Hedda Hopper, October 17, 1944. Hedda Hopper Papers, Special Collections, Margaret Herrick Library, Academy of Motion Picture Arts and Sciences, Beverly Hills, CA.
——. Letter to Marion Meigs Woods, July 27, 1951. Edward Sheldon Correspondence, Houghton Library, Harvard University.
——. "Lionel Barrymore Looks Back to Days of 'Leaping Tintypes.'" Undated newspaper clipping from the Museum of the City of New York.

Bibliography

———. *Mr. Cantonwine*. Boston: Little, Brown, 1953.
———. "Music in Hollywood." *Picturegoer*, January 5, 1946, 9, and *Hollywood Reporter*, December 31, 1945, 296.
———. "On *A Christmas Carol*." *Guideposts*, December 1949. https://www.guideposts.org/better-living/entertainment/books/guideposts-classics-lionel-barrymore-a-christmas-carol.
———. "On *The Piker* and the Reviewers." *New York Herald Tribune*, January 25, 1925, C13.
———. "The Present State of the Movies." *Ladies Home Journal*, September 1926, 25, 205–206.
———. *The Shakespeare Club*. Samuel Colt Collection. University of Southern California Library Archives.
Barrymore, Lionel, and Cameron Shipp. *We Barrymores*. New York: Appleton-Century-Crofts, 1951.
"Barrymore Out of Winterset." *New York Times*, July 23, 1936, 24.
"Barrymore Recovers from Hip Injuries." *San Bernardino Sun*, September 15, 1939, 14.
Basinger, Jeanne. *The "It's a Wonderful Life" Book*. New York: Knopf, 1986.
———. *The Star Machine*. New York: Knopf, 2007.
Beasley, David. *McKee Rankin and the Heyday of the American Theater*. Waterloo: Wilfrid Laurier University Press, 2002.
"Before the Cameras and Microphones." *New York Times*, July 16, 1933, X3.
Belfrage, Cedric. "He's in Pictures for the Money." *Motion Picture Classic*, November 1928, 58, 87.
Berger, Spencer, to Margot Peters, November 3, 1987. Spencer Berger Collection on Film, Theater, and Music, *House of Barrymore* folders. Yale Collection of American Literature, Beinecke Rare Book and Manuscript Library.
Billboard, September 12, 1942, 6; November 12, 1949, 9.
Blum, Daniel. Questionnaire, Clipping File, Lionel Barrymore Folder 1, Wisconsin Center for Film and Theater Research.
Boomerang Bill Clippings. Folder 22 [Clippings about Lionel Barrymore (ca. 1920s–1930s)], Box 5, Collection 2145. Collection of Scrapbooks, Stills, and Ephemera about the Barrymore family, 1900s–1960s, University of California at Los Angeles Library, Special Collections.
Brideson, Cynthia, and Sara Brideson. "Harry Davenport." In *Also Starring*, 147. Duncan, OK: BearManor Media, 2012.
"Bringing *Song* to Light." *Moving Image Review*, Winter 1999, 9.
Briscoe, Johnson. *The Actors' Birthday Book*. 3rd series. New York: Moffat, Yard, 1909.
Broun, Heywood. *New York Tribune*, September 7, 1919, 7.
Brownlow, Kevin. *Hollywood: The Pioneers*. New York: Knopf, 1979.
———. *The Parade's Gone By*. Berkeley: University of California Press, 1968.
Buffalo Courier-Express, September 28, 1928, 1.
Burbankbob. "The Barrymore Family Tour, Part One, 1878–1925." NitrateVille. Posted October 16, 2010. https://www.nitrateville.com/viewtopic.php?t=7421.

Bibliography

Bureau County Democrat, March 27, 1936, 7.
Calexico Chronicle, February 12, 1935, 3; October 14, 1936, 3; November 20, 1936, 3; March 18, 1938, 3; May 9, 1939, 3.
"Cal York's Gossip of Hollywood." *Photoplay*, September 1938, 76.
Capra, Frank. *The Name above the Title*. New York: Macmillan, 1971.
Carey, Gary. *Anita Loos: A Biography*. New York: Knopf, 1988.
Cavendish, Henry. "Medicine-Man on the Wilderness Trail." *New York Times*, May 24, 1953, BR24.
Center for Oral History Research, University of California at Los Angeles Library, Special Collections.
Chicago Daily Tribune, October 1, 1917, 20; February 9, 1920, 20; September 14, 1920, 18; November 10, 1920, 20; February 27, 1921, F1; March 19, 1921, 14; April 3, 1921, F3; May 11, 1923, 1; November 4, 1923, E1; January 25, 1925, G1; September 22, 1930, 5; July 19, 1931, C6; October 7, 1933, 17; March 24, 1934, 16; October 22, 1935, 13; October 24, 1946, 32.
Chierichetti, David. "Mitchell Leisen, Charles Brackett, and Billy Wilder: A Strained and Successful Collaboration." *Films of the Golden Age*, Spring 2013, 25.
Clark, Agnes. "Ethel Barrymore Colt Holds a 'Family Reunion.'" *Women's Wear Daily*, May 6, 1974, 32.
Closeup on Lionel Barrymore. Tucson, AZ: Motivational Programming, 1969. Cassette recording of 1954 radio broadcast.
Coffin, Leslie L. *Lew Ayres: Hollywood's Conscientious Objector*. Jackson: University Press of Mississippi, 2012.
Collier, Constance. *Harlequinade*. London: John Lane/Bodley Head, 1920.
Columbia Center for Oral History Archives. Oral History Research Office, Rare Book and Manuscript Library, Columbia University, New York.
Commercial Appeal, September 6, 1936, 38; August 30, 1936, 41.
Cooke, Alistair. "*The Cinema*." BBC, September 30, 1935, and April 27, 1936. Reprinted in *Alistair Cooke at the Movies*. New York: Open Road, n.d.
Coronado Eagle and Journal, February 24, 1932, 7; May 18, 1933, 2.
Cox, Stephen. *"It's A Wonderful Life": A Memory Book*. Nashville: Cumberland House, 2003.
"Craig to Replace Johnson in Role." *New York Times*, October 11, 1946, 37.
Crichton, Kyle. "Barrymore the Lionhearted." *Collier's*, March 26, 1949, 21, 36–37.
Critchlow, Donald T. *When Hollywood Was Right*. Cambridge: Cambridge University Press, 2013.
Crowther, Bosley. *Hollywood Rajah: The Life and Times of Louis B. Mayer*. New York: Holt, Rinehart, and Winston, 1960.
———. *The Lion's Share*. New York: E. P. Dutton, 1957.
Current Biography, 1943, 28–31. New York: H.W. Wilson, 1943.
D'Arc, James. Lew Ayres Oral History Interview (1978). Folder 1, MSS OH 852, Brigham Young University Oral History Project. L. Tom Perry Special Collections Library, Harold B. Lee Library, Brigham Young University.
DeMille, Cecil B. Papers. Folders 10 and 12, Box 111. Special Collections, Brigham Young University Library.

Bibliography

Desert Sun, July 28, 1950, 6.
"Director Thorpe Seeks Aid in Missing Dog Mystery." *Bureau County Democrat*, March 27, 1936, 7.
Downing, Robert. "Lionel Barrymore." *Films in Review*, January 1955, 8–12.
Drew, John. *My Years on the Stage*. New York: E. P. Dutton, 1922.
Drew, Louisa Lane. *Autobiographical Sketch of Mrs. John Drew*. London: Chapman and Hall, 1900.
Du Bois, W. E. B. *Black Reconstruction*. New York: Library of America, 2021.
Eagle Rock Sentinel, April 22, 1932, 4.
Ellenberger, Allan R. *Margaret O'Brien: A Career Chronicle and Biography*. Jefferson, NC: McFarland, 2000.
Episcopal Academy records.
Evening Star, October 4, 1943, B–12.
Exhibitors Herald, June–August 1923, 27.
Exhibitors Herald-World, June 15, 1929, 97, 115; June 29, 1929, 104, 105; August 17, 1929, 27, 34; August 31, 1929, 40.
Eyman, Scott. *Hank and Jim*. New York: Simon and Schuster, 2017.
———. *Lion of Hollywood: The Life and Legend of L.B. Mayer*. New York: Simon and Schuster, 2005.
———. *The Speed of Sound*. New York: Simon and Schuster, 1997.
Farber, Manny. *Farber on Film*. New York: Library of America, 2009.
"Film Reproduces Small Village in New England." *Daily Herald*, May 1, 1936, 8.
"Final Act: The Bankruptcy of John Barrymore." *National Archives at Kansas City Newsletter*, October 2018, 4, 7.
Finding Aid for the Lionel Barrymore Music Manuscripts, ca. 1920–1954. University of California at Los Angeles Library, Special Collections.
Fowler, Gene. *Minutes of the Last Meeting*. New York: Viking, 1954.
———. Papers. COU:4381. *Good Night Sweet Prince*. Box 2, Folder 6, Part 2, Special Collections and Archives, University of Colorado Boulder Libraries.
Fowler, Gene, to Harold Thomas Hyman, January 13, 1944, 5. Folder Hyman, Harold Thomas—Correspondence re John Barrymore and Ben Hecht, 1944. Series II: Gene Fowler Files, 1915–1963, Subseries B: Office Files, 1915–1963, Box 32, Folder 30 Hy. William Randolph Fowler Collection. California State University, Northridge, Library, Special Collections.
Fowler, Will. *The Young Man from Denver*. Garden City, NY: Doubleday, 1962.
Gargan, William. *Why Me? An Autobiography*. Garden City, NY: Doubleday, 1969.
Genealogical records: Ethel Barrymore: Paris, France, Births, Marriages, and Deaths, 1792–1930; passenger manifest for the SS *Pennsylvania*, arriving August 6, 1909; Philadelphia, Pennsylvania, US, Death Certificates Index, 1803–1915; New York State Undertaker's Certificate; Pennsylvania and New Jersey, US, Church and Town Records, 1669–2013. Mary Barrymore: New York, New York, US, Birth Index, 1910–1965; New York, US, Death Index, 1852–1956; cemetery record for Mary Barrymore, buried March 21, 1917.
Gill, David, and Kevin Brownlow, dir. "End of an Era." Episode 13 in *Hollywood*. Thames Television, broadcast April 1, 1980. New York: HBO Video, 1980.

Bibliography

Gish, Lillian, and Ann Pinchot. *The Movies, Mr. Griffith, and Me.* Englewood Cliffs, NJ: Prentice-Hall, 1969.
Golden, Eve. *John Gilbert.* Lexington: University Press of Kentucky, 2013.
Goldrup, Tom, and Jim Goldrup. "Richard Simmons." In *The Encyclopedia of Feature Players of Hollywood*, vol. 3. Duncan, OK: BearManor Media, 2012.
Gordon, Herb. "Royal Trio, Part Two." *Classic Images*, no. 84 (June 1982): 36–37.
Gordon, Shirley. "We Beard Lionel in His Den." *Radio Life*, July 28, 1946, 30–31, 35.
Gottlieb, Robert. *Garbo.* New York: Farrar, Straus and Giroux, 2021.
Graham, Sheilah. "Hollywood Today." *Citizen-News*, October 2, 1946, 7.
Greene, Graham. *The Pleasure-Dome.* New York: Oxford University Press, 1980.
Hall, Barbara. Laraine Day Oral History Interview (1998). MSS OH 1900, Academy of Motion Picture Arts and Sciences, Oral History Program. L. Tom Perry Special Collections Library, Harold B. Lee Library, Brigham Young University.
Hall, Gladys. "The Barrymore Voice Is a Curse on the Air." Gladys Hall Papers, Special Collections, Margaret Herrick Library, Academy of Motion Picture Arts and Sciences, Beverly Hills, CA.
———. "Hollywood's Greatest Love Story." Gladys Hall Papers, Special Collections, Margaret Herrick Library, Academy of Motion Picture Arts and Sciences, Beverly Hills, CA.
———. "I Am a Renegade in Hollywood: Ruth Chatterton." *Motion Picture*, July 1929, 97.
Hall, Mordaunt. "Greta Garbo Explains Her Picture." *New York Times*, July 28, 1929, 101.
———. "Lionel Barrymore and Gregory Ratoff in a Film Version of a Novel by Lester Cohen." *New York Times*, March 24, 1933, 22.
———. "Loyalty of a Family: Lionel Barrymore's Stirring Acting." *New York Times*, February 18, 1934, X5.
———. "Marie Dressler and Lionel Barrymore." *New York Times*, November 25, 1933, 10.
———. "*Night Flight* an Absorbing Film." *New York Times*, October 15, 1933, X3.
Hammond, Percy. "Eight Good Actors." *[Omaha] Sunday Bee*, January 25, 1925, 6-C.
Harris, Mark. *Five Came Back.* New York: Penguin, 2014.
Hay, Peter. *MGM: When the Lion Roars.* New York: Turner, 1991.
Healdsburg Tribune, Enterprise and Scimitar, April 9, 1943, 3.
Henderson, Robert M. *D.W. Griffith: His Life and Work.* New York: Oxford University Press, 1972.
———. *D.W. Griffith: The Years at Biograph.* New York: Farrar, Straus and Giroux, 1970.
Higham, Charles. *Merchant of Dreams: Louis B. Mayer, MGM, and the Real Hollywood.* New York: Donald I. Fine, 1993.
Hoffman, Carol Stein. *The Barrymores: Hollywood's First Family.* Lexington: University Press of Kentucky, 2001.
Hofstadter, Richard. *Hofstadter.* Edited by Sean Wilentz. New York: Library of America, 2020.
Holliday, Kate. "The Old Man." *Maclean's*, May 1, 1948.

Bibliography

Hollywood for Dewey Scrapbook. Scrapbook 68, Box 91, Collection 155, A Collection of Scrapbooks, 1830–1960. University of California at Los Angeles Library, Special Collections.

Hollywood Reporter, May 14, 1934, 1; also see page 4.

Holston, Kim. *Richard Widmark: A Bio-Bibliography*. New York: Greenwood, 1990.

Hopkins, Arthur. "Hollywood Takes over the Theatre." *Screen Guild Magazine*, April 1937, 6–8, 10, 23–28. Reprinted in *Celebrity Articles from the "Screen Guild Magazine"* edited by Anna Kate Sterling, 141–159. Metuchen, NJ: Scarecrow Press, 1987.

Hopper, Hedda. "Eleanor Forbids Barrymore in Role of FDR in Movie." *Chicago Daily Tribune*, June 7, 1946, 1.

———. Interview with Lionel Barrymore, December 21, 1953. Hedda Hopper Papers, Special Collections, Margaret Herrick Library, Academy of Motion Picture Arts and Sciences, Beverly Hills, CA.

———. "Lionel Barrymore Tells Important Events of Life." *Chicago Daily Tribune*, December 25, 1953, A2.

"H.S. Bucquet Dead; Film Director, 54." *New York Times*, February 15, 1946, 22.

Huston, John. *An Open Book*. New York: Knopf, 1980.

Image, December 1954, 63.

Indianapolis Journal, February 15, 1903.

Internal Revenue Service (IRS). Rejection of a Freedom of Information Act (FOIA) request for any information about the income tax situation of Lionel Barrymore, August 18, 2021.

Inter-Ocean, September 14, 1902, 35; September 28, 1902, 36.

"Irene Fenwick Buried." *New York Times*, December 29, 1936, 21.

"Irene Fenwick Fails to Reopen Big Suit." *Evening Star*, March 10, 1929, 23.

"Irene Fenwick Joins Famous Players." *Moving Picture World*, October 28, 1916, 533.

"Irene Fenwick, Wife of Lionel Barrymore, Dies: Actor at Bedside." *Chicago Daily Tribune*, December 25, 1936, 20.

"Irene Frizelle a Divorcee." *Chicago Daily Tribune*, October 26, 1909, 6.

"John Alden Had a Word for It." Script for *Mayor of the Town* (ABC), February 4, 1948. Agnes Moorehead Papers, Wisconsin Center for Film and Theater Research.

Johnson, Erskine. Columns for *Los Angeles Daily News*, February 2, 1945, 31; May 11, 1951, 35.

Jordan, David M. *FDR, Dewey, and the Election of 1944*. Bloomington: Indiana University Press, 2013.

Kalavros, Philip. "I Remember Lionel." *Fortnight*, February 2, 1955, 17–20.

Kaufman, George S., and Edna Ferber. "The Royal Family." In *Kaufman & Co.: Broadway Comedies*. New York: Library of America, 2004.

Kiser, Brett. "Ginny Simms." In *The Pin-Up Girls of World War II*. Duncan, OK: BearManor Media, 2013.

Knoxville Journal, September 21, 1936, 6.

Kobel, Peter, and the Library of Congress. *Silent Movies: The Birth of Film and the Triumph of Movie Culture*. New York: Little, Brown, 2009.

Bibliography

Kobler, John. *Damned in Paradise: The Life of John Barrymore*. New York: Atheneum, 1977.

Kotsilibas-Davis, James. *The Barrymores: The Royal Family in Hollywood*. New York: Crown, 1981.

———. *Great Times, Good Times: The Odyssey of Maurice Barrymore*. Garden City, NY: Doubleday, 1977.

Kotsilibas-Davis, James, and Myrna Loy. *Myrna Loy: Being and Becoming*. New York: Knopf, 1987.

Larson, Robert W., and Carole B. Larson. *Ernest L. Blumenschein: The Life of an American Artist*. Norman: University of Oklahoma Press, 2013.

"Late Actor Owed $40,000 in Taxes at Time of Death." *Valley News*, July 21, 1955.

Lawrence, Edward. "A Golden Jubilee for Lionel Barrymore." *New York Times*, May 16, 1943, X3.

———. "Hollywood's Jacks of All Trades." *New York Times*, November 17, 1940, 140.

"L. Barrymore, Beery Appeal on Income Tax." *Chicago Daily Tribune*, August 20, 1935, 6.

Library of Congress. Copyright Office. *Catalog of Copyright Entries, 1928 Dramatic Compositions* . . . Vol. 1, part 1. Washington, DC: Government Printing Office, 1928.

Lindsey, Estelle Lawton. "Mob, War Films Teach Children Valuable Lesson." *San Pedro News-Pilot*, July 20, 1936, 6.

"Lionel Barrymore." PowerPoint presented at the Chatsworth Historical Society, November 20, 2018.

"Lionel Barrymore and His Films." *Picture Show*, March 14, 1936, 20.

"Lionel Barrymore and Miriam Hopkins in 'The Stranger's Return.'" *New York Times*, July 28, 1933, 18.

"Lionel Barrymore and Wife Named in Income Tax Lien." *Chicago Daily Tribune*, August 16, 1935, 5.

Lionel Barrymore Clippings. Theatre Collection, Free Library of Philadelphia.

Lionel Barrymore Collection. Accession 1716 M828 (885). Louise Pettus Archives and Special Collections, Winthrop University [Rock Hill, SC] Library.

"Lionel Barrymore Marries in Rome." *New York Times*, July 15, 1923, 24.

"Lionel Barrymore Revealed as Expert Etcher." *Chicago Tribune*, November 6, 1937, n.p., Ingalls Library, Cleveland Museum of Art, Lionel Barrymore File.

"Lionel Barrymore Sent to Arizona by Tax Rate." *Illustrated Daily News* [Los Angeles, California], January 18, 1936, 10.

"Lionel Barrymore, Stage Great, Dies." *Los Angeles Daily News*, November 16, 1954, 10.

"Lionel Barrymore to Wed Irene Fenwick, Is Rumor." *New York Herald*, December 24, 1922, 12.

"Lionel Barrymore's Art Treasures to Be Sold." *Los Angeles Times*, October 28, 1955.

"Lionel Barrymore's Nurse Sole Heir to Actor's Estate." *Los Angeles Daily News*, December 2, 1954, 3.

Lompoc Review. Re: *Laugh, Clown, Laugh*. February 14, 1928, 8.

Longstreet, Stephen, to Mary Astor, October 1, 1958. Boxes 5 and 6 (*My Story*), Mary Astor Collection, Boston University Library.

Bibliography

Lopez, Sammy. *Barrymuch, Barrymore, Barrymost: Lionel Barrymore, Obsessively* (blog). Accessed December 19, 2023. https://lionelbarrymore.blogspot.com.
Los Angeles Daily News, reviews of *The Copperhead* on March 4, 1926, 21; March 13, 1926, 19; March 14, 1926, 34; March 28, 1926, 26; April 4, 1926, 52; tributes to Irving Thalberg, September 15, 1936, 12.
Los Angeles Evening Citizen News, April 13, 1949, 1.
Los Angeles Herald, April 3, 1898, 13; May 24, 1903, 1; March 11, 1904, 11; January 2, 1910, 2; September 15, 1910, 5; August 27, 1911, 7; June 17, 1916, 15; October 20, 1917, 15; February 18, 1919, 28; February 9, 1920, B5.
Madera Tribune, January 2, 1930, 2; June 28, 1933, 2; January 26, 1934, 2; November 1, 1948, 4; April 14, 1964, 3.
Maltin, Leonard, ed. *The Real Stars*. New York: Curtis Books, 1973.
"Making Scenes for a Talking Film: So Different." *New York Times*, April 7, 1929, X8.
Mank, Gregory. *Hollywood's Hellfire Club*. Los Angeles: Feral House, 2007.
Mantle, Burns. Reviews in *Chicago Daily Tribune*, February 28, 1918, C1; January 25, 1925, G1; May 31, 1925, D1; April 24, 1932, F1.
Marshall County Democrat, April 3, 1902, 4.
Marx, Samuel. *Mayer and Thalberg: The Make-Believe Saints*. New York: Random House, 1975.
Mary Pickford Papers. File 362, *New York Hat*, Special Collections, Margaret Herrick Library, Academy of Motion Picture Arts and Sciences, Beverly Hills, CA.
"Maurice Barrymore's Son Arrested." *New York Times*, August 23, 1895, 1.
McBride, Joseph. *Frank Capra: The Catastrophe of Success*. New York: Simon and Schuster, 1992.
———. *Frankly: Unmasking Frank Capra*. Berkeley, CA: Hightower, 2019.
McGilligan, Patrick. *Young Orson*. New York: HarperCollins, 2015.
McLellan, Dennis. "A Hollywood Reputation." *Los Angeles Times*, May 28, 1995, 1.
MGM Radio Scripts. *At Home with Lionel Barrymore*. Script written in April 1949. Script 28, Box 5, Collection 2411, University of Southern California Special Collections, 7.
"'Milt Shanks': A Masterpiece." *Chicago Daily Tribune*, December 5, 1918, 6.
Mitchell, Greg. *The Beginning or the End*. New York: New Press, 2020.
Morning Press, May 6, 1920, 6.
Motion Picture Herald, September 8, 1934, 32.
Motion Picture News, April–June 1917.
Movie Pictorial, March 1915, 17.
"Movie Stars Fight Income Tax Levies." *New York Times*, August 20, 1935, 24.
Moving Picture World, November 9, 1912, 541; March 13, 1915, 1621; October 28, 1916, 533.
Muir, Florabel. "Profile Must Produce—Quick—Stage Is Out." *New York Daily News*, October 10, 1940, 26.
Mullett, Mary B. "Lionel Barrymore Tells How People Show Their Age." *American*, February 1922, 37–39, 84, 86.
Napley, David. *Rasputin in Hollywood*. London: Weidenfeld and Nicolson, 1989.
Nashville Banner, September 1, 1936, 15.

Bibliography

Neuman, E. Jack. "The Long Boyhood of Mark Twain." *Hallmark Hall of Fame*, radio show for CBS, January 17, 1954. Collection PASC 71, Hallmark Hall of Fame Scripts and Production Information. University of California at Los Angeles Library, Special Collections.

New York Herald, December 24, 1922, 12.

New York Times, reviews and stories, May 5, 1906, 9; September 7, 1913, X3; June 20, 1915, X4; February 9, 1920, 10; February 15, 1921, 8; December 22, 1922, 1; May 27, 1923, X2; July 15, 1923, 24; October 28, 1923, X2; May 27, 1923, X2; July 15, 1923, 24; September 24, 1924, 19; October 28, 1923, X2; June 27, 1928, 25; July 22, 1932, 18; July 16, 1933, X3; July 28, 1933, 18; February 9, 1935, 11; November 24, 1935, X4; July 23, 1936, 24; September 13, 1936, X3; December 25, 1936, 23; December 29, 1936, 21; April 20, 1937, 29; September 13, 1943, 19; June 7, 1946, 16; April 11, 1949, 3; April 22, 1949, 20; September 18, 1950, 23; November 16, 1954, 1; November 17, 1954, 32; November 19, 1954, 32.

New York World-Telegraph, November 13, 1937. Lionel Barrymore File, Ingalls Library–Cleveland [Ohio] Museum of Art.

Norden, Martin F. *The Cinema of Isolation: A History of Physical Disability in the Movies*. New Brunswick, NJ: Rutgers University Press, 1994.

Nugent, Frank S. "An Objective War Film." *New York Times*, August 6, 1936, 22.

NY Philharmonic Shelby White and Leon Levy Digital Archives. Artur Rodzinski to Bruno Zirato, October 15, 1945. "Radio Membership Speeches 1945–46: Membership Appeals; Zirato Correspondence." October 10, 1945–March 31, 1946 (ID: 027-01-15). https://archives.nyphil.org/index.php/artifact/ea3240e7-9cbd-4251-9519-135e93525fbf-0.1/fullview#page/1/mode/1up.

———. Bruno Zirato to Artur Rodzinski, October 10, 1945. "Radio Membership Speeches 1945–46: Membership Appeals; Zirato Correspondence." October 10, 1945–March 31, 1946 (ID: 027-01-15). https://archives.nyphil.org/index.php/artifact/ea3240e7-9cbd-4251-9519-135e93525fbf-0.1/fullview#page/1/mode/1up.

———. Lionel Barrymore to Bruno Zirato, December 31, 1945. "Radio Membership Speeches 1945–46: Membership Appeals; Zirato Correspondence." October 10, 1945–March 31, 1946 (ID: 027-01-15). https://archives.nyphil.org/index.php/artifact/ea3240e7-9cbd-4251-9519-135e93525fbf-0.1/fullview#page/1/mode/1up.

O'Brien, Scott. *Ann Harding: Cinema's Gallant Lady*. Albany, GA: BearManor Media, 2010.

———. *Ruth Chatterton*. Albany, GA: BearManor Media, 2013.

O'Leary, Dorothy. "Barrymore's Scrooge." *New York Times*, December 21, 1947, X13.

Othman, Frederick C. "Hollywood Isn't Any Fun, Says Barrymore at 65." *New York World-Telegram*, April 28, 1943, 23.

Pacheco, Manny. Interview with Margaret O'Brien. In *Forgotten Hollywood* short film. Premiered April 13, 2022, Los Angeles. https://www.youtube.com/watch?v=JO26F1nWCFA.

Pacific Coast Committee on American Principles and Fair Play. Japanese Americans—Evacuation and Relocation, 1942–1945. Folder k63b65kr-FID1, Clippings File, University of California at Berkeley Library.

Palos Verdes Peninsula News, August 24, 1950, 9.

Bibliography

Parker, Dorothy. "The New Plays—If Any: The Actors' Strike Has Seriously Cut In on the Theatrical Season." *Vanity Fair*, October 1919, https://archive.vanityfair.com/article/1919/10/01/the-new-plays-if-any.
Parsons, Harriet. "He Hitches His Houses to a Star." *Movie Mirror*, November 1933, 44–46, 84.
Peters, Margot. *The House of Barrymore*. New York: Knopf, 1990.
Pettey, Tom. "The Barrymores Vie for First Screen Honors." *Chicago Daily Tribune*, March 13, 1932, C8.
Philadelphia Times. "Posing for Pictures." Reprinted in *St. Paul Daily Globe*, December 25, 1882, 5.
Photo-Play Review, August 28, 1915, cover, 7.
Poe, James. "Lionel Barrymore." *Hallmark Hall of Fame*. Radio show for CBS, June 6, 1954.
———. Papers, 1940–. "Lionel Barrymore" Folder, Box 9, Collection 878. University of California at Los Angeles Library, Special Collections.
Pomainville, Harold M. *Henry Hathaway*. Lanham, MD: Rowman and Littlefield, 2016.
"Posing for Pictures." *Philadelphia Times*, reprinted in *St. Paul Daily Globe*, December 25, 1882, 5.
Press Democrat, June 21, 1921, 3; April 14, 1949, 4.
Pringle, Henry. "Late-Blooming Barrymore." *Collier's*, October 1, 1932, 27–28.
Profiles in History. "Debbie Reynolds: The Auction Finale." www.profiles in history.com.
Rabwin, Marcella. "Harlow: This Lady Was No Tramp." *National City Star-News*, March 3, 1977, B1.
Rankin, McKee. *Confusion*. D-179 Davenport, Folder 18, Box 16. Edward L. Davenport Collection. University of California at Davis Library, Special Collections.
The Real Stars. Edited by Leonard Maltin. New York: Curtis Books, 1973.
Review of *Mr. Cantonwine*. *Evening Star*, May 24, 1953, E-7.
Richmond Palladium and Sun-Telegram, December 14, 1907, 5.
Riverside Daily Press, March 17, 1922, 3.
Robinson, Edward G. *All My Yesterdays*. New York: Hawthorn, 1973.
Rollyson, Carl. *The Life of William Faulkner*. Vol. 2. Charlottesville: University of Virginia Press, 2020.
Ross, Steven J. *Hollywood Left and Right*. New York: Oxford University Press, 2011.
Rothwell, John H. "Lewis Stone: Perennial 'Prisoner of Zenda.'" *New York Times*, June 1, 1952, X3.
"Royal Family." *Wisconsin State Journal*, June 20, 1933, 16.
Ruff, Loren K. *Edward Sheldon*. Boston: Twayne, 1982.
Sacramento Union, October 14, 1917.
Salmi, Markku. "Lionel Barrymore." *Film Dope*, March 1973, 95–98.
San Bernardino Daily Sun. Re *Laugh, Clown, Laugh*. February 12, 1928, 10, and February 16, 1928, 7.
San Bernardino Sun-Telegram, February 15, 1948, 25.

Bibliography

San Francisco Call, March 30, 1905, 9; October 27, 1910, 7; December 23, 1922, 1.
San Francisco Dramatic Review, October 29, 1910, 16; November 5, 1910, 10; December 3, 1910, 5.
San Luis Obispo Tribune, July 10, 1923, 1.
San Pedro Daily News. Re *Laugh, Clown, Laugh*. November 30, 1927, 5, and December 31, 1927, 7.
San Pedro News-Pilot, October 11, 1921, 8; March 16, 1932, 4; March 4, 1933, 6; December 19, 1933, 2; February 23, 1934, 10; June 12, 1934, 6; November 21, 1934, 1; August 6, 1936, 1; October 15, 1936, 8.
Santa Rosa Press-Democrat, June 2, 1918, 2.
Schallert, Elza. "Who Else Is a Man of Mystery? Lionel Barrymore!" *Motion Picture*, August 1934, 35, 86–87.
Scheuer, Philip K. "A Town Called Hollywood." *Movie News*, August 25, 1933, 5.
Schmidt, Jackson. "On the Road to MGM: A History of Metro Pictures Corporation, 1915–1920." *Velvet Light Trap* 19 (1982): 46–52.
Schriftgiesser, Karl. "The Drews and the Barrymores." In *Families*, 200–243. New York: Howell, Soskin, 1940.
Screen Guild Magazine, March 1935, 8, 15; November 1936, 4, 13, 23.
"Sees Theatres Scrapped: Lionel Barrymore Predicts Television Will Displace Them." *New York Times*, May 11, 1928, 33.
Selznick, David O. *Memo from David O. Selznick*. Edited by Rudy Behlmer. New York: Viking, 1972.
Selznick, Irene Mayer. *A Private View*. New York: Knopf, 1983.
Sennwald, Andre. "Lionel Barrymore and a New Screen Version of *The Return of Peter Grimm*." *New York Times*, October 4, 1935, 25.
———. "Morning after a Dream." *New York Times*, October 13, 1935, X5.
Seton Hall records.
Seward Daily Gateway, March 20, 1929, 5.
Shadowland, November 1919, 71.
Shaffer, George. "Easy to Keep a Barrymore Down on Farm." *Chicago Daily Tribune*, May 19, 1933, 19.
———. "Ginger Rogers Given Rating of Full Star: Studio Buys Story for Her First Solo Lead." *Chicago Daily Tribune*, June 4, 1936, 18.
———. "Knoxville '05 Gets Big Play in New Movie: *Ah Wilderness* Sets Taken from High School." *Chicago Daily Tribune*, October 4, 1935, 28.
———. "Mary Pickford Will Speak at Easter Service." *Chicago Daily Tribune*, April 6, 1935, 19.
———. "Six Foxhounds Being Tested for Film Lead." *Chicago Daily Tribune*, November 8, 1935, 32.
Shaffer, Rosalind. "Actor Calls Hollywood a Prosaic Town." *Chicago Daily Tribune*, January 12, 1936, D4.
Shipp, Cameron. "The Most Unforgettable Character I've Met." *Reader's Digest*, August 1957, 117–22.
———. "1954: The Gable Saga." *Cosmopolitan*, June 1954. https://dearmrgable.com/?page_id=3488.

Bibliography

Shulman, Terry Chester. *Film's First Family: The Untold Story of the Costellos.* Lexington: University Press of Kentucky, 2019.
Silver Screen, October 1939, 12.
Slide, Anthony, ed. *D. W. Griffith: Interviews.* Jackson: University Press of Mississippi, 2012.
Smith, Frederick James. "The Loneliest Man in America." *New York Herald Tribune*, May 4, 1941, 10, 17.
Smith, Ronald L. *Horror Stars on the Radio: The Broadcast Histories of 29 Chilling Hollywood Voices.* Jefferson, NC: McFarland, 2010.
Spaltro, Kathleen. "Who Was Ned Sheldon?" *Illinois Heritage* 24, no. 4 (2021): 33–37. https://www.wellesnet.com/who-was-ned-sheldon/.
Steele, R. Vernon. "The Squire of Chatsworth." *Pacific Coast Musician*, March 16, 1946, 3, 14.
Steen, M. F., comp. "Lionel Barrymore." In *Celebrity Death Certificates*, 21. Jefferson, NC: McFarland, 2003.
Stevens, Ashton. Ashton Stevens Papers, Newberry Library.
St. Johns, Ivan. "The Barrymore Mystery." *New Movie Magazine*, July 1932, 50, 90, 92.
Stockton Independent, March 4, 1924, 6.
Stone, Amy Fay, to Katherine Fay Stone, September 30, 1922, 2; October 24, 1922, 3–4; October 30, 1922, 4; December 5, 1922, 1. 78-M105—96-M100. Fay Family Papers, 1800–1967. Schlesinger Library, Radcliffe Institute, Harvard University, Cambridge, MA.
The Story of Dr. Kildare radio program. Accessed December 19, 2023. https://www.rusc.com/old-time-radio/articles/The-Story-of-Dr-Kildare.aspx?id=512#:~:text=Kildare%2C%20the%20radio%20program%2C%20came,Leonard%20Gillespie.
Strange, Michael [Blanche Oelrichs]. *Who Tells Me True.* New York: Charles Scribner's Sons, 1940.
Strauss, Richard, to Lionel Barrymore, January 1, 1947. Collection 0329, Miklós Rózsa Collection of Music Letters, Photographs, and Other Material. University of Southern California Library, Special Collections.
Sturges, Fiona. Review of *Madly, Deeply: The Alan Rickman Diaries. Guardian*, October 12, 2022. https://www.theguardian.com/books/2022/oct/12/madly-deeply-the-alan-rickman-diaries-review-inside-the-actors-world.
Sullivan, Ed. "Looking at Hollywood: Column on Gable." *Chicago Daily Tribune*, April 1, 1938, 23.
———. "Looking at Hollywood: Portrait of an Actor." *Chicago Daily Tribune*, May 4, 1940, 15.
Talmey, Allene. *Doug and Mary and Others.* New York: Macy-Masius, 1927.
Tarbox, Todd. *Orson Welles and Roger Hill.* Albany, GA: BearManor Media, 2013.
Tax Treatment of Single Persons and Married Persons Where Both Spouses Are Working: Hearings before the Committee on Ways and Means, House of Representatives, Ninety-Second Congress, Second Session . . . April 10 and May 1, 1972. Washington, DC: US Government Printing Office, 1972.
Taylor, Frank J. "A Christmas Message from America's Scrooge." *Better Homes and Gardens*, December 1940, 15–17, 98.
The Theatre, October 1916, cover.

Bibliography

Thomas, Bob. "Hollywood." *Santa Cruz Sentinel*, April 24, 1953, 15; April 29, 1954, 9.
———. "Hollywood Roundup." *Belvidere Daily Republican*, April 28, 1954, 2; November 20, 1954, 2.
Thomson, David. *The Big Screen: The Story of the Movies*. New York: Farrar, Straus and Giroux, 2012.
———. *Showman: The Life of David O. Selznick*. New York: Knopf, 1992.
Tildesley, Alice L. Interview with Lionel Barrymore. Lionel Barrymore Clippings, Theatre Collection, Free Library of Philadelphia.
Tillotson, Steve. "1942 John Barrymore Afghan Hound." *Afghan Hound Times*, December 2015. https://afghanhoundtimes.com/barrymor.htm.
Time. "Cinema: The New Pictures." January 11, 1943. https://content.time.com/time/subscriber/printout/0,8816,884767,00.html.
———. "The Theatre: Ethel's 40th." February 17, 1941. content.time.com/time/subscriber/article/0,33009,851030,00.html.
Tranberg, Charles. *I Love the Illusion: The Life and Career of Agnes Moorehead*. Albany, GA: BearManor Media, 2007.
Turner/MGM Scripts. "English Family." File T-623, That Forsyte Woman. Margaret Herrick Library, Academy of Motion Picture Arts and Sciences, Beverly Hills, CA.
Variety, March 12, 1910, 16; March 19, 1910, 18; September 16, 1911, 18; September 30, 1911, 26; May 31, 1913, 8; March 5, 1915, 20; October 12, 1917, 40; July 26, 1918, 15; January 31, 1920, 22; March 19, 1920, 58; February 2, 1921, 13; February 18, 1921, 16; February 25, 1921, 12, 16, 22; March 4, 1921, 14, 15; September 23, 1921, 17; September 8, 1922, 16; September 29, 1922, 18; October 6, 1922, 12; May 10, 1923, 1, 47; May 24, 1923, 13; June 28, 1923, 3; July 16, 1924, 21; January 14, 1925, 19; January 21, 1925, 24; September 30, 1925, 18; October 7, 1925, 5; March 31, 1926, 14; April 21, 1926, 12; October 6, 1926, 78; January 18, 1928, 49; July 4, 1928, 42; August 22, 1928, 98; October 3, 1928, 50; February 13, 1929, 13; May 15, 1929, 5; June 12, 1929, 5; August 28, 1929, 54; January 22, 1930, 14; February 26, 1930, 10; September 24, 1930, 2; February 16, 1932, 62; April 12, 1932, 42; August 23, 1932, 3; April 18, 1933, 42; September 12, 1933, 2; October 10, 1933, 2; December 12, 1933, 26; February 6, 1934, 49; February 13, 1934, 17; February 27, 1934, 48; June 26, 1934, 41; July 3, 1934, 47; January 22, 1935, 60; August 21, 1935, 2; November 27, 1935, 2; April 8, 1936, 35; September 16, 1936, 3; October 21, 1936, 61; December 9, 1936, 4; December 23, 1936, 5; February 10, 1937, 2; June 23, 1937, 44; August 11, 1937, 21; May 4, 1938, 27; August 24, 1938, 45; November 9, 1938, 55; November 23, 1938, 4, 45; December 14, 1938, 14; January 4, 1939, 10, 55; January 18, 1939, 54; April 26, 1939, 5; June 28, 1939, 5; August 23, 1939, 18; September 20, 1939, 54; November 22, 1939, 55; January 29, 1941, 3, 54; April 23, 1941, 1; June 3, 1942, 14; August 12, 1942, 3; September 2, 1942, 35; September 9, 1942, 28; September 23, 1942, 2; September 30, 1942, 27; December 16, 1942, 16; May 26, 1943, 36, 38, 55; September 15, 1943, 4; September 20, 1944, 2; October 4, 1944, 1; November 1, 1944, 38; November 27, 1946, 3; December 18, 1946, 43; October 1, 1947, 53; January 14, 1948, 70; May 19, 1948, 21; January 5, 1949, 42; April 27, 1949, 62; June 22, 1949, 26; May 10, 1950, 53; June 11, 1952, 3; April 8, 1953, 26; February

Bibliography

17, 1954, 18; November 17, 1954, 70; December 1, 1954, 27; March 2, 1955, 25; September 21, 1955, 32; March 12, 1958, 74; September 3, 1958, 61; November 30, 1960, 17; December 14, 1960, 33; January 4, 1961, 10.
Vidal, Gore. *Palimpsest*. New York: Random House, 1995.
Wagenknecht, Edward, and Anthony Slide. *The Films of D.W. Griffith*. New York: Crown, 1975.
Walker, Alexander. *Stardom: The Hollywood Phenomenon*. New York: Stein and Day, 1970.
Wall Street Journal, August 3, 1932, 3; March 25, 1933, 3; December 18, 1933, 3.
Washington Times, December 23, 1922, 1.
Werner, Wade. "Screen Life in Hollywood." *Alton Evening Telegraph*, October 9, 1928, 7.
Wheeler, Benson. *I, Becky Barrymore*. New York: Robert Speller, 1959.
Whittaker, James. Review in *Chicago Daily Tribune*, February 27, 1921, F1.
"Wife of Lionel Barrymore Sued for $3,641,452." *Chicago Daily Tribune*, June 27, 1928, 16.
Wilder, Robert. "On the Sun Deck: Gasping Comment on a Breathless Moment—Miss America's Boy Friend." *New York Sun*, December 14, 1937, 28.
Willson, Meredith. Meredith Willson's script for *The California Story* by Jack Moffitt. Meredith Willson Papers Collection, Great American Songbook Foundation. Digital collection hosted by Indiana Memory, Institute of Museum and Library Services, Indiana State Library. https://indianamemory.contentdm.oclc.org/digital/collection/p16066coll91/id/1788.
Wilson, Edmund. Review in *New Republic*, March 9, 1921, 47–48.
Wodehouse, P. G. "The Barrymores, and Others." *Vanity Fair*, April 1918, 51.
Woolf, S. J. "Old Scrooge to the Life." *New York Times*, December 19, 1943, SM18.
Woollcott, Alexander. Reviews in *New York Times*, September 20, 1919, 18; February 29, 1920, X5; March 14, 1920, BR5; February 20, 1921, X1; October 18, 1921, 27.
"Yesterday in New York." *Hollywood Reporter*, February 2, 1934, 3.
Young, Gwenda. *Clarence Brown*. Lexington: University Press of Kentucky, 2018.
Young, Stark. Reviews in *New York Times*, January 16, 1925, 14; April 15, 1925, 16.
———. *Theatre Practice*. New York: Charles Scribner's Sons, 1926.
Zádor, Eugene. "The Musical Barrymore." *Music Journal*, March 1967, 59.

Index

Académie Julian, 17, 22, 23
Academy of Motion Picture Arts and Sciences, 74
Actors' Equity, 39–41, 71–73
Actors' Equity News of Hollywood, 71–73
Ah, Wilderness! 83–84
Alias Jimmy Valentine, 66
America, 51
American Film Institute, 1, 143
American Society of Composers, Authors, and Publishers, 152
American Society of Etchers, 152, 154–55
American Theater Hall of Fame, 152
Anatomist, The, 58
Andy Hardy film series, 125–27
Arnold, Edward, 40, 86, 113–14, 141, 155
Arsène Lupin, 86–87
Art Students League, 17–18
Association of Motion Picture Producers, 74
Astor, Mary, 34, 58, 64, 106–7
As You Like It, 18
At Home with Lionel Barrymore, 114, 128
Ayres, Lew, 127–29

Bacall, Lauren, 145–46
Bad Man, The, 132
Bannerline, 140
Barnum, George, 113
Barrier, The, 57
Barrymore, Blanche (Michael Strange), 23, 44–45
Barrymore, Diana, 109
Barrymore, Doris Rankin, 14, 21–25, 37, 39–41, 43–45, 48–49, 99–100, 160

Barrymore, Elaine Barrie, 12, 103, 106–9, 136
Barrymore, Ethel (daughter), 22, 34, 166
Barrymore, Ethel (sister), 3, 11–13, 16, 18, 20–22, 24–25, 30–31, 38–42, 73, 86, 109, 112, 119, 140, 151, 153, 159–61, 166–67
Barrymore, Georgiana Drew, 11–16
Barrymore, Irene Fenwick, 39, 43–51, 58, 93, 99–103, 153, 165–66
Barrymore, John, 1, 3, 5, 12, 14–15, 18, 35–38, 42–43, 45–48, 58, 85–89, 103, 106–12, 119, 123, 145
Barrymore, John, Jr., 153
Barrymore, Katherine, 46
Barrymore, Lionel: and acting, 4–6, 20–21, 23–24, 29–30, 34, 38–39, 53, 113, 162–63, 167; and Actors' Equity, 39–41, 71–73; artistic values, 6–7, 22–23, 51–53, 68–69, 168–70; art training and artwork, 17–18, 23–24, 154–55, 169; as character actor, 1–7, 19, 28, 43–44, 80, 94–95, 162–63, 167; daughters, 22, 34–35, 39, 44, 152, 166 (*see also* Barrymore, Ethel [daughter]; Barrymore, Mary); death, funeral, and burial, 164; as director of movies, 3, 29, 32, 57, 66, 69–71, 75–78; disability, 104–5, 111, 123, 125–27, 130–31, 133–36, 138, 145; divorce, 39, 43–45, 48–49, 52–53; education, 12–13, 15–17; in fights, 13, 15–16, 18; financial and tax problems, 104, 119–22, 154; identity and introversion, 7, 146–47, 165–66; lifetime contract with MGM, 63; memoirs, 14–15,

Index

160–61, 169; and MGM pay cuts in 1933, 73–74; and movie acting, 32, 69, 168; and movie quality, 29, 32–33, 52, 66, 68–69, 167–68; music training and composition, 18, 129, 156–58, 161–62, 169; novels, 159–60; and Oscars, 75, 79, 94; pain management, 136–38; perfectionism, 6, 95, 162–63, 166–67, 169–70; political views, 122, 149–51; and radio acting, 117; and radio appearances, 111–24; remarriage, 50–51; as reporter for *New York Telegraph*, 159; residences, 104, 121, 152–54, 158; and Screen Actors Guild, 74–75; and silent films, 28, 30, 41; and the sound boom, 76–77; and sound films, 57, 63, 65–66, 69–71; Speech Arts Medal, 111; and stage acting, 6–7, 18, 32, 38, 116; and star system, 2–3, 68–69, 86, 94–95, 167; and television, 70, 123, 165; tributes to, 1, 147, 113–14, 164–65; in vaudeville, 24–25, 53, 59; as widower, 103–4; will, 154; wives (*see* Barrymore, Doris Rankin; Barrymore, Irene Fenwick); writer of scenarios, screenplays, and plays, 29, 159

Barrymore, Marie Floyd, 17
Barrymore, Mary (daughter), 22, 34, 39, 166
Barrymore, Maurice, 11–17, 21, 28, 35, 41
Battle, The, 28
Baxter, Warner, 94
Beery, Noah, 72
Beery, Wallace, 73
Beginning or the End, The, 147–48
Belasco, David, 50, 71
Belfrage, Cedric, 64
Bells, The, 57
Bennett, Richard, 37
Best of Friends, The, 20
Binyon, Conrad, 115
Biograph, 25–27
Blumenschein, Ernest, 23
Bob Acres, 24
Body and Soul, 57–58
Bogart, Humphrey, 145
Bondi, Beulah, 140

Boomerang Bill, 41
Brasselle, Keefe, 140
Briggs, Edward, 15
Brixton Burglary, The, 20
Broken Lullaby/The Man I Killed/The Fifth Commandment, 84–85
Brooding Eyes, 57
Brown, Clarence, 81, 83–84, 89
Browning, Tod, 81, 90, 93
Bucquet, Harold, 70, 130
Burglar's Dilemma, The, 29
Burke, Billie, 131
Butler, Frank, 19, 113

California Story, The, 117–18
Camille (film), 63, 85, 104
Camille (play), 18, 40
Capra, Frank, 141–44
Captains Courageous, 131
Carey, Harry, 27, 120
Carney, Art, 131
Carolina, 90, 94
Chadwick Pictures Corporation, 51, 53
Chatterton, Ruth, 70–71
Cheri Beri, 77
Children of the Whirlwind, 57
Chodorov, Frank, 149
Christmas Carol, A (film), 123–24, 126
Christmas Carol, A (radio series), 119, 122–24, 180
Christopher Bean/Her Sweetheart, 90
Christopher Columbus, 157
Claw, The, 43–44
Collier, Constance, 36
Colt, Ethel Barrymore, 153, 155
Confession, 76
Confusion, 24
Conway, Jack, 81, 87
Cooper, Jackie, 59, 90
Copperhead, The (films), 37, 41, 81
Copperhead, The (stage play), 4, 20, 37–38, 40, 53, 57–59, 77
Costello, Dolores, 109
Crawford, Joan, 86–88
Cromwell, John, 81
Cukor, George, 63, 64, 69, 81, 82, 84
Cumnor, Bill, 87
Curious Conduct of Judge Legarde, The, 30

Index

Daniell, Henry, 85
Dark Delusion, 126
Davenport, Harry, 21, 31, 35, 126
Davenport, Phyllis Rankin (a.k.a. Gibbs, Phyllis Rankin), 21, 126
David Copperfield, 90
Day, Laraine, 129, 163
Death's Marathon, 29
Decameron Nights, 50–51
de Cordoba, Pedro, 118
Delmore, Ralph, 113
DeMille, Cecil B., 73, 150
Devil-Doll, The, 90, 93
Devil's Garden, The, 41–42
Dewey, Thomas E., 149–51
Dinner at Eight, 87, 89
Dorn, Philip, 128
Down to the Sea in Ships, 146
Dragon Seed, 117
Dressler, Marie, 5, 90, 93
Drew, Gladys Rankin, 21
Drew, John, 4, 12–13, 40
Drew, Louisa Lane, 1, 11–14, 18–19, 130, 141
Drew, Sidney, 18–19, 21, 24
Dr. Kildare (radio series), 114, 126, 128, 180
Dr. Kildare (TV series), 128
Dr. Kildare/Dr. Gillespie (film series), 4, 125–31, 140, 179–80
Dr. Kildare's Wedding Day (musical score), 129, 199n5
Drums of Love, 58
Duel in the Sun, 2, 67–68, 139, 144–45
Dumas, Alexandre, 85
Dunn, Emma, 129

End of the Tour, The, 18, 31, 34
Enemies of Women, 50
Enemy of the People, An, 42
Episcopal Academy, 12
Eternal City, The, 50–51

Face in the Fog, The, 41
Family Affair, A, 125, 131
Faulkner, William, 85
Fields, W. C., 36–37, 40
Fifty-Fifty, 57

Fires of Fate, The, 24
Fiscus, Kathy, 166
Fleming, Victor, 81
Forsyte Saga, The, 81–82
Fountain, The, 43
Fox, 81
Fox, William, 62, 67
Free and Easy/Estrellados, 66
Free Soul, A, 77, 79–80
Friends, 28
Frohman, Charles, 20, 24, 100

Gable, Clark, 59, 77, 140
Gaige, Crosby, 58
Garbo, Greta, 78–79, 129
Gargan, William, 89
Gilbert, John, 75–76
Gillmore, Frank, 71–73
Gilmore School, 12
Girl from Missouri, The, 90
Girl Who Wouldn't Work, The, 57
Gish, Lillian, 5, 27–29, 64, 67, 144, 155
Gone with the Wind, 126
Gorgeous Hussy, The, 90
Goulding, Edmund, 81
Grand Hotel, 86–88
Great Adventure, The, 41
Greenstreet, Sydney, 141
Griffith, D. W., 25, 27–31, 51, 144
Guilty Hands, 66, 76, 78
Guy Named Joe, A, 133

Hadley, Henry, 18, 156
Haines, William, 66, 102, 154
Hallmark Hall of Fame, 112–14, 164–65
Harlow, Jean, 89–90, 131
Harris, William, 58
Hat, a Glove, a Mantle, A, 58
Hathaway, Henry, 146
Hawks, Howard, 81, 84–85, 89
Herne, James A., 19–20
His Father's Son, 34
His Glorious Night, 75–76
Hollywood for Dewey, 149–51
Hollywood Playhouse, 112
Hollywood Revue of 1929, The, 66
Hollywood Walk of Fame, 111, 152

Index

Hopkins, Arthur, 4–5, 37, 43, 64, 110, 159, 162–63, 167
Horton, Edward Everett, 165
Hot Cross Bunny, 130
House of Darkness, The, 29
Hunter, T. Hays, 30
Huston, John, 145

I Am the Man, 51
Ickes, Harold, 148
In Diplomatic Circles, 29
Isman, Felix, 45–46, 100–102
It Can't Happen Here, 81
It's a Wonderful Life, 1, 139, 141–44

Jest, The (film), 38
Jest, The (play), 35–38, 169
Jim the Penman, 41–42
Johnson, Van, 128
Jones, Jennifer, 131–32
Judith of Bethulia, 29

Kalavros, Philip, 167, 169
Kant, Immanuel, 170
Key Largo, 139, 145–46
Keystone Literary Club (Rock Hill, SC), 155
King Lear, 112

Lady Be Good, 131
Laugh, Clown, Laugh, 50, 53, 58
Laurel, Stan, and Oliver Hardy, 76
Let Freedom Ring, 131
Letter of the Law, The, 39, 41
Life's Whirlpool, 31
Lion and the Mouse, The, 66
Lionel Barrymore Concert Hall, 112
Little Colonel, The, 84
Little Dorrit (proposed film), 130, 141
Loew, Marcus, 61, 66
Lone Star, 140
Looking Forward/Service, 83
Loos, Anita, 28–29, 62, 129, 159
Los Angeles Central Labor Council, 73
Lowe, Edmund, 102–3
Loy, Myrna, 64
Lubitsch, Ernst, 81, 84
Lucky Lady, The, 57

Lux Radio Theater, 112

Macbeth, 42–43
Madame X, 70–71, 75, 130
Main Street to Broadway, 140
Malaya, 140
Man of Iron, A/Iron Man, 57
Man or Devil, 51–52
March, Fredric, 79
Mark of the Vampire, 90
Master Mind, The, 41
Mata Hari, 78–79
Mayer, L. B., 2, 30, 60–63, 73–76, 104, 126–27, 136
Mayor of the Town, 114–17, 118–19, 180
McCaull, Angela, 21–22
Meddling Women, 51
Menjou, Adolphe, 150
Metro-Goldwyn-Mayer (MGM), 60–64, 73–74
Metro-Goldwyn-Mayer Story, The, 57, 140
Metro-Rolfe, 30–31
Millionaire's Double, The, 34–35
Modern Magdalen, A, 30
Moorehead, Agnes, 115
Morgan, Agnes, 18, 156
Morris, Chester, 90
Mortimer, Roger, 49
Motion Picture Distribution and Sales Company, 26–27
motion picture industry development, 26–28, 59–61, 63
Motion Picture Patents Company (MPPC), 26–27, 59
Mr. Cantonwine, 159–60
Mummy and the Hummingbird, The, 4, 20, 113
Mysterious Island, The, 66

Napoleon the Wonder Dog, 58
Navy Blue and Gold, 131
Never the Twain Shall Meet, 77
New York Hat, The, 28–29
Night Flight, 86, 88–89
Nishimura, Mark, 109

O'Brien, Jay, 45–46, 49–50
O'Brien, Margaret, 129–30, 141

Index

Old Buddha, 159
Old Lady Shows Her Medals, The, 112
Oliver Twist, 77
Olympia, 77
On Borrowed Time, 125–26, 133–34
One Man's Journey, 83
O'Sullivan, Anthony, 29
Other Girl, The, 20
Owen, Reginald, 123, 126
Ozu, Yasujiro, 82

Pantaloon, 20, 38
Paradine Case, The, 81
Paramount, 81
Paris at Midnight, 57
Peck, Gregory, 147
Penalty, The, 131
Peter Ibbetson (play), 34–37
Peter Ibbetson (proposed film), 38
Pickford, Mary, 27–28
Piker, The/Four Knaves and a Joker, 6, 51–52
Preston, Frances, 93
Public Hero No. 1, 90

Rankin, McKee, 19, 21, 24–25, 29
Rasputin and the Empress, 86–88
Ratoff, Gregory, 82–83
Reagan, Ronald, 126
Redemption (film), 76
Redemption (stage play), 37
Return of Peter Grimm, The, 90, 92
Reunion in Vienna, 81
Richard III, 35–36, 42–43
Right Cross, 140
Rivals, The, 18–19
River Woman, 66
RKO–Radio Pictures, 81
Road House, 66
Road to Glory, The, 85
Robinson, Edward G., 145
Rock Hill (SC) Public Library, 155
Rodzinski, Artur, 157
Rogers, Ginger, 150–51
Rogue Song, The, 76
Romance of Elaine, The, 30
Rooney, Mickey, 131

Roosevelt, Eleanor, 147–48, 151
Roosevelt, Franklin D., 147–48
Roosevelt, James, 147–48
Royal Family, The, 79, 167

Sadie Thompson, 58
Sag Harbor, 19–20
Saratoga, 104, 131
Schary, Dore, 1, 63
Schenck, Nicholas, 61–63, 147
Schulberg, B. P., 57
Screen Actors' Guild, 74–75
Sea Bat, The, 76
Seats of the Mighty, The, 30
Secret Heart, The, 139–40
Selznick, David O., 62–63, 67, 81–82, 131, 144, 150
Seton Hall Academy, 13, 15
Shakespeare Club, The, 160
Shearer, Norma, 80
Sheldon, Edward, 35–36, 100, 107
Should Ladies Behave, 84
Show, The, 58
Shubert, Lee, 20, 37
Shubert, Sam, 20, 37
Silas Marner, 81
silent films and the coming of sound, 63–66
Simmons, Richard, 114
Since You Went Away, 131–32
Skidding, 81
Small, Maury, 53, 57
Some of the Best: 25 Years of Motion Picture Leadership, 57, 140
Span of Life, The, 30
Splendid Road, The, 57
St. Aloysius Academy, 13, 15–16
star system in movies, 27, 66–68
Stewart, James, 131, 142–43, 147
Stone, Amy Fay, 48–49
Stone, Lewis, 63, 71, 83, 125, 141
Stranger's Return, 82
Strauss, Richard, 158–59
Stroheim, Erich von, 90
Sullivan, Ed, 30, 77
Sullivan, John L., 15
Sweepings, 82–83

Index

Taps, 52
Tashman, Lilyan, 102, 103
Taylor, Robert, 125
Tchaikovsky, Pyotr Ilich, 15
Temple, Shirley, 84, 132
Temptress, The, 57
Ten Cents a Dance, 76
Tender Hearted Boy, The, 29
Tennessee Johnson, 132–33
Test Pilot, 131
Thalberg, Irving, 61–63
Thirteenth Hour, The, 57–58
This Side of Heaven, 84
Thomas, Augustus, 37
Three Wise Fools, 141
Timber Line, 81
Tracy, Spencer, 88
Treasure Island, 90
Trevor, Claire, 115,
   145–46
Twain, Mark, 15, 112–13
Twentieth Century–Fox, 81

Unholy Night, The, 76
United States v. Paramount, 63
Unseeing Eyes, 50

Vajda, Ernest, 74
Valedictory, 81
Vallee, Rudy, 108
Valley of Decision, The, 139
Van Dyke, W. S., 81
Veiller, Bayard, 78
Vengeance of Galora, The, 29
Vidal, Gore, 142
Vidor, King, 81–82,
   144

Voice of Bugle Ann, The, 90, 92–93
von Stroheim, Erich, 90

Walker, Robert, 131
Walsh, Raoul, 81
Warfield, David, 37
Warshawsky, Sam, 58
Washington Masquerade, 89–92
Watson, Bobs, 133–34
We Barrymores, 14–15, 160–61, 169
Welles, Orson, 107–8
West of Zanzibar, 66
Wheeler family, 152–54, 164
White Slaver, The, 24–25, 34
Whitman Bennett, 41
Widmark, Richard, 146
Wife Tamers, 57
Wildfire, 30
Williams, John D., 37, 42, 48
Wilson, Edmund, 42
Winterset, 81
Wodehouse, P. G., 5
Wolheim, Louis, 72
Woman Who Did, The, 50–51
Women Love Diamonds, 58
Wood, Sam, 81, 90
Woods, Al, 36
Wrongdoers, The, 57
Wynn, Ed, 40

Yank at Oxford, A, 81, 125
Yellow Ticket, The, 66
You Can't Take It with You, 125–26, 133
Youssoupoff v. MGM, 88

Zádor, Eugene, 129, 156–57, 169
Zanuck, Darryl F., 146

Screen Classics

Screen Classics is a series of critical biographies, film histories, and analytical studies focusing on neglected filmmakers and important screen artists and subjects, from the era of silent cinema through the golden age of Hollywood to the international generation of today. Books in the Screen Classics series are intended for scholars and general readers alike. The contributing authors are established figures in their respective fields. This series also serves the purpose of advancing scholarship on film personalities and themes with ties to Kentucky.

Series Editor
Patrick McGilligan

Books in the Series

Olivia de Havilland: Lady Triumphant
  Victoria Amador
Mae Murray: The Girl with the Bee-Stung Lips
  Michael G. Ankerich
Harry Dean Stanton: Hollywood's Zen Rebel
  Joseph B. Atkins
Hedy Lamarr: The Most Beautiful Woman in Film
  Ruth Barton
Rex Ingram: Visionary Director of the Silent Screen
  Ruth Barton
Conversations with Classic Film Stars: Interviews from Hollywood's Golden Era
  James Bawden and Ron Miller
Conversations with Legendary Television Stars: Interviews from the First Fifty Years
  James Bawden and Ron Miller
You Ain't Heard Nothin' Yet: Interviews with Stars from Hollywood's Golden Era
  James Bawden and Ron Miller
Charles Boyer: The French Lover
  John Baxter
Von Sternberg
  John Baxter
Hitchcock's Partner in Suspense: The Life of Screenwriter Charles Bennett
  Charles Bennett, edited by John Charles Bennett
Hitchcock and the Censors
  John Billheimer
The Magic Hours: The Life and Films of Terrence Malick
  John Bleasdale
A Uniquely American Epic: Intimacy and Action, Tenderness and Violence in Sam Peckinpah's The Wild Bunch
  Edited by Michael Bliss

My Life in Focus: A Photographer's Journey with Elizabeth Taylor and the Hollywood Jet Set
  Gianni Bozzacchi with Joey Tayler
Hollywood Divided: The 1950 Screen Directors Guild Meeting and the Impact of the Blacklist
  Kevin Brianton
He's Got Rhythm: The Life and Career of Gene Kelly
  Cynthia Brideson and Sara Brideson
Ziegfeld and His Follies: A Biography of Broadway's Greatest Producer
  Cynthia Brideson and Sara Brideson
The Marxist and the Movies: A Biography of Paul Jarrico
  Larry Ceplair
Dalton Trumbo: Blacklisted Hollywood Radical
  Larry Ceplair and Christopher Trumbo
Warren Oates: A Wild Life
  Susan Compo
Helen Morgan: The Original Torch Singer and Ziegfeld's Last Star
  Christopher S. Connelly
Improvising Out Loud: My Life Teaching Hollywood How to Act
  Jeff Corey with Emily Corey
Crane: Sex, Celebrity, and My Father's Unsolved Murder
  Robert Crane and Christopher Fryer
Jack Nicholson: The Early Years
  Robert Crane and Christopher Fryer
Anne Bancroft: A Life
  Douglass K. Daniel
Being Hal Ashby: Life of a Hollywood Rebel
  Nick Dawson
Bruce Dern: A Memoir
  Bruce Dern with Christopher Fryer and Robert Crane
Intrepid Laughter: Preston Sturges and the Movies
  Andrew Dickos
The Woman Who Dared: The Life and Times of Pearl White, Queen of the Serials
  William M. Drew
Miriam Hopkins: Life and Films of a Hollywood Rebel
  Allan R. Ellenberger
Vitagraph: America's First Great Motion Picture Studio
  Andrew A. Erish
Jayne Mansfield: The Girl Couldn't Help It
  Eve Golden
John Gilbert: The Last of the Silent Film Stars
  Eve Golden
Stuntwomen: The Untold Hollywood Story
  Mollie Gregory
Jean Gabin: The Actor Who Was France
  Joseph Harriss
Otto Preminger: The Man Who Would Be King, updated edition
  Foster Hirsch
Saul Bass: Anatomy of Film Design
  Jan-Christopher Horak
Lawrence Tierney: Hollywood's Real-Life Tough Guy
  Burt Kearns
Hitchcock Lost and Found: The Forgotten Films
  Alain Kerzoncuf and Charles Barr

Pola Negri: Hollywood's First Femme Fatale
  Mariusz Kotowski
Ernest Lehman: The Sweet Smell of Success
  Jon Krampner
Sidney J. Furie: Life and Films
  Daniel Kremer
Albert Capellani: Pioneer of the Silent Screen
  Christine Leteux
A Front Row Seat: An Intimate Look at Broadway, Hollywood, and the Age of Glamour
  Nancy Olson Livingston
Ridley Scott: A Biography
  Vincent LoBrutto
Mamoulian: Life on Stage and Screen
  David Luhrssen
Maureen O'Hara: The Biography
  Aubrey Malone
My Life as a Mankiewicz: An Insider's Journey through Hollywood
  Tom Mankiewicz and Robert Crane
Hawks on Hawks
  Joseph McBride
Showman of the Screen: Joseph E. Levine and His Revolutions in Film Promotion
  A. T. McKenna
William Wyler: The Life and Films of Hollywood's Most Celebrated Director
  Gabriel Miller
Raoul Walsh: The True Adventures of Hollywood's Legendary Director
  Marilyn Ann Moss
Veit Harlan: The Life and Work of a Nazi Filmmaker
  Frank Noack
Harry Langdon: King of Silent Comedy
  Gabriella Oldham and Mabel Langdon
Charles Walters: The Director Who Made Hollywood Dance
  Brent Phillips
Some Like It Wilder: The Life and Controversial Films of Billy Wilder
  Gene D. Phillips
Ann Dvorak: Hollywood's Forgotten Rebel
  Christina Rice
Mean . . . Moody . . . Magnificent! Jane Russell and the Marketing of a Hollywood Legend
  Christina Rice
Fay Wray and Robert Riskin: A Hollywood Memoir
  Victoria Riskin
Lewis Milestone: Life and Films
  Harlow Robinson
Michael Curtiz: A Life in Film
  Alan K. Rode
Ryan's Daughter: The Making of an Irish Epic
  Paul Benedict Rowan
Arthur Penn: American Director
  Nat Segaloff
Film's First Family: The Untold Story of the Costellos
  Terry Chester Shulman
Claude Rains: An Actor's Voice
  David J. Skal with Jessica Rains

Barbara La Marr: The Girl Who Was Too Beautiful for Hollywood
    Sherri Snyder
Robert Herridge: A Television Poet
    John Sorensen
Lionel Barrymore: Character and Endurance in Hollywood's Golden Age
    Kathleen Spaltro
Buzz: The Life and Art of Busby Berkeley
    Jeffrey Spivak
Victor Fleming: An American Movie Master
    Michael Sragow
Aline MacMahon: Hollywood, the Blacklist, and the Birth of Method Acting
    John Stangeland
My Place in the Sun: Life in the Golden Age of Hollywood and Washington
    George Stevens Jr.
Hollywood Presents Jules Verne: The Father of Science Fiction on Screen
    Brian Taves
Thomas Ince: Hollywood's Independent Pioneer
    Brian Taves
Picturing Peter Bogdanovich: My Conversations with the New Hollywood Director
    Peter Tonguette
Jessica Lange: An Adventurer's Heart
    Anthony Uzarowski
Carl Theodor Dreyer and Ordet: *My Summer with the Danish Filmmaker*
    Jan Wahl
Wild Bill Wellman: Hollywood Rebel
    William Wellman Jr.
Harvard, Hollywood, Hitmen, and Holy Men: A Memoir
    Paul W. Williams
Clarence Brown: Hollywood's Forgotten Master
    Gwenda Young
The Queen of Technicolor: Maria Montez in Hollywood
    Tom Zimmerman